LIONESS

AUGUST ANDERSON

authorHOUSE®

AuthorHouse™
1663 Liberty Drive, Suite 200
Bloomington, IN 47403
www.authorhouse.com
Phone: 1-800-839-8640

This book is a work of fiction. People, places, events, and situations are the product of the author's imagination. Any resemblance to actual persons, living or dead, or historical events, is purely coincidental.

© 2007 August Anderson. All rights reserved.

No part of this book may be reproduced, stored in a retrieval system, or transmitted by any means without the written permission of the author.

First published by AuthorHouse 9/4/2007

ISBN: 978-1-4343-3221-9 (sc)

Library of Congress Control Number: 2007905946

Printed in the United States of America
Bloomington, Indiana

This book is printed on acid-free paper.

TEA PARTY BOOKS
P.O. Box 706
Black Hawk, SD 57718
(605) 787-6486 Fax: (605) 787-6203
www.teapartybooks.com
email: teaparty@sturgis.com

This book is dedicated to Jesus Christ – Quite possibly the most misinterpreted Man/God/Prophet in history!

TABLE OF CONTENTS

PROLOGUE: THE LION, THE MAN, AND THE LOVER

The Salty Taste of Blood 3
David 9
Pierce – Falling 15
Lioness – Running 20
David – My Beautiful Wife 28
Pierce – The Beginning of the End 33

BEFORE THE DAWN OF TIME

History of the Universe 41

THE BEGINNING OF THE END

Lioness – Fear 47

THE BOOK OF PIERCE

Pierce – Fear 59
Pierce – Curiosity 72
David – Educating 83
Pierce – Being Initiated 91

THE BOOK OF ANNE

Pierce – Their First Caribbean Trip 97
Back to Reality 114
Pierce – Back to the Present 115
David – Dinner from David's Point of View 121
David – Continuing The History Lesson 134

THE BOOK OF JAMES

Pierce – Courage 147
James – Courage 151

Pierce – Harney Peak..................................157
David – Bitterness and Shock.........................162

BOOK OF BART AND TOM

Pierce – Looking Up, Looking Down......................169
Richard – Fear..183
Pierce – The Green Grass of Home........................193
Pierce – The Gardens of Home............................197
Pierce – Looking Down...................................201
Pierce – Deciphering the Moons and the Stars 208
Pierce – The Globe......................................213
Pierce – Moving On......................................220
Pierce – Traveling......................................225

THE BOOK OF PAUL

Paul – Salt Lake Connection 233
Santorini 237
The St. John Ruins 242

MEANWHILE, BACK IN THE UNITED STATES

David – The Presidential Debates Raged On 249

YEARS EARLIER

Lioness – Curiosity...................................263
Lion's Theme Song.....................................270

LION - ROARING HER WAY TO THE SENATE SPEAKING

Of God and Souls and Free Will 275
The Role of Government and Taxation...............279
Lion – Of war and peace 286
Lioness – Of Rights and Responsibilities.................291

YEARS LATER: BACK TO THE FINAL PRESIDENTIAL ELECTION

Richard – The Domestic Debate 305
Political Advertising..321

MEANWHILE, BACK IN TURKEY THE BOOK OF JOAN

Pierce in Ephesus...331
Mary's Home..342

THE BOOK OF MO

Oh Ancient Wonder of Ephesus 347
Pierce – Beneath The Star Of Ephesus.....................351
Pierce – Running...359
Pursuit 362
Lioness on Light and Dark 365
Stopped In Mid-air 367
Turkish Escape 376
Woman President..378
Mary – The Unknown Years 387
The Rest Of The Story...390
Venice, Italy – St. Marks..399
Enter St. Mark's Cathedral 405
Meanwhile Back At The Ranch 414

THE BOOK OF ANDREW

Pierce in Hell 421
Rosenburg Castle, Austria 424
Moons, Stars, and Flags...428
Deer In Headlights Moment 435
Altenburg Monastery 440

THE BOOK OF THEODORE JUDE CHAMPELLA

Onward to Egypt 451
Andrew to the Rescue 458
In Flight 463
Solving Puzzles 467
Living Kings 471
Cairo 473
The Empty Search 479
Invasion In The Night 482

THE BOOK OF MATHEW

Memphis 489
The Step Pyramids 492

THE BOOK OF MARGARET

Australia 499
Sister Meade's Final Secret 502
Dissappointment At The Rapid City Airport 504
The Terror Of Sexual Betrayal 508
Gathering Of Strangers 510
Excerpts From The Final Debate 513
The Gathering Of Angels And Devils 530
The Final Seating Arrangement 537
The First Breakfast 540
The Mystery Unveiled 543
The Cup Runneth Over 552
Whom Can You Trust? 558
The Answers At Last 560
Death Revisited 563
From Murderess To Heroine In Less Than A Day 568
The Final Chapter 573

PROLOGUE: THE LION, THE MAN, AND THE LOVER

THE SALTY TASTE OF BLOOD

The lioness stretched and yawned in her sleep. Her tawny mane scrunched under her neck and her long golden muscles expressed sinewy power in their smallest twitching movements as she dreamed. She dreamed of cubs, she dreamed of her King, she dreamed she was running free across great expanses of golden African grasslands. She dreamed of Freedom.

Her den was comfortingly warm, cozy and moist. She rolled over onto her back bathing in the luxurious feeling that morning sun would soon to be breaking around her. She savored the feeling of being wrapped in fur and warmth. Wet. Fuzzy. Warm. Glorious. Almost like floating in her mother's womb.

Must she really awaken? It was so heavenly just lying here being a lioness. All 138 pounds of her muscles stretched again. She coughed slight phlegm, releasing a small hairball as she reached out her rough red tongue to lick the liquid on her forearm. Her hypnotizing eyes remained closed, hesitant to open and take on the task of living. Were those magnificent orbs open, they would mesmerize all who gazed deep into their magic-large, innocent waters. Compassion and passion danced in the rainbow mist of those eyes that slanted up in the corners just enough to reveal her dangerous soul. But for now, those haunting eyes were on the brink of sleep and she did not want to strain to open them just yet.

The magical eyes, ever changing in color like an old fashioned "mood ring", remained pleasantly closed. She was licking her own forearm. Her bumpy tongue roughly massaging her muscles as she licked the delicious warm liquid from her limbs. Salty. Warm. Blood. Nothing lovelier than the salty taste of blood.

Blood? Blood? Holy Shit, Blood! She quickly sat up in the foreign bed and those huge golden eyes sprang open. *Crap. Crap. Crap. Blood. Blood. Blood. Help. Help. Help.*

Her thoughts were short and panicked and the eyes turned bright green, then ocean blue, as she was in utter confusion. She saw the dead, sliced up body of a formerly lovely woman beside her. The bedding was covered in the woman's blood. The sheets, her own body, everything covered in blood. *YUCK*. She had licked it. *GROSS*! Waves of repulsion flooded her body. Panic married repulsion in her gut producing together an explosion of an odd sort of orgasmic heat, flooding out from her groins and through her body to her brain. *Shit.*

Her life was over. Her destiny was over. The Presidential election was over. As of last night she was going to be the first woman President of the United States in just two weeks. Now she woke up like this!? She could kiss her life's work goodbye. She could kiss her life's purpose goodbye. Her Republican Party could kiss the Presidency goodbye.

What happened? Where were her people? Where were her clothes? Where was her damned, irritating cell phone when she needed it? Should she call her campaign manger, Levi Henning, from the bedside phone? No, she'd leave incriminating fingerprints on that phone.

Where was she anyway?

She looked wildly around her, the great eyes throbbing and straining. Ah, she recognized her suite in the Watergate Hotel. Dizzily she remembered a private reception for her top campaign contributors being held there. What was the important announcement friends and foes had gathered to hear? Was it last night? Was it here in the historic Watergate? She needed answers. But first she had to get out of here before the press and the FBI surrounded the place.

She spotted her gown from the night before. The exclusive Versace designed especially for her – Lioness Godfrey – future president. Inspiration to women around the world. The gown designed by the female Versace sibling in honor of her brother who had shocked a nation when he crossed over so many years ago.

No, surely, it couldn't all be ending like this, could it? She had worked so hard and given so much. She had waited so long. Longer than the world would ever know. *No. No. No.* Something was wrong with this picture and she would get out of here and she would find out what really happened.

The Lioness roared inside - *she knew her own soul like no one else in the world knew their soul.* She could not commit a murder. Uh, could she? Not of her best friend!

Even if her best friend had tried to blackmail her last night? Bits and pieces of blurry memory were painfully, fuzzily forming in her mind. Many people had feared Lioness in her life, but this was the first time she feared herself.

First things first. *Get out of here!*

Lion, as her friends all called her, looked around and saw her nylons were as bloody as the dress. She had looked so fantastic last night that when she looked in the mirror, she took her own breath away. She knew she took all her oppositions' breath away. When she entered any room she heard the collective gasps followed by dead silence of men, and jealous whispers of women as her fans and enemies alike took in the sight of her extraordinarily unique and wild version of beauty.

Golden hair softly curling around her neck and face, then flowing toward a triangle down her muscular back, ending between her withers. Tan shoulders gleaming under soft white satin - thanks to lovely times at that Atlantic Hotel in the Bahamas where her campaign team often met when absolute offshore privacy was needed. The white gown had a Grecian goddess style draping over her right shoulder and showing off her tall slender silhouette all the way down. Jagged hemline with slits up to her thighs had accented the long brown super muscular legs. Ah, movie stars couldn't have done it better.

Focus, Lioness, focus. Get out of here. The press will be looking for you soon. In any case, the stunning dress was ruined. Covered with blood. As were the nylons. She really did not even need to wear the uncomfortable stockings anyway as she had such long tan legs. She flushed the hose down the toilet. Fortunately, her white heels were not bloody and not too high - at least she could make her exit in the almost practical (if you ignored the stripes of gold and fake diamonds dressing them up) white pumps.

Having stayed there often, Lioness knew the Watergate Hotel furnished plush robes in every room for its upper class patrons, so she approached the closet. Luck was with her. She grabbed a robe and wrapped it snuggly around her muscular brown body. She also knew, as one of those regular Power Patrons, she could take the elevator down to the lobby in the robe without arousing any suspicion. Many times she had worn the familiar thick robes down to the basement gym for an early morning work out before a long session in the Senate. Congressmen, Arab Princes, you name it, accepted this among their peers at the Watergate, so she could pull this off.

She wrapped her hands in thick, soft wash cloths, then she used those and the shoe shine cloth to wipe her fingerprints off everything. Phone, door handles, toilet seat. Anyplace she might have left a print, she rapidly, yet thoroughly, scrubbed it down. She grabbed the two broken, blood covered wine glasses that were obviously used to hack her best friend to death and put them in the pocket of the robe. She tied her bloodied gown around her flat, toned waist under the robe then retied the robe tightly around her nervous, sweating body.

The clock beside the crimson stained bed signaled 5:00 a.m. Good. Still dark and the press would be sleeping.

She crept to the elevator and noted she was on the 6th floor. She pushed Lobby and rode the elevator down, not daring to look at her own reflection in the elevator mirrors that morning, with a towel covering her head and hair, she hoped she would not be identifiable by security's elevator camera. Turning from the mirrored wall and camera, she could only hope she looked like a featureless man going down to the basement gym for an early morning swim, rather than the goddess from the previous night, escaping untellable sins.

Oh, *what a difference a day makes*!

Lion's heart and brain raced wildly as the elevator slowed. Peering out the elevator door Lion saw no one at the reception desk. She saw a sleepy concierge talking to an equally sleepy porter so she darted out the heavy door, unseen and into the dark, pre-dawn night.

As she crept toward the street, the sun began to peer over the horizon turning the sky grey. Lion picked up her pace. A few minutes later, Mr. Sun rapidly began streaking the clouds with fingers of color. Deep rich fingers of red light announcing the arrival of morning painted the sky with the color of blood. It was as if the Great Painter were using the richest of watercolors to announce to the world *the time of blood* had arrived. As mankind slept, the final betrayal had encountered the hand of the Lion. How did the sky already know?

Lioness ran like she'd never run before.

DAVID

My sister always thought she was hot shit. Even before the polls showed she had a chance at becoming President.

But I knew better. I have always known she was a skanky, murdering bitch and the headlines in today's Washington Post just go to prove it. Of course, they only list her as one of about a dozen suspects, but I happen to know that power-hungry wench would stop at nothing to become President. *To defeat me.* Isn't that her very reason for living?

People act like she is the Second Coming. I, for one, know better. In fact, quite the opposite. Really. You see, I was there even for her birth. It was a nothing extraordinary birth in the Rapid City, South Dakota Municipal Hospital. Mom screamed. Dad paced. And the ornery, stubborn little brat refused to come out. Finally, they pulled her out by C-Section, then she got everyone's attention by refusing to cry. They thought she was going to die, because they were not sure her lungs would clear for breathing. Too proud to be born. Too proud to breathe. Too proud to cry. The little bitch was always too proud. Worse still, she was always getting all the attention that belonged rightfully to me – the first born son of the wealthy and powerful Godfrey family of South Dakota.

The only thing significant about the ugly little yellow scrunched faced baby, besides the facts that she was too stubborn to cry and too ugly to look at, was that she chose, of all days, my own birthday as the day she would be born. Yup, the little wench was a copy cat from day one, so the name Lion fit her perfectly. I did not get a fourth birthday party that year, needless to say. And every April 21 from that day forward, I never had my own party. I had to share it with the evil little cat. Yes, in many ways I have hated her since the day she was born. But now she was a murderer.

Revenge will be mine.

Where did such powerful, bone chilling evil come from?

It was rumored that the prior two generations of Godfreys were South Dakota's original self-made billions. Supposedly, the Homestake Goldmine in Lead wasn't the only mine making a fortune in gold back in those Wild West days. It was the only mine the public knew about. The Homestake Mine was one of the most productive *known, publicly held* goldmines in the world. But back then there were all the *unknown, private* mines, such as the Godfrey mine. Let's face it, the Black Hills were streaming rivers of gold in those days. Today there are large caverns where tourists love viewing stalactites and stalagmites – but many of those caves were not exactly made by Mother Nature. No siree; rumor has it many of those caves were made by employees of the great Godfrey family. Black market, gold rocks. What a combination! But, of course, those are only rumors, which I, naturally, deny.

By the time Lioness and I had our first sibling fights the family money had been laundered sufficiently to be as clean as a whistle. The Godfrey family had ownership in three movie production studios, seventeen large newspapers, two monthly magazines, (it is important to own the press, you know, if you want to become President in modern times), diamond mines in South Africa, Oil Wells in Venezuela, internet hosting sites, buffalo ranches as far as the eyes can see, ruby and sapphire mines in Thailand, Stock Market interests in Hong Kong. You name it, we dabble in it. Unfathomable wealth. But what good is such wealth without unfathomable Power? That is what the Godfreys seek now. Power. Unfathomable Power. Money, Fame, and Power. The dream of everyman. We have the Money. We would rather not have the Fame, but that comes with the territory. Now we seek Power. Not for the sake of Power itself. Rather, Power for righteous purpose – power for the purpose of helping all mankind.

Lioness and I were groomed for this divine purpose by dad from the moment we each were born. Still, in those humble cold dark hills, Lioness and I somehow managed to have what mom wanted – a private, obscure, and relatively normal upbringing.

Lioness always followed in my footsteps. If I got wire rimmed glasses, she got wire rimmed glasses, even though she had perfect eyesight. If I tried marijuana, she tried marijuana. If I inhaled, she inhaled. If I got a new car, she got a new car. When I became a U.S. Senator, she became a U.S. Senator two years later. It really pissed me off.

Copycat. Copycat. Lying little Lion.

South Dakota was a red state - Republican all the way. South Dakotans believed in lesser government, so they fell for the standard Republican lie - that Republican administrations would tax and regulate less than Democratic administrations. Yet, there I was – a nice young Democrat sweeping the state by storm. Convincing the South Dakota people to send me back to the East Coast, where I preferred to be, on their own dime. Handsome, rich, educated, and popular with the ladies. Naturally, I got elected to the Senate my first try. I had soundly trounced my Republican opponent with moderate, centrist views that I had learned to sell to the people, while covering my more educated, left wing plans. South Dakotans liked to be lied to and they and would elect Democrats every time, if the Democrat learned to talk conservative and promise more free money to them one and all.

South Dakota bragged about being a welfare state – that the Feds sent them more money than they gave the Feds. This drove Lion to the brink of madness and played nicely in my favor.

My Harvard debating style could convince anyone that I was their man. I trounced my opposition. When he ran for the Republican nomination two years later – thanks to MY earlier trouncing of the poor man - Lioness was able to barely squeak into the position of Republican candidate instead of him. Riding on my coat-tails, as always, and taking advantage that she ran as a Republican in a Republican State, she was elected by the skin of her teeth to the United States Senate. I was appalled. She doesn't even really belong in Congress. Now I have her dogging me even in Washington, D.C., where I belong, and she has no business hanging out. Lioness belongs back in South Dakota.

So, that is how the Lion and I went on to rock the Senate with our outrageous debates! Sibling rivalry was carried out in its most adult form in the world's most public of forums - the floor of the United States Senate. Not to mention the bloodletting and disputes we had behind the scenes. I was South Dakota's senior Senator – a Democrat, and Lioness was the junior Senator – a Republican.

Republican, my ass, Lion was a Libertarian if ever there was one.

We made history then, in any case. The first Brother and Sister to ever hold seats in the United States Senate... Democrat and Republican. We were hailed as the new generation of Kennedys. Rich, beautiful, and charismatic, but as different as salt and sugar. Blonde gal and brunette brother, both of us as wholesome as apple pie. Smiling hand in hand at the cameras from CNN to FOX to ABC, CBS, NBC and more. But we were different scary in our differences. We both knew it. And under the smiles, we detested one another. At least I think I detested her, in spite of SOME begrudging respect. No one ever really knew for sure what the Lying Lion was thinking.

I started to muse earlier that there was nothing holy about her birth. The opposite, indeed. But fourteen years after the fact of her birth, there was one startling piece of news none of us can understand to this day. At the age of fourteen, Lion was in a serious car accident and needed a blood transfusion. Fearing the possibility of transmitting A.I.D.S., hepatitis, or other diseases through a transfusion of stranger's blood; the family all got genetically tested and ultimately dad was cleared to donate blood for the transfusion (meanwhile Lioness emerged from the coma and refused a transfusion). But those genetic blood tests proved something rather odd. Mother, was not the mother of Lioness!

We ran further genetic tests after that illogical little bit of information. Sure enough, they all came back indicating it was genetically impossible that mom was the mother of Lioness. Yet, Mother painfully recalls giving birth to her!

Dad and I recall painfully watching the birth of the ugly, hairy, yellow little child.

And now, if being a lifelong copy cat just doesn't take the cake, Lioness simply had to go out and get herself a movie star boyfriend. As if someone like Pierce Hanson could possibly like a self-centered, weird looking copy cat like Lioness! Don't tell me, it isn't our Hollywood and Black Hills production studios he really has his eye on! But Lion is not above using her position to get a date.

Yes, all in all, Lioness is totally devoid of morals.

Oh, and did I happen to mention the woman whom that she-devil murdered was my own beautiful wife?

Yes, vengeance will indeed be mine.

PIERCE – FALLING

I fell in love with her physical beauty the first time I saw her. I will never forget the moment the world stood still and I knew love at long last.

Of course, I'd known lust plenty. A tall, blue-eyed, dark haired Irish movie star has plenty of "groupies" to select from twenty four hours per day. Been there, done that!

However, I wasn't famous the first time I saw her. Still, I had women after me from all facets of life even then. We all knew I was destined for stardom. As fate would have it, I was one of many, many "extras" on the set of Kevin Costner's "Dances with Wolves" when it was filming in South Dakota. Naturally, every tourist and "wanna be actor" from Costner's set had to see Mt. Rushmore when they were in South Dakota; hence, there I was, doing my trek to South Dakota's Mecca With Four Faces; when just outside the small, old-fashioned western town of Keystone, I saw something go galloping by on a white horse. At first I thought it was a white cloud swishing by like the horizontal lightning you spot only in South Dakota occasionally in your peripheral vision.

But no, it was a horse streaking by carrying only a rider with no bridle or saddle. I kid you not. They do that in South Dakota. Not just the Native Americans. It seems everyone rides a horse like a maniac and half of them have no regard for tack of any sort.

Now, I was trained extensively to ride dressage, jumping, and eventing after I left my poverty stricken childhood home back in Ireland. In fact, I'd once come close to making the Irish Event team for the Sydney Olympics Games. An American, David O'Connor, won the gold that year with brilliant riding, but I often wonder if I could have procured any of the other medals had I not suffered a broken leg when my horse fell on me during the Irish Olympic Selection Trials.

There is nothing like the power of a big Irish Thoroughbred rolling his back up under you as he gallops across green fields (often chasing the hounds who are chasing the fox – or now that foxhunting has been outlawed, I should say chasing the hounds chasing the scent of the fox) with horse and hound leaping anything that gets in the way. If a horse jumps higher than about four foot, they have to snap their backs to get over the jump. This creates a snap in the steed's back resulting in a rush of power like you would not believe. It feels like your horse is catapulting you to the stars. You pray the saddle, your decades of lessons creating balance, and the reins somehow keep you somewhere near the horse's mighty back upon landing. You gallop on, wind ripping the breath from your lungs and tangling hair into a frenzy, knowing your are as close to a religious experience as a man will ever know

But Ireland, horses, and my Olympic Dreams – those all took a back seat when my destiny to be an actor when America called me to that large, wild, and still uncivilized country.

Oh, what man can land upon the unbridled shores of America and not feel the awe? Sense the infinite opportunity there for the grabbing? Smell the vastness? Adore the unending variety of Her landscape? Yearn for America's loving arms of freedom borne of blood and pain centuries ago to enfold and protect you? Taste the air? Feel at the stress? Observe the melting pot of people? Hear the excitement of ever expanding souls? What man could set foot upon that sacred land and not know it was a land created at the hands of Almighty God? Ruled by a government put in place by Himself? Oh, America! Rapturous beauty that you are! A country and a people worthy of being saved!

Yet, when I set foot upon America's generous bosom, I was disturbed to find that She, America, was – just like all great civilizations – crumbling around Her edges, and destructive forces were destroying her ideals – from the rugged coastline inward toward those vast golden plains. I shuddered in the private knowing that unworldly potential was going down in the flames of a greedy government that America's founders never intended.

But I digress. Back to Lioness. When I witnessed with jaw dropping amazement, that white streak of lighting, it was not like any style of riding I had ever seen growing up. There was no jumping involved. No studied, on the edge but always in control dressage. It was a flat out mad gallop of an insane horse being ridden by an obvious lunatic. A white horses stretching for all it was worth taking 14 foot strides that would have never managed a good Irish Stadium jumping arena. Those courses are designed for the typical 12 foot stride.

Precisely where was her saddle? How did she stay on? Where was the bridle? How did she steer the white streak of a horse? And did my eyes deceive me? Was that some kind of Indian war paint on her white horse and her own golden face? Surely the knots would never come out of that mess of hair streaking behind her. Nor would the knots ever come out of my stomach after watching such a sight. After my heart came back out of my throat and settled in my chest where it belonged, I concluded surely this vision was surely an actress in Costner's movie. Certainly I would meet her on one of the sets.

Thus, I began searching everywhere for the unmistakable face, unbelievable body, and that unearthly spirit.

I never did see her near the set. She was one of the only South Dakotan's not an extra in Dances with Wolves! And she was not to meet Kevin Costner until years later when I introduced them at a political function.

But there was something about her. Untamed, galloping, wild and unobtainable. Something about her that would haunt my daily fantasies to the very end.

David, my dear, bitter, jealous would be brother-in-law (if only I could persuade Lioness to marry me) would claim that the haunting Lioness was a worthless copy-cat, at best, and an evil power hungry woman capable of even murder, at worst.

But I knew better. For I am the one she chose of her own Free Will to stand at her right hand through all eternity. I am the only human being on this earth who knows the real Lioness. For I have come to her nest and know what lies inside the Beast they call the Godfrey family. This knowledge gives me unspeakable horror for all mankind--for in this knowledge I have seen the future of mankind on planet earth.

Wash this knowledge from my brain, please God. I am not strong enough to bear it.

LIONESS – RUNNING

Legs were stretching, reaching, pulling. Long, golden, powerful. Pumping blood, now famous for its unknown origin, throughout the entire athletic golden body.

Dawn was stretching, reaching, pulling the morning clouds away. Long, golden, powerful rays of sun were just beginning to pump throughout the slightly polluted air of Washington D.C. as the Lioness bolted through the park.

FBI Agent, Tom Smith, was stretching, reaching, pulling the phone toward his ear. There had been a murder at the Watergate.

Lioness was stretching, reaching, pulling - galloping full speed through the park. *Crap.* She was one block from where the dead body of Chandra Levy had finally been discovered years ago. Interns and Congressmen! The inevitable mix of crushes, affairs, power. Never a good combination-just ask any member of the Godfrey family, especially David before he was wed. But Lion would not sink to that level of campaigning. Lions are very, very good at keeping secrets-even to the grave and beyond.

Why? *Because the public simply can not handle the truth.*

For instance, take her now dead best friend, Anne. She was not just Lion's sister-in-law. Lioness had arranged for the entire matter of her brother meeting, falling in love with, and marrying, her best friend. It was convenient, not to mention highly useful, to have a set of eyes in Dave's house. Although Lioness had made the introductions initially to help out Anne's husband in a legal matter, Anne and her brother falling in love came in handy when the campaign came to fruition.

By putting her associates in just the right places, Lioness could have eyes everywhere, in every color, watching everything. Her eyes could then match the color of the eyes of her associates and she could see clearly what they were seeing without even being there. For example, Anne had dark almond eyes. When someone speaking to Lion saw her eyes mysteriously turn brown, little did they know Lioness was observing exactly what Anne was observing. At the same time Lioness viewed the world, often hundreds of miles away from Anne's setting, Lion appeared focused completely on her own conversation.

If Lion's eyes turned blue, she was seeing through Pierce's eyes, no matter where he was in the world. Lion was the queen of multi-tasking and could easily take it all in. Any observer never realized Lion could see through the eyes of outsiders at the same time she saw through her own eyes. Observers merely saw the Lion's own eyes constantly changing color. They did not realize she was matching minds with a green eyed person when her eyes turned green. Audiences merely saw the liquid pools of ever changing light in Lion's eyes.

Lion had worked long and hard to organize her own brain in such a manner. The queen of multitasking, she would work two separate computers, while doing her taxes, while also watching ten different news channels on ten television sets and still yawn with boredom.. This allowed Lioness to be in more than one place at a time – ever watching the drama of the human race unfold its final destiny from many different angles at one time.

Lioness had studied techniques to tap into different parts of her brain.. She was urgently trying to learn to tap into the final portion wherein lay cosmic consciousness and the secret to the creation of the universe. The Ultimate Creator was still creating and was always constantly recreating his creations. Big changes were on the horizon and Lioness could afford no mistakes right now. Especially big mistakes like last night's death of Anne.

Lioness found multi-tasking, multi-observing, and multi-thinking all at the same time quite easy because rather than using the 8% of her brain that most humans used, she had learned to tap into 89% of her brain. The 11% Lioness Godfrey was denied access to was the direct line to the Universal Intelligence that controlled life and death.

The human race was staring extinction right in the eye and did not even realize it. Lion urgently needed to tap into the death controller or life was over as she knew it during this incarnation. And the problem was, she needed to be backed by the majority of mankind.

Senator Godfrey feared the majority might just be too apathetic to rise up to the occasion and grab onto truth and life.

Apathy, is indeed, the devil's greatest weapon.

Brother Dave was the elder Senator Godfrey. His eyes were quite the opposite of Sister Lion's eyes. Dave had his serious, silvery brown eyes focused on nothing but the acquisition power from the moment Lioness had been born. Dave overwhelming craved the attention that the ugly, fuzzy little baby had wrongfully stolen from him when the cat first entered the world.

The cat had been dubbed by David as the most stubborn being ever born. From the doctors who paddled her butt, to the childhood swats for bad behavior, Lioness was known for one thing special in throughout her childhood – that she was so stubborn she could not ever be made to cry. Never in her life had she shed a tear. She would try to explain that she was only half human and that Lions do not cry, but everyone found that simply silly. It only made most reasonable people question her parents' choice of name for her - supposing that a name like Lioness probably warped that young girl's sense of self in some extraordinary way.

People were wrong, as usual. Knowing she was the Lion gave her a profound sense of self. A purpose filled life. A passionate drive to succeed where all women before her had failed. Equality was not enough-she would be the leader of the free world.

Yet, now something had gone terribly wrong with the Destiny that had been planned from way before her birth. She always knew she served a purpose far greater than herself, yet the plan was crumbling around her right as she was entering its final stages.

Running. Running. Lungs pumping. Air filling her great lungs, then exhaling into a puff of steam in the cool of the morning. Droplets of sweat soaked her stolen white robe, yet her breath was on the verge of chill.

She saw the homeless – *the Forgotten Men and the Invisible Women* - by the fire turn to stare in sleepy surprise. One shaggy looking man gave her a toothless leer and started to stand. Darting over to their fire, Lioness opened her robe and untied the bloody gown from around her waist. She stopped to catch her breath for just a moment as she made sure to witness every last shred of her Versace gown burn to ashes. The stench of burning blood filled the chilly morning air.

The homeless men, five in all, plus two women, both equally toothless and aged and grey beyond their years, awakened to witness, in a sleepy blur, their fire being used as some weird alter by a wild-haired, wild eyed ghostly beauty. The "one's the world forgot" turned their noses from the retched smell of whatever was burning. Did that flaming white cloth reek of burning hair and blood? In the dead silence and coldess of the dawn they watched their fire rise up in ugly smelling flames, engulfing the white flag that had once been a gorgeous designer gown.

The Forgotten groggily came to their senses. They slowly eyeballed the stranger in the strange land in a flowing white robe using their fire for an unknown purpose. Were they dreaming? Some felt a small pounding in their chests as if a minor heart attack might relieve them of their bodily burdens. Four eventually fell back to old habits and instinctively began a half-hearted, tired attempt to beg for a dollar. The lustful one came toward the Lioness with bad intentions in his heart. She stepped sideways with the grace of an animal and he fell to the ground. Alas, with blood stained dress entirely burnt, Lioness darted off leaving the other four men and shortly thereafter the two women sprawling on hands and knees gathering the multitudes of hundred dollar bills that were dancing in the small breeze of the wake the mysterious creature had left behind.

It has been as if an energy field had come into their presence, then darted right out. Wherever Lioness entered, the energy could be sliced with a knife, and when she exited a place, there was a void that all felt but only the honest admitted.

When the Forgotten Ones stood to watch the disappearing streak of white running in the distance, they heard a great voice fill their hearts and their minds,

"You are not Forgotten, you are precious spirits. Go fly upon the wings of this miraculous gift called life."

Suddenly something internal was changed in each of them. One remembered he had a sister in Toronto and he longed to hear her voice. Another said to himself, "Now is the time to get my education". The man of lust decided he'd like to cleanse himself and join the priesthood he had once dreamed of joining. One man thought of a homeless shelter where he could sneak in a shower, get a set of clean clothes, and perhaps, still could get that job at the fast food joint that he had so often dreamed of owning in his youth - before hardship, drugs and alcohol deprived him of ambition. Now he had a certainty he could work his way up from the bottom and still realized the dream. Another simply knew it was time to return home. Home

August Anderson

to Kansas. The women brought out a comb and began to take turns picking at one another's tangles, while they talked of the possibility that if they pooled their new found money they could share a small apartment, buy some nice clothes, have their hair colored, and maybe look for a job.

Something had changed inside each of them at the sight of the running woman.

They had no way of knowing, everyone was effected internally when they encountered the presence of the Lioness.

Rather than plan their next meal, each of the Forgottens had enough money and inner strength now to plan their new lives. The seed of hope had been planted in the hopeless. And now, each one had a little money with which to start to unleash their changed hearts.

Something always changee in the heart of people in the presence of the Lioness. Sometimes it was goodness and inspiration that were borne of her presence. Often it was deep, dark and ugly – jealousy and hate aroused by her mere presence. Good or Evil took flame when she entered a room. It was all too often based on gender lines. Men were inspired to become great. Women were inspired to hate and looked for a reason to sue. Surely they deserved some of the Godfrey money. But whom did they hate? Lioness for being the Lion? Or themselves, for not being her? For better or for worse, Lioness left no one unchanged.

FBI agent Smith picked up his phone and was getting dressed and running out the door barking orders in less than five minutes. This was history in the making. He could feel it in his gut. This was no ordinary murder, but rather the murder in the family of America's "royalty".

Lioness ran, sure the last of her gown of bloody evidence turned to ashes. *Burn fire burn. Burn blood burn. Burn evidence burn.*

DAVID – MY BEAUTIFUL WIFE

My beautiful Thai wife. She is dead now. My heart is simply numb for this newfound knowledge of the pain of being human. My brain is blurred in anguished sorrow and filled with only excruciating memories of Anne. Tears streaming down my face, I see people surround me, but it is surreal. I don't really see or hear them. I just wander around in shock and anguish. Who would have ever thought being born human could possibly have been this agonizing, this devastatingly cruel, this unpredictable, this tumultuous? I can not catch my breath, and my eyes sting with tears.

Oh, heart of mine, please quit beating in my chest. For what is life without love?

Who would ever choose to be born, knowing they all would, at some point suffer, some related form of this sort of torment? How brave is Everyman to go on living? How cruel is the creator of life to allow such horror? Why? Spare me of the very root of these tears.

Lioness

Anne, my treasure, my darling, the mother of our two perfect children, had only two faults that I know of. First, Lion is the one that introduced us. Second, Anne was married when we met.

I was a young lawyer. I had already graduated from Harvard Law School and served my time in the Peace Corps.

I had been hired right out of Harvard by one of Boston's most prestigious firms – Anderson, Bastile, and Cooke. ABC as we like to call the firm – but never in front of the partners, of course.

Anderson Bastile, as they were commonly known in the industry (Cooke had passed on years ago, but his name was still on the stationery) was famous for grabbing the best of the best as they graduated from ivy league law schools. The partners would train fresh faced ivy leaguers to become the most powerful of the powerful. ABC had nurtured four U.S. Senators, two Governors, sixteen Representatives and innumerable state officers on the east coast in the past thirty-five years. There were no more respected lobbyists anywhere in the world than the lawyers at Anderson Bastile. Now ABC was looking to expand their powerbase to the Midwest and overseas, especially the oil rich middle east. Never was I so glad to be fluent in both Russian and Arabic as the day the partners interviewed me as a young law student.

I was perfect for the only law clerk position they were hiring for that year. I was from South Dakota – the heart of what ABC clientele affectionately called "fly over country". I was valedictorian of my graduating class at Harvard. I was a member of Phi Beta Delta law fraternity, holding its secret scholarship key. I played basketball with finesse and was the star of the swim team. After majoring in Political Science, I had served two years in the Peace Corps in Africa. Then I returned to Harvard to procure my MBA followed by my Juris Doctorate. I had written for Law Review: "The Constitution – a Grant of Immeasurable Power" and later became a Law Review Editor. I had won every Moot Court competition I had ever entered. And I won Am Jurs in no less than five different subjects – Constitutional Law, Remedies, Evidence, Contracts, and Torts. Better still, I was a Democrat. I also had overwhelming political ambition and the family money to back up my ambition.

In short, I was perfect in every way for a career with ABC. And why not? I had secretly been eyeballing Anderson Bastile from the time I entered Harvard, so I made sure I was perfect in every way. I had very thoroughly researched my future employer. I knew what they looked for and I studied and worked myself into the ground to make certain I molded myself to fit their every ideal.

When I received the phone call requesting an interview for a clerkship after my second year of law school, I danced a happy jig. It was the first happy jig I ever danced. My second happy jig was the day Anne agreed to marry me. Other than that, I, David Godfrey, am way too professional to jig!

There is one thing, however, that to this very day continues to irk me about my hiring on as a clerk, then as an associate to the esteemed ABC law firm. Anderson himself told me that it was a tough decision between me and some black chick from Princeton who would have fulfilled affirmative action hiring quotas; thus, gaining

ABC additional esteem as an equal opportunity law firm. They would have hired her, but the deciding factor in my favor was that darned Law Review paper I had written, "The Constitution – a Grant of Immeasurable Power" that revealed to Anderson himself that I was destined to be their single associate hired that year.

Anderson would never know my dirty little secret. I only wrote that article because Lioness, who never even attended law school - heck I'm not even sure she ever graduated from college - had been published a year prior to my being published. Hers was a little known Law Review Article published from South Dakota's only law school. If you graduated from the University of South Dakota law school in the olden days, you could become a lawyer without even taking South Dakota's Bar Examination. So that must explain how Lioness, who never even attended USD, got published! How dare she get published before I did?

That idiot girl, *Lioness the Kiss Ass*, had written an article called "The U.S. Constitution – A Strict Limitation on Power". No one ever read the damned article except me. I do not even think Lioness read her own article. It was boring, opinionated, and inaccurate. But I was so covetous that she was published before I was that I hastily wrote "Immeasurable Power" just to spite the little wench. I went on to become famous for "Immeasurable Power" which was passionately written by me in less than two hours and for the sole purpose of harassing Lioness and to show her that she was an absolute idiot.

After it was published in Harvard's Law Review, "The Constitution – a Grant of Immeasurable Power" was picked up by the New Yorker. After that I became famous as "Power" was then published in about every Liberal think tank and magazine in the world.

And now, the irony was that the article I hastily penned in hate only to spite my kid sister, was the very article that would be the founding corner to launch my own brilliant legal and political career.

PIERCE – THE BEGINNING OF THE END

I heard her heavy breathing at the other end of the phone and I knew this was the Beginning of the End. Lions breathe deeper and slower than humans when they have just finished a run. I recognized the breath even though I was across the raging Atlantic Ocean from her and the phone line was full of static.

Listening to that breath sent memories flowing through my mind. How breathless I was two decades earlier when I saw her riding bareback on that galloping white horse. My search for her every moment I was on or off the set in South Dakota. My nearly giving up ever finding her. I still remembered my walking into the Godfrey production Studio years after that first unforgettable glimpse of an angel galloping by on a churning cloud from heaven.

By the time I finally met Lion, I had already won my second role as a leading man in my now blockbuster spy series. I was the "flavor of the month" and riding high on newfound fame, wealth, and popularity.

August Anderson

When we met, I was not in Hollywood. I was back in South Dakota for two days shooting a small scene where I was supposedly scaling the face of Mt. Rushmore with ropes to escape my pursuer – a terrorist who wanted me dead before he would blow up the monument. Seven of America's most sacred monuments were going to blow at midnight in this film and only I, Luke James, Super Stud Spy, of course, could save them. While simultaneously seducing whichever actress was Hollywood's newest "female flavor of the month".

At that time it was my co-star, Anabelle Lee, who was definitely the hottest actress in Hollywood in a decade. Pregnancy would end her career instantly when her affair with my stunt double would start the ruination of her figure. She got pregnant right as our filming of Sweeter than Sweat was completed. It seems 38-21-33 figures are hard to maintain after one gives birth! And Anabelle was so content to drop out of the spotlight and become a mom she quickly gave birth to three more children without losing the weight in between. I saw her recently, glowing, radiant, and surely topping 300 pounds. Life is the great equalizer, though, and my former stunt double has a paunch and is bald. There was a peace to be found in their normal family life that I would envy, but never have the chance to enjoy for myself.

In any case, we were done shooting for the day because my stunt double, the future Mr. Anabelle Lee, had taken quite a fall. As I returned to my trailer I noticed a stretch limo pulling up, but initially did not give it much thought as I knew our producer was scheduled for a visit.

As I cleaned up in my portable dressing room, I glanced out the small window and again saw the large black limo, but when it pulled directly onto the set, I caught my breath because I instinctively knew something important was about to happen. Moments earlier when the accident rendered my double useless, he was hauled off in the studio's private ambulance. No sooner had the ambulance left my sight, but the limo had pulled into my limited view. I do not believe in coincidences, so some small part of my mind suspected a relationship between the accident and what was about to take place. The timing of the limo arriving just as the ambulance departed seemed suspicious to me.

As I continued to peer out the small window of my trailer, I froze! It was not a limo from our studio. I realized it was from Godfrey Productions because of the design of a crest etched like crystal into the windows with the initials G.P. formed in the shape of a lion. I knew even back then that Godfrey Productions was the only major studio ever to headquarter in South Dakota. The lion insignia had been stamped on many blockbuster movies for years. Rumor had it that Godfrey Productions was run by a mysterious C.E.O. who did not like to leave the State of South Dakota any more than necessary. It was the age of information and technology, so any business could be run from anywhere. Personally, I still had the romantic view that Studios should be in Hollywood, but whatever.

I had the self-confidence instilled in any man born handsome, talented, and athletic. I had the heart of steel born into anyone severely abused as a child. My cocky coolness was triple enhanced by my newfound fame and fortune. Why then, were my legs trembling when I learned the limo was sent for me? Why then, were my palms sweating when I exited the limo and walked into the plush offices of Godfrey Productions – not knowing why I was being so summoned? Or who was doing the summoning.

When I entered the C.E.O.'s office, I felt my breath fly from my body as if a large boulder had hit my chest. My heart pounded in my ears so hard, I was sure strangers could hear its wild throbbing as far away as Sturgis.

My heart fluttered like a bat out of hell.

My throat felt parched, and my head began to spin.

Seeing *her* behind that huge desk in a strict business suit with hair in a harsh bun, a lesser man might not have recognized her, but for those slanted golden green eyes, that told me even then, this creature was not human.

"I hear you've been searching for me," the voice purred and the eye color changed to a deep dark blue akin to the color of the deepest ocean waters. Those eyes would change colors like the ocean dancing in the sun. Aqua one moment, violet the next. It was not possible to pull away from the eyes-you felt they looked not at your body, but were staring into your very soul.

I felt like I was being hypnotized and was really quite dizzy.

Where I had just flushed with heat, I now felt a bone chilling cold tingle down my spine. Was I to gain my composure to speak to this odd and glorious creature?

"I don't know how you could hear that I was searching for you. I've never told a soul." I could hear my own voice and was amazed at how calmly it answered; because internally I was anything but calm.   I was a mess and I was pretty sure I was having heart failure. I know not how I could control the trembling of my voice within my

Lioness

own throat. I could not breathe. I was sure the sweat coming through every pore of my body would leave my Armani suit soaking wet before this meeting was done.

"Precisely." She whispered back, "I know men's secrets that are never told to another." Her whispers would always sound like roars within in my own ears. And her roars would sound like whispers. The voice was indescribable, but it passed sexy miles ago and was somewhere in a new sound range. Did this woman have this effect on all men?

It is now long after that initial meeting. I am now shooting in Europe, my sixth movie and she is a US Senator running for President. Yet when I hear that same sexy, low whisper I had fallen blindly in love earlier, I now know the answer. Yes, her voice has that effect on every man. Her voice seduces while her eyes hypnotize.

Crossing the Atlantic there was some static on the line, so I knew the lines were bugged. Further, global warming and a rise in Ocean depths had interfered with transatlantic phone reception. Most relied on satellite transmissions these days, but when we wanted privacy, we still called one another land line to land line, which meant oceanic interference.

"Code Red. Atlantis." I knew it was a whisper, but it sounded like the familiar roar in my ears leaving my head hurting so bad it was spinning. It hurt. It hurt so good. But there was no time to fantasize about her today.

The time was upon us. I knew what I had to do and I was filled with dread. I hung up the phone and dialed Paul, the pilot to my private jet. I was headed to the Bahamas and this was not going to be pretty.

It is now thirteen days before the Presidential election and all our fears had been realized. The enemy would stop at nothing to defeat us. Right at the finish line, he had taken the boldest step. The enemy had killed.

The only question was, did the enemy live inside or was the enemy outside.

The end was now upon us. Would I thrice deny her this time around, or would I find the courage to serve her through the end?

BEFORE THE DAWN OF TIME

HISTORY OF THE UNIVERSE

Long before man invented time, long before he scribed his first word, bright flaming orange lava exploded from the center of the earth to break up the blackness of the planet.

Land was formed. Water separated from the land, sky from the sea. The acidy smell of sulfur filled the air.

Dinosaurs ruled the planet, Plesiosaurs ruled the sea. Over millenniums, the scent of hard wood penetrated the acid and filtrated the air into a new and glorious atmosphere. Creatures began to walk erect and thumbs became opposable. The smell of cedar wood filled the newly formed atmosphere.

Creation evolved a large brain, and walla, a soft and magnificent housing had been developed for souls to both occupy and engulf. Soft housing shed its scales, then shed its wooly coat and became so touchable it was worthy even to house part of the great Universal Intelligence Himself. A lonely God would never need to be lonely again. The perfume of flowers filled the air.

Life replicated and vibrated upon the planet. Life took millions of forms, all beautiful, to the joy of the once lonely Creator. Add to that, the vibrations of sounding trumpets, the pull of magnets, the intelligence of the creative forces and the result was that pyramids, cities, and all sorts of great wonders took over the planet. The lands smelled of sweat.

In the beginning was the Word, and the Word was with God and the Word was God.

Two thousand and twelve years before the Father of Creation would breathe life worthy of claiming His own bloodlines, man created the written word. Through the written and spoken word, man became more than animals, if still less than gods. With the advent of the word, spoken and written, Mankind was slowly separated from all knowledge he had possessed in the time of creation. Over generations, he used more and more of the word part of the brain, less and less of the creation part. By the time civilization reached its midpoint, when the Son was born, the naked apes would operate theretofore on only one tenth of their original brain power. Most mankind's brain would continue to shrink due to non usage over the centuries. Hence, the brains that built the pyramids no longer existed in the human form. They stayed only among the stars. Only the shadow of those original brains remained - the portion that housed man's languages, that portion that could only view time as lineal, the brain parts that could not peer past death's cloak —only that part of Mankind's original brain survived. Shrinking, shrinking, forevermore shrinking. Man lost sight of the knowledge of the creative God, of world's beyond the earth, of divinity of Man's purpose. The human brain shrank and it shrank. It shrank not so much physically as in its ability to access its greater parts. Yeah, even the desire to access the rest of the brain, simply disappeared. What was the need? They had language.   The air took on many smells.

Man named all those smells and everything else left behind by creation. He named and described them all through Words. Words were first spoken, the written, then spread throughout the lands, they became many tongues. Words had separated Man from the Creator. Now the different tongues separated Man from Man. Words became the most powerful of all weapons. Man learned to hunger for power. Words spoken and written, exploded like the ancient lava around the world. Words resulted in war and peace. But never again did men find divinity of purpose. The air lost its smell.

Throughout history, some men and women, through creative forces would tap into that long dormant, now ancient, nine tenths of the brain. They were visionaries, inventors, artists, revolutionaries and prophets. As sure as the world initially loved them, the world would eventually turn on them and the messages they tried to deliver from the nine tenths of untapped human intelligence were deemed offensive. The messengers, throughout earth's history, were always persecuted or prosecuted.   The air smelled of blood.

Civilization, wrapped in the Word, was born, lived and died, with little understanding of the divinity of individual life; then…

Two thousand and twelve years after the written Word came to Power, He came to earth to clarify Everyman's very sacred purpose.   He was crucified and it rained. The air contained the clean odor of ozone as earth was purified.

Thundering hoof beats were heard on crusades that rushed out distorting His original truth. Noses again smelled blood.

Man learned to live in peace, then there was no smell.

Civilization took on great manners, people wore extravagant clothing, and art and architecture was at its finest since the times of the Ancient Ones. These allowed for a great variety of smells from newly tasted spices to newly woven clothes.

Fighting and work ensued. The earth smelled of sweat.

In times of peace, man again smelled flowers.

Houses were built of wood and forests were cut down to house the great population that appeared all over the globe. The earth smelled of cypress and smoke blowing through pine trees.

Two thousand and twelve years after the truth was delivered at the price of a crucifixion, the final war was launched and people existed in a perpetual state of fear. Their great spirits failed to live in greatness and their minds retreated into even smaller brains as they sold their bodies into prostitution, or perhaps worse, their souls into welfare. It was time for the lamb to return. But the lamb was sorely disappointed. The lamb was angry. The lamb would return as a lion. And, once again, as it was in the beginning, it would be in the end - that the acidy smell of sulfur lingers in the air.

THE BEGINNING OF THE END

LIONESS – FEAR

Her round ears were perked forward. Her slanted eyes were huge with wonder. The golden irises were surrounded with sky blue today and they opened wide around the slits of her pupils. Her nostrils twitched, as the mighty head followed the motion of the fish. Her great jowls were open, the pink tongue swished across her fangs as she salivated in anticipation of the hunt and the feast.

Lions like only one thing more than raw red meat. They love fish. And before her very eyes was the most amazing display of fish she had ever witnessed. Her long elegant claws opened and closed around the calloused pads of her paws in subconscious anticipation of the catch. Every muscle in her body was taunt and ready to pounce. She paced and swished with excitement.

There was only one problem. Fear.
Lionesses have no fear. Or do they?
She was not afraid of flying. Not afraid of heights. She always landed on her feet.

She was not afraid of lightning, thunder, or wind. In fact, she loved the scent of the storm and the way her adrenaline rose to chase the smells brought into her nostrils by the great and powerful wind.

Lionesses are not afraid of creatures in the night, for their acute night vision gives them every advantage.

Lions are not afraid of the moon or the stars. Their spirit longs to howl like a wolf in honor of the wonderment of the great vastness of eternity.

Lionesses are not afraid to be alone. They travel faster that way. They are not afraid to work in a group – they hunt better with their pride. They don't care if they have a king or not – a king is just one more big, lazy, opinionated, conceited jerk to feed.

Lionesses are not afraid of terrorists. Terrorist fears were severely overplayed at the turn of the century for wrongful political gain. Trembling little fools surrendered their rights in exchange for the politico's baseless promises of security.

Lions are not afraid of governments, knowing if an official blockhead attacks you, you attack back at the jugular. Lioness never hesitated to attack the very power base of anyone who attacked a Godfrey business.

A Lioness simply has only one fear. And that fear is huge.

All cats are afraid of water. Deathly afraid of the water. That was her problem today as she stared hungrily at the amazing colorful feast swimming before her very eyes. It was rumored that God Himself had given the Devil jurisdiction over the water! Lioness could not shake her fear of water. She could not fish if she had to go in. She could only pace nervously at water's edge.

She could not swim very well, except to scramble herself quickly to shore anytime she fell, or was tossed as the case may be, into water. She would flail her limbs wildly toward the closest exit so she could fling herself, devoid of her usual grace, onto shore, viciously shaking the burning water off her body. She would never enter the devil's wet underworld voluntarily.

Hence, on that day, she could only gaze in twitching hunger at the mind numbing selection swimming before her.

"Gosh Lioness, you'd think you'd never seen an aquarium before!" Pierce's deep Irish brogue interrupted her thoughts. Startled, she jumped back out of her private thoughts and back into her own skin. Into the here and now. Pierce laughed at having caught her so off guard. She had to laugh, too, because her actor boyfriend rarely let his well trained actor voice slip into the Irish brogue. Hanson had trained for years to eliminate the Brogue and sound as American as if he were born in her country.

"I've never seen an aquarium like this one before!" They were at the formal dinner table next to the huge, famous and amazing Aquarium at the Atlantis Hotel in the Bahamas. Pierce had flown them down there soon after they met in the Godfrey Production Studio. It was her first time in the Bahamas and that world traveler had to confess she was in complete awe at the display of fish in the humongous aquarium beside their table.

Drawing her attention away from that mesmerizing display, she tried to focus on her boyfriend gleefully watching her amazed expressions.

What was he asking of her?

Why was he on the floor? Her fur rose around her neck and her back arched reflexively, ready to fight in his defense. While she had been staring at the multitudes of fish in the aquarium, someone had driven her boyfriend to his knees. She bared her teeth and whirled, ready to attack any foe.

But the sparkle of the huge diamond Pierce held out toward her rendered his purpose clear. Pierce was asking her to marry him!

"Pierce, my love, my joy. My right hand. Sit back down you silly man. You know I adore every cell in your body, every thought in you head, every stirring in your soul, but you know I can never marry you."

Pierce was aghast. He went white. Other diners looked over to see the famous movie star being coolly rejected by the most stunning of all women. Helen of Troy could not have been more beautiful, they mused. Cleopatra could not have looked more dangerous.

Later, when she would run for President, the public's awe would turn to criticism, naturally, for there is nothing Everyman enjoys more than watching the press turn people into heroes, then turning on the heroes like a pack of hyenas and dragging them back down. Raise stars up, then pull them down – that was the very job of the press. It fed the masses and kept them content with having smaller lives than they should have been living. Keeping the masses down was very important to maintaining a power base.

Jealous people felt justified in living very small lives when they watched the mighty fall. It was modern day sport and the masses practiced envy when they should have been practicing life. Seeing heroes come and go was the modern day coliseum where masses watch the doers fall from grace just the same way the Romans watched the Christians being devoured. Something about watching spectacular failures of great achievers always made small achievers feel somehow smugly superior. Or at least grateful that such attention was not turned on themselves. Being invisible and meek look like a most viable option to most people in the modern times of wimps being dominated political gluttons.

The planet had become a planet where most people were living dead. Waiting. Just waiting. For what? For a savior? For the end? For a welfare or unemployment check? To win the lottery? For their parents to die and leave them an inheritance?

"Live, just live." Lioness would roar out to crowds on her campaign trail. "This life is not a dress rehearsal. This is your chance at life. Seize it. Because you may not have tomorrow. You may not have another life. Give this one all you have. Take the risk. Sow the rewards. Live with a passion that borders on violence, but never cross the line unto violence. Merely cross the line unto a vivacious life."

"She advocates violence," her opponents would attempt to launch with the usual onslaught of misquotes and partial quotes.

"Nay, I advocate living life to the fullest," the cat would constantly attempt to correct.

Pierce was remembering their first time in the Bahamas, now, as he flew there for what he knew would be his last time. When he first took Lioness there, she was not yet a Senator.

Pierce had publicly proposed in front of the great aquarium. Now he did not know what to say, but he begrudgingly admitted to himself that he'd known, deep down in his gut, this would be her response. He had simply denied it to himself while searching for an engagement ring stunning enough to do her justice. Stunning enough, he hoped, to change her mind on the subject of marriage.

Pierce had argued with himself all the way to the Bahamas, but he knew that he could not sleep again in his life, if he did not at least ask her to marry him. Pierce did not believe in going through life wondering "what if". And, he was taking Lion's own advice to try. Try and fail. Try and fail a thousand times, but continue to try until you finally succeed.

He understood fully that *one loses many battles on the way to winning the war.*

Further, his stubborn pride could hardly accept that there was a woman alive that could resist him, although resist him Lion always had. Still, he had to be true to his heart – he had to ask her.

Some of the on looking diners were amused. Others were surprised. Pierce could read his audience out of his peripheral vision (body language and peripheral vision often became a seventh and eighth sense in children violently abused). Some of the onlookers grabbed their cell phones to tell the press what they were witnessing or to take photos they could later sell. Others phoned home to tell their loved ones. Some just looked sad that they no longer loved so passionately.

Before Pierce and Lioness returned to the United States, the failed proposal was all over the tabloids. Photos and all. Darn those cell phones that took pictures, anyway.

Lioness was the only woman who had ever said "no" to Pierce on anything. And Pierce was a man already accustomed to getting everything he wanted. He was not just strikingly handsome, he had an air of power and eloquence borne only by a Prince that defied his wretched, poverty stricken childhood.

All his life, in order to survive, he had fine tuned his instincts, his cunning, and his looks to survive. As an adult, he now combined all this inner strength with an uncanny intelligence to promote the enterprise he created out of Pierce Hanson. He was now an irresistible force among men and women alike. The charisma of the Kennedys had nothing over his own.

Yet, Lioness constantly and continually said "no" to him - on every subject. Was she making up for any wrong he had ever committed against any other woman – starting from denying, then abandoning his own mother? Was her denial the subconscious root of his fascination for Lion. Did he only want her becuase she did say no to him where every other woman said yes? Did he absolutely have to have her, simply because she could not be had?

"Of course, you can marry me. We are a grown man and woman. I love you. We can have it all. Give me one good reason you will not marry me." He slowly rose from his knees and his tight, horse back riding, famous rear-end somehow found his chair.

"There are more reasons than we have time to discuss right now. Not the least of which is my obligation to the women of the world. They need to know there are highly moral and successful women who make it on their own without a man. Without a husband many women are convinced they are unsuccessful. Women need to clearly understand that their only purpose in life is not to marry and reproduce. Not to serve a husband. These can be a purpose, but it is not the only purpose of women. I owe it to women everywhere to demonstrate that a woman can be successful, happy, and fulfilled off her own efforts – with or without a husband or children. Female humans are told by schools, jobs, parents, bueurocrats, churches and society that marriage and children are their greatest options. I'm here to say that those options can be great, but all too often those options are modern day versions of slavery. Beatings, humiliations, working like a dog for no pay are all too often the price women pay for loving a man. I am here to say with the demonstration that is my life, that women can achieve their full potential without marriage and reproduction – should that be their choice. And should they chose to marry and reproduce, by first having discovered and fulfilled their divine calling they will be far more exciting partners to their husbands and far more stimulating parents to their offspring. Women must learn to garner and encourage lifetime respect and love from the man they chose. It should be an honor for a man to be faithful to his wife, not something easily discarded by a man when menopause approaches or the going gets tough."

"But you have already lived that example, my Princess, and I will always respect you as the intelligent businesswoman and golden hearted beauty that you are. You have told me all public reasons you will not become my wife. You have not told me a single personal and private reason why, following your own heart, you will not marry me."

He asked for the blunt truth, but was Pierce ready to hear it?

Ask and ye shall receive.

"I am only half human, dear. Lionesses do not marry mortals. I am already married to my purpose here on earth."

"Don't be ridiculous or I'll make you change your name once and for all. I'm still waiting for a single good reason we should not marry. I *KNOW* you love me, as I love you-from the beginning to the end of all eternity."

Lioness nodded warily in agreement. Her own distress at saying no was reflected in those great eyes, which were now emerald green.

"Then why not?" Pierce hissed the question with a dangerous power he usually reserved for self-defense.

"*Because it is not my destiny.* You know that, My Immortal Beloved."

THE BOOK OF PIERCE

PIERCE – FEAR

Pierce's mind reflected back, as it so often did, to their very first meeting at the Godfrey Studios in Spearfish, South Dakota.

"What is the real reason you called me here?" Pierce was sweating profusely from nerves. His instinct told him this was a woman who would respect courage, but could eat you alive if you showed any sign of weakness. He determined then and there he would always be courageous for her.

"I need a favor."

"Sure. Anything. Just ask."

I hope it involves sex.

"No it does not involve sex."

Wait a bloody minute, I didn't say the sex thing out loud, did I? Damn, I hate women who can read my mind!

"That is too bad because yours is really easy to read!" She was mocking him.

"Well quit it then."

"Thine will be done."

"So why am I here?" Pierce somehow summoned his voice, although it reverberated oddly in his own ears.

"I knew you were thinking of me since the Costner shoot so long ago. I have a confession. I've been thinking of you since years prior to that, since childhood and beyond. Some day you will remember many things. In this carnation, we met in Ireland as children. Mercifully, your memory was wiped clean, but I've remembered your hair, your eyes, your pain for all the days of my life."

She cleared her throat and continued, "You haunted me right to the date I saw you ride in the Rolex Three Day Event. I was always enamored by you, but thought it best I only watch from a distance. I attend Rolex as a spectator every year. The year you competed, many horses were spooking on the course at the scent of a lion, so I made sure to go to a distant hill and watch your ride from afar so as to not overwhelm that brilliant red mare you rode. I watched several amazing cross country rides; but, when I saw you ride at Rolex I was knew the overwhelming yearnings, at long last, of being a human woman. I felt a kind of love for you I've felt for no other. I was awe struck with emotion, with you, your horse, your ride, and your win. Watching your ride that great chestnut Irish Thoroughbred galloping like the Devil Himself was chasing you, I felt what the Italians call, 'Thunder Struck'. I knew a passion that was so human as to be embarrassing."

"I have felt your presence over the years and sneaked peaks at the world through your eyes. I felt your presence in Keystone when you were a young extra on the set of Dances with Wolves. Later I bought the video and watch the scene you were in over and over, until the tape literally wore out in that spot. I've seen every movie since then that you ever starred in. But on that day in Keystone, I

Lioness

wanted you to see me. I felt your approach all the way from Rapid City, so I ran for my white mare and leaped upon her back without taking time to groom, or saddle and bridle her. I would be flying by when you drove toward Mt. Rushmore and my timing had to be perfect if you were to see me. I wanted the seeds of my existence to be replanted in your head because I knew you had forgotten our childhood encounter.. I knew when you saw me ride by on my white mare. I knew you were looking at me then and looking for me since that moment. I could stand it no longer, I rode by you on purpose that day that you were to see me flying buy in Keystone. I felt it was time to plant in your mind and heart the possibility that I did exist, even though I recognized you were not destined to meet me yet. You and I both had our own careers, our own destinies, our own characters needing to fully develop so I had to stay away. We could not meet until you were strong enough to carry out your own divine purpose in the plan for the human race. When you finally were in my home state shooting this time, I really felt your presence and your power and looked insed you and your were a fully developed strong and confident man – just in time for us to meet."

Pierce confessed, "The possibility of meeting you has haunted me year after year after year - from that day to the moment I walked into this office. I often thought that I just conjured you up out of my vivid imagination."

"I know. But your existence has haunted me since before we met as children."

"I don't get that. We've met before as children? No way. I'd have remembered you!"

"Your memory of our childhood meeting was blocked by the beating you received at the hands of the man you believed to be your father. He was not. When I watched your cross-country gallop later at Rolex as an adult, I recognized that the boy had turned into a heckuva man. And I knew you were the one. Actually, I've always known."

"What one?"

"The one who would stand beside me through the end."

"What in heaven's name are you talking about?"

Heaven's name might just be the right instinct!

"I'm talking of things so deep, so serious, so beyond your imagination that I could not begin to tell you of them right now. First, you, as a cautious man, do not know me, so you would have no way of knowing if you could believe me. You would simply walk out of here and call the nuthouse. Second, a mind can only take in a little totally new information at a time."

"Well, then let's start with today. Why, dear Princess, have you summoned me today?"

"I want you to teach me to ride."

"I saw you riding that white horse. You don't need me to teach you to ride. You have a natural seat that defies belief. Indeed, defies even gravity."

"But I don't have an *educated* seat. Sure Compassion – that is the name of the white mare you saw me on - allows me the joy of becoming one with her for mad gallops, but she does not know, neither of us knows, how to execute a flying change on command. A half pass to the beat of music...What are judges looking for in the rein back? What is your audience looking for in the musical

Lioness

freestyles? Where is the right spot to jump from? What pace is the proper pace into water, jump across a spread, down a steep hill?"

"Whoa girl, whoa with the questions. I get it. OK. But it takes years to learn jumping and dressage."

"I have years. Don't you?"

"If they are to be spent with you, I'll find them. Do you have any other horses?"

"I thought you'd never ask."

So off the star and the lion whisked in the GP stretch limo to her stable in the hills near Keystone. They entered a glorious barn with huge stalls and indoor arena surrounded by runs, pastures, trails, outdoor arenas, cross country courses….in short everything needed to ride in comfort all year round. Everything needed to ride any of the Olympic Disciplines. The GP insignias, for Godfrey Pruductions, were tastefully on blended into the buildings and landscape. One was on the rod iron gate when entering the one hundred acre estate, another on a stadium jump, while another was on the barn at its very peak. The odd couple was greeted by a heard of three tail wagging huge white dogs. Great Pyrenees, naturally. One was actually named G.P., short for Great Pyrenees, Lion explained;.

Later over their dating years, Pierce would see the sign all ove rthe Godfrey empire - from business cards to yachts.

One of the other huge white dogs was named Madonna, and the final huge white beast was named The Saint.

It turned out the Lioness had four horses and would begin her lessons that very day. Pierce would learn that

Lioness never put off until tomorrow anything she could accomplish that day – it was almost as if she saw the time clock of the entire world ticking rapidly out of control, spiraling ever faster toward an eternal midnight.

The White Mare, Compassion, was almost thirty years old by now and was the only horse that willing let Lioness even sit on her back! They were going to have a challenge with the three others.

Upon merely thinking he needed some breeches and boots, a groom appeared, seemingly from out of nowhere with breeches, boots, and a T-shirt for Hanson. The groom directed Pierce to the tack room with mirrors and Pierce had never been so glad to strip out of a suit in his life. The suit was soaked with sweat from the excitement of meeting her in the studio."

A quick rinse in the sink in the tack room and a change in to riding apparel made the star rider feel right at home and her was ready to meet the rest of the horses.

The Red Gelding, Peace, reared up in terror and threw her off the minute Lion's seat hit the saddle. At 18 hands and trained to Grand Prix level of jumping, Lion was launched before her right foot even found its stirrup. Pierce was sure she was going to die. Oddly, as she flew through the air she twisted her body to almost defy the very force of gravity and somehow she landed with grace in a crouched position on her hands and feet. For just a moment, Pierce was convinced he was looking at a cat immediately before she gracefully arose to an erect position.

Pierce decided to mounted Peace, to teach him some manners, but the horse was such a perfect gentleman for him. The surprised and happy man even did a small stadium course just to show off a little for his new princess. The big gelding performed with perfect rhythm, perfect form. He displayed fantastic scope and bascule. Obviously, someone had put some mighty big bucks into buying some of the best horses in the world, already trained. Pierce could not help but wonder why this perfectly trained horse had launched Lioness, yet was butter melting to his aids when Pierce was on his back.

Lioness needed study how to connect with that exquisite European training, he concluded. Yes, in fact, she did need Pierce as an equestrian teacher. Pierce was glad she needed him for that. Lioness struck him as such an independent woman she probably did not need any man for much of anything else. Except, perhaps, to warm her frigid body he mused? He thought he detected a glare when he galloped by imagining her naked.

Pierce felt an inner sigh of relief knowing she needed him for something. A more independent woman had never been created on this earth.

Bringing Peace in to a halt, the great red beast was barely breathing because the horse was so fit and the course had been so easy for Peace to negotiate. It reminded Pierce of the horse he had ridden for his famous Rolex win. Unfortunately, it also reminded him of his broken heart when the owner of the horse, his sponsor, had pulled it out from under him to give to the owner's mistress. Pierce determined then and there he would make enough money to own his own horses from that point on. Never again would his heart be broken by losing an equine partner he had spent years training. But one movie after another came along and Pierce had not ridden since that time.

It felt ecstatic to experience this powerhouse fire breathing dragon under him that was so uncannily like his Rolex event horse.

Hanson begrudgingly turned the great red beast over to an awaiting groom to cool down, bathe, and return the powerful creature its stall. As a trainer Pierce had so loved the grooming part of bonding with a horse. The smell, the nostrils, the silky flowing tail. Indeed as President Ronald Regan had once quoted, *"The outside of a horse is good for the inside of a man"*.

There were not enough hours left in that perfect sun filled day for Pierce to groom. That slice of heaven awaited him for many more days in the future. But today, another groom brought in the next horse belonging to Lion.

The mount was a smaller Grand Prix dressage stallion, Eternal Hope. Hope was a shocking looking bugger as he was Cremello. He had inherited the "golden" dilute gene from a palomino sire and a palomino dam, so he had spooky looking blue eyes and was so pale as to look almost the color of bubbling Champagne. Hope was so well disciplined in dressage, that in spite of initially nervously objecting to having a lion on his back, after a few crow hops he did finally settle down and allowed her to experience some of his impeccable European trained flying changes. But when Lioness asked him to skip along doing a flying change of lead every stride, Hope kept doing them every other stride.

"You must TRUST your horse. He knows his job. You are not asking fast enough, or in the correct rhythm. He is giving you twos because you are asking for twos," Pierce coached. "If you want ones, you need to be asking him for the second change before he has even given you the first change. Trust he'll give you the first one and ask for the second one before the first one is completely executed - and just keep asking...." When she finally got two single tempe changes in a row she had worn the poor, noble horse out and quit on that great note. Hope would teach her a lot. And that great lesson was a sign of the many, many more fabulous horse filled times the two of them were going to experience over the years. Pierce was happy. Lioness was happy. They both glowed at one another.

The final horse, Lion did not even attempt to ride as night was approaching. It was a large black thoroughbred gelding named Joy's Pride. That was an understatement! He had turbo engines on his ass such that he exploded with joy and he was trained to the Advanced Level of eventing. The horse was dynamite and his short fuse was already lit. Pierce knew of the horse because he was virtually undefeated in Eventing at five star events under his former owner, Joe Norman. About a year prior, the great horse had disappeared off the event scene and no one knew why – except Mr. Norman who had been a dead broke horse trainer before the horse had disappeared off the show circuit. Norman had gone on a world wide spending spree and never rode again, having plenty of money to retire. There had been speculation of fowl play that perhaps the great black horse had been destroyed and Joe was spending the insurance money. Pierce never did believe that of the man with the talent to train and ride "The Black", as the Eventing world had all called Pride. What a great relief to see this magnificent blue black beauty was healthy, shiny and breathing fire in this spectacular stable. The riddle was finally solved for

Pierce. Eventing's superstar was living a quiet and private life in the Black Hills of South Dakota. Pierce was glad – the horse had earned the right to live in horse heaven right here, right now. Joe had earned the right to spend tons of Godfrey money having raised and trained one of history's greatest competitors. Pierce was dying to know how much money was involved, but his manners kept him from asking.

Lion called the great black Joy, but Pierce chose to call him by the name his thousands of Eventing fans had always called him – The Black. Or Black Pride as others had dubbed. The Black seemed to recognize his name when Hanson stroked his neck and called to him. He held his head high on a powerful neck rising high out of the withers. Watching the horse gallop he almost put no weight on his front end and the long legs grabbed at air gave him the appearance of spider legs in front, while the huge, muscle toned rear pushed powerfully. The horse looked like he hovered over the ground rather than touching it when he moved he was so light and extravagant on his feet.

The white of Pride's eyes revealed fear when Lioness neared. He obviously did not want Lion on his back. They agreed that Pierce would ride Pride and Peace for awhile and give the lessons to Lioness on the other two. Wow! What an animals they were.

Pierce had ridden horses for the previous 20 years of his then 34 years of life and had learned from the best of the best in Europe. It was going to take every ounce of my Olympic Caliber skill to ride Pride. There was no freaking way Lioness would handle that hot steed for

Lioness

years, if ever. Pierce couldn't wait to have that beast explode cross country underneath his famous arse!

Pierce left Lion's ranch that night the happiest man on earth. H ran the joyous memories over and over in his brain as the limo transported him back to his hotel room in Rapid City. Every flinch of her seat, every smile, every response of the horses, the sound of her laughter, the cute innocence of her horses' names: Compassion, Hope, Peace, and Joy. *How lovely. What a lovely woman, inside and out!*

What beautiful horses. White, Red, Black, Cremello. *One of every color*, Hanson mused.

Kind of odd choice of colors for a woman who could buy any horse she wanted in the world. European standards were bays, blacks and chestnuts. She must have really searched Europe to find such talent in such odd colors.

White, Chestnut, Black and Cremello.

White, Red, Black and Pale.

Pierce floated into his hotel room at the Alex Johnson. He was happy, fulfilled. He had met the woman of his dreams. He imagined his every fantasy with that woman. He wanted her. He wanted her for his life and for his wife. All others would forevermore fail in comparison with Lioness. She was rich, brilliant, and breathtakingly beautiful. And she loved horses as Pierce did! Compassion, Hope, Peace, and Joy. Pierce could not even begin to wipe the stupid "I'm in love" smile from his strikingly handsome face.

High cheekbones, piercing blue eyes, dark thick hair with a mere hint of auburn highlights. His reddish highlights were more pronounced when he spent time in the sun. His shiny hair was just wavy enough to drop sexily across his intelligent brow and fall into his eyes. The star was famous for the tossing his own great mane out of his eyes before he seduced starlets in his movie. Pierce knew he could seduce most mortals on that single gesture.

Lioness had not shown any reaction when he tried all his subtle movie star moves on her. The seduction of the lion was, indeed, going to be a challenge. A challenge Hanson was completely up for.

Pierce knew that very first day he had to have Lioness. *As my wife. As my eternal soul mate.* He already knew that no other woman would ever compare. Athletic. Intelligent. And a beauty that defied description. And, oh, those lovely horses.

White, Red, Black, and Pale. America's favorite sex symbol threw myself happily down on the hotel room bed; in spite of the fact that Lioness was not joining him there. Happy pictures of horses and the most striking woman he had ever seen galloped through his head.

"JEEEEZZZZUUUUUSSSSSS HOLY SHIT!!!" Pierce cried out to know one in his empty room as he sat up so fast he snapped his strong, muscular, and tan neck. "Ouch, damn it," he cursed. He lunged toward the bedside. Oh, thank goodness for the Gideons! There was a bible there. He flipped to the back to the book of Revelations and started skimming fast, trying to remember from his Irish Catholic childhood, what Revelations contained. Reading rapidly, fear and sweat poured out of his being.

A brown piece of parchment paper floated out of the Bible and landed on the carpet by my bed. Pierce absentmindedly picked it up, then noted interesting markings on ancient looking yellow/brown paper. The angular yellow lines looked like the papyrus paper, or the imitation banana paper, of the Egyptians. It had some sort with burnt edges with both hieroglyphics and Greek looking writing on it. Pierce thought for a spit second about the Rosetta Stone that translated Ancient Egyptian to Ancient Greed. He wondered, was it in the Cairo museum in Egypt?

Pierce was in a hurry to get back Revelations of the bible, so he tossed the strange parchment into his open suitcase. He hurriedly returned his intense focus back to the Gideon Bible before him. He knew exactly what he was searching for.

He got to Revelations 6 and slowed down his reading to a crawl as goose bumps erupted all over the 6 foot 3 inch tall, sun bronzed and muscular body.

Goosebumps reveal spiritual truths.

HOLY SHIT. HOLY SHIT. HOLY SHIT. Pierce turned green as he ran to the bathroom, fell to his knees and began to wildly vomit into the porcelain toilet bowl.

White, Red, Black, and Pale! Had he just met the four horses of the apocalypse? Had Pierce just danced with the devil? *White horse to conquer, Red horse for war, Black Horse for greedy trade, Pale horse for death with Hades to follow! The Apostle John had written of these visions of the end of the world.*

NO! NO! NO!

The dream, at that very moment, suddenly turned into a nightmare.

PIERCE – CURIOSITY

Pierce had carried the yellow stained paper with him everywhere he went for many years. He dared not speak of it, but he always had it near him.

He had carried it from the hotel that night, onto every set, wherever he traveled, and through the years of falling ever deeper in passionate love with Lioness.

For all the years the paper haunted Pierce and traveled with him he had shown it to no one. Now, he was about to show the paper that swooped out of the bible the night he met his true love to a total stranger.

Pierce suffered a minor anxiety attack accompanied by stomach pains as he climbed the steps of the language department at Harvard. He was inhibited by Ivy League colleges since he never had the opportunity to finish high school. All his life he studied – languages, horses, geography, fencing, shooting, acting, art, architecture, and drama. But those learned in writing, philosophy, physics, and law – they still demanded awe in Mr. Hanson. Yet, Pierce had to know what his parchment said.

The movie star was currently on to a set at the Boston Harbor. Hence, in spite of his inferiority complex about university learning, Pierce found himself climbing the steps at Harvard, leading to the language department. And toward Ms. Johnson, the Ancient Languages Department Head, who had sounded more than willing to indulge a famous movie star with his silly little piece of paper.

Pierce's mother had taught him to read, do math, and write. After running away from home, he only sought to deny and defy his childhood roots of poverty and abuse, so all learning institutions of great repute made him nervous.

At night Hanson had taken classes at community centers – foreign languages (he worked hard to lose his Irish accent as he knew from birth his destiny was to be an actor in America), acting, playwriting, self-defense and more. During the day, he worked a minimum of 14 hour days. He started his mornings, seven days per week in stables mucking out stalls, driving tractors, feeding and watering horses. At the end of the day, too tired to stand, Pierce always sought to expand his mind. During the morning hours, he did all he could to learn the ways of horses. Noon hours Pierce waited tables in the nicest restaurants he could find in order to learn the manners and mannerisms of the wealthy. Afternoons were reserved for any acting and modeling jobs he could land. Evenings were reserved for "book learning" except when Pierce was performing in plays.

In Pierce's mind only Noblemen rode horses, so he was determined, he too, would be a great rider – a Knight in Shining Armor – not the son of an alcoholic gardener and a poor abused Irish maid. Determined to take his weaknesses and make them his strengths, Pierce's sharp mind craved the education he could never afford, so he did his best to learn at night school and wherever else he could. The majority of his education came from the school of hard knocks.

At the stables, though, the thin, quiet young man showed such talent with horses he was soon promoted to groom and eventually got to hack out some of the lesson horses on their days off. His talent was then spotted by the head master and gradually part of his meager pay was taken in the form of a daily riding lesson. Lunging round and round for months before he could touch the reins, he developed the seat and posture of a Prince. Eventually he became one of the top Event riders in Ireland, then he could write his own ticket and get a nice paying job at any top stable in the world. That he did, throughout Europe until he had seen the world – horses during the day, any bit part in a play or commercial whenever he could sneak it in at night. He worked his way from homeless waif to superstar over decades of blood, sweat, and tears. He had the calluses to prove it. Later, as a superstar Pierce would often joke that it took him twenty years of hard work to become an overnight success.

Pierce felt that his "doctorate in the school of hard knocks" rendered him profoundly qualified for anything and everything.

But was he qualified to be one of the Lion's chosen ones? Could anyone be so qualified?

As he slowly conquered the great marble steps to the Ancient Languages Department, he felt the lump in his throat – for a lifestyle he would never know? Or knowledge he did not have the time to absorb in this lifetime?

Years earlier he had placed the browned paper into his suitcase in South Dakota, but from that moment on, the paper seemed to haunt him. Every time he opened his suitcase, it had somehow managed to float to the top of his clothes, even when he specifically remembered placing it at the bottom of his suitcase. He was drawn to it and its strange markings. The paper was different shades of beige, yellow and brown. Lines ran at ninety degree angles, up and down, back and forth. Edges crinkled and burnt looking. He constantly looked at it. A disturbing warmth flooded his body each time he held it in his large hands or stroked it with his long, straight, elegant fingers.

Once, during a one day shoot in Kansas City, he did not see it immediately because it fell onto his hotel room bed when he opened his suitcase and he felt a panic in his heart. In a Bozeman diner he held it in his hands turning it around and around, dying to know what those marks met. Often he just felt like walking among down to earth people so he would go to a local diner as inconspicuously as possible. He did show it to some farmers in the diner. Those were the only eyes to see it before he climbed the Harvard steps that day. The Montana farmers merely shrugged and said it looked Latin, Greek, or Hebrew.

Several suggested that he consult a leading expert on languages.

When Pierce had learned he would be going next to shoot in Boston, he made some preliminary phone calls. When he found Himself on location in Boston, and he had the afternoon off, he mused-what would it hurt to visit the rumored "queen of ancient languages" at Harvard?

August Anderson

The women before him looked like a typical librarian. Thick glasses. Crooked teeth. Pale skin. Probably forty something. Old enough and ugly enough, she would fall into that category of invisible women. American men tended to ignore the old and the ugly women. Older men in America seemed not to see their own paunched stomachs, pale skin, wrinkles and baldness as a problem and often were under the delusion they were entitled to a supermodel. The over forty women on the other had were often so lovely in intellect and spirit that they were the true beauties of the world. The wiser among the American older women, simply sought companionship outside the United States once they reached the "disposable age" – usually about the time they hit forty. Fortunately, foreign men saw the treasures hidden within intelligent, successful older women that American men so often discarded for hot young idiots.

Pierce shook his head wondering if he had become Americanized because of his negative thoughts about professor Johnson's physical lack of attractiveness. Yet, he justified, she even had a hint of a moustache! And those nose hairs – YUCK!

Johnson was so thin she could be anorexic. *So unlike the muscular Lioness.* And the ugly professor was literally shaking as she gazed at Pierce's yellow-brown paper.

"My gosh, where did you get this?" Ms. Johnson whispered in awe. She trembled so badly, Pierce thought she might have Parkinson's disease.

He repeated the story to her for about the third time, the first two tellings had been on the phone convincing her to see him. Twice on the phone she had indicated she was too busy to look at some simple piece of paper discovered in a hotel room in Podunk Town. When he told her he was Pierce Hanson, her tone suddenly changed. "Yes, please bring it in the moment you get to Boston."

Star power had its advantages.

Pierce was naturally becoming irritable as he repeated his story for her again. Was the woman stupid? Or was she so awe in being in the same room with a Superstar she simply could not think?

Deciding the professor must be a bit daft, Pierce arose and reaching for his parchment stated, "Maybe coming here was a mistake…"

The ugly bespeckled woman's speed with which she snatched the paper out of Pierce's reach caught him by surprise. Yet she continued to mutter like an idiot, complete with drool creeping out of the left corner of her mouth, "Oh my. Oh my. Where did you get this?"

Crap. Not again. "I think I'll just take it and go." He reached for the delicate brownish document, but Johnson again surprised him with the speed at which she yanked it away. She dove for brighter light while Pierce worried aloud that it might crumble, if she were not more careful with it.

"It appears to be an ancient Aramaic language with touches of Hebrew and Greek intermixed. Yet, it appears to be written on Egyptian papyrus. I've only seen one thing like it in the world. It is very, very old. My guess would be a couple of thousand of years. Would you mind if I keep it and send it down to our labs for age testing?"

"How long would that take?"

"Less than a week."

"Good, I'll still be in Boston then. Will they take really good care of it? I've never left it since it fell out of that bible years ago."

"Absolutely. Our labs are the best in the world and you won't even see any difference when I return this to you."

It made Pierce nervous to think of his pet paper not being with him, but he had to know why it haunted him, "I suppose that would be OK, if you first tell me what is written on it, and promise to return it to me the very moment the testing is done."

"I promise. But I suspect it should be in a museum. Perhaps in the Vatican."

"Say, What?"

"I think you stumbled across a small part of the Dead Sea Scrolls!"

"What Dead Sea Scrolls? In a hotel in South Dakota? Not possible. Never mind. Just write down what it says for me, I have to get back to the set."

Ms. Johnson licked her lips, adjusted her glasses, then slowly, neatly penned her best interpretation of the text:

The Second Coming will begin at the end. The end shall begin with the final war launched by a king at a time when five living kings have come before and one king comes after. A Savior shall rise to power to enlighten mankind only after the Apostles, lead by Peter, recognize and identify The Savior unto the world. The Link to the Power of the Universe houses His Holy blood and has been scattered to the Four Winds of this World by the twelve Apostles. The Sacred Vessel awaits Peter's enlightenment to bringing the pieces together. May the moons and the stars be his guide.

"This is my best educated guess for the time being."

"What do you mean for the time being?"

"Until I find a Rosetta Stone of sorts, or someone more skilled in ancient languages…"

"I thought you were the world's leading expert."

"That is what some say, but as I explained to you on the phone, if it is a language I am not familiar with, there is a lot of guessing as to correct interpretation."

Pierce painstakingly read the words aloud as Dr. Johnson took more than an hour trying to figure out the most accurate way to translate this bizarre combination of ancient scribing. Even the Bible had been open to so many possible translations, and this did resemble some of the ancient biblical texts she had seen when she studied in the Vatican library for a year under the disguise of a being nun.

"That's it? That's all it says?"

"That is not exactly all. These marks encircling the text on the left, the right, the top and the bottom of the paper also have meaning."

"What do they say – write it down just as it is presented."

On top she slowly penned: He Who Finds This is Hereby Called

On the bottom Johnson interpreted: Truth is Opposite the Second Time Around

Johnson turned the document sideways. On the left hand side was written sideways, from bottom to top: Time is not Lineal

On the bottom, after turning both the original document and the paper she was carefully preparing for

Pierce upside down, she scrolled down the paper: Let the Triangles lead you to the moons and the stars

She was shaking so hard, both her pen and her glasses fell to the floor beside her writing table simultaneously. He nose was running and her ugly little beady eyes were growing wider by the minute.

For the fifth time she stuttered, "Oh my gosh, where did you get this?"

Before Pierce could answer for the umpteenth time, she continued, "Who are you, anyway?"

The esteemed scholar stood up straight with anxiety and began backing slowly way from Pierce with a new found fear being revealed in her squinty little eyes. Her hooked nose gave her the appearance of a hawk and her skinny fingers appeared as claws as she clutched the document to her flat chest. Yup, she definitely looks like a hawk, Pierce decided. Unpleasant little hawk girl screeched out with an equally unpleasant little voice, "I once found a similar paper in Rome."

She hesitated, considering if she should reveal her secret to this man who stood before her with the beauty of a god. What the heck, he had trusted her with his secret so Johnson took a deep breath to gather her courage and decided to take a chance. "It was in an ancient bible at the Vatican. I was amazed because it appeared to be written in Hebrew and Greek woven into Aramik on paper similar to your papyrus, here. I had pulled out this dusty old bible from behind some other ancient books. As I opened the bible, a paper dropped to the floor and I instinctively put it in my pocket to carry out with me. Don't get me wrong, I'm no thief and I'm no Catholic. I was in Rome on a secret project to prove the church wrong

- by accurately interpreting the ancient books the Vatican so carefully guards. It was an acting job better than any you have ever done; my convincing the Swiss guards I was a nun. Anyway, I digress. I was not stealing the paper, because I intended and did return it. I just wanted to study it alone. When I returned to my hostel room that night, in the ancient part of Rome, I transcribed, "The bearer must stand beside the seeker." It had no meaning at the time. I had nearly forgotten about it, until you walked in and showed me this. What if I were the Bearer of that paper and you are now the Seeker?"

Pierce was agitated, confused, and cruel, "Sorry, sister, where I'm going, you can not stand beside me. It is a Lion I choose to stand beside me anyway, not some skinny little hawk."

Was that hurt or disappointed he saw in the hawkish face of Joan Johnson? Perhaps he should not have been so harsh.

The little skeleton of a woman had gone from pale, to paler, to an odd sort of green coloring. She looked as if she were about to faint. Pierce reached for a glass of water that was surrounded by clutter and discarded sunflower seed shells on a nearby desk.

"Are you the seeker?" she sank into her chair as far from Pierce as the messy office would allow.

Ms. Johnson gulped the water Pierce was shoving at her and slobbered gratefully as she tried to regain some semblance of composure.

"What does this mean?" Pierce looked puzzled at the simple transcription that did not make an ounce of sense to him.

"I can't be sure, but if you ask me, since you are the one who found it, perhaps you are the one who is supposed to figure it out," the spectacled one seemed to be regaining some semblance of composure.

"I have to get back to work. Here is my cell phone number, call me when you determine its age and authenticity - and let me know when and where I can pick it up when you are done," Pierce scribbled down his private cell number. He reached toward his wallet and said, "Can I pay you for your transcribing services?"

The pale one shook her greasy brown hair so violently that a cloud of dandruff hovered before falling to her narrow, slumped shoulders, "No. Just mention me with kindness in history."

"Say what?"

"Never mind," Ms. Johnson looked suddenly very old and very exhausted as she handed Pierce the white paper with the puzzling words transcribed into English.

Pierce darted out the door and just before closing it, he glanced back at the frail, exhausted woman with small, bloodshot eyes. He could have sworn he heard her whisper, "May the moons and the stars guide you, Peter."

DAVID – EDUCATING

Hanson had an easy afternoon of minor retakes on the set in the Boston Harbor. A modern day tea party scene was being shot for his latest movie.

Pierce got nervous toward the end of the shoot because he knew he was going to face a far shakier situation than his one earlier in the day past those marbled steps of Harvard. He trembled in anxious anticipation of the meeting he had that night. By the time the shoot wrapped for the day he was positive the pain in his stomach meant he was developing an ulcer. All for the love of his mysterious woman.

It would be over by 4:00 the next morning at the Koh Samui Restaurant in Boston. Not a single person who was lucky enough to be dining at Samui's at 7:00 p.m. the previous night when the two gods walked, had departed the restaurant. As soon after the two forces had entered, no one came, no one went.

Those lucky enough to be in the room with the two most gorgeous men of modern times were not about to leave. The waiters were not about to leave. The restaurant owner was not about to leave, nor let any more diners in.

The diners recognized the powerhouses instantly. They cell phoned the press, their families, and their colleagues. They whispered brief reports, clicked and transmitted cell phone photos, then hung up quickly. Ordering one more dish of sticky rice with fresh mango. One more dish of thai soup. They'd nibble on anything to keep their places in a restaurant where they sensed history in the making.

Inch by inch, chairs and tables and ears moved closer to the two men. The public's strongest desire was to overhear any snippet of conversation between these giants. It was not just the facts that they could sell their stories to the press the next day and that they would have fantastic fodder for conversation at dinners and at parties for years to come. That, too, but there was more to it. In Koh Samui that night there was something in the air you could almost slice with a knife – a sinewy sexual energy between the men. A spiritual magnetism that described description resembling a controlled explosion of pure energy. A soft aura of light so powerful that eyes almost dared not look upon the men surrounded and stroked the diners. Like a black hole, the diners longed to be sucked to the center of the light where the two men intently talked.. But like a hole for souls, no on was sure they would emerge alive if they got too close to the hazy light.

There existed an uncanny feeling of history in the making. Although the diners would never truly be able to describe that night, there was one thing of which they were certain. Men and women alike were devoid of any desire, indeed virtually devoid even of ability, to leave that room. Trips to the restroom would find them darting back two minutes later and asking in hushed, yet excited, whispers, "What did I miss?"

"Senator Godfrey uncrossed his legs and Pierce Hanson said something that made them both laugh."

"I heard the words bucking horse, but not much more."

"I think Pierce Hanson looked right at me!"

However, mostly through the night and until wee hours of dawn, the audience settled into quietly straining to overhear the two gorgeous hunks of mankind.

At the beginning of the night, a couple brave souls had approached the men for autographs, but it was almost as if that gentle aura of strange light provided a protective shield around the stars' table.

The circle of light around the men might have been imaginary, except that the diners each saw and commented on it and further it picked up on all the photos they e-mailed from their phones. It was presumably from the overhead lighting above the table. There was a special soft lighting that engulfed the two men and surrounded them about seven feet around in all directions. When the autograph seekers got near the point of the gentlemen's soft light, something made them freeze and back away.

A force so gentle it was powerful.

Closer observation of photos later showed that it was technically two different auras merging in the center of the table between the two men. Senator David Godfrey seemed to be protected by a silvery light, whereas a dim turquoise haze surrounded the movie star.

When approached by fans early in the evening, the men would glance sideways almost simultaneously with a look that said, "Not now. Not tonight, we're busy."

Autograph seekers immediately backed away.

Further, both men had bodyguards inside Koh Samui and outside, so if anyone dared to try to brave the circle of light, a bodyguard stepped out of the shadows and quietly nudged the fans away. After the first couple hours no one tried for autographs, but merely strained to overhear.

Diners still edged in closer inch by inch over the course of hours, but it was as if an invisible force field was keeping them at a polite seven feet distance from the intently speaking men. One woman got too close and felt faint. She quickly stumbled away and pretended she needed to use the restroom where she caught her breath. Another came to the edge of the light and simply fell to her knees then literally crawled back to her table. A man scrunched his chair too close and wet himself. Covering his embarrassment with a napkin, he dared not budge the rest of the night or into the morning.

Only the waiter seemed unaffected by the protective auras, from inception to end, serving the two men's every need, quietly, efficiently. Refilling their waters without asking, retrieving their dishes invisibly. Placing steaming bowls of spicy food before the hungry men without them needing to order. The waiter had been with the restaurant from the beginning and had earned the right to exclusively serve only the three best tables in the house. Thai food was the latest rage in Boston, so celebrities often dined at Koh Samui and this waiter knew the art of serving without invasion. Quiet, polite, almost reading the minds of his diners, he anticipated the needs of the great men and their bodyguards without a word being spoken. There when they needed nothing more, the awesome waiter awaited alert a polite distance away. Waiters such as this made a fortune on tips, and tonight would be no exception. He was the best in the city and over years of serving the rich and the famous, he had earned the right to be serving these two powerhouses. Better still, whatever he overheard never passed out of his smiling lips.

David knew this and this was part of the reason he selected that restaurant and that table for the encounter with Pierce. They had met repeatedly over the years at social functions, but had only entered into casual conversations. Tonight was going to be their first time alone and both men had agendas for this private and intense discussion.

The other reason David chose Koh Samui was that for some strange reason he had a craving for the unique flavoring of Thai food that night.

Everyone in Koh Samui spoke in hushed tones that evening, if they spoke at all; except David and Pierce who were carrying on very serious conversation with one another.

David wanted to educate Pierce about who he was dealing with here. Actually, he wanted dearly to persuade Pierce to break up with Lioness, but he felt that any pressure put in that direction would force Pierce closer to her and would alienate Pierce from David. Hence, David decided he would do what Pierce had requested when Pierce had asked The Senator to dinner. David would educate Pierce about the Godfrey family so that Pierce would call off the damned detectives he had hired to investigate the family.

And with a little luck, Pierce would decide it was his own idea to break up with Lioness rather than recognize it as David's propaganda.

There were, of course, many skeletons in the Godfrey family closets, as there are in the closest of all great men – *skeletons being part of what make a man or woman great.* Still, it would help neither sibling's political career if Pierce's paid professional spies dug too deeply. A bunch of amateur journalists were one thing, but Pierce had hired some darned good detectives, and it was imperative they be taken off the Godfrey case. Pierce agreed that he would dismiss his detectives, if David would answer all his questions blatantly and honestly that night. David agreed, for least he could tell Pierce the truth in the light most favorable to the Godfrey's dark, mysterious, and multi-faceted family history.

David determined to tell Pierce the gentlest part of the truth and just to hope Pierce would learn soon enough on his own that Starlets were far more pleasurable that Lions. David anticipated the star would dump the Lion on his own, when the time came; and hopefully crush her in the process. After all, women were so easy to ruin. Easy to drive to suicide, drive to anorexia, drive to welfare, drive to low self-esteem, drive to drugs. A man like Pierce had surely ruined many fine women.

Yes, women were easy to ruin, David mused to himself. You could destroy a woman's self-esteem by looking at other women and making admiring comments to your date of the other woman stranger. You could have wild, passionate sex with a woman, moaning vows of love and false promises, then simply never call her again. You could swear you loved a woman one day and break up with her the next. You could deny the child was yours. You could go out with the boys on New Year's Eve, an anniversary, or Valentine's Day. You could criticize a woman's hair, make-up, or clothing. You could let a woman discover you were cheating on them. You could simply lie about the smallest thing then stand back and watch a gal turn the molehill into a mountain.

Yes, women could be so easily devastated by a man. Men could crush a woman's heart for life without even thinking about it. Or they could do it deliberately. Easily. For sport. Pierce could wipe out Lioness without any assistance from David. David would just sit back and enjoy the show:

The Destruction of the Virgin by the Movie Star.
This live performance was going to be entertaining indeed!

David sometimes wrecked women on a bet. Sometimes on a whim.

But then, along came Anne - destiny would present him a Thai woman of indescribable beauty. Suddenly the world as David knew it changed. Anne would turn the tables on David. Anne would ultimately avenge all woman-kind, through her death. As she had redeem all womankind to David through her life.

Anne had showed David why people chose to live inside these weak, mortal bodies. Why heroes sacrificed all for passion, principal, and love. Anne turned David's world upside down through the vehicle called love. From the moment David met Anne, he was never going to hurt another woman again, for through her, David had become human.

As a result, for the first time in David's life, he was going to hurt. Hurt like hell. Hurt for having at last known true love.

PIERCE – BEING INITIATED

Pierce sat before David that night already knowing the anguish of loving someone with all his heart and soul. Pierce knew the pain of too much tenderness. Both men were learning of the fiery hell of loving unconditionally.

Pierce's heart would never be the same for having met Lioness, yet he had to know, what was the strange object of his every passion? Frankly, he had to know if he was dealing with a devil of unspeakable evil or an angel of unfathomable sacrifice. Tonight's conversation was revealing that perhaps Lion's brother, David, believed Lion was the former. Still, sibling rivalry was a powerful force and Pierce had seen it distort perspectives before. Although there were constant jabs and jealous undertones, there was also a hint of respect and awe when David talked about his sister.

David talked of their lovely mother, Evelyn, and how she ran a house full of love, but strict discipline. He talked of her desire to bring her children up amidst infinite wealth as normal as possible. Like all mothers she never believed her children were normal. Evelyn adored and spoiled her two very different children. David glowed as he talked of his mom and of how she would take them to Europe every summer to expand their appreciation of their other cultures and how they would affect their own role in the history of mankind.

Lioness never wanted to leave her Black Hills of South Dakota and would violently resist leaving on those European travels, but once she was gone, she would have a blast.

"Why does she so hesitate to leave the Black Hills?" Pierce was baffled, "Our Cat is obviously terribly curious; hence, one would think she would long to explore the planet."

"I suppose it has something to do with the safety, peace and familiarity of home. South Dakota is a nice place to disappear – if you don't run for public office, that is. Lioness still doesn't ever really want to leave. She says she leaves only because she must to fulfill her calling, but she'd much rather be running through green fields with South Dakota wind blowing her mane and South Dakota sun shinning down upon her."

"It sounds like you'd rather be there, too."

"In many ways, yes. But South Dakota is not quite Cosmopolitan enough for me. I like cities. I like seeing the masses of humanity surround me; human beings racing through life without realizing that the bigger picture would stop them dead in their tracks. Men can not see the forest for the trees, and perhaps that is lucky for mankind. I, however, like to observe them in action moving among the trees, and since I can clearly see the forest. I enjoy watching mankind from above - watching them scurry about like little rats in a maze running in all the wrong directions gives me a perverse satisfaction. It reminds me of my own purpose - I know that I can show them a better way. And I will. Someday soon. Someday, the souls of man will follow me, they will fall to their knees before me, and I will release the masses from their ignorance, poverty, and pain."

I think I'll let that slide. I don't think I want to know what he interprets about the masses he serves, thought Pierce. Back to simpler subject – why does Lioness so hesitate to leave the Black Hills.

"Surely, it is not the weather that makes Lioness want to stay in South Dakota. Let's face it, the four seasons there are cold, colder, coldest, and hotter than Hades."

"It is the hot season I most enjoy. Nothing like a hot August night in the Hills – just ask the hundred thousand motorcyclists who make their Mecca to the Sturgis Motorcycle Rally every year. I simply adore the heat and the hum of 100,000 motorcycles in the air that time of year."

David focused his grey eyes on Pierce's blues. The Senator knew the Star wanted to know about his sister, not about his would be brother in law.

"But that is not what Lioness likes. She actually detests the noise and the heat and the sweat and the raw sexuality of the place during the motorcycle rally. August is the precise time of year when it is easiest to talk her into going abroad. No, my sister's outlook is entirely the opposite of my own. She says she only feels complete and safe at home when she resides within the Sacred Triangle. That is why she has moved all our business headquarters back there. So she can headquarter inside the Sacred Triangle."

Pierce shot up straight in his chair and fumbled that piece of paper in his pocket. Every since his meeting at Harvard, he was on the alert for the word triangle.

"Sacred Triangle? Is that something like the Bermuda Triangle?"

Chills ran down Pierce's spine when David showed a bemused smile at this comment.

"Maybe. Maybe Cat's Sacred Triangle is to souls as the Bermuda Triangle is to ships."

THE BOOK OF ANNE

PIERCE – THEIR FIRST CARIBBEAN TRIP

"Details, man, give me details." Pierce was fascinated.

In a flash, Hanson remembered the most sacred night of his life. Soon after meeting, He and Lioness had both called into work claiming to be sick day after day for for nearly two weeks. Passion drove their desire to learn all there was to know about one another. Years later, though, Pierce still felt he did not understand who or what she was and alas Pierce felt compelled to hire detectives. How could he have traveled with a woman for a fortnight and come home knowing still nothing about her? How could he have known her for years and found her a deeper mystery now than the day he met her?

Something was wrong with the picture.

It took Senator David Godfrey less than 24 hours to find out about the detectives and to mentally call Pierce to dinner. The bargain was that David would give Pierce details and Pierce would call off the detectives.

While David excused himself to use the restroom, Pierce recalled those two long ago when he was able to be with the Cat twenty four, seven. Those weeks where he learned so little about the love of his life, but still his obsession with her grew into a choking force he constantly felt in his chest.

They had first visited the Bahamas where Piece had failed in his marriage proposal. From there they flew on down to Puerto Rico and in the middle of the night and had kayaked into the luminescent bay at the tip of the Bermuda triangle.

The air was warm and still. The stars were bright overhead with just a sliver of moon shining silver upon the waters. Lioness sat in the kayak in front of him, paddling to match Hanson's powerful rhythm. Through the channel toward the bay, slowly with every stroke of the oars began to cause a blue-green glow in the water. The glowing algae, lit up by the disturbance of the oars stirring the warm water was simply unbelievable. The closer they got to the bay, the more brilliant the lights in the tepid waters of the tropical night.

In the bay itself, life was silent and still. Time stopped.

Pierce leaned back in the kayak, taking in a deep breath of the salty air. He looked up at the sky. The vastness of the Universe and the number of stars overwhelmed him.

"May the moons and the stars be his guide".

That doesn't make sense. There is only one moon. Johnson must have misinterpreted. But now, Pierce was obsessed, looking up for some sort of meaning in his part of the ancient scroll. His gut somehow knew this was a message delivered through time to him personally.

"Time is not lineal."

Pierce almost felt naked knowing he had left his original papyrus back at Harvard. He kept his fingers constantly stroking the paper housing Johnson's rough interpretation as had become his habit with the original for years.. Now that it was interpreted, Pierce constantly had to shake its haunting words from his head. Would he forevermore search the sky for the meaning of the puzzle on that paper? Surely Johnson had done a poor job interpreting. Or maybe he sought meaning where there really was none.

He shook his head and continued to remember the voyage with Lioness in their early courting days. His mind wandered back to the warm bay where he experienced total happiness and bliss to the point of near cosmic consciousness.

Hanson lowered his eyes to the water surrounding him and ran his palms through its warmth. He smiled in peace at the green glow. Then he looked toward the golden beauty before him. If anything could distract a man from the moon and the stars, it would be Lioness.

Pierce could smell the musky scent of the Cat. That scent was notorious for driving men out of their minds. As they entered the silence of the bay, Pierce could resist no longer. He had to have her, lest his heart explode from his chest.

He leaned forward and gently placed his lips on the curve of her perfect neck. He licked her and breathed in the very deep, strange animal like smell of her. His arms engulfed her as she turned with a light moan and their mouths hungrily sought hunger's salvation in one another. They devoured the taste of each other's tongues.

She clung to his well toned biceps and he thrust his full body weight toward her slender, strong being. As they leaped toward one another, their long controlled passions were now out of control. In their longing to become one, Lioness wrapped her lengthy, muscular golden legs around Pierce's body and groaned out loud with longing. Panting wildly, before they knew what was happening, the kayake flipped over and the two untamed animals were suddenly two green glowing circles in the iridescent bay of warm waters.

Lioness spat in horror as she swam, wildly flailing limbs, toward the kayak in total panic. She hated water. It burned. And every stroke released a spooky green glow more and more brightly from disturbed algae. The more it glowed, the more she panicked, which in turn released more bright green terror with her every increasingly out of control fear. She was in a Catch-22 and surely she would burn to death in these swirling green waters.

Hysterical, Lion caught hold of the kayak and tried to leap up, but it kept flipping over.

She glanced over her left shoulder toward Pierce. He was laughing, back floating, flipping, enjoying the fact that he was a big mass of glowing green in the foreign waters. Lioness wanted to hate him at that moment for being so oblivious to her own horror. She glared icily at Pierce displaying his childlike antics, ignorant of her agony.

After she had a secure grip on the kayak and realized the water was not in fact going to kill her, she overcame her fear and started to enjoy watching Pierce splash, laugh, and show off. Watching his joy and his lack of terror, Lioness had to forget herself for a brief moment and her burning skin and simply giggle at the man she was blessed to have loved.

Lioness surrendered the last of her horror, and with great courage, finally splashed noisily toward Pierce. She knew her own awkwardness and grinned thinking what a klutz she would look like to her brother David – former star of the Harvard swim team – as she lunged onto the glowing green mass that was Pierce rolling in blue green algae. She pushed him under with a hardy laugh. He sputtered to surface yelling, "Quit trying to drown me!" Pierce chased her wildly back to the kayak. Lioness was sputtering and flailing with Pierce laughing hysterically beside her, when they looked up in surprise to see they were no longer alone in the glowing bay.

A young couple in a canoe had paddled up and held the kayak upright while Pierce and his Lion struggled like a pair of flopping fish on a foreign shore to awkwardly remount their wobbling kayak. Pierce gave Lioness a boost up from behind and could not help but think how muscular her sexy arse was as he pushed. She flopped clumsily onto the kayak landing on her belly on its wet floor and was breathing heavily. Now that she was safely out of the water, she could freely laugh so uncontrollably she was almost crying.

Being human feels so darned good sometimes.

Pierce did a sideways kayak mount like he was leaping up onto a horse's back and landed with slight grace, but for the fact that he was facing backwards. After awkward scrambling through a one hundred eighty degree turn, the couple looked toward the tinkling laughter of the dry couple in the canoe. Eventually, the wet couple on the kayak at last settled down long enough for introductions.

The man in the canoe introduced himself as Bill, the woman was Anne. They talked of the origin of the fascinating blue-green waters, the beauty of the night, the miracle of nature. The two couples became instant and forever friends as they made plans to visit all three luminescent bays in the world - one in the U.K., and the second one in another part of Puerto Rico. Anne had also heard of some glowing waters off the coast of Mexico the two couples determined to investigate.

Much to the delight of all four friends, Lioness and Pierce learned that Bill and Anne were joining their very same cruise ship in Puerto Rico. It would not leave for other islands until 9:00 p.m. that evening, so they stayed up talking and rowing in their turquoise haven until almost dawn.

The two couples marveled at every glowing stroke of the oars. They talked of the vastness of the universe and the wonder of the moon and the stars above.

May the ancient moons and the stars be his guide.

Pierce must have time traveled in cosmic consciousness when they rolled out of the bay and into the Atlantic Ocean where they would beach their kayak and canoe and watch the sunrise. He was suddenly wide-eyed as he now remembered asking the group year ago, inherently knew he could ask these new friends anything, "What would you think if someone spoke to you of moons, not just a moon, but of moons in the plural, and stars to guide you?"

Time is not lineal.

Lioness

Was he time traveling to the future then. Or did he travel back in time from today to ask the question?

He seemed to recall Lioness jerking her head up so fast Pierce thought for a moment she had been shot with a bullet. She looked so deep into his eyes, that although it was still relatively dark under the Puerto Rican sunrise, he could see her eyes gleaming bright yellow and he felt blinded by her eyes as if he were looking at two suns!

Bill broke the spell when he calmly replied, "Hmmm. I would think I was on another planet. Doesn't Jupiter have like eight moons or something.

Lioness, still giving Pierce the most intense look hissed something that sounded like, "Opposites". Pierce went into mild confusion, not even understanding where his question had come from until today.

Yet he now remembered Lion was looking like the Cat who swallowed a mouse and knew more than she was willing to admit. Slowly, Lioness did what he was learning Lion would often do, she said something that did not make an ounce of sense until he later digested it. "Perhaps you have been looking up when you should be looking down."

The three, Anne, Bill, and Pierce looked around puzzled for an awkward moment or two. Pierce stared down into the water. He saw a reflection of the night sky.

Then Anne squealed with delight, pointing down at the warm salt water. "Look, at the reflection of the moon in the water. It looks like two moons!"

Pierce sighed with relief and stared into the reflection of the moon upon the water. It did look like there were a couple of moons dancing upon the gentle little waves that churned up with the warm breeze. He had searched the waters looking for a clue as to why he had even asked such a question. Now he knew he was obsessed with more than one moon. But back then, why had he asked?.

Then he searched the face of the Lion. Was she looking at him like he was some sort of idiot? In any case, the passion that had overwhelmed them earlier in the night had definitely disappeared and had been replaced with frustrated confusion.

They were soaking wet, and a tad miserable. And frankly, Pierce felt like he was missing something that was blatantly obvious to every one out there on the dark waters, except to him.

The two couples turned their conversation to each other as they paddled their vessels back through the channel toward the open ocean and out of the Bermuda Triangle housing the peaceful glowing bay.

They learned about each other's history. Bill was British Citizen, so he and Pierce had much in common. Their accents were very similar, whenever Pierce unwittingly slipped up and dropped his learned American accent. They had traveled by train all the same places around Europe as teens using Euro-passes. Soon they forgot all about moons and stars and were chattering away like a couple of teenage girls.

Bill was a thin and benign looking man. Pale, handsome and with very kind, sad brown eyes. He was an international banker currently living on the Isle of Man. Anne was an exquisite looking woman – as strange looking in her own right as Lioness. She was from Thailand and the couple had met when Bill was stationed at a large bank in Bangkok three years earlier.

Anne had the same elegant cheekbones, perfect smooth dark hair, and a remarkable resemblance to Jacqueline Kennedy Onassis. The glorious face, though, was carried by a proud neck, so long it reminded Lion of the long necked women of Northern Thailand. Although Lioness knew it was the necklace that stretched out, plus gave an additional illusion of length, the necks of those lovely natives, Anne's neck appeared unnaturally long without the artificial aids of the rings of jewelry. Anne's long neck was matched by incredibly long, thin and graceful limbs. All who looked upon Anne had the feeling they were looking at a graceful giraffe in human form.

Anne's height was strange for a Thai woman. Her father was tall for a Thai man. He gave tours around the King's summer palace for a living, but did both Thai boxing and Thai dancing on the side.

Anne laughed as she described her father's right hand looking as if its belonged to a woman - having long nails and being so double jointed he could fold the elegant fingers back at least a 90 degree angle. His left hand looked like it belonged to another persona completely – masculine, no nails, hard and muscular, it was the fighting hand of a powerful man. Anne's father had the right hand of a woman and the left hand of a gorilla. Grace and power were the yin and yang of her amazing father.

Anne's mother was a towering golden goddess from Sweden. Decades earlier, the lanky pale blonde Swede was visiting Phuket as a typical European tourist trying to turn her creamy pale skin into an all over tan. She simply burned and freckled instead. When it was time to return to her native land, the divine Swedish goddess landed in

Bangkok where her plane was late and she missed the connection back to Stockholm. The airline informed her she could not catch another flight out for 5 days. She was thrilled – she longed for an excuse to stay in Thailand and learn some Thai massage. She had been a sought after massage therapist in Sweden, but she really adored the Thai massage she had experienced in Phuket, so she wanted to study those techniques to add to her own Swedish Massage techniques, and perhaps teach, when she returned home. Thai massage, "lazy man's yoga", was a heavenly, unique combination of stretching and massage.

Missing her plane, she re-ticketed for five days later. By the end of those 5 days, Anne's mother's life changed such that she never saw her home in Sweden again. "With love," she would advise Anne, "One is wise to never look back."

Anne's mother had explored Bangkok and found a place she could take a three day course in Introduction to Thai Massage. She signed up for those massage classes, experienced some magic mushrooms, dined at the Joy Luck Club, and was having the time of her life sleeping with a different man every night. She was keeping a journal, as she deliberately sought out a man from a different country to bed each night. On her final day in Thailand, she signed up for a day trip to the ancient ruins and King's summer palace.

All her wanderlust and adventuresome sex ended for Anne's mother the very moment she saw Anne's father, her tour guide to the summer palace that day. Between riding trams with a dog, climbing towers, admiring bushes carved like animals, and all the golden decor of the palace,

Anne's mother found in Anne's father her soulmate. They recognized this immediately and soulmate status was confirmed for the rest of both of their lives.

"Mother saw in father all the beauty of a woman and all the strength of a man. He saw in her a golden goddess unlike any Thai woman. It was love at first sight for the former Buddhist monk and for the wild Swedish beauty."

Anne was born nine months later and had herself never left the peaceful beauty of her native Thailand until she met and married Bill.

Sharing their childhood histories, the two couples expressed awe at meeting someone they could relate to out in the middle of nowhere in a bay so far away from each of their respective homes. Bill and Pierce spoke of business and banking interests, of queens and religions and palaces of Europe. Anne and Lioness spoke in Thai and Anne glowed at being able to communicate in her native tongue after three years away from the "land of peace" and the "city of angels" she missed so much.

Lioness talked of the Godfrey interests in Sapphire and Ruby mines in Thailand. She openly discussed her management of the Godfrey's Thai interests in everything from the mining operations to gem cutting to the jewelry outlets that were famous world-wide. Lioness had improved the salaries and working conditions of thousands of Thais and was very honored when she walked among these gentle people.

Ah, Thailand. *Land of Peace.* Ah, Bangkok. *City of Angels. The lessons all the world could learn from the teachings of Buddha.*

August Anderson

Breathing in the warm moist air at 4:00 in the morning, the four sipped on some German Riesling wine and nibbled on cheese and crackers that Bill and Anne had been wise enough to pack in a picnic basket. They had slowly rowed away from their glowing bay through the channel, out of the Bermuda triangle into the open ocean. They arrived back at the beach just in time to see the spectacular sunrise. The rays of the Puerto Rican sun cemented their friendship.

The moments the four of them had shared together that night, were such deeply spiritual moments that would make up eternal memories of peace, tranquility, and friendship that in the hardships to follow, none would ever doubt the faithfulness of the their other companions.

Doubt, divorce, murder, suicide. That all would come later, but for now, the bonds of friendship were simple bliss.

The two couples joyously learned they were about to embark on the same cruise to South America, so they decided to arrange their diner at the same table at the same time and to make sure all their day trips coincided. Their Penthouse suites were just two doors apart, so they were in and out of one another's cabins for the entire journey.

Although Pierce originally arranged the trip in hopes of having Lioness alone long enough to convince her to make love to him, or maybe even get lucky enough to have the ship's captain marry them, it did not work out that way. Explorations during the day with shore excursions on every island, and Broadway type shows well into the night left them all so exhausted at every day's end, it was all they could do to wander into their cabins and collapse.

Lioness

A couple nights, they even found themselves sleeping on lounge chairs on deck all night. Staring at the night sky, they would talk until they could talk no longer, then would pass out to the lull of the ship cutting through the waves, the hum of its mighty engines, the stars smiling brightly down upon them, and the smell of ocean breezes that ruffled their hair.

Arguing politics, solving the world's problems in theory only, by night and playing in waves off a new Caribbean Island each day, it was a if they all four understood this was the last of the good times before the battle to save the souls of man and the planet herself would begin in earnest.

The ancient moons and the stars will guide him. What moons? Pierce was not resolved that the moons in the luminescent bay were the answer. He was becoming more obsessed by the minute with the words scribed by Johnson earlier that day. He wanted the original papyrus back. He wanted someone else to write the interpretation in case Johnson made a mistake.

He saw David had exited the restroom and was talking seriously into his cell phone near a distant table, so her let his memories of the cruise with Lion and their new friends flood over him once again. In some ways it seemed like yesterday, in some ways it seemed a lifetime ago.

The four continued their adventures around the Caribbean – biking in Barbados, river rafting in Grenada, swimming with the dolphins (the girls declined and watched from ashore) in Isla Margarita, then heading to Aruba – scuba diving for the men, and more bicycling for the women. In Martinique, they had rented a private sail boat and sailed into a bat cave over a cove in the ocean. Thousands of bats hung upside down squeaking and flapping. Anne thought them gross while Lioness licked her chops.

Sailing around the point from the cave, all but Lioness donned snorkeling masks and came up describing flowing clouds of fish where a hundred thousand fish swam in exquisite harmony, as if guided by one brain. After returning the rented sail boat, they walked along the beach and into town. On the stroll back to the cruise ship, the other three shopped, Lioness renewed her soul by darting off the beaten path for a fantastic run through the amazing rain forest.

Lioness often took to her own adventures as she was neither a swimmer nor shopper, like the other three. Lion hiked around and visited the turtle farm while in Grand Caymans while the other three visited "Hell" and then swam with the stingrays. Lioness never did fit in anyplace in the world, but at least these three allowed her to be herself without sitting in negative judgment of the things that made her so different.

The four formed bonds that would bind them for all eternity – closer perhaps than many bonds of marriage.

When the trip was over, Lioness shook her head sadly. She tried to explain, "I am honored by the pledge of faithfulness, yet distressed by the knowledge that this pledge would lead to your ultimate destruction."

Pierce had ignored the statement at the time, but remembering from this perspective of hindsight he was covered with goose bumps. He could swear he heard a voice in his head saying:

What a shame their love for me will be their very undoing on earth.

Lioness

He remember Lion then shaking her curling mane as if trying to shake gloomy thoughts from her brain.

A happier Lion had changed the subject and salivated as she described the tens of thousands of turtles of all sizes and shapes swimming before her in their round pools just off a great Caymen beach. It would have been so easy to grab a turtle and devour it raw and whole. She held back from the temptation. She had once been in jail in America, she had no desire to try out a Caymen cell!

Pierce was remembering an evening setting on the top deck of the cruise ship. The four were on lounge chairs watching the full moon cast a silver shimmer across the almost still ocean. Pierce became aware as the two lovely woman spoke that he felt as if he were hovering above his body. He looked down and saw the four of them below them on the deck whispering softly about the secrets of the Universe. He became aware of all things in the Universe and their beautiful connection to one another. He had the profound feeling of understanding everything from the beginning to the end of time. From creation to destruction. It was all so plain. It was all so simple. He must remember these, the simple truths and go tell it to the world.

Was he experiencing cosmic consciousness, or was he experiencing death?

Whatever he was experiencing, he decided to remember this experience and put it into words he could repeat. Just as he tried to form words, he felt a tug on the back of his neck and was slammed back into his body and was back on the deck with a terrible neck ache.

He was agitated and cranking and disappointed. He could not form truth to speak to his friends.

Reading his mind, Lioness leaned forward and whispered, "I lift up y eyes to the hills, From whence does my help come? My help comes from the LORD, who made heaven and earth. He will not let your foot be moved, he who keeps you will not slumber. Behold, he who keeps us will neither slumber nor sleep. The LORD is your keeper; the LORD is your shade on your right hand. The sun shall not smite you by day, nor the moon by night. The LORD will keep you from all evil; he will keep your life. The LORDE will keep your going out and your coming in from this time forth and evermore. Psalms 12:1-8"

Somehow her purring comforted Pierce, but his neck still hurt like a sonofabitch.

Anne, who had been trying to teach her friends the philosophy of Buddha, as she had been a Buddhist all her life, naturally, in Thailand used this opportunity to tell them that the early Buddhists had Psalms of their own sort. One of her favorites, Anne had noted summarized the Buddhist philosophy quite succinctly, "Be loving, be kind; And follow the ways of goodness. Committed, and longing for the goal, Always keep going with courage. To dally and delay will not help you. But to be ardent is sure and safe. When you see it, cultivate the path, So you will touch and make your own The Deathless Way."

"You see now, my love," the Lioness purred over Pierce's aching body, "The TRUTH is the TRUTH, although it tries to express itself in many ways, through many religions, it simply can not be put into words. But words can dance around the truth."

Then the two stunning women leaned over Pierce, one on each side of him and whispered in a duet as if in stereo, as if well rehearsed, "Bhagavad Git 16:1-3 directs you: Be fearless and pure; never waiver in your determination or your dedication to the spiritual life. Give freely. Be self-controlled; sincere, truthful, lovoing and full of desire to serve. Realize the trust of the scriptures; learn to be detached and to take joy in renunciation. Do not get angry or harm any living creature, but be compassionate and gentle; show good will to all. Cultivate vigor, patience, will, purity; avoid malice and pride. Then, Arjuna, you will achieve your divine destiny."

It did not help Pierce that the truth he had suddenly realized is that Anne and Lioness were united in Sisterhood somewhere long ago and that they had used this entire journey to prepare him for his role in the future.

It sort of pissed him off at the moment.

BACK TO REALITY

The four returned to Puerto Rico. Anne and Bill had flown back to London, then were to fly on to the Isle of Man while Pierce and Lion returned to South Dakota. That cruise was the last moment any of the four had normal lives.

Destiny was to take over from that point forward.

In less than three days from their unpacking, Pierce received the call that Bill had been struck by a bus in London. Anne had never made it back to the Isle of Man, instead, she had turned and fled to the last safe harbor she had known-the arms of Lion and Pierce. She was calling from the Rapid City Regional Airport.

PIERCE – BACK TO THE PRESENT

David was hanging up the phone and approaching their table. This jolted Pierce's memory back to the present evening and how he came to be in this Thai restaurant in Boston with Senator David Godfrey.

"OK. OK. I admit it," he confessed earlier, "I've had detectives investigating Lioness."

"Save your money. That simply won't be necessary. I can tell you everything you want to know about *her*." He seemed to spit the word "her".

They were having dinner in Boston's popular Thai restaurant. The paparazzi were outside, as were screaming fans, all doors being blocked by BOTH their bodyguards! It had been quite a spectacle that night on the streets of Boston.

David agreeing to have dinner with Pierce was the modern day equivalent of Apollo dining with Dionysus. Both their fans had gone nuts and press was everywhere from the skies to the streets.

Pierce, now shooting his third of his famous spy series, had two scenes to shoot in Boston. One, was the necessary rope climbing, falling swinging on tall buildings of Boston. His stunt double, naturally did all those scenes, until the close up where the famous spy crashed through a skyscraper window and naturally fell into the arms of a gorgeous executive. The other, was much more interesting scene. It was a modern day re-enactment of the Boston Tea Party being shot right in Boston harbor. That was nice. Pierce loved ships of every kind. Ocean water in any place so attracted him he often joked he had salt water running through his veins. The Boston skyline from the harbor and the gentle rocking of the waves made Boston one of his favorite locales.

Bored when his double was being shot, Pierce had impulsively called David at Anderson, Bastile, and Cooke and was more than a little surprised when David readily agreed to meet.

The limo took them to Koh Samui Thai, the latest rage in Boston's restaurants. Naturally two of the world's most gloriously sexy men could not possibly walk through the courtyard without being surrounded by flashing bulbs and screaming fans, but they both laughed that the helicopters above were a bit much.

It was nice to escape to the cool, relative privacy of the restaurant.

Pierce had movie star looks and a passion for the people that the masses could not resist either on screen or off. But Pierce had severely underestimated the man now sitting in front of him.

David Godfrey was simply the handsomest man Pierce had ever encountered. Greek God kept springing to mind. *Apollo perhaps?* This man reflected the slender musculature of the former Harvard Swim Team champion he had been years before. He wore his expensive suit even better than Pierce. The sophisticated graying at the temples could not have painted a more perfect picture of a Senator or President. David made no bones about his intention to be President.

The tan was not too dark, not to light. It reflected off his face like a youthful athlete. The eyes resembled Lion's in no way, shape or form. She had burning, bright greenish eyes with flecks of gold that constantly changed colors. Brother David had silvery eyes that defied description. Grey to blue to darkly brooding, you had the feeling the man could see right into the depths of your soul.

He studies you. He reads you. He charms you.

This man was highly disconcerting. Pierce was not one to let a man inhibit him, but this man was inhibiting beyond anything Pierce had ever encountered.

Still, they chatted easily about the Godfreys.

David seemed a charming and open book when answering all Pierce's questions about the Godfrey family history and Lioness. This conversation that would last until the wee hours of the morning – long after the restaurant closed to other guests – would save Pierce hundred's of thousands of dollars of detective fees.

"It is obvious you want to shag my sister, but why so obsessed?" David inquired of the movie star.

"I guess, being her brother, you can't see her overwhelming attraction."

"I hear she is attractive, but she has no effect on me. Other than I find her irritating."

"Why?"

"Well, for starters, she was born on my birthday. Then she tried to imitate everything I do. Everything I do, she tries to do better. She always falls on her face because she can not begin to follow in my footsteps."

"For example?"

"For example, she couldn't get into Harvard. She skipped so many classes in high school, she was lucky dad got her into the local School of Mines. She had no useful skills, so she could not get into the Peace Corps when I joined. I loved my two years of Peace Corps service in Africa. At last I was hands on helping people and half a world away from my nemesis, my kid sister. Those two years in Africa were the happiest two years of my life because I was on the far side of they world from Lion. But still, I felt she was watching me from the bushes. Every time any of the large cats watched us from the bushes, I was creeped out – like she was there. And what really irritated me is sometimes, she would walk right out of the bushes. Here she was supposed to be learning the Godfrey businesses back home as private industry would never hire her…"

"Why do you say that?"

"No college degree and too good looking. No woman would hire her as they are pathologically jealous of her looks and money. There is no solidarity between women. Precisely women's downfall in the business environment. And no man would hire her as every wife in the country flatters themselves with the false belief that Lioness is sleeping with, or would sleep with, their husband. Men never hear the end of glancing sideways at her from their wives or girlfriends. Nope, short of being a movie star, like yourself, Lioness could not survive in the world. She is lucky dad lets her work for him."

"You were saying she was with you in Africa?"

"She was not supposed to be in Africa during that time. Eevery once in awhile she would simply appear from out of nowhere. Abusing the Godfrey jets, I'm sure. She always had an excuse to walk into my camp. Hell, I often did not know where I was, so how could she always find me? She'd show up shooting a documentary in protest of female circumcism. Or she would show up with food and clothing for starving tribes. Occasionally she would simply show up to appear the Heroine while I was there working in the dirt, hunting, protesting, teaching, helping with calloused hands and exhausted body day after day for two years. Yet all the publicity was about her philanthropic trips to Africa – with Godfrey financing, of course. I would educate about sex and AIDS for days, then she would show up, put her hands on some fool, and tell him he was healed. That sent a very wrong message to people about sexual responsibility. I hated her then. I hate her now."

"She simply adores you. Imitation is the sincerest form of flattery."

"Well she can go imitate someone else."

I sensed the steamy passion inside the man and I wanted to change the subject because David's piercing eyes were changing colors and freaking me out.

"Tell me about your dad." I tactfully moved on.

"The legend or the man?" David inquired dryly. Still studying me, but the heat radiating from his inner conflict cooled instantly as he flashed me the most perfect smile I had ever seen. Perfect white teeth. Gorgeous dark hair with just the right amount of curls and graying at the temple. Wow. David took your breath away. And his intellect simply radiated out of the man. He obviously cared for people with a near dangerous passion, yet with a slightly distant feel of one born to aristocracy. No wonder women were drawn to him like moths to a flame. He was simply irresistibly perfect in every way. Even I felt drawn to him.

Gosh, I hope I'm not gay.

He threw back his ruggedly handsome face and laughed.

Did I say that out loud?

Now David's grey eyes sparkled gleefully at Pierce who nervously wondered if the brother had the same mind reading abilities as the sister.

As David continued talking openly and warmly about himself and his heritage, Pierce felt a nervous fascination for who this man was and for who he would become. His strong jaw line, his magnificent body (did Michelangelo picture this David when her carved into marble the original gorgeous David?). The proud, arrogance of his stance. President seemed a natural calling he could wear with ease. Power simply oozed out of the man. Still, something crawled way down deep in Hanson's gut and it wasn't the ginger in the divine Thai soup. Then it slowly dawned on Pierce.

I am looking at the most dangerous man I have ever met.

DAVID – DINNER FROM DAVID'S POINT OF VIEW

Book learning came easy to David. Life came easy to David. He was genetically blessed with great looks, health, and brains. Doing the right thing comes easy to David. His mother had raised him strictly, but with tons of love.. David did have a curiosity that had him agitated and unfulfilled for a few years now. A curiosity about the man his sister would have stand beside her through eternity. And a curiosity about the woman my sister would have stand beside me, my beloved wife Anne.

So David agreed to dinner with Pierce that night in Boston. He opened up about the Godfrey family. OK, so he omitted how much I hated the crazy bitch born on my birthday, but a man in love doesn't want to know the object of his affection is a crazy bitch. Pierce could figure that out on his own – and Pierce opened up to David who truly saw the "Star" in the man. Gosh, Hanson was good-looking. His deep voice with a hint of a British accent blended with a bare hint of an Irish accent certainly deserved the acclaim it was getting world-wide as they sexiest male voice on earth..

Yes, David could see what Lioness saw in Pierce – simple irresistible sex appeal combined with a strong, heroic self-discipline and a surprisingly high I.Q. This powerful combination shook David a bit, as this was David's claim to fame.

If I am going to destroy her, I do not need this tower of strength standing supportively beside her. But now is not the time. I will wait until the last minute to discredit them both before the entire world. Vengeance may be sweet, but we Godfrey's were always taught by Adam, himself, "revenge is a dish best served cold"

"Adam likes to think of himself as Jewish," the Senator was explaining to the gorgeous Celt before him. "The fact is, dad is only ¼ Jewish. He exploits his German accent, I'm sure he adds curling gels to his hair and he certainly has displayed his race's knack for making money – obscene amounts of money."

"Which you don't mind helping them spend…" Pierce boldly pointed out. Pierce was rewarded with a flash of anger shooting like lighting across David's chiseled face before David clearly consciously brought his fire under control.

"I only spend on good causes. And only for the betterment of mankind. My education, my service in the Peace Corps, my travels, and my political races, current and future, all cost millions. But this does not put a dent in the Godfrey budget, and my rise to power will be the very redemption of this planet. Consider it a bargain. Money well spent."

"So, you were saying your father, Adam, is ¼ Jewish, making you and Lioness 1/8 as Evelyn has no Jewish blood?"

"Well, no one knows quite for sure what Lioness is," David smiled slightly revealing his perfect white teeth, "I told you about the strange genetics test when she was injured as a teen. But, yes, I will be the first Jewish president of the United States WHEN I win. I will run, of course as a Catholic, just like President Kennedy, whose charisma and looks the press likes to compare me to. I was baptized Catholic by my mother when I was ten against howling protests of my father. But my father would kneel down and eat buffalo chips if mom asked it of him – he simply melts in her presence. Apparently, she was s real looker in her day – looked just like Jacqueline Kennedy I am told."

"Ah, as does your Swedish/Thai wife, Anne!"

"Yes, they do say men are attracted to women who remind them of their mothers. I hate to admit to ever being typical, but I suppose in that regard I am a typical man. Anne is a young sexy version of my own mother."

"Well, your mom's Jacqueline Kennedy features helps explain the magnificent cheekbones on both her offspring," Pierce commented, wanting to get and stay on David's good side. *I'll appeal to their vanity, no problem.*

Now Dave laughed out loud. "And I'll try to always appeal to YOUR vanity, which could certainly compete with my own."

Damn, I'll have to watch what I think around these two siblings!

"Don't worry about it. Lioness and I both find life far more interesting when we don't read minds, so we rarely do it."

"You read minds? Come on, man, you don't expect me to believe that," Pierce was getting uptight.

"Now. Now. Cool your drawers. Everyone does it. Faces reveal so much of what a person thinks. So does body language. Study animals. Study those horses you love so much. I am sure you have very, very extensive communication with them without ever saying a word. Reading minds is merely combining body language with instinct. Anyone can do it with a little practice."

"Well, you are, in fact right. I know when the horses are hungry, tired, thirsty, fearful, willing to please, have a belly ache, want to run….yes, perhaps over a thousand communications without a single spoken word. Some sort of universal body language, I suppose."

"Precisely. Take the fact that Lion and I grew up on a buffalo ranch and we were surrounded by animals, and combine it with years of us playing a game we called 'Guess What It Is Thinking' and we have amazingly refined the art of reading people. It was probably good practice for going into politics later in life. Who needs the polls to tell us how the people feel?"

"So as children you would guess what horses and buffalo were thinking for fun?"

"Hey, there weren't many kids ever invited to play with us. And it wasn't just horses and buffalo. We played a game we invented and called 'Guess What It is Thinking'. We played it on everything from worms, to snakes, to bees, to cats, to dogs, to people. We refined it to an art. Lioness says we probably opened up parts of our brains that normal people never develop in a lifetime, just by playing that game so often as children when I brains were in a formative stage. Just as it is easier for children to learn foreign language, it is easier to learn to read minds if you do so for endless hours as a child.. Lion contends that the brain is so formed by the time it is five years of age, that by five, you almost predetermine which amounts of the brain and which locations within the brain you will tap into for the rest of your life. She thinks by five years of age, you have either enlarged your brain significantly to succeed in life, or you've allowed it to shrink so much that brain diseases, from Autism to Alzheimer's are already pre-determined before the time your reach grade school."

"That is certainly a negative thought that goes against all her speeches on Free Will!"

"Well, in a way, yes. In a way, no. Never mistake the brain function for the soul. Although there is the general capability of the human brain based on early usage, we can never underestimate genetics, drug and alcohol use, brain exercise later in life, souls, destinies, or our relationships to the whole – remember 'the butterfly effect.'.

Pierce could not help but think how brilliant this man was and that he was glad he would never have to publicly debate the man. The Godfrey intelligence was as notorious as their money. As far as Pierce could see, the only person he had ever met sharp enough to debate Senator David Godfrey, was the junior Senator, Lioness Godfrey!

David continued explaining, "For example, although we learn 'ESP', horse riding, bike riding, foreign languages, and so many more things much better as a young child, there is ample evidence that later in life you can learn such things if you consciously apply yourself. Children learn with subconscious ease, adults learn with applied effort. Therefore, you still can control your destiny with your will. You still can enhance your brain later in life, but you are usually too busy participating in the rat race to do so. Anyway, this is all Lioness talk. She is the one recognized as an expert on the brain. I'm just telling you what she has told me, in layman's terms. She is the brainiac, not me."

"So I've heard. What is her I.Q. anyway?"

"It can't be measured by standard tests. Those just put her in the genius range, as well as I. But where Lioness distinguishes herself is in the I.Q. tests that measure the varying degrees of genius. She is at the top. Whatever number that is. I lurk around 155. She and Albert Einstein, it is guessed are closer to 168. Others test higher intellectually, but where she and Einstein departed from numbers is their apparent ability to tap into the Universal Intelligence. They both sought to know the mind of God, and it is claimed they have genius spiritual I.Q. in addition to intellectual. Which separates them out to a degree from Social I.Q. Sometimes, Lioness appears to be socially 'retarded' as she is so busy living in the ideal world, she doesn't see the real world! I try to live equally in both worlds – hoping to have enough of each to get me to the Presidency."

"You probably have double what most elected officials have displayed over the years!" Both gorgeous hunks laughed at that. Fellow diners continued to stare in awe at the two men. Some wondered aloud that the famous almost-brother-in-laws appeared to lack jealousy and were actually bonding

"Why did Lioness get bad grades and never get a college degree?" Pierce wondered out loud.

"She's hyperactive in case you didn't notice. She rarely attended class. She runs around from one fascination to the next like a little ferret. No one can keep her still very long. And she said school bored her to death."

"Was she ever given drugs for her hyperactivity?"

"Thankfully, no. She declared them to be an evil oppression of children from very early on. She and dad have always been actively anti-drug and anti-alcohol of every kind. To the point of extremism. Lioness doesn't just decry street drugs. She decrys prescription drugs MOST of the time and even refers to doctors as 'licensed drug pushers'. I've seen her literally spit on a doctor. That will cost her the votes of all the medical practitioners some day. Dad long ago convinced her that hyperactivity is a sign of pure genius and that any drug to reduce it is a chemical lobotomy."

"Even the drugs that are for preventative medicine?"

"And precisely how many of those are out there? Really? 1% of the health practitioners? The doctors and the drug companies rely on the government to give them legalized drug monopolies. The government relies on doctors and drug companies to give them money to keep them in power. By keeping the masses drug dependant, hence financially dependant, voters will re-elect incumbents every time! Medicine and Government are married through their symbiotic relationship. It is this relationship that Lioness decries. I find it an opportunity to exploit the people into giving me the power I need to direct them."

The American people don't want to be free. The people want goods and services to be free

David continued gloating, "Without the support of the doctors and pharmaceuticals, Lioness will not ever get elected even to dog catcher."

"Can't the voting public see that the marriage of medicine and money is killing people, destroying families financially, creating a generation of drug addicts and getting bad people into office?"

"Ah, do you and Lioness give the masses far too much credit!?" Dave's grin was almost evil in his smug knowing *that people were not about to revolt and bite the hand that feeds them.* David's Democratic Party was absolutely the hand that feeds them.

Barely enough to stay alive. But never enough to thrive.

Buying the votes to keep the system staggering down the same lane toward infinite power it has since before David was born:

Thank You F.D.R. for the recession driven power grab. Thank You Osama for the fear driven power grab.

Pierce kept hearing words that David was not saying. Was he loosing his mind? He shook his head, then asked, "Why is Lioness so obsessed with the workings of the human mind?"

"Ask her yourself. Her big mouth is never too shy to ramble on and on and on about her version of the Truth. Me? I suspect it has something to do with the fact that she was autistic as a child."

"Oh my gosh, she never told me that!"

"Yup. The little wench never cried in her life. And she never spoke a word until she was three years old. She just would stare at you with those creepy, creepy eyes and you would know there was a creature looking out at you from somewhere inside that silent, yet active, body."

"Did your parents treat the autism?"

"Oddly, Dad kept saying she would grow out of it and, by gum, she did. Right on her third birthday – my seventh – she started yapping that trap of hers and has not shut up since! She started screaming, right smack dab during my baptism ceremony that Dad had so objected to. I had just been baptized and my skin was literally welting up from burns caused by something in the holy water – some of the water in Piedmont has long been hazardous to your health, causing everything from welts to brain tumors, but the people do not heed the warnings and just keep on drinking and bathing in it – right from birth to early death. Well, anyway, my skin was welting before our very eyes and mom was dragging Lioness up to the alter. Cat was planting her feet, pulling away, and struggling like a wild woman. Suddenly to the shock of the priest, the congregation, the choir, my parents and mostly me, the Lioness roared!"

"Water. Burn. David. No. Water. Burn. Water. Poison. Bad. Water. Burn. David. No. Water!" She pulled away from mom and flew out of the church.

"We sat there in total numb shock as we had never heard her voice before. We lost total focus on the welts on my head, as always she stole attention away from me in my special moments. Her voice was an odd voice. But it was distinctly yelling those words. We searched for her until well after midnight. The dogs from Search and Rescue eventually found her back on forest service land laying on a bed of snow under some bushes, panting, drooling and gaunt from hunger and thirst. Her small body had virtually no fat to protect her from the cold and she was sick for the next week."

I heard mom ask dad, "Shouldn't we take her to the doctor? With this kind of fever she could die or be brain damaged."

Dad rarely was gruff with mom but flatly stated, "If you take her to the doctor she will be better in a week. Otherwise it will take seven days." Dad was right, as always. Dad hated doctors. To this day, he claims his secret to youthful eternal life is that he has never been to a doctor or hospital, except to witness the birth of his children."

David paused to nibble some food, then continued.

"All I know is that she had succeeded in ruining still another birthday for me. Every year, from the day that yellow little monkey was born to this very day, she has ruined every birthday of my life." Pierce saw the heat of some unfathomable hate starting to rise in David again.

"Speaking of her birth, how did your parents come up with such a name for her?"

"They didn't. I'm the one who named her!"

"What!?!"

"Well, I told you of her unfortunate birth, right? How mom was in labor for 15 hours. How she had ruined mom's body by making her eat tons of raw meet and cauliflower and shrimp and cabbage during the pregnancy so mom gained 90 pounds and only ever lost 80 of it? She almost killed mom. She was huge. There was no way that big head of hers was ever going to exit mom's body the way I did, so when mom's blood pressure shot through the roof, they did an emergency C-section to save mom's life."

"Well, they pulled this horrid little creature out who refused to cry and would only make this odd purring sound when dad held her. Her eyes shifted wildly back and forth as if taking in the whole world, so we knew she was alive. But no sound would emit from her mouth. Not from the spanking. Not from the tying of the cord.

"Worse, it was my fourth birthday and she was ruining the big party we had planned. There I was watching this hideous creature come into the world and my party was cancelled.

"We are talking Ugly baby. And I mean Ugly with a capital 'U'. Double Ugly. Dare I say triple Ugly?" David shook his head remembering and both men laughed.

"It looked a little like a monkey I'd seen in a visit to the San Diego zoo. Some sort of Gibbon. With really long arms. I could swear I even heard whispers of a tail that needed to be cut off. They whisked the yellow creature out of the room and when they brought it back, I could swear it looked at me with eyes screaming in pain. Her birth was simply the most horrifying experience of my life!"

The Senator looked absolutely serious. He continued, "Anyway. She was yellow. I swear to you, it was the worst case of jaundice ever seen in the history of medicine. The doctors kept trying to treat it and mom kept setting the yellow baby in the sun until it was this gross shad of pink and yellow. And let's face it. She even looks yellow to this day. Fortunately for her, as an adult, it simply looks like she tans all year. Trust me, she never tans. She is simply that color."

"And I love it," The Movie Star interrupted.

"Well, anyway, she looked like a very hairy little baby yellow baboon. But the face, what can I say? It was scrunched, hairy (thank goodness for laser hair removal, huh?), and it was yellow. The nose looked cat-like. Heck the whole face looked like a yellow Persian kitten. And there it was making purring sounds in dad's arms. Further there were those slanted, yellow and green speckled eyes. So, it looked like a cat's head on a monkey's body."

David paused, looking as if the memory of his sister pained him.

"I remember thinking, why does dad look so proud? He should drown and it and keep its Ugliness away from the whole world. Maybe he'll hide it in the back shed."

Pierce was turning green. This was the love of his life that David was calling an "ugly it".

"Suddenly I realized my parents were looking at my horrified face and asking ME what to name it!?!?! YUCK!

"Too stunned to think of any reasonable response, I mumbled 'name it lioness. It looks like a lion'. So, bingo, there you have it. I unwittingly named the hideous little creature."

After the men both quit laughing Pierce simply had to ask, "But surely your parents would have picked out some names before hand. After all, you are David Godfrey the III, your dad is Adam Godfrey the III. Your Grandad was David Godfrey the II. Your great Grandpa was Adam Godfrey the II and so on. It is not as if your family doesn't plan its names, in fact, for generations in advance!"

"Yes. Father, in his Jewish pretenses, brags that he traces his family tree right back to King David himself and from there we can theoretically trace our family tree all the way back to Adam and Eve. I find it hogwash, of course. But to answer your good question, why were they 'unprepared to name Lioness?' Everything about Lioness leaves everyone unprepared, I suppose."

"I'm sure they were not prepared for her to refuse to be born. I'm sure they were unprepared for her profound Ugliness. But the REAL reason no one had even thought of a single name for a baby girl was that Godfreys do not give birth to girls that live! They always have sons, or daughters that die within their first day of life. Some sort of genetic defect on the Godfrey line, I suppose. Just like calico kittens are always born female, Godfreys are always born male. Not an uncommon occurrence among some mammals. Further, every single ultrasound taken throughout mom's pregnancy confirmed: Lion was supposed to be born a boy. The ultrasounds all showed a rather long private part down there. Since she was born without, I can only surmise that she was born with a tail and it was cut off at birth. The reason we had no name prepared....you can not imagine our shock when the doctor said it was a girl!"

DAVID – CONTINUING THE HISTORY LESSON

It was getting very, very late. Dawn would show her lovely face soon and Pierce seemed to be going in and out of consciousness as he tried to consider all David's shocking revelations about his girlfriend.

"Hey, are you with me man, or zoning out on me?"

Pierce snapped back to his restaurant meeting with David.

Time is not lineal.

"Oh, I'm sorry. I was just remembering when I took Lioness to the Bahamas to propose and after she turned me down how we had a great two weeks exploring the Caribbean. In some ways it feels like another lifetime. We started in the Bahamas where she had so much fun sliding down the slides at the Atlantis…"

"What? You got her to go into the water? No freaking way. She hates water."

"I know. She was a hoot to watch at the Atlantis Resort - she would leap onto the inner tube and go down that water slide being ever so careful not to get wet. It would splash her a little, or the tiny water falls at the bottom would drip on her and she would scream such that you would think she was dying. But she was in absolute heaven as she slowly drifted through the tube that protects tube sliders from the surrounding water and the fascinating sea life. In the tube, you are totally dry, but surrounded 360 degrees by fish. She loved gazing at the sharks and fish swimming all around her from the dryness of the inner tube and the safety of the thick plastic as she floated through the center of the great aquarium.

"Over and over and over she would barrel down the slide on her tube, laughing hysterically and shaking off water and screaming as if it burned her skin. Then she would drift, mesmerized, watching the sea life in utter fascination with the same awe that you and I look up at the stars. At the end of the ride, she would leap to the steps trying not to get wet. Laughing hysterically, she would grab another new inner tube and dart back up the stairs two or three steps at a time to the top of the water slide pyramid only to do it again and again. We would stop to eat, dance, play shuffle board, walk along the beach at night. It was heaven. But day after day, Lion would ride that tube through the shark pool with an almost wicked smile on her face."

"I can imagine. But Sis does have such a pathological fear of water, I marvel that she actually enjoyed the Bahamas. Or even let you take her on a cruise."

"Well, the only time she did actually end up totally submerged in water was in the luminescent bay in Puerto Rico. After days of watching her go through the tube at the Atlantis, I was ready for a change of pace, so we flew to San Juan to catch a Cruise and while we waited to

August Anderson

embark, we found ourselves in an old bus heading for a glowing bay everyone said we simply must visit. Our first night we kayaked into the tip of the Bermuda triangle to the luminescent bay."

"Which is fortunate for me, because that is where you met my beautiful wife, Anne. Anne has told me all about your adventures from her perspective. But, Hmm. A romantic cruise. Did you at least get a honeymoon out of Lioness?"

"No. She had an excuse every night. On her period. Falling asleep outside on the deck. Anne and Bill dropping into our Suite at inopportune times. Exhaustion from our day trips. Whatever. As far as I know, your sister is still a virgin!"

The Senator raised a doubting eyebrow, "As far as the rest of the world is concerned, she has slept with every man in America. Frankly, I don't know rumor is true or which I prefer to believe. Maybe she just isn't into good looking movie stars."

"Thanks, buddy."

When David teased, it was almost as if there was movement within the glowing silvery light softly filling the space around him with heat. It reminded Pierce of the purple aura that seemed to frequently surround Lioness. You could especially see the glowing auras surrounding both Godfreys when you watched them on videotape in slow motion. It was things like this that had driven Pierce to detectives and then to David to try to find out exactly what he was dealing with in the woman who had so totally stolen his heart. Now as he felt the calm, yet overwhelming power of David, he also wondered nervously just what powers he was dealing with in his "would be brother-in-law".

Pierce shook the pondering from his head and felt compelled to tell David of their night in the luminescent bay, "Anyway, that night we paddled into the tip of the Bermuda Triangle, I was overwhelmed with an eerie feeling of spirits surrounding us. It was not possible for night air to be that profoundly still. I was covered with goosebumps in spite of the tropical heat. I had the feeling we were being watched. There really was some odd feeling about the Bermuda Triangle. Then our kayaked toppled over and we went for an involuntary swim, I began laughing hysterically. But Lioness, well Lion was so horrified and looked so cute, like a little drowning rat, it made me laugh even harder. What was really strange though, in hind sight was, I had not seen, nor heard, Bill and Anne canoe into the bay. It was almost as if, they simply appeared out of thin air. The night was creepy as hell. Sacred. A blast. Planting eternal memories. But creepy all the same."

"Yes. Lioness can creep a person out. Especially with those crazy eyes of hers."

"I melt into those eyes and I beg her to take my very soul into her glorious depths when she focuses them on me. They leave me so utterly helpless! I would rather gaze into those eyes than have sex with a thousand starlets."

"Yeah. Yeah. Whatever. Just remember, she is nothing special. She merely had a case of severe jaundice as a baby that left her skin and eyes with that yellow coloring which affects the way her eyes reflect light. It is nothing for everyone to get so exited about. Yellow in the eyes can combine with blue and make green or other colors-just depending on the way the light hits it – or reflects off any other object near her face. It is not the miracle or the wonder people make it out to be. She was just a sickly, ugly little baby. I suspect the hospital gave her some contaminated blood and that explains everything about how odd she looks and her blood tests not matching Mother's blood. It is not a big deal. She is easily explained by medicine and science. It was jaundice. She lived through it. It was just jaundice," David repeated almost as if to convince himself more than to convince Pierce that Lion's 'goldeness' was nothing more than the malady of an infant.

"OK. Well, we survived the Bermuda Triangle experience, so please tell me about the other sacred triangle."

May the Triangles guide you.

"Well, although business necessities, and our own mom, have mandated that Lioness and I travel all over the world, Lioness is always a little nervous unless she is at home. She says that she is not really an African Lion, but rather a smaller version - a Mountain Lion. She believes that the Black Hills of South Dakota is the natural home of the Mountain Lion. She says that is why she is so small for a lion. She only pretends to be an African Lion to fit in when she is in Africa."

"So have you ever had a shrink explain to her that she is a woman, not a lion?"

"Some of the best in the world have tried. Over the course of many years. Their diagnosis has ranged from 'she is so looney she should be checked in to a nuthouse' to 'she is just plain evil' to 'it is just a cute game she plays to explain her odd looks' In any case, Bro, my advise to you would be to run – run as far from her as possible. She is not good news. The psychiatrists – well, some are so terrified of her they refuse to see her again. Others she refuses to see. The problem is, she is very smart and who is to say if she is crazy or if it is everyone else who is crazy? And that fine line between genius and insanity is an easy one to cross back and forth."

"I have found her brilliant, rational, fun, successful, and idealistic. I guess if that is crazy, then the whole world should strive to be crazy."

"Precisely what our dad would say."

"Who is to define sane anyway? Some short, fat, chain smoking shrink with a drinking problem that will die of a heart attack before 50? Or someone like Lion that seems to dance with the light of God and the joy of life? Healthy, charitable, idealistic, successful, and happy to the core of her being. If that be crazy, then viva the crazy!"

"Just because she thinks she is a damned Lion because I accidentally, sarcastically, named her that, and because she pathologically fears water, is no reason to think her nuts, huh?"

"Well, let's call her eccentric."

"Oh, yes. If you look up the word eccentric in the dictionary, there will be a picture of my sister!"

"And are you eccentric?"

"Aren't we all in our own way? Some people just have the balls to be more visible about it."

"Or the honesty to be themselves. Or the money to wear their eccentricity out in public."

"Yes, you, Sis, and I certainly all do that very well now, don't we?"

"Anyway, back to sacred triangles, then we must go. It is nearly four o'clock a.m. already and we are both going to be worthless at work today. Not to mention all our fellow dinners who seemed to have slowly circled in pretty close and have strained to overhear our conversation all night!"

The fans heard that as Pierce turned toward them and spoke loudly, for the first time acknowledging the small crowd. All the exhausted, yet mesmerized, diners sort of sat up as one with that acknowledgement. They had heard very little of the low conversations between the two god like men all night, but the little snippets they were able to hear would be fodder for the tabloids, gossips, and family for months, if not years, to come. They would stay up another full night if the Movie Star and the Senator were up for it. But exhaustion was overtaking all in the restaurant, along with the worry that they must somehow function at al their respective jobs that day.

Pierce turned his focus back to listen intently to David once again. Odd, the Senator, too, had slightly strange colored eyes when you looked real close. The Senator looked every part of his proud Jewish heritage. Dark curling hair, very thick with a distinguished graying around the temples. Large, dark, piercing eyes, but upon closer examination the outer rim of the dark irises reflected a silver circle. It was almost as if his aura of silver light was radiating out from the Senator's eyes. What a powerful man he was. With a large, strong frame to house the undercurrents of his brilliant and strong soul. A totally confident man, with the look and air of a President.

Pierce had goose-bumps from head to toe. He certainly would not want to go up against David in any contest. The man was strength and charisma embodied.

"OK. Basically, Lioness says that if you draw a line from Bear Butte to Harney Peak to the Devil's Tower, you draw a perfect triangle around the spiritual center of the world." The strong, deep voice brought Pierce back to the here and now.

"Tell me more," Pierce noticed he actually had goose-bumps on his goose-bumps. Koh Samui should turn off the air conditioning. Now the diners were feeling a chill in the air, too, as David deliberately spoke a little louder so that some of the closer men and women could hear part of the story.

"Legends abound within the triangle. The Lakota Indians have declared Bear Butte holy and hold many sacred rituals there. Lioness has been seen attending their "sweats" at the foot of the mountain and I swear there must be some funny weed in those peace pipes they pass around. Bear Butte is amazing because it sticks up out of the South Dakota Prairie as if it was dropped onto the flat lands from the skies above. To watch lighting surround and light up that mountain from afar, one would almost have to think there was something going on beyond the powers of man on that Butte.

"Then there is Harney Peak. The highest point in America east of the Rockies. When you hike to the top of Harney Peak you arrive at an old rock Park Service Tower. From there you can look around on a clear day and see five states – North Dakota, South Dakota, Montana, Wyoming, and Nebraska. It is said that at the turn of the century, the Aquarians and other crystal carrying nutcases gathered at the top of Harney Peak to welcome in the end of the world. The Y2K guys were sure the planet would go black that night. Seems they had their time line a bit wrong, huh? Scientists have proven that the time line based on the life of Jesus is actually off by maybe a dozen years. The fools did not realize they should not have been on Harney Peak to welcome in the beginning of the end of mankind on January 1, 2000, but rather, the date and time they were searching for would be closer to April 21, 2012." David stopped as if he realized he had said too much and quickly moved on to the third point of the triangle.

Pierce said nothing, but shivered to realize the date that David named as the end of time, was the very next shared birthday for the Godfrey siblings.

David hurried to move the subject on, "Then there are all the legends of the Devil's Tower, ranging from UFO encounters down to the all those deaths of any who would attempt to rock climb the Tower. So you draw a line from the Devil's Tower to Bear Butte to Harney Peak and there you have it – a perfect triangle. Bottom line, Lioness only feels truly at peace, truly at home, only when she is within the boundaries of the Sacred Triangle."

"And you?"

"Me? I've been to the top of all three and enjoyed the views."

David is certainly pragmatic enough to be President.

"So tell me. What I really want to know about the woman who owns my heart. I've heard all the rumors. Some say she's got Angel and some say she's got Devil. Which is it?"

"You tell me. You were born and raised to be her soul mate, were you not?"

Pierce shivered. He did not want to look into his childhood years where one might argue he fought his way out of poverty like a little demon, or he endured abuse with the help of angels. He preferred to think that his charity, compassion, and gift of entertainment of the masses would raise him to a level closer to angels rather than sink him to the sins of devils. But he knew, like all people, he was overcoming the influences of both.

"Why don't you just ask ***her***? You know perfectly good and well she has seen both the fear and the adoration in your heart. She reads people very well as you know."

"OK. I'll do that. The next time I see her, I'll say, 'hey, are you a little devil or a little angel?' That will go over like a ton of bricks, I'm sure."

"Give it a try. It is not as if she isn't crazy about you. She'll give you some sort of answer. She has a big mouth and has not yet learned the art of tact – she doesn't know how to answer a question by changing the subject completely – that is why she is such a rotten politician. But let me give you one little warning, lest you never learned this from your Irish Catholic upbringing. The devil is very, very clever. Two things it would behoove you to remember about the devil. One: it is said that he/she is the most beautiful angel to every have sat at the hand of God. Two: he/she mixes truth with lies so cleverly that you never know whether you are hearing the truth or a lie."

Pierce felt terror engulf him, pressing so hard on his chest he felt that he could not breathe. The pounding of his chest and the roar of his ears was so deafening he dizzily saw the room spinning around him, the faces of his fans hideously, silently mocking him as they whirled around his head just before he passed out from the horror inside his own brain.

THE BOOK OF JAMES

PIERCE – COURAGE

Thank goodness for body guards. Pierce woke up hours later in his Boston hotel. James Running Bear, the big strong bulky Native American, Lakota, had been hired years earlier in South Dakota shortly after the Dances with Wolves phenomenon. Pierce and the big bear of a man had become friends as extras on that set, so when Pierce's career took off like wild fire, he immediately contacted Running Bear to be his bodyguard. James could be depended on to stay quietly by his side through thick and thin. For a big man, James was able to stay mysteriously invisible with one eye on Pierce and the other on his fans whenever Piece went out in public. When they were alone on the road, James and Pierce had great and enlightening discussions about the "spirit in the sky" and the ways of Native Americans.

Invisible, except when needed, James had carried Pierce over his huge shoulders out of the Koh Samui Restaurant when Pierce apparently passed out from exhaustion. He dragged his boss to their Boston Hotel Suite, tossed him on the bed, then went to the living room couch to catch some sleep himself.

Hours later, the men awoke, both feeling totally refreshed. James went to the balcony to smoke something in his pipe and Pierce grabbed some coffee when he sat down to make a call. It was crystal clear he needed to talk frankly of his concerns to Lioness just as soon as his movie wrapped up in Boston. He could then judge in person by her reactions to his questions, what the truth might be about her and her handsome older brother. Heck, the entire Godfrey family was intriguing, but brother and sister opposing each other for President, well that was too much to imagine all by itself. But the mysterious looks, the way Lioness acted, her fear of water; as much as he loved her Pierce was fascinated and nervous about her. After those two weeks in the Caribbean years earlier, he felt like he did not know her at all. Most women were willing to spill their guts on every subject. Lioness often set silently giving him her Cheshire cat grin or a wink that turned him on, but answered no questions.

As soon as the final scene was shot over the Boston Harbor, Pierce and James were on his private jet heading back to the small, yet busy, Rapid City, South Dakota airport.

James was arguing that political leaders should return to the Lakota the entire Black Hills. White man had stolen it from his people and they wanted it back. Pierce submitted that in modern times, the way to get it back would be to quit accepting welfare, get jobs and buy it back. After all, the Natives had stolen it from the buffalo, who stole it from….

James rolled his eyes and said Pierce would never understand the ancient ways. Pierce asserted that since they were in modern times, perhaps James should accept the modern ways.

"No one will ever give you back the Black Hills. Politicians who promise you that are lying to you just to get your votes. Further, when they give you the free houses, free legal, free medical, they again are buying your souls on the cheap. And your people think theses gifts are to uplift? They are to keep you forever poor and on the reservation so that you drink and get diabetes. They are not trying to uplift you, they are trying to keep you forever in poverty, so you will forever re-elect them."

Pierce suspected the large man with hair to his waist, covering half his three hundred pound body, and dressed in a tanish orange tunic with lots of fringe and beads already knew this for he seemed sad about his people. Never had Pierce heard James laugh, nor go out of his way to rejoice. James was cool. Totally cool at all times. The perfect body guard, Running Bear never seemed to be bothered that the job of body guard involved sitting around doing nothing. With Mohawk and a single eagle feather on top of his head, and long braids often donning his silky black hair with grey streaks, Running Bear did draw attention to himself - unlike most guards who donned dark suits and sunglasses.

Yet, in ways this look was a great surprise, no one noticed the mysterious necklace he wore under the beads around his neck. And no one ever suspected the fringes around his pants covered a loaded gun strapped beneath his huge belly, nor the knife strapped to his thigh. His weapons were invisible, yet instantly accessible.

As the jet hummed its ways over Minnesota, Pierce turned his bright baby blue eyes to focus on the mountain of the man who had so gracefully carried Pierce's tall slender body out the Bostonian restaurant the night before. Pierce noticed the green colored beads on the front of the great man's shirt formed the shape of a tree on the orangish/oatmeal colored back ground. James seemed to always wear the same shirt. Pierce had to wonder when and how the man ever washed it.

Suddenly the movie star's crystal clear eyes sprung wide open, "James, tell me about all those stars on your shirt."

JAMES – COURAGE

The great lined face showed a look of slight bemusement, like he finally beheld a child waking up, "I was wondering when you would finally ask!"

"We'll start with the shirt. The tree is sacred to my people as its arms are constantly uplifted toward the stars in heaven. I wear the stars on my shirt in honor of my mother who was a Cherokee. The Cherokee talk of Time and Untime being symbolized by the stars. The Cherokee's Rattlesnake Constellation took on a different shape in 2004. This was the time of the rise of woman. The Rings of Time shall move as circles backward and forward. The time of woman started with the Morning Star in 2005 and the time of the Cherokee Calendar ends with the Evening Star in 2012. That is when the Pale One will come again. Your Jesus came to the North America's after his crucifixion, now he is back. In shocking form and probably angry! Anyway, the entire Milky Way is viewed by my people as a tree. Trees are sacred to my people. The smell of cedar chips burning at a sweat purify the air and visions are great. A tree is always in a state of prayer. When we put our prayer ribbons on trees, as you'll see will all over the climb to the top of Bear Butte and some on the way up Harney Peak, the wind of life blows the prayers across our planet lifting them up to the Great Spirit."

Pierce was listening hard now. Two of the Lion's three Sacred Triangle Points had just been mentioned and he was determined that by this time tomorrow, he would be climbing one of those mountains and drilling the Lioness about its powers. He knew it would not bee in Wyoming, the Devil's Tower looked too steep to climb and would have to wait, but Harney Peak was close to the Lion's Den. "Tell me about the Devil's Tower."

A slight grin crossed across the proud man's face revealing yellowed teeth that were rarely seen. "Legend has it that the Devil's Tower was once a great tree. The Tree of Life is the symbol of our communion with the whole Universe which we experience not through thoughts, not through words, not through actions, but though pure feelings. Well, the Devil's Tower was the greatest tree ever witnessed on earth when it is rumored that seven Lakota Sisters, some say representing our seven spiritual goals, were chased up this humongous tree by their brother who had been turned into a bear. The seven sisters climbed the great tree into the sky and became the big dipper, while the burnt remains of the tree became the Devil's Tower – a great cosmic tree which links heaven and earth. Others believe the sister are the constellation of stars that reached its highest point in the sky at the beginning of the end – a few years back. Perhaps, the year you met your Lion?"

Pierce shivered.

"Tell me. Is the triangle formed from lines drawn between the Devil's Tower, Bear Butte, and Harney Peak supposed to be sacred to your people in some way?"

The wise man nodded sadly, "Isn't the whole earth sacred? Our ancestors do have Sacred Sites, including the Black Hills of South Dakota. But if you look at the earth from heavens above now that you can study satellite photos, you will see that the Black Hills of South Dakota is shaped, not like a triangle, but like a heart. Although the triangle is, indeed sacred, the Black Hills herself is the heart of the entire world. If you fast forward your satellite photos you will see the Black Hills looks like a pumping heart."

Shaking his head in fascination, Pierce could now envision why his Lion love was so enamored with the Black Hills. He could barely whisper from his dry throat, "Fascinating. Now I think I start to see why the Lakota want the Black Hills returned to them. I'm sorry I was so haughty earlier. Ignorance can do that."

"But," his wise friend and guard continued, "Do not be fooled into thinking that the Black Hills are the only Sacred Sites in the world we wish to protect from the destruction of the white man. Look at any satellite photos and you will see what my people have known for centuries before you put those birds called satellite into space. Our ancestors have tried to protect the Big Mountain, as it is the liver of the earth and the coal extractions are poisoning her. The Aborigines warn of global warming's effect on the Coral Reefs which are Mother Earth's blood purifier. The Indigenous people of the rainforest have for thousands of years held that the rainforests are the lungs of the planet…"

"You are making me almost sorry for every time I used the term 'environmental terrorist.'"

"Don't be, my friend. We have learned that extremist self-righteous behavior has given the truth of our cause a bad name. But on the other hand, apathy and white man's welfare dollar have kept my people, who should be guardians of the planet, planted in front of the television drinking alcohol and given themselves diabetes and other illnesses for way too long. Somewhere in between the destruction of rights and the destruction of the planet lies the true path. I have called upon all Native Americans to rise, to live, to fight. They have responded by asking for more money. Free money is killing my people's great spirit."

Shaking his head sadly Pierce commented, "I'm afraid you call upon your people to bite the hand that feeds them,"

"Then my people must learn to feed themselves," commented the wise old bear.

"Tell me of the seven sacred rites your once mentioned and of Jesus visiting the Americas."

"Ask our pilot about Jesus in the Americas. It is well documented in the Book of Mormon."

As if on cue, Pierce looked up to see Paul stretching his legs while the co-pilot took a shift as they neared their destination at the Rapid City Regional Airport.

Paul was nodding in agreement while Running Bear continued his story. "Legends abound about the White Buffalo Calf Woman. Some thought she was Sioux. Some believe she was the Virgin Mary herself – that is after the first Roman Catholic missionaries visited the Lakota! In any case, she is the one associated with presenting our people originally with the sacred pipe that we should smoke in times of prayer as the smoke from our pipe carries our prayers upward to the Great Spirit, Wakan Tanka. Legend was that she was the most beautiful woman ever seen – with pure white skin and long shiny dark hair. She proclaimed children to be the greatest possession of any nation. She said life was a circle without end. She said it is the work of the hands of a woman and the fruit of their wombs that keep people alive and sacred. She preached of love and healing and as she sang a song she changed into a magnificent white buffalo calf and galloped into the prairie's setting sun. As for the seven rites she instructed our people in, they are briefly: Keeping of the Soul, The rite of Purification through Sweat, Crying for a Vision, The Sun Dance, the Making of Relative, Preparing a Girl for Womanhood, and Throwing of the Ball. I think what you will find so interesting about many of our Sacred Rites have there own version in Latter Day Saint beliefs."

Paul, their faithful Mormon pilot interjected, "God once told Joseph Smith that no one religion was completely true, but that all religions contain some truth. I think if we reconciled and studied the founding principles of most religions, we would be shocked at how many common truths there are. Now, of course, we Christians believe in one great God with Jesus as our Savior, but Muslims believe both Jesus and Mohammed were great prophets of the one great God. The Book of Mormon tells of Jesus visiting the Americas after his resurrection. The common things all religions agree on, are usually the good things. All religions seek to make us better human beings and to cope with the inevitableness of death. These commonalities must be acknowledged. Where we differ is that Lakotas believe in many Gods or spirits. Yet both the Bible and the Book of Mormon reference gods!"

Before Paul could continue, his co-pilot turned and hollered for Paul that it was time to land the private jet.

This flight had been the most Pierce had even heard Running Bear Speak. It was the most he ever would.

PIERCE – HARNEY PEAK

Pierce sat before the most beautiful of all angels at the Aspen Inn in the lovely old town of Hermosa where dogs and their sleds ruled the streets in the winter and tourists flocked in the summer.

It was a delicious early dinner that simply melted in their mouths. From there, they were going to climb Harney Peak and spend this balmy June night in sleeping bags at the top of the rugged limestone peak, among the mountain goats. Pierce had determined to explore all points of the alleged triangle.

"Your brother said I should ask you something outright," Pierce gathered all his courage, took a deep breath and plunged right in.

"Did he?" Lioness barely raised a tawny eyebrow and looked relaxed as she licked her chops, waiting for Aspen Inn's legendary desert to be served.

"It was a question I put to David the other night when we dined in Boston. A question he either could not or would not answer."

Pierce had already told her many details of the Bostonian dinner. They had always been honest with one another, and had he not confessed, she would have read about the evening in all the tabloids anyway.

"Well, then, spit it out."

Pierce could tell she already knew the question, just as David had suggested.

"Are you the devil?"

A few beats of silence ensued as Lioness clinched her mighty jaw, then relaxed it with a twinkle in eyes that were as green as emeralds at the moment.

Hadn't she said her eyes only turned green when she was angry?

"Would you even be able to love me if there was a drop of evil in me?

"David warned me that smart politicians often answer a question with a question."

"Pierce, my love, my heart. You've been with me for time immemorial. What do you think? Have you ever once seen me do a single act of evil?"

Remembering from the brief report of his recently dismissed detectives, Pierce stuttered feeling slightly ashamed. "No. But your employees have horrible things to say about you."

The detectives had reported almost infinite acts of charity and reports of near sainthood in her business practices. The only negatives they had dug up on the Lion consisted of jealous, hateful hearsay from the mouths of many former employees.

"I beg your pardon? Every one of my current employees only raves about me. Surely, you are talking about my **X**-employees. **X**-employees always have bad things to say about **X**-bosses. Because they refuse to admit to themselves that they are responsible for their own firings. It is THEIR lack of self-responsibility, lack of honesty, lack of work ethic, lack of self-motivation, or any other lack that gets them dismissed from a great paying career with a future. Rather than learn and make it a positive experience, it seems to turn most X-employees into jealous and embittered welfare recipients. It is not a lack of compassion, but true love and compassion for my fellow man, that drives me to try to get my associates to do their best. To be all they can be. To give opportunities and teachings to those most of the rest of society has given up on and won't even hire in the first place. Look at my hiring record – I hire women, minorities, felons, and the aged. I strive to give opportunities to those no one else would consider giving a job to – what more a career opportunity. I teach them then to do great things. But I expect them, then, to do great things. Unfortunately, some people have been raised to be the least they can be. This breaks my heart. I try to light the fire of life into each of them and, sorrowfully, some try to avoid and deny their own inner greatness it at all costs. They leave work at 3:00 p.m. sharp. Head for the beer and the television. When I lecture them about going the extra mile to find their own inner greatness, they call me a slave driver. I pay double for overtime, yet some work minimum wage second jobs rather than overtime for me. I am not the slave driver of popular rumor; I am the one who offers infinite opportunity to those who would work for it. You try being the boss someday. You try being the female and the boss. You will automatically be dubbed 'The Bitch'."

Lioness had a point. Successful women through the ages would always be disdained by the non successful.

It played nicely into the success of men to keep brilliant women down, and young lovelies thinking their only potential was to marry young and help a man build an empire. This subconscious plot carried out by modern society kept women down when young, then discarded them when they aged. Someone like a Martha Stewart or a Hillary Clinton or a Lioness Godfrey would come along and upset the apple cart temporarily, but then they must be destroyed one way or another. Women of intelligence and independent means were a definite threat to men. A threat to other women who believed they "were owed". A threat to the very structure of society. One way or another, successful women would be made to look like fools or criminals.

Still, Pierce was compelled to return to the original subject of conversation as Lioness seemed to be doing what David suggested a politician would do - hide her direct answer behind an evasive truth.

"I really need a straight forward answer now my love. Who are you?"

She looked right into Pierce's eyes now with dancing light blue eyes to match his own and he felt so weak he was grateful to be sitting, for he knew he could not stand.

"Well, I am who you say I am. I am who you think I am. I am your Lioness, of course."

She had still not answered directly! She was a better politician than David gave her credit for! But Pierce suspected he knew his answer. He knew precisely what he had to do. He had to solve the riddles contained on a single piece of paper in his shirt pocket. He instinctively knew all the answers to the question of Lion's identity were somehow contained on that paper. Once he solved that riddle, he would know precisely who or what he was dealing with here. Then Pierce's only question would be, did he have the strength to stand beside her? One thing he knew for sure, at that moment, with his blood coursing throughout his body, he did not even have the strength to move. Thank goodness desert arrived at that very moment.

Seeing her lick her chops at the sight of the divine sweets almost made him weak. Pierce had always stored his stress in his taunt stomach which gave him a gorgeous six pack without sit-ups. Watching Lioness lust for desert made his stomach clench.

What is this kicked feeling in my gut a result of - fear or lust?

DAVID – BITTERNESS AND SHOCK

I had no fear before Lioness killed my wife. Death was not part of my thoughts. Ever. I felt immortal all my life and I know without question that life is eternal.

Before the wench murdered Anne, I never stopped to think of the pain of losing a loved one. It just did not happen in my perfect world. I would rule in this world the way I had learned to rule. With my loving guidance, all would have food, medicine, clothing, housing and education. There was no need for all the suffering in the world. I would be Robin Hood. I would rob from the rich and give to the poor and all the world would adore me.

I promised my constituents a redistribution of wealth and as President, it would happen. I would be so loved.

Control has always been key for me. I control the events of my life. I control my surroundings. I control my emotions. I control my destiny. I control the people, animals, and things in my life. I, like Lioness, have a genius I.Q. and I know what is best for the masses of people.

I suppose that is part of why I have always considered Lioness my nemesis. Things are always totally out of control around her. Lion drones on and on and on about Free Will. Frankly, what she doesn't realize is people neither deserve, nor do they even want, Free Will!

Free Will is too much work. Free Will is too much responsibility. Free Will requires effort and thought. After the teenage years, people lose their yearning for freedom and they simply want to be taken care of. The masses will vote for me because I offer them health care, retirement, welfare and entitlements. The masses will not vote for Lioness as she offers them nothing but the freedom to explore opportunities and to create their own lives. Let's face it, the masses, being poor, long for a redistribution of wealth. They want their fair share (as Lioness would say, without working for it). They want me to be their Robin Hood. Lioness claims that once wealth is redistributed society will crumble under its own lack of motivation. She believes Americans will become fat, apathetic, drug users, riddled with heart disease and diabetics. Well, I have news for her. They have already become that. Now they are looking for a hero to support their easy lifestyle and I am it. I do not fear my future as Robin Hood. I look forward to it.

No. I had no fear. Simply disdain. But now, for the first time in my mortal life, I understand Fear.

Fear of Death, perhaps? *Death is the ultimate lack of control.*

Fear of Pain? *Who would think a human heart could hurt this bad?*

Until Anne died, certainly not I.

Now I must surely question all that I previously believed in. I agonize over all that I was born to do. Because for the first time in my eternal life I understand the absolute horror of being born mortal. I appreciate the full terror of not being able to see behind the curtain of Death. I feel a pain beyond physical that can not be soothed.

To know the anguish of wondering if your loved ones are OK or even exist on the other side of the curtain. That uncertainty never hit me before now.

To question: Will I be alone in all the Universe when you pass through Death's dark door?

To not know what lays beyond this life! How cruel a God would make each man wonder about mortality itself?

Oh, Lord, why have thou forsaken mankind?

What makes you think I have forsaken my children? Are not you all at a part of me? A part I would not, nor could not, forsake? Then why should you fear? I am in each and every one of you. Yeah, I am in you even in your darkest pain.

Shaking those thoughts from my head, I know I must remain strong. If for no other reason, to keep mankind from the fear and agony I now feel with the loss of my beloved Anne. How would I ever find her? How would I ever embrace her now that her glorious body was gone from my bed? From this planet? Gone to ashes blowing across the golden prairie? Where in the infinite Universe would I look for the spirit that had been unique only unto my beloved wife?

I now understood how hard it is to bear unbearable sorrow. I lost the woman who would share the White House and beyond with me. I lost the hope of having children. I lost my motivation, my love, my beauty, my inspiration, my better half.

Lioness will suffer. Lioness will learn the true meaning of fear for this. Death is too good for her for what she has done. Vengeance will be mine.

No, my son, Vengeance is Mine alone.

Who said that? Am I losing my mind?

You know who said that. I exist even in you.

Oh the pain. Oh the agony.

Focus. *I have a planet to save from the ravages of death. From the ravages of Free Will.* Well, I guess I'll get the sympathy vote. My advisors tell me this kind of sympathy garnered by the death of a spouse immediately before election day can guarantee me a good 10% of the vote.

Fear? Maybe fear of failure. Failure is not an option, yet I fear for mankind if Lioness wins this Presidential election.

BOOK OF BART AND TOM

PIERCE – LOOKING UP, LOOKING DOWN

Pierce lay at the top of Harney Peak with the Lioness at his side starring at the magnificent stars in the sky. There were two college kids camping out beside them on the balcony of the old Forest Service Lookout – much to the frustration of Pierce.

Bart and Tom were from Maine and they were hitch-hiking across America. Bart was a member of some small cult calling itself the Aquarian Church. Tom was dragged to church along with Bart, in spite of being a Science Major, because he seemed to enjoy Bart's company. They were crystal worshiping fruitcakes as far as Pierce was concerned, and as usual, a tactful way for Lioness to avoid sex with him, in one of their rare moments where they could have been alone together. The boys sat cross-legged displaying the sacred crystals that Bart claimed were the result of the tears of his noble and glorious Aquarian leader, who was now an X-patriot hiding somewhere in the Himalayans.

Yup, Bart claimed that their prophet had shed tears of actual crystal!

"That I'd like to see that." Pierce said sardonically.

"I don't believe it either," said Tom, "Yet I've seen the videotape that the government released to the public during the prophet's trial for fraud, just before his disappearance, and it sure did look real. And painful!"

"It takes all kinds," Pierce shrugged.

Lioness was wearing one of her all knowing grins that, frankly, was starting to piss Pierce off. If she knew so much, she should just spit it out and let him get on with getting on.

Bart had explained that the Aquarian Church leader had given parishioners each their own crystals from his tears before disappearing a decade ago. He had told Bart to take the remaining crystals high upon a mountain top and The One would chose the crystal out of the thirteen.

The crystals were large, looking like huge diamonds and sapphires crudely cut by an amateur. Costume jewelry thought Pierce.

The fakes were sparking in the moonlight and in the reflection of the night sky, for a moment Pierce imagined he saw moons and stars being reflected up at him. He jumped a little taken aback by this thought. He felt for the transcription in his pocket and thought to himself he had given Harvard's Dr. Johnson enough time to verify age and authenticity and that he would have to get the original back from her as soon as he could make the trip to Boston. Common Sense told him that he should not trust his parchment to any outsider. He did not feel right from the very moment he had given it's custody over to Johnson.

The crystals of every size, shape and color were laid out before them in the dual light of the full moon and a kerosene lantern. They did have a mystical sort of glow that gave an illusion of the crystals themselves radiating a soft blue light. Pierce knew it was simply a reflection of the brightest night sky he had ever seen in his life, but still it was a little eerie.

The two boys constantly looked warily at Pierce throughout the night's discussions. They must have never met a movie star in their lives. Further, they were sure having a blast flirting with his girlfriend. Lioness seemed fascinated by their talk of their screwy religious beliefs, that they thought they once saw a U.F.O. and man had been placed on earth by UFOs, and by all the other spooky tales of travel that a little wine atop a mountaintop would inevitably bring out in almost anyone.

The real surprise of the night for Pierce was that when he asked when the Aquarian Church of Maine had been founded, the boys said and date. He and Lioness exchanged such deep looks. Pierce was surprised and Lioness looked smug and all knowing. The boys could not help but wonder what was up and begged to be in their secret.

Tom and Bart subconsciously scooched nervously a little further away from the older couple when Pierce explained that the day the Aquarian church was founded was the very same day was the date Lioness was born.

Desiring to ease the tension in the boys Lioness reached a casual paw toward the crystals, and picking up a lovely blue one yawned, "I would like to have this crystal."

Bart and Tom fell instantly on their knees bowed low before her with hands folded as in prayer.

"That won't be necessary, my children," Lioness purred softly. "How would you boys like to end your travels now and come to work for me on my campaign? There is an easier way to see the world than hitchhiking."

They nodded excitedly, still unable to actually speak. Hmm, what was that about Pierce wondered.

Further, a business woman and politician had that effect on these kids, yet they've barely acknowledged me, a movie star is among them tonight?

"Is there something special about the blue crystal Lioness chose?" Pierce asked, perplexed.

"Well, um, yes," the boys barely had their voice, but seemed to regularly talk in unison or over one another, constantly finishing one another's sentences.

Bart, the taller, red-headed one cleared his throat and said, "Before our prophet left us, he gave us these crystals and told us they each have their own master. This one is mine and the one over there is Tom's".

"How can you tell, they all look alike, except the one Lion picked?" Pierce was genuinely interested.

"Well, mine has this little nick on the side. Tom's radiates a soft pink while mine radiates a soft yellow."

Pierce picked up a crystal examining it, and it just looked like a clear piece of cut glass to him. "That one is yours – it is the clearest white," Bart continued.

Pierce put the crystal back in the pile, but Tom grabbed it and forced it back in his hand, "No, no, you must keep it always. It is yours. Because you picked it.

Lioness

"Or rather, the crystal picked you." Bart corrected.

"Whatever," Thomas rolled his eyes.

Pierce didn't know what to say or do, but he did not want to insult these kids. They seemed to act like they were giving him a dear and valuable treasure, so he tucked it into his pocket, beside his translation of the scroll and thanked them.

They continued talking of the crystals as if they were somehow magical.

"What is so different about the one that Lion picked?"

"It is the only one that reflects both clear white and blue light depending on who is looking at it and when and where they are looking," Tom explained.

"Reminds me of Lion's eyes," Pierce remarked casually.

Bart shot Tom a look that Pierce could not understand. Then the two college age kids began to bicker between themselves as if Lioness and Pierce were not even there.

"Tell him," Bart hissed under his breath.

"No. You can't be sure. It is probably a coincidence. Surely this is wrong. Surely the Master would not be a woman."

"All the prophesies are coming true, Tom, when are you going to admit it?"

"And if we are wrong and we've given the crystals to the wrong people?"

"The prophet said the crystals would find them, not that we would…they picked them Tom, we did not hand them over. There is no way two strangers would have picked the two correct crystals…"

"We're sticking close and watching them like hawks and you better promise me if you are wrong, you'll get those crystals back so we can find their proper owners."

"OK. Thomas. My Thomas, My doubting Thomas. I promise."

"What is this amazing piece of blue glass with gemstones?" Pierce asked about some cut glass that fell out of Bart's backpack; more to change the subject than for any other purpose.

Did Pierce see Lioness sit up with wide eyes out of the corner of his eyes? Was that a small gasp or growl barely audible coming from her throat?

"Oh, that is kind of a funny story."

"Let's hear it." Pierce said. He was dominating the conversation now with the boys simply because Lioness was being quiet for a change.

Bart started in. "Tom and I went to Cancun to get wild for spring break our senior year of high school. One day we were climbing around some ruins about sixty miles south of Cancun that a native cab driver took us to on the request of our host family. We were far back in the rainforest. Birds and monkeys were squawking, strange sounds enveloped us from all directions, and these ruins were absolutely divine. There was a carving near that top our host family indicated was in honor of the sun god. Kinda circular with multiple squiggly arms representing the sun. We left there in time for a swim, so we asked the Cabbie to take us to a beach for a swim. He took us to the Mayan Ruins of the ancient town of Tulum. We had never seen such a magnificent green sea. We swam and laughed in the huge waves, then rested on the beach just to the north of the ruins. Afterwards, we were exploring the ruins which displayed the Mayan god of the winds."

"Eventually, just before evening when it was time to go, we came upon the Temple of the Descending God." On the façade in original Mayan Pigments is a figure head down that is thought to be a deity of the ancient cult."

Lioness let out a huge gasp.

Pierce stared at her shocked face, "What is it, honey?"

"The Apostle Peter. He was crucified head down."

The comment did not make that much sense to the group at the time, so Bart continued his story, "Well, I saw this flash of blue and when everyone else had their back turned and were returning to civilization, I told them I had to take a leak. I promised to catch up. I reached toward the blue light shining through the sun symbol. Imagine my horror when the rock near the paintings head crumbled under my touch. I had destroyed an ancient artifact! I wasn't sure, but I thought I could go to jail for that so there was no freaking way I was going to admit this to anyone. I might still be inside a Mexican prison to this day had I been found out! Anyway, I quickly thrust this beautiful blue piece of cut glass deep in my backpack and went running after our group. I dared not tell anyone, not even Tom about it until a month later, long after we had safely returned home. In fact, I almost forgot about it until we were unpacking safely back in Maine. It fell out of my backpack, so I showed Tom and we washed it off in the sink."

The four stared at the beautiful way the cut glass was reflecting the dim light of the stars above Harney Peak. It cast a glorious bluish glow for a good seven feet around.

Each of the faux diamonds, rubies, sapphires, and emeralds radiated its own light. In some ways, it reminded Pierce of a piece of a disco ball – popular for lighting up dance floors decades earlier in the way different colored lights sparkled off the glass. The smoothness of the cut, the curvature of the glass, made it exquisite, even if it was a piece of junk. If it were real, it be worth millions of dollars Pierce mused. It had a smooth tongue running up one side and a matching groove up the other. Pierce knew it was a piece of something larger, but what he did not know.

It looks so familiar.

Ah, Pierce did remember. It looks like a present Anne had quietly given Lioness on the cruise when they initially met. Pierce did not pay an ounce of attention at the time because on the sets of movies he had grown accustomed to seeing magnificent jewelry, all fake and worth less than a couple hundred dollars.

Still, it seemed beyond coincidental that two different people that Lioness had just met in his presence would be showing her identical pieces of fake jeweled glass, allegedly found at opposite ends of the earth. As Pierce recalled Anne had brought her gift to the Cat from Thailand. And now Tom was offering her the same sacrifice he had found in Tulum. Odd. Very odd. What a small world, after all.

"Did you ever have it looked at by an expert to see if those gems are real?"

"No. When the prophet showed us his crystals, we showed him our Mexican Temple find," replied Bart, fully wanting to claim his interest in the "find". "The prophet advised us to keep it with us at all times, never let the authorities know it existed and to basically guard it with our lives. So we've hauled it all over with us. He told us it was a part of a whole and it would reveal its purpose when the time was right."

"Lioness is a bit of an expert on gems. Why don't you take a look at it, Honey?"

"Honey?" Lioness had backed way up against the stairs of the old lookout tower and was looking at the cut glass and gems with wide, almost fearful, eyes. The same way, Pierce now remembered, Lioness had looked when Anne had given her a matching piece.

"I'll bet it is made in India or China and there are 10,000 of these scattered by tourists all around the world," Pierce tried to reassure his girlfriend, as well as himself, it was nothing much and there was no reason to fear.

"I'm sure you are right," agreed Thomas, "cuz I found one just like it when I was scuba diving in Tahiti. "Bart was not with me, as he had measles when I went to Tahiti with my folks for Christmas. I joined a group of divers that claimed they found wreckage of a two thousand year old ship from India. That I had to see, so I dove deeper than I ever had before. There were the most interesting carvings on pieces of old wood and stone that could certainly have been centuries before our time. They were sort of like fish. You know, like a sideways eight sort of, but not closed on the right. Akin to the bumper stickers Jesus Freaks plaster on their cars"

Thomas continued with flourish, "Well, I was just pondering the possibility that an ancient ship could have been decorated by Jesus Freaks, but such a ship should never have found its way to Bora Bora. Just then a gleam of light caught my eye. My diver's light reflected off it with such a brightness that the turquoise seemed blindingly bright to me and seemed to streak right up to the ocean's surface. Still, none of my fellow divers noticed it, for unbeknownst to me they were signaling me in a panic.

"Blissfully ignorant of the danger that surrounded me, I took my divers knife and chipped away at the fish carving to access the glass reflecting beneath. I was chilled to the bone and had a feeling of disbelief that I would see glass there on the bottom of the ocean, akin to what Bart had found a year previous in Tulum!"

"Just as I grabbed the beautiful gem covered glass, I realized why none of the others had seen it. They were ascending at a dangerous speed, in fact, two ended up with the bends because of their rapid ascent. They were also frantically trying to signal me that I was surrounded by sharks. And not just little sharks that tourists like to feed, but sharks larger than me and dozens of them. The first one approached me and I could see large jagged teeth and I knew I was a goner. Things sort of went into slow motion. I prayed my death would be swift and painless and that I would transcend unto heaven rapidly. At the same time, my body instinctively started swinging all four limbs wildly toward the attacking sharks. I had my knife in one hand, the glass in another, and somehow I scored bulls eyes with both hands. I ht the large, closest shark squarely in his left eye with the glass and squarely in the right eye with the knife. Now I am a gentle animal lover by nature, and I tell you I could not have consciously done that. It was pure reflex – almost as if I did not own my body.

"I don't know who looked more surprised, me or the blind shark as he swam backwards away from me. Yup, I didn't know sharks could swim backwards, but I tell you he and all his pals did that day! For as I whirled around at the dozens of other sharks that had encircled me from three sides, either their wounded buddy or the light flaring off my glass souvenir scared them all something furious. Backward they swam, honest, all of them, until they were a safe distance from me. Then they swirled around and swam off at great speed.

"I swam to surface as quickly as I dared without blowing out my lungs, and breathing out at a steady pace as I gained altitude. I was constantly looking below me and whirling around in terror, hoping I could surface before the sharks came back.

"In any case, I've never let my glass out of my possession. And needless to say, you could not possible talk me into scuba diving again in this lifetime. No siree, Bob, not for all the tea in China as my dad used to say!"

"Wow. That is a heckuva story."

"It is all true. I'm telling you." Tom seemed pale in remembering it such that Pierce guessed he was in earnest.

"Yeah, I've heard Tom tell that story a dozen times, but I'm still convinced he is just jealous that I'm the one who found the matching piece in the Mayan ruins, so he either had a copy made, or found a cheap piece of glass in some tourist joint and just didn't tell me so that I would continue to think mine was special."

"Hu uh," Tom vehemently denied with an anger and a pout reminiscent of a lover's quarrel. "Want to see mine?"

"No. Some things are best left a mystery." Lioness had found her voice and it was clear she did not want a closer look at either of the boys' lovely blue glass.

It dawned on Pierce that it had started Lion's mind racing about things he knew nothing about, but that obviously made her nervous. Pierce shrugged. She must have her reasons – she always did.

Turning off the lantern, they finally lay flat on their backs looking up at the night sky and changing the subject to the stars and constellations they talked through the night and well into the early morning hours.

"See the Seven Sisters how they are almost directly overhead?" Bart pointed up to a small cluster of stars directly overhead. "It is said that when they are directly overhead in the night sky, it will be the end of time."

Pierce commented, "So, my Native American bodyguard has told me. Do you think that is directly overhead? Or that they have just been overhead? Or that they are about to be overhead? How can you tell? From what part of the world, does this legend references as a viewing point and at what time of night?

"Not to be a trouble maker," Tom affectionately agreed, "But which night sky? They may be directly overhead here, but they are not directly overhead in the Australian night sky."

"Every party loves a pooper, that's why we invited you," Bart was still pouting at Tom's putting a damper on everything Bart said. Still, you could see the affection ran deep between the two friends, probably because they had a shared history of being friends most of their short lives.

Shared history. More binding, perhaps, than wedding bells.

And so they talked. From the mysterious to the mundane, the four were becoming friends. Eventually, sleep slowly overtook the four on top of that sacred mountain – a corner point of Lion's sacred triangle, inside Her sacred country – the United States of America.

Pierce was awakened with in chill of the morning by the dawn streaking sunlight across his face. He sat, looking around he saw the Lioness breathing deeply and twitching in her sleep. Dreaming of things only Lions might dream of, he mused.

He noted, almost with a tinge of jealousy, that their new young friends, Tom and Bart were sound asleep *between* Lion and himself.

Are they protecting me from he, or her from me?

Pierce stood up, yawned stretched, then caught his breath up short. What lay beyond his eyes was beyond description. The view from atop Harney Peak – in all directions, surely he could see forever from up here. And the always outrageous South Dakota outdid herself this morning. The bright orange sunrise, melted an orange hew across Pierce's view of forever.

Forever to the east. Forever to the west. Forever, up above. Then he looked down at his large bare feet.

The moons and the stars will guide him. Truth is Opposite.

Jeeez. He simply could not shake the words from his head. Over and over and over he could hear the thoughts as if spoken out loud.

"Oh my gosh!" Pierce cried aloud awakening his companions. It was so simple. It was right there before him as simple as could be. He had been looking up when he should have been looking down! How many different ways did it have to hit him in the head before the understood the simple truth?

"The truth is simple. Now I see it. Get up, you guys, get up. I must get off this mountain and go home. I have to get to Dublin, NOW!"

The boys looked around confused with sleep in their eyes. "Dublin? Where's Dublin?"

"Dublin, Ireland, idiots!" Pierce exclaimed. "Where I was born. I must return there NOW!"

Lioness sat up fresh and beautiful and ready to go. The way her eyes twinkled deeply into his, Hanson understood that she knew exactly that he had finally figured out that part of the puzzle.

Lion had an important meeting to attend to while Piece flew out to learn what he had to learn in order to find the rest of his answers.

She looked proud when she looked at her boyfriend. She winked at him behind the boys' back, as the three of them waved goodbye as he darted toward his private jet.

Had she known all along what he had just figured out?

RICHARD – FEAR

Lioness could smell fear. It reeked of a person's individual body odor amplified by about tenfold when it hit her sensitive nostrils. Lioness could smell lust. It smelled like fear with a slight pine scent thrown over the top of the fear scent, like icing on the cake of the underlying stench of fear.

Lioness often smelled fear and lust when any man sat across her table or stood in her presence. She was caught completely by surprise when she smelled neither fear nor lust as Richard stood before her snarling smile. She could take him down by the throat. He was one great leap away from her. Her fangs would be sinking into the major vein of his soft neck before he knew what hit him. She could devour his flesh before he would emit a sound from his mouth. So why didn't he fear her? Why didn't he want to bed her? Why did he have the smug smile on his face as he looked at her with his large, brown, loving elephant eyes?

What pleasure would it bring to devour him anyway? The ugly little man was not exactly a juicy morsel of plump monkey meat. In fact, he looked to be all bones and cartilage. Especially cartilage. My gosh, what is with those huge ears? He could play Dumbo the Elephant in a movie. Although lions do not fear elephants, they certainly respect them. A lion must use great care in the presence of elephants. Even homely, scrawny little elephants like the one standing before her. Elephants can be very dangerous to a lion alone.

"To what do I owe the pleasure of this meeting?" Richard asked as he sat down across from her at the huge, finely carved rosewood table in the fabulously decorated and famous Godfrey dining room. He easily sipped on a cup of coffee as he played lightly with his salad and pondered if Lioness really was going to eat the slab of raw meat her servants had placed in front of them.

Sure enough, Lioness was gobbling the thick, barely seared meat with bloody au jour dripping out - without displaying a sign of the manners you'd expect from the wealthy. She wolfed the red meat down in glee without hesitation right in front of him and was washing it down with that cup of wine that oddly looked like purplish red blood. Richard, the vegetarian, felt a wave of nausea overtake him as he looked at Lion's choice of lunch. Surely the woman should weigh 300 pounds eating that crap. It boggled his mind that she maintained her gorgeous tall slim figure of a fashion model, combined with the sinewy muscles of a weight trainer. Must be her daily runs and working out at the gym, he mused. Everything about Lioness bemused Richard.

She is a study in dichotomies – that is why she is so fascinating to the world. So loved, so hated. So hideous as to be beautiful. So loved by men that women hate her. So deeply kind as to be a dangerous idealist; therefore, thought to be evil. Often misinterpreted, but never ignored.

"Richard, Richard, Richard," Lioness let out a low purr.

"Lion, Lioness, Whatever. Can we get straight to the point? We are two of the busiest people in the world, so might I suggest we do not beat around the bush and get straight to the reason you called this meeting?"

My. In spite of his lack of lust and his lack of fear, the man does have a blunt directness to be admired.

"I like directness and honesty in a man. And courage. I see all three in you."

"Thank you. But I think you'll find I'm one man completely immune to your obvious charms. Further, if I have to watch you eat any more of that grotesque lunch, I will simply vomit, so would you mind if we get right to whatever point it is you have to make? I have a campaign to run."

David is right. This man might just be straight forward enough to beat them both in the election!

"OK. Here it is, then. I have to select a vice-presidential candidate this week. I'd like you to drop out of the race for President and run as my choice of Vice-President instead."

"No can do." Richard said without even a moment of thought or hesitation.

"What do you mean, 'no can do'?"

She started to penetrate his mind with her's but was met by a solid steal block. She could not read a thing and her eye color could not change to his brown.

Drat, he is a powerful warlock. I should have taken the warnings more seriously.

"No thanks. First, I plan on beating you on my own and becoming President. Second, the legalities of switching parties could not be effectuated in time. Third, I would be betraying my people, my country, my principals, my truth, my children-who deserve a choice. Godfrey vs. Godfrey is not a choice. Fourth…"

"Whoa. Whoa. Whoa. Let me take those objections one at a time. There is a choice. David is a Democrat all the way. I'm a Republican most of the way."

"My butt. You are a 'do gooder' socialist simply disguised as a Republican. You and David are both Democrats."

"Funny you should accuse me of that, when at the very same time David accuses me of being a Libertarian just like you!"

"So, what are you really?"

"I am what you think I am."

"Then you are a troublemaker because you swing both ways! You are fiscally conservative yet socially liberal."

"Ah, then that is what I am. But we were talking of differences and free choice now were we not? In the case of Godfrey vs. Godfrey for President, there is a helluva a choice and a heckuva difference. David and I are as different as night and day. Man and woman. Beast and mortal. Don't tell me there is no choice. There is plenty of choice. We are opposites, for Chriminey sakes. As for the legalities of your switching parties to be my running mate, Godfreys have access to the best attorneys in the entire world. I'll get them working on it within seconds of you saying yes."

"Don't hold your breath or pick up the phone. It is not going to happen."

"What if I told you the future of mankind depends on the outcome of this election?"

"Isn't that what they say about every election?"

"Legend has it that In the End of Times, one third of the people will follow the devil. One third of the people will follow the Christ. And one third of the people could be persuaded to go either way. The polls indicate David has 1/3 of the vote, you have 1/3 and I have 1/3. I submit to you, Richard, that this is the End of Times -- as prophesized from the very beginning."

"Precisely why I will not only hold onto my 1/3, but I will seek intelligent souls to steal from both you and David, then I will win the Presidency."

"Join me, Richard, and together we will win. We will have the 2/3 we need to take over the most powerful nation in the world."

"You are a little slow, Miss Lion. This is precisely the proposition David made to me last week."

Rats! That bastard!

"Don't worry," Richard seemed to be almost able to read her mind. This angered her because ESP was her own little trick. "I turned him down just as I'm turning you down."

Lioness could tell there was no changing Richard's mind. It was time for a new approach. She would shake his unshakable confidence.

"Richard, you know perfectly well a Libertarian – or any third party candidate for that matter – can't possibly ever win the Presidency of the United States."

"My parents taught me there is no such thing as a 'can't'".

"Be reasonable. People think Libertarian and they think Marijuana. Marijuana is no campaign issue to win on."

"Before they started listening to me that may be what they thought. But people may be brighter than you think or David thinks, Lion. I believe people realize now Libertarian means freedom, liberty, human rights and personal responsibility, dignity, Constitutionalism and Original Intent of our founding fathers. You know – all those things you claim to believe in."

"You know perfectly well I believe in all those things. We think alike, Richard in way more areas than you realize. But if either of us is to win this final election, we must join forces for the sake of all humanity. You are correct in all your ideals, but you also know that Libertarianism in its purist form can not work as it borders on anarchy."

"With the waste and corruption in government today, what is wrong with a little anarchy?"

"Do you fear nothing, Richard?"

"Yes, you already know what I fear. I have never, in all my life feared a terrorist. Yet, everyday of my life I have feared my own government. I fear governments who rob people of their rights and their money. I fear daily the persecution and prosecution of local, state and federal government. It is the government interference with life, liberty and property that is the very enemy of mankind. So I aim to take the enemy down."

"You can not take down the United States government. Our Constitution and Bill of Rights was inspired by the Hand of God, Himself. Rather than take it down, let's work together to return this great country to the idealisms it was founded upon. Let's return to the Original Intent which gave birth to America."

"Well at least we agree this Republic was founded on the sanctity of life, liberty, and property. Unfortunately over the years the Sacred, God Given Rights have been corroded and eroded by courts, legislators, and wannabes. Corrupt elected officials at all levels of government took all the sacred rights away. I'm here to bring them back."

It was time to bitch slap a little reality into this pure idealist.

"I respect your message, Richard. I even agree with most of your message. But do you think for a minute the majority of people respect your message? Let's get real. You got elected Governor of Virginia only because of your name."

"And you don't think you got elected to the Senate because of your name? You don't think Swarzenegger was elected governor of California years ago because of his name? You don't think Kennedys got elected for decades because of their name? Never underestimate to power of a name, Lioness."

"That is different. You have just referenced all great families who've EARNED RESPECTED names. Your name, Richard, well frankly, it is borderline obscene."

"Hey, you don't think the things you and your brother say are obscene? You should thank your First Amendment, as I thank my First Amendment, daily for free speech – for the right to use my name in my campaign."

"But as a Libertarian you pulled in only 1-2% of the vote when you ran under Richard. It was not until you changed your campaign signs to your nick name, Dick, that you started winning elections. You did not change your message, you changed your name and the disgruntled public, packed full of disdain, disbelief, and a twisted sense of humor elected you by an overwhelming majority ONLY because of your SIGNS! Don't you want to be remembered for something greater, something nobler?"

"History will remember me for the clarity of my beliefs, the steadfastness of my intellect, my love of all living creatures, and my profound blunt honesty and humor. No matter that I exploited the perverse humor of the voting public to get elected. What matters is what I do when elected. And I aim to restore America to her proper role – the protection of rights. Under me we will not be the most taxes or the most jailed people in the history of the world. I shall set the minds, bodies, and souls of man free. That is how history will remember me! How will history remember you?"

Lioness shook her head sadly, slowly. She already knew that answer.

Richard continued, "I may get elected because I have a humorous name. It doesn't matter, does it? What matters is that I get elected, then I can fix this country. I remember watching a man get elected to City Counsel and mayor of Encinitas, California, decades ago. His real name was James Bond and I was convinced people only voted for him because of his catchy name. He did not resemble the movie character at all – but you know what? The misfortune of his name became his good fortune. What he was teased about as a child – his name – ended up getting him elected by a public who enjoyed the amusement of a man being named James Bond. And you know what else? He turned out to be a good man and a good leader. I learned from watching him. I have turned my merciless childhood teasings from a weakness into a strength. What matters is that I get elected and restore rights, freedom, hope, love, and dignity to the American people."

"There is no dignity in your name, Mr. Head. However, I can definitely relate to the merciless childhood teasings you surely received.. You may have been teased about your name, but I've been harassed about my name all my life, as well as my looks!"

"Perhaps there is dignity in the very humor of our names and how we handle our childhood traumas. Let the world be inspired by how we both took our weaknesses and turned them into strengths. Do you know that when I ran for Governor in Virginia after finally **learning with grace to accept** what people called me behind my back, not only did I win by overwhelming margins, doing my Libertarian party very proud, I did not have to sell my soul or surrender my principals to do it. Every college dorm room in the State of Virginia has one of my campaign signs on its wall. People could not buy, steal, or display my signs and bumper stickers fast enough. I challenge you to walk into any dorm room or to find any car driven by an 18-28 year old in my state that does bear a bumper sticker with my name. Let's face it, my name assures I'll win the under 30 vote hands down."

Lioness knew she was not going to convince Mr. Head to either join her or to change his name. She had to hand it to her beloved humankind, they did, indeed have a warped sense of humor. A warped sense of humor is worth saving.

She shrugged her shoulders, shook his hand, and braced herself for the signs and bumper stickers that would shortly follow:

DICK HEAD FOR PRESIDENT.

Oddly, that was going to be a hard act to beat even with all her ideals, her intellect, and all her money!

PIERCE – THE GREEN GRASS OF HOME

The white stretch limousine had been selected in Dublin out of the several available limits merely for the etching of horses in its windows. The comfortable limo wound through roads caressing the green, green grass of home. Yet Pierce was on edge. Further, Pierce could not help but think that Ireland was turning into one huge golf course. Since Ireland joined the European Union years earlier, it's economy had boomed. It was the place to go for jobs, for luxury living, for divine horses, for easy passports, for green pastures that were rapidly being converted to playgrounds for wealthy golfers in lieu of galloping fields for wealthy fox hunters.

Fox hunting was outlawed years earlier. But in altered form, the tradition continued with the hounds chasing a scent dragged behind a motorcycle, rather than a pursuing and shooting a live animal. The hunt was not as wild, for the path was planned through friendly terrain long before the event. But modern times called for modern concessions and modern compromises.

Hanson's ever faithful bodyguard, James Running Bear doubled as Pierce"s driver whenever this limo was employed. Pierce did not particularly like to drive. Running Bear was skilled. "Soon Ireland will just be one big golf course," Running Bear mused aloud, echoing Pierce's own thoughts.

The poverty stricken boy from a starving and war torn land was returning a wealthy man to a wealthy country. Hanson was highly uneasy by all that had changed – inside his country and inside himself in a matter of just a couple of decades.

Pierce was filled with uncomfortable trepidation, rather than the joyous anticipation most human beings feel when returning to their childhood home. There were no fond memories for Pierce, simply dread. Whereas Ireland was just beginning to emerge as the new economy for some when Pierce was a child, Pierce remembered his childhood hunger and abuses as the fodder on which horror movies could be based.

Sure the hunger, the cold, and daily beatings of his youth had made him the strong, successful, and determined man he was today. But he had also vowed, never to return home again when, as a skinny teen with large blue eyes and a shocking amount of dark brown hair, he had left so long ago. He was simply appalled now to find himself suddenly going back voluntarily.

The moons and the stars will guide him.
Truth is opposite.
Perhaps you should be looking down instead of looking up.

If the words of his ancient papyrus did not continue to haunt him day and night, he would not be returning against his teenage vow. But, now it was crystal clear to him where he should be looking to solve the puzzle of the papyrus. He fumbled with the crystal and the paper where Johnson had penned her interpretation in his pocket near his heart. It was odd that when he touched the piece of cut glass, he felt a soothing warm wave of emotional courage and mental clarity.

It's just cut glass. Logic tried to tell him this. But how did cut glass create a warm, clear stirring inside his soul, when he rubbed its smooth surface? Not to mention a clarity of purpose.

A purpose driven life – the only way to live!

Pierce was not a drinking man, but he noticed his white stretch limo came with the usual wine and glasses, so he selected a merlot and sipped nervously as his driver slowly guided the ostentatious vehicle toward the majestic Powerscourt House.

Thousands of tourists annually visit the Powerscourt Gardens to marvel at 47 acres of the most beautiful landscaping on the planet.

Hanson had worked so hard to erase every aspect of his childhood, that he nearly forgot the amazing beauty of the gardens.

None would even think he had been here in his childhood, he had so erased it from his very being. He had studiously studied his American accent such that he could easily pass for a "damned Yankee". He did a strictly British accent for his spy series without missing a single beat. And he enunciated in perfect German when he did the Hitler documentary. But for an occasional accidental "blimey, mumsy, or bloody hell," even Pierce's voice denied his Irish upbringing.

The Limo pulled into the massive drive of the Powerscourt Castle. Sure, over here it was simply called a House – the Powerscourt House, but by most world standards, by gum, this was a castle. The House was a formidable palace of delicious taste and grand in size. Visitors by the busload would tour a small portion of the house, shop for knitwear and souvenirs in the specialty shop, stand in awe of the furnishings, attend a wedding, or dine at the terrace café. But this was peripheral to why they came by the thousands to stand in wondrous awe of the place he knew like the back of his hand. The wonder of Powerscourt was her gardens – some of the most beautiful grounds the human eye could ever behold.

Pierce exited the Limo and told the driver to feel free to walk around while he waited for Pierce to return, as he expected this was going to take hours.

Pierce yearned to go straight to the spot. It was as if an invisible force was pulling him toward the spot. But he fought the force with all his inner strength. First he had to make peace with his memories. He decided to take the long path to walk around the heavenly gardens while facing the demons of his childhood. He would end up ended up standing on top of the destiny he had denied all his life.

He would stand atop of the moons and the stars soon enough.

PIERCE – THE GARDENS OF HOME

The smells of the gardens were unique to anyplace in the world. Not the sweet smell of the Hawaiian islands. Not the rice water smell of Thailand. Not the dried greens smell of pines of South Dakota. The gardens, well, the gardens there smelled like a mellow blend of them all! Surely this is what heaven smells like; although Lioness always contended heaven smells like Hawaii.

Ah, so I do have SOME fond memories of these gardens!

Still, Pierce could not help but flash back though to the terror of hiding in secret nooks and crannies of the castle, trembling at the fear of his drunken father, a maintenance man who lived in a one bedroom servant's cottage with his wife, who had been a maid at the Great House, and his gangly, irresponsible son. The stench of booze on Pop's unwashed body always spelled of a beating for either Pierce or his mother.

By the time Pierce ran away, his mother had long since ceased to even try to stop Pops from beating Pierce. If she interfered, Pops would beat on Pierce even worse, then turn and give her twice the beating. Mumsy, too, would try to become invisible to hide from his wrath when Pops was drinking. And Pops was drinking every time either of them got paid. Booze took priority over food. You could smell him coming from a hundred yards away as he failed to bathe but once every week or two. A razor was a foreign object to Pops.

Outside the anguish of the cottage, in this large parcel of sheer heavenly gardens, yes, indeed you could hide. But sooner or later you would get cold or hungry and when you crept out of your secret crevice looking to satisfy those terrible pangs and shivers, Pops would, more often than not catch you and give you the beating you deserved for being the cause of all his unfulfilled dreams.

If Pierce locked himself in a room of the Master House, Pops would break through the door or come in through a window in an even greater rage and beat him until he coughed up blood. If Pierce could hide out in the gardens, though, he might be safe, albeit cold, when the Irish Mists turned to pouring rains. Seeking shelter would eventually drive him into their small stone house heated by an old wood burning stove - and into the arms of a raging bull and a horrified Mum.

Now returning as an adult, Pierce Hanson left the great house and wandered the familiar gardens and he was surprised at the details he now recalled from his long stifled childhood memories. He still felt the pain of the beatings and the tightness of his gut at the thought of his father. Yet he felt an acting softness in his heart when he remembered the warm embraces of his mother.

The star was glad he left his bodyguard waiting for him in the limo. He needed to be alone with his emotions; alone with his memories; alone with his reconciliation; and alone in his search for answers.

Pierce looked at the fountain surrounded on either side by the two magnificent Pegasus statutes. Wings of flight, powerful necks high, striking mirror images of one another, the Pegasus artwork loaned a sense of power to a peaceful background of water and calming greens. This fountain and its winged horses gave Pierce a hope of flying away on the back of a horse. This essentially had become his own self-fulfilling prophecy.

Little wonder he loved the creature called horse from his earliest memories. No wonder he adored the pas de deux of dressage where two magnificently trained horses danced in mirror image of one another. These Pegasus at the fountain were performing the original pas de deux. Art mimicking the life the young Pierce could only dream of. The life he would obsess over until he found a way to create it for himself.

Dream until you dreams come true.

Staring at the inspirational horses of flight framing the still waters, Pierce deliberately made sure he did not look down. He was not ready for the moons and the stars quite yet. First he must find his inner peace and strength. Then he would step into his destiny. His gut told him when he looked down he would be launched toward solving the mystery of his own part of the Dead Sea Scrolls.

Hanson needed just a few more minutes of being a rich and famous movie star wandering through quiet gardens, because once he looked down, he knew full well he would no longer be that man he had spent so many years creating. Instinct told him that when he looked down Pierce Hanson the movie star would cease to be and would turn into Her servant.

He took the long outer path around the gardens. He needed an extra hour to simply savor being Pierce Hanson the gorgeous Superstar one last time. Soon enough he would revisit his childhood nightmare which would launch into his adulthood nightmare.

Pierce shivered as he realized his childhood anguish had been mere training for what was to come.

PIERCE – LOOKING DOWN

No tourists were taking the longer, outer pathway at the time, and no cameras or autograph seekers were there. Pierce sucked in only peace as he listened to the birds chirp, the insects buzz, and the slight breeze rustle the bushes and tease the tall trees.

Pink and yellow flowers lined the path. Trees and bushes were trimmed yet overwhelming in their size and years. The grooming of the gardens remained impeccable for tourists year round. He remembered his mum with gloved hands on her knees in the dirt, quietly humming hymns in her happiest hours. She loved the gardens and although technically a maid at the big house, she was allowed to work the gardens quite often, too.

He went down toward the path to the old tower he had claimed as a child and pretended to be a knight in his own castle. He had talked one of the wealthy boys from the big house into teaching him to fence and they would spend hours defending their "mighty" castle. The rounded two story rock structure with windows and curving staircase looked just as it did when he would hide from his father there decades ago. Lightning flashing, rain pounding, father cursing flashed through Pierce's memory banks. He shook off the dread that filled him at the very memory before he climbed to the top and looked out at the extraordinary greenery that surrounded him. That vast and multi-faceted country he now called home, America, in all her wilderness, golden plains, and majestic mountains, still would never know green like Ireland's green. Nor know gardens like the great gardens of Europe.

Reluctantly climbing down from the old remnants, Hanson continued exploring the famous gardens that had not changed much at all since his childhood. Deep in reminiscents and rapidly recovering memory, he still knew all the different paths around all the different theme gardens that added together became one of the greatest gardens of all of the United Kingdom. He past the pond with lilies so abundant you almost felt you could walk across the water, lily pad to lily pad. He wandered on down below to the Japanese garden that rivaled anything he had ever seen in Japan. The delicate walkways, the little bridges. The stairs, the plants, everything was done in perfect detail. Pierce could not help but wonder if Walt Disney's attention to miniature detail had ever taken inspiration from this site. Hanson strolled on toward the famous rock grotto, where two rock archways formed a magnificent heart with purple flowers peeking out shyly from the crevices.

Here was earth marrying civilization to join in an eternal bond of immortal union whose beauty would forever defy description.

Yes, here was Pierce's ideal picture of heaven.

Why then, did he remember it as his childhood hell?

A hymn from childhood began to fill his head so clearly it was as if his ears heard angels strumming a golden harp and singing only unto him. *"Softly and tenderly Jesus is calling. Calling, oh sinner come home."*

Pierce fell to his knees directly under the heart shaped grotto, shaking the music from his head, and prayed out loud with tears running down his cheeks, "Dear Lord, your sinner has come home. Guide me please. Help me to humble my proud temper and give me the strength and the intellect to discover and perform Your Great Will."

Touching his crystal and his translation of his Dead Sea Document in his pocket, he found peace and purpose as he stood tall, raising his arms to heaven. An inner strength took over his anguished soul and he stood strong ready to take up pen and sword and finish his job.

No longer a star, at that moment Hanson was transformed to a man on a mission, Pierce marched up the hill, past the fascinating, if a tad macabre, animal cemetery. The Powerscourt family had erected tombstones to rival those of man over the graves of their family pets. Hanson looked for the tiny gravestone he had erected when he placed his dead puppy beside the beloved animals of the wealthy Powerscourt heirs. In the upper right hand corner remained the tiny unmarked piece of granite among the larger dedications.

He had buried her secretly and alone in the moonlight when he was just becoming a young man – just a shadow of the future superstar. Mitzy, the little white mix breed that had followed him everywhere from the time one of the gardeners had given the five year old Pierce something of his own to love, until the day his father beheaded her with a shovel merely because he could not find Pierce to beat at that moment.

Hanson shook the heartache from his body as he left the animal cemetery and strode determinedly upward toward the famous, magnificent rose gardens. The fragrance filled his nostrils with a sweetness that contradicted the dark stench of his worst memory in his lifetime - finding Mitzy beheaded.

Pierce slowed his stride slightly at the heavenly scent as he continued forward and he passed the phenomenal displays of roses. He ended up back toward great rolling green yard below the castle, then stopped dead in this tracks.

He felt dizzy at the memory that was forming in his mind. The memory of a little blonde girl with a strange face rolling down those grassy green hills laughing, laughing, laughing. Her mother rolling with her laughing and her older brother standing embarrassed with his arms crossed, eyes glaring in disgust at his mother's and sister's outrageous and embarrassing public behavior.

Pierce froze in place as he remembered. The girl beckoned to him. "Peter come roll with us". Her kind and lovely mother beckoned to him, too.

What? Be frivolous? Laugh? No, that simply was not allowed. He had to help mums and father earn a living. Besides, his name was Pierce, not Peter.

But she was such a pretty little thing. All kinda golden and glowy. And three days ago pops had killed Mitzy, so what did he care about anything anymore, anyway?

He remembered looking into that cute little blonde's happy carefree face and seeing eyes that looked more like

Mitzy's eyes than like a human's eyes. He abandoned his gardening equipment, his rake and his hoe, and began to roll down the hill with the American girl and her mum.

Running up and rolling down – over and over again. The odd looking little girl, the lovely mom and Pierce. It was the only time from his childhood that he remembered laughing. Laughing so much his stomach hurt. When they were too tired to climb up and roll down another time, covered with grass stains and sweat, the girl exclaimed, "Let's get some ice cream, Peter."

"The name is not Peter. My name is Pierce."

"Whatever," said the girl shrugged her shoulders with the arrogance of an American, "I shall call you Peter." Just then her mum walked out of the house and handed them each an ice cream that would melt in their mouths.

Only the wealthy tourists were privy to the joy of the ice cream from the souvineer shops. Pierce's mouth had so often watered as he watched them licking the sweet delights while Pierce was covered with mud and sweat helping his mother in the great gardens.

"Where'd your brother go?" the mother of the boy's new strange little blond friend worried.

"Who cares?" said the girl. "Let's go eat our ice cream down there." The blonde girl had pointed down the stairs toward the archway above the two Pegasus.

They had walked down to the heavenly inlays and were halfway through their ice cream when the little girl danced upon the carvings, pulled the boy aside and whispered with confidence, "Don't worry. Your puppy is not dead. There is no such thing as death. Always look inward as well as outward. Always look down, as well as up."

The girl was talking pure nonsense. How did she know about Mitzy? What kind of gibberish was she muttering?

Whop. Pierce was struck across the head and knocked out cold by the same shovel in his dad's hand that had killed his Mitzy three days prior. Until this very day, decades later, he had so blocked the emotional and physical pain form his mind that this was the very first time he remembered the incident.

Now Pierce knew why the woman he now knew and loved had said they had met before. Lioness and David had not been knocked out by Pops that day, so they both remembered it clearly! He wondered why David had not mentioned it at dinner in Boston. Lioness confessed to recognizing Pierce from their visit to these gardens. Did David not remember, or merely have no desire to bring it up? Only Pierce had forgotten, due to the sharp blow to his head from a shovel wielded by his retched alcoholic father who could not stand to see his son happy on that day.

The adult still hurt, so many years later. The pain in his chest from his broken heart remembering the undying courage and love of Mitzy was unbearable, yet sweet, at the same time. His head actually ached from remembering the brain concussion that left him vomiting when he came to. Not to mention the embarrassment of his first crush seeing his humiliation right where Lion had danced a moment.

Pierce moved still further from the rose garden and back toward the central pond. He had to get to the very spot he had last seen the sister and brother. Of course his own dropped ice cream and spilled blood had been washed away so long ago, but he felt he must stand exactly where he stood before shovel encountered head. He was there.

"Always look down as well as up."

As he stood on the spot the young boy had experienced his only moment of joy, where he had felt laughter and tasted ice cream and had the dizziness of his first childhood crush, he looked down. There before his now very adult eyes, he saw the meaning of the universe clearly spelled out in the carved stones beneath his very feet.

He saw the planets, the circles, the squares, the triangles. Yes, they had been there to guide him all his life, but he had simply never really paid attention to these guides. He had no reason to ever return before now.

Now surrounding his very large famous movie star feet, Pierce saw it all, including the moons and the stars.

And the moons and the stars will guide him.

PIERCE – DECIPHERING THE MOONS AND THE STARS

It is one thing to locate the moons and the stars. It is still another to decipher their meaning.

Pierce stared and stared, but did not quite understand. He darted up to the large castle-house and purchased a disposal camera in one of the gift shops. What the heck, "throw in an ice cream, too, if you don't mind," he told the clerk who was staring at him in recognition and with such a powerful crush Pierce believed she would faint. He had that effect on women. His looks had taken him far. It was now time for his spirit and brains to take him the next step.

He sat on the very steps where he had endured his final beating at the ripe old age of thirteen. After he got out of the hospital that time, he would never again return to his childhood home - until this very day. He felt awful leaving, nay abandoning, his mum to the hands of the abusive alcoholic, but by gum, he would not suffer the same fate as Mitzy. He determined before the hospital released him, that he would survive. He would escape poverty and abuse and he would rise to the top of the social ladder. He would see the world, then he would have it all for his own.

His new life started the night before he was to be released from the hospital. He climbed down the vines three stories, then made his way to the Dublin docks. He was already in England before his angry father realized he was missing from the hospital. His mum knew in her heart she would not see him again on this planet, in this lifetime.

With help from none, but on his own profound inner will, he learned to fight with fists, shoot a gun, and perfected his execptional fencing skills. He learned to read and write and recite. He learned to ride and speak languages without a hint of his Irish accent. And he learned to act. He would work all night as a janitor in theaters, work the stables all day, study and take classes in the evening. On four hours of sleep per night, he crawled his way up and out and around society over the years. Pierce had crawled down out of the hospital window in mere seconds. He climbed up out of poverty over year. He would claw, charm, and think his way up the social ladder. Twenty hours per day, seven days per week, for twenty years, Pierce worked like a dog never taking a single day off.

Now, he stood at the top of society in a fine Armani suit, ready to take on the world as a highly skilled and stunning looking man. He was brilliant, successful, well traveled and about to marry a future President, whether she accepted this concept or not.

He had fought his way to the top with help from no one.

Surely now you can take on the world with help from twelve.

Who said that? Who exactly were the twelve? Was Lion one? Was his bodyguard? Some thoughts filled his head from out of nowhere as he gazed at the moons and the start. Still, he needed more information.

For now, Hanson was back where he started. Eating the ice cream and smiling to himself. He got it. All those years of training were indeed for a mission far greater than the child could have ever fantasized. He had been in training from the beginning. All the suffering. All the anguish. All the hard work. All the studying. All the auditions. All the hard earned money now wisely invested. It was all for the far greater purpose on which he was now about to embark.

Looking down at the coded message in the stones of his childhood, Pierce saw two half moons surround circles, surrounding stars, surrounding more circles.

Life goes eternally outward unto the heavens and eternally inward through the cells of man, therefore, **man is indeed the center of the universe,** *as was alleged from the beginning.* **As it was in the beginning, it will be in the end.**

Pierce kept thinking he was hearing things and had to consider the possibility he was losing his mind.

Hanson starred at the stars carved so carefully into the granite walkway beneath his feet. Stars with eight arms, rather than the usual five or six. Eight arms. Where in heaven or earth had he seen eight armed stars before? What did they symbolize?

He pulled the now worn translation of his Dead Sea Scroll out of the pocket of his classic pin striped suit. He read it for the umpteenth time, straining to understand.

"May the Triangles guide you." Each of the eight arms of the stars pointed away from the inner circle at the heart of the stars. The arms were in the shape of triangles pointing away from the internal circle. Where were they pointing?

"To all the corners of the earth?"

It flashed across his mind that the triangles forming the stars might be pointing to seven continents. That could not be right. There were eight triangles.

He wandered the grounds looking for understanding. Throughout the carefully laid rock sidewalk were circles, squares, and elliptical designs that could either represent the rings of Saturn or the orbits of planets around the sun. He photographed and photographed as his head ached to figure out what mysterious message was portrayed in the rocks beneath his feet.

He kept returning to the triangles forming the eight armed stars. They were simply too powerful, just too precise, magnificently too centralized, far too repeated in theme, and much too obvious now to not have significant meaning to whomever painstakingly and with precision carved these patterns and laid this rock foundation of the garden's sidewalks.

On Christ the solid rock you stand.

Who said that? Pierce again thought he heard some tender voice whispering to him, but there were merely birds and the sound of tourists whenever he looked over his shoulders for an unidentified speaker. He pondered if he was losing his mind.

Then, again, he looked down at the moons and the stars.

Pierce pulled out Johnson's interpretation of his Dead Sea Scroll. The final words she had penned read, "Let the Triangles lead you to the Moons and the Stars." Of one thing Hanson was now certain – the paper making that statement was meant for his eyes only. Hanson stood on top of the triangles, moons, and stars carefully carved into the Powerscourt sidewalks to guide him to his destiny.

All who looked down from above could appreciate the beauty and harmony of the message, even though they failed to comprehend the message itself.

Viewed down from the heavens, viewed up from the earth, these shapes were now obviously historically sacred and inspirational.

Mankind was meant to see these. Mankind was meant to figure these out. The gardens were one of the most visited sights in all of Ireland and these patterns were eye catching and blatant. Why had so many hundreds of thousands tread to this amazing place to view these gardens, including Pierce himself, and not realized they trod upon holy messages begging to be interpreted?

Pierce was so deep in thought he was caught utterly by surprise by the mob suddenly surrounding him.

PIERCE – THE GLOBE

Pierce normally saw his fans coming. Normally, he had body guards to warn and ward. Normally, giggling and whispers warned he was about to be surrounded.

Today he had no warning. Alone with his thoughts so deep he was not normal today, he had forgotten about the gal in the gift shop. She must have called her entire high school! Suddenly the Movie Star forgot the more important Stars upon which he stood and pondered that day. Pierce was surrounded by a mob of hysterical girls thrusting their pens and papers asking for an autograph. One woman lifted up her shirt as she handed him a pen and asked him to sign her bare breast. This was too much intrusion. In the midst of his spiritual epiphany Pierce was being intruded upon by the baseness of the masses. This was not acceptable.

Cameras were clicking, gossip was spreading. James, his trusted bodyguard, was sleeping in the limo under orders not to intrude on his solitude. What solitude?

Without a single bodyguard, he had no choice. He took off running like a bat out of hell.

Dodging through bushes, rolling down a hill. Running. Running. Running. For all he was worth, he ran and lost the crowd behind him. He could outrun them all and lose them for his childhood survival instincts had kicked in and he ran as he had run time and time again to dodge the danger that was his daily childhood experience. Instinct and old memories were his guide. Run from your dad. Run. He has been drinking again. "Run, Pierce, Run." He could almost hear his mother's voice urging him to self-protect. To survive the abuse that eventually would kill her.

He was there. Out of breath he found himself in the one bedroom cottage of his childhood nightmares. Dust was everywhere. There was a pot on the cooking stove. There was one dingy, filthy window that let in sacred light. The corner where he slept and the slightly offset room where his poor mother endured the ravages of his hideous father were even filthier than when he had left so many years ago. The stench of the cottage was almost unbearable. He wondered how long his father had lived after mum had died in the "accident".

Fell, my butt, he pushed her and killed her as sure as I am standing here today. Forgive me mum, for leaving you alone here with him. Forgive me for not returning to your funeral. My survival instinct was just too overwhelming and raw since I left here.

Right below the dingy window, where it had set for decades, covered in dust was the only treasure he and his mother ever had. There was the large round object supported on top of the Triangle base that opened into a box where mother hid their only secret treasures from father.

Pierce removed his handkerchief and began fondly dusting off the old globe that he had so idolized as a child. Pierce and his mom had found this humongous, ugly old globe thrown out in the garbage during one of the many remodelings of the great house. They had somehow talked three of the gardeners into taking it to their tiny cottage and placing it by the window so when the light shown in, they could talk of all the marvelous places in the world they would visit some day. Of course, pops hated the globe because it made his family happy and he assured them at all times they were such losers their dreams would never come true. He would have destroyed the big old ball on many occasions, but it was indestructible and too heavy for him to remove.

And pops never did know that the triangular stand holding the globe up could be opened. It was Pierce and mum's little secret. Mum would place a pretty trinket in there for Pierce. Piece would leave a pretty flower in there for mum. Mum kept her bible and her necklace that had been handed down for generations – the only two objects of any value or meaning mum had left to own after marrying the man who had impregnated her out of wedlock.

As a child Pierce would gaze upon the precious globe for hours upon hours dreaming of the countries he would explore one day when he became rich and famous. He would leave Ireland and he would see the world.

Ah, the power of the self-fulfilling prophecy.

He had now done what he had always dreamed of doing.

He had seen China, Russia, Hawaii, Argentina…. he had seen the world and left the filthy, little dirt poor starving boy far behind.

He brushed the dirt off every bit of the humungous globe, marveling how in his lifetime the names and boundaries of countries had changed. The iron curtain had come down and the boy had grown into a man. The countries and their boundaries had changed over the decades, but the land itself stood firm.

"The boundaries drawn upon the land do nothing more than show, the void within the minds of man that make these cancers grow."

The last part of the globe he dusted off was Ireland herself. What the heck was that!?! Right outside Dublin, there appeared a tiny hand drawn likeness of the eight armed stars he had just been pondering in the gardens above! The little miniature star had never been there before! Had his mother left that as some kind of message him before she died?

One of the itsy bitsy arms of the stars pointed north - to the very point where he was standing at just that very moment. Right outside Dublin Ireland! The other seven triangles formulating the rest of the star seemed to have faint lines penciled out away from their point to encircle the entire globe. Pierce had absolutely no remembrance of seeing the star or the lines extending outward from the star's eight arms in his early days of anguish and fantasy.

The triangle opposite the north pointing star had a line drawn through Paris France, northern Africa and all the way straight toward Antarctica.

The star's line to that line's left seemed to touch the Canary Islands before ending up near Rio de Janeiro

Lioness

The next one counterclockwise cut its way across the Bermuda triangle and through Puerto Rico to its final destination in the Costa Rica area.

The line sketched to the right of the southernmost arm of the star cut across eastern Europe, then through the Greek Islands or Turkey.

The one to the right of that seemed to cross through Dubai on its way to Austraila while the next one up went straight to Asia – right to Bangkok, Thailand.

One went to Africa – in the area of Cairo, Egypt.

And one of the lines presumable sketched by mums shot out the arm of the star directly through western South Dakota and continued on to the Salt Lake City area.

"The Seven Clues are on the Seven Continents."

Who said that? Hanson looked fearfully around the creepy little cottage.

Pierce knew he had found one of the referenced triangles in North America. It was sacred Triangle in the Black Hills that David had told him about. The moons and the stars had guided him to the stars with eight arms. The eight arms of the stars must surely be guiding him to sacred triangles.

Obviously the Bear Butte, Devil's Tower, Harney Peak triangle was one of the eight triangles.

Did the Bermuda Triangle house another clue?

Clues on seven continents. Why then did these stars have eight arms pointing?

There were no famous triangles in Ireland that he knew of.

Wait a darned moment!

Pierce fell to his knees and frantically wiped the triangular box beneath the globe that housed his mother's treasures. He began to dust the base. Right where you lifted the secret lid to his mum's private box was carved another eight armed star! The northern most arm pointed directly to the hidden latch to open the box at the base of the globe. His mum must have known he would return in search some day. She must have left these to guide him one day.

Pierce opened the box and fondly lifted out his mother's well worn bible. An Irish Catholic to the core, every hour not spent cooking and cleaning, mum's gained her meaning and solace from reading the bible.

Neatly underlined in red were her favorite passages. To have this sacred part of his mum's life as his only heirloom just made the entire trip back to Dublin worth his while, even if all else was simply his imagination gone wild.

Perhaps his unfulfilled lust for Lioness was driving him to the brink of madness, perhaps not. But he was glad he was here now, holding something his mother had cherished and relied on for strength until the end of her miserable excuse for a life.

It was hard to breathe as his deep sobs erupted from his body, missing his mum and so sorry he had left her alone with the Beast.

Streaks of tears running down his cheeks combined with the setting sun that no longer penetrated the soot streaked window were making it difficult to see anything now. He barely spotted the envelope labeled "for my chosen Son" in the triangle box just as a faint breeze caused the dust to stir from the bottom of mother's triangular box.

Pierce squatted to retrieve the envelope in the last moment of grey light and as darkness invaded the horrid little house.

Pierce jumped erect and his body erupted in chills. He heard the squeaking of the loose floorboards behind him too late.

Pierce recognized the putrid smell of stale alcohol and body odor. He instinctively knew he was not alone in this house of unforgotten tortures and that the Beast stood between him the doorway. There was no way to escape.

PIERCE – MOVING ON

Whirling to face the aggressive abuser of his childhood, all six foot three inches of his magnificent being raised itself ready for the fight. Before him stood the monster of his childhood-his own father. His breath came up short.

What stood before Pierce, the huge monster of childhood terrors who regularly tormented Pierce to within an inch of his life – from electrocutions to beatings – was a shrunken, unshaven, smelly old drunk leaning over his cane and looking so feeble he could barely stand. Surely a strong wind could blow the little skeleton away. This was the source of his first decade's agony?

"Hello, Son, I knew you would return for those some day," the skeleton glanced at the envelope Pierce held in his hand.

Pierce clutched tighter. Whatever these documents held, he must cling to them with his life for they were all that gave meaning to the hopeless life of his hopeful mother.

"Sit down, Son," Dad sank to his old rickety rocking chair as he motioned to the filthy chair in front of it.

Pierce silently did as told, studying the object of his fear and wondering how such a weak and putrid little creature arose from the ashes of his big and scary father. To ashes he would soon return and Pierce suddenly felt only pity and forgiveness in the area of his heart where he for a lifetime he had housed hate, fear, and unfathomable determination to escape and succeed.

Those emotions had served him well. They had turned him into a fighter – fists and swords. They had turned him into a rider – Olympic Caliber. They had turned him into a millionaire – many times over. They had turned him into a Super Star – the flavor of the month for more than two years now. They had led him to her – Lioness.

Unfathomable drive is borne out of childhood deprivation.

"As God is my witness I shall never go hungry again," had been the famous words of Scarlet O'Hara upon returning home to Tara after war-inflicted deprivation in "Gone With the Wind" – Pierce's favorite movie of all time. Pierce had landed in America years prior with his fists clenched and raised to the skies crying out, "As God is my witness I shall never go hungry, I shall never go unnoticed, I shall never go in fear, and I shall never go without my heart's every desire again." These yearnings of his heart and mind and soul had been so powerful that the entire Universe had no choice but to yield to them!

But, standing before his tormentor on this day he could only shake his weary head and ask, "Why?"

Pops knew exactly what he was asking and he held his head in shame, "I don't know, Son. Perhaps jealousy. Once you were born, your mother went into her own world. She shut me out. You and Abby were a team.

August Anderson

I was the outsider, expected to provide food, but never privy to your secrets, you laughter, your love. Perhaps my alcohol addition. Perhaps it was your own fault for never being grateful for what I did provide – clothes, a roof over your head, food enough to stay alive, anyway. I saw you as lazy and ungrateful. Perhaps my own lifetime of being an orphan - poverty, hunger beyond imagination, losing my arm in a war for an ungrateful country. A cause without a purpose. An anger without a reason. I don't know, Son, but I do know my only emotion was rage. After your mom virtually abandoned me for the love of you, I felt only anger and hate. There was no love, no life, no joy. I could only cover it all in booze. Mine was a purposeless life. At least you had purpose. I hated you for taking her heart - and your brother for breaking her heart."

"I don't have a brother, Dad," Pierce felt deep, dark pity, and he whispered in a choking voice to the pathetic, confused, shrunken little creature before him.

"Look at those papers your mom left you. She cried over and over again for you when you left her. She had visions, your mother did. Lots of visions. She was crazy as a loon. She said you had a divine purpose and the globe and the papers would reveal it. She said at the right time you would return and you must have the secrets the globe housed for you. With her dying breath she ordered me to live until you returned and to make sure you got the globe's papers. She repeated these things a thousand times, then she died. I'm sure she cries in heaven to this day that you did not even return for the funeral."

Pierce lowered himself to a rickety old chair as his old man lit an oil lantern on the table. Pierce sat the papers

Lioness

beneath the flickering lamp and his father pulled an old rocking chair up beside Pierce.

As he spoke, Pierce thumbed through the papers. He came upon two copies of his birth certificate. There before his weary eyes he could make out in the semi-darkness a copy of the birth same birth certificate he carried with him the original at all times.   Pierce Hanson, born blah, blah, blah...

But the shocker was there was another almost identical birth certificate – this one an original with all the information exactly the same, except this one had the name of Peter Hanson upon it.   "Why do I have two birth certificates?"

"You don't son. You had a brother. You were a twin. That is why you are left handed. All left handed people have a twin your mum would always say. Your twin died at the age of three days old of pneumonia. Your mum cried for three years. I took up drinking. Abby clung to you like you were life itself. She acted as if you were the savior Himself for having lived when Peter died." His breath from a lifetime of smoking was choking him as he said these words. He sank deeper in the rocker and then quit rocking all together.

"You two looked exactly alike. No one ever could tell you apart."

Pierce did not even know what to say or do, so he sat there numb and dumb. All he could think was that he must have gotten his good looks from his mother, not this ugly little man with a humped back before him. He knew it was both wrong and shallow to think only that, but he was in shock.

Also, he was starring at the other documents from his mum's tiny legacy he had placed on his lap. He opened a tightly sealed, large manila envelope, addressed "To My Beloved Son" in mum's handwriting and glanced inside. He saw a faint blue shine emitting from under the envelope that made him gasp. He thought he knew what it contained, but he was not about to bring out the source of the blue light in front of a man who thought anything of any value must be sold for cheap booze. He would examine it later. He resealed the envelope quickly. He must be allowed to walk out of there with this envelope.

He saw the envelope was covered with small flags she had stuck to it on the back side. Instantly he knew exactly where he must go and knew he must go now. He brought out his cell phone and ordered the jet be waiting and called James in the limo and said he would be there in less than ten minutes. He went for the door when he heard his father's voice, "Goodbye Peter."

Before he could reply "I'm Pierce, not Peter" the tormentor of youth had slipped to a lifeless heap upon the filthy floor. Pierce knew he had died without even stopping to take his pulse.

As he darted out the door, Pierce looked toward the heavens, "Father forgive him, for he knew not what he did." It was his first, last, and only prayer for the soul of his earthly father.

Pierce had business to take care of. He had to get to Turkey. And fast.

PIERCE – TRAVELING

Hanson's private jet, the Cosmo 2011-the latest in flying luxury, from sleeping rooms to Jacuzzis, was sitting on the runway with engines roaring, ready to take off the moment he and James set foot in his air cabin.

Pierce was halfway to Turkey when his pilot, Paul, came back and set in the luxury seat across from Pierce.

"We can not get clearance to land in Turkey."

"What are my options?" an exhausted Pierce did not want to deal with paperwork or political complications.

"You could land in Santorini, Greece, then take a private yacht into the harbor of Turkey at either Izmur or Kusadasi. Kusadasi is a very short drive to Ephesus, but Izmur is closer to the airport where you wanted to land.

Pierce was grateful that he had spent so much time around the Aegean Sea before coming to America in his early twenties.

That glorious warm summer he traveled around the Greek islands with a Shakespearean Troop was one to be remembered. The troop lived like gypsies. Staying in hostels, YMCAs and even in open fields, they traveled throughout Greece and Turkey, putting performing "As

You Like It" over and over until they could perform it in their sleep. They ate, drank, partied, and performed to full houses around one of the most historical and beautiful places on the planet. No matter the native language, the audiences were always great. The troop always played to a full house and all seemed to understand and enjoy the play immensely.

They had appeared at the Parthenon in Athens. None could argue with Athena's temple and Pierce marveled at the other ancient ruins; however, air pollution, traffic, graffiti and crime made Athens less than Pierce's favorite part of Greece.

Oh, how they had all loved Santorini. Holy red wine resulting from the miracle of time's effect on green grapes wrapped in sacred vines. The one wine Santorini did not export. How sweet the sacramental wine was to the tongue. Liquid desert. Riding donkeys up and down the cliffs to the white houses with blue roofs was a scene out of many movies. Riding the donkeys up the steep cliffside was standard for tourists, but if you wanted to laugh hysterically while fearing for your life, you rode the donkeys down the steep and slippery cliff to the aqua colored harbor. Little hooves would scramble to keep you upright as they slipped on donkey urine and Pierce would envision himself tumbling over the rock wall to the sea below.

They performed before massive crowds in Istanbul. Visiting both the Asian and European part of the City and its many mosques, was an adventure that went on for weeks.

Then they had traveled south and had appeared in Ephesus at the great theater beyond the library – below the ruins of the Temple of Artimisne of the seven wonders of the ancient world. Even while Pierce performed on the ancient stage that had once overlooked the great harbor, he had an eerie feeling that part of his destiny was here. He knew he would return. He did not know when or why.

Now Pierce was crystal clear that he was being called to return there. Why? Because he held before him the cut out of flags carefully taped on the back side of his mum's package for him.

The first flag was the Irish flag or his youth displaying the familiar green, white and orange vertical bands.

The next flag was the red flag with a crescent moon and single star – recognized around the world as the national flag of Turkey. Instinct told him he was to proceed from Ireland to Turkey and he was heading there as fast as he could go.

He wasn't sure why mum's hand would so direct him from beyond the grave, but he figured it had to do with the Dead Sea Scrolls and pieces of cut glass with fake jewels.

"Can you make the arrangements on the way to Santorini so that a yacht is completely stocked up with food and has a crew waiting for the minute I land? Kusadsi is closer to both Santorini and Ephasus, so charter the yacht to take us to that Turkish harbor."

"Can do, boss," he strode back to the cockpit and started the radio while his capable co-pilot flew the jet through the quiet evening sky. The short bespeckled international pilot was paid double what any airline would pay him and he was worth every dime of it because of his "can do attitude." No matter what Pierce's request – from a yacht take him to Turkey to lemonade and donuts for after sex snacking with his latest starlets, to middle of the night flights, Pilot Paul, as Pierce affectionately dubbed him, always found a way to make it happen. If Pierce desired it, it was always there waiting as if somehow Paul knew what Pierce would want even before Pierce did. Employees with ESP were simply the best! Paul was so good at anticipating every need on the Cosmo 2011 that there was no need for a flight attendant. Paul had been with the jet from the beginning, but the co-pilot was new and usually stayed in the cockpit. Paul spent time with Pierce and James, seeing to their every need whenever they were on longer flights.

Pierce often reflected on the value of a friend and employee like Paul. Any man on earth could be wildly successful at any career he wants. He/She simply needs to make one's self indispensable. Flexibility, a good attitude and doing the job are really all any one ever needs to please a boss. So simple, yet so rare in the current work place.

Pilot Paul, with his honesty, work ethic and talent never let Pierce down. Today was no exception. Paul came back to the plush interior of the Jet to let Pierce know the arrangements had been made. Seeing Pierce standing at the sink, washing off something giving off a familiar blue glow, he jumped back in surprise, "What do you have there, Pierce?"

"Something my mother left me in an envelope just before she died," Pierce held it out toward the Pilot. Paul carefully examined the glowing blue glass, smooth as a baby's bottom on the inner side of the curve; covered with sparkling jewels on the opposite side.

It had this note taped to it. That is my mother's handwriting – the pale and confused star explained to on of the man he trusted the most in this world. Paul read out loud:

To my darling Son,

The angels gave me this the night I am to die. They told me that they took it out of St. Peter's very tomb from beneath His Bascilla in the center of St. Peter's square in the Vatican. The Angels told me it belongs to The Son. Please guard it with your life. Find its missing mates, and all will be clear to you. Know that I love you forever and await your ascension into my arms when heaven and earth are at last one.

You loving mummy, for all eternity.

These words were followed by her familiar scrawl of a signature.

"It appears that my mother had lost her mind on her death bed. Who could blame her, married to an abusive alcoholic. And, I, her only child, abandoning her there with him. Yet, I've seen something like this before! Have you ever seen such a thing?"

Now it was Pilot Paul's turn to go white as a ghost as he lowered himself into a cozy, leather chair. "I think you better sit down. Perhaps your mother did not lose her mind at the end. Pierce, I have to tell you, I have seen such a thing as this!"

He started his story, completely unaware that his co-pilot could hear every word through a hidden microphone as they flew through clear skies toward the blue green waters of the Greek Isles.

THE BOOK OF PAUL

PAUL – SALT LAKE CONNECTION

"You know, of course, that I hold the Malchestic Priesthood in the L.D.S. Church."

Paul was a Mormon. This was common knowledge and it was part of the reason Pierce had trusted Paul from the day he purchased the Cosmo Jet and instantly took their recommendation that Paul be his personal pilot.

Latter Day Saints were commonly referred to as Mormons. Honest as the day is long. Don't drink or smoke, so Pierce knew they would always fly sober. They pay 10% of all their income in tithing to their church, so petty theft would never be an issue. Religious as heck in their own way. Centered out of Utah, but growing in numbers worldwide, especially South America. Famous for bigamy, when in fact it is actually forbidden in the modern church, but practiced by just a few outsiders-just enough wierdos misusing religion to feed their own perversions to give Mormon's a bad rap among the other Christian religions.

Paul would contend that his was the truest of the religions. Practicing actual Christianity seven days a week, twenty four hours per day – rather than hypocritical Christianity where people practiced their religion one hour per week then spent the rest of the week in self-righteous negative judgment of others.

"Some of my friends expect to see people with horns when they see Mormons," Pierce would laugh as he patted Paul's balding, obviously unhorned head.

"Yeah. Yeah. We're just as Christian as the next," Paul would patiently explain. "Ninety-nine percent of our beliefs are the same as Catholics or any other religion. We believe in the Bible. We believe in Jesus Christ. We believe in peace, love, chastity, kindness, family, sanctity of life, service to our community, and eternal life. The only difference between Mormon and other Christian religions is just one prophet. Joseph Smith. We believe that God did not stop granting visions to Prophets or talking to his people when Christ died. We believe in modern Prophets, especially our founder, Joseph Smith, who was the interpreter of the Book of Mormon. Like all great prophets, he was a persecuted stranger in his own home town, but a hero outside to any who would be truly enlightened."

So their talks would go anytime they were on a long flight and Paul needed to take a break from his cockpit.

But now the conversation took a more serious undertone.

"Pierce, I have a piece of glass exactly like the one you show me now that your mother claims to be from Angels raiding the Vatican!"

"No way! Where? How? Why?"

Lioness

"I was a young priest just out of high school and preparing to go on my two year mission-like so many other young Mormon men, prior to attending college at Brigham Young University in Provo, Utah. Before I was sent on a mission, all the way to the ghettos of Los Angeles, I was accepted into the Priesthood and had certain rights and keys to heaven given to me in the Salt Lake City Temple. Well, part of the rites included being taken to the center of the temple, where women can only enter when marrying a holder of the Malchestic Priesthood. We were trainees with pure and true hearts. There were twelve of us. Dead center of the temple we were given a pair of sacred undergarments that were to protect us as we traveled on our missions and beyond."

Pierce had frequently noticed Paul was wearing some sort of white undergarment with strange markings sewn into the cloth. It was a one piece garment that had short sleeves yet seemed to go nearly to his knees. Paul wore it under his suits, no matter how warm it was outside. He wore it in modesty when changing clothes. He slept in his sacred garments.

"Well, when they handed me my garments, wrapped inside a cloth cut like a star with 8 arms was a piece of glass, identical to this one. I looked toward my fellow young Missionaries assuming they, too, received something similar, but not a single one of them had anything but the basic garments. Instinct told me not to talk about it and each of them promised they would tell no one, but suggested I hide it at the bottom of my briefcase and carry it with me always until I was told why I was given such an object."

"Later that week I received my patriarchal blessing – a blessing elders recite to members of the church when the time is right. It talked of how I would meet a lovely woman of Zion to bear me children and so forth, but one thing stands out in my patriarchal blessing, that none of my friends' transcripts had. My blessing indicated that I had just received a gift that was of infinite value so I should guard it with my life for it would guide me to help unite the religions of the world."

None of my fellow missionaries nor I could ever make sense of this. But I figured it had something to do with the piece of bluish glass and gemstones I received in the temple the week prior.

A little stunned, Pierce said nothing, as he watched Paul rise and go toward the cockpit. Coming back with his familiar old, battered briefcase, Paul turned the dials to his secret code and opened it. Sure enough, there among Paul's charts, maps, and other papers was a piece of glass identical to the one Pierce held in his hands!

"What do you suppose this means?" Pierce whispered.

"I've no idea. But now I believe even more than ever, that I was destined to be your Pilot."

"Do me a favor, will you?"

"Of course."

"Keep mine locked in your briefcase with yours until we can get them back to the others."

"There are others?" Paul asked in shocked surprise.

"Three that I know of, and I suspect there may be more!"

SANTORINI

Pierce turned his eyes toward the window to see the sun coming up and realized he had not slept in nearly twenty four hours. Vividly orange, the majestic star, giver of all life, broke through the night sky driving away the darkness.

Soon he saw the beautiful island of Santorini with its white houses and blue roofs lining the steep cliffs. He could make out the donkeys already carrying their first loads up the side of the mountain. He yearned to take the twenty minute donkey ride down the cliffs as he had done in his early acting days, but today he did would not have time. He was a man on a mission and a man in a hurry to get back to South Dakota, so instead of the absolutely hysterical donkey ride with breathtaking views, he elected the quick ride down the Cliffside via the tram.

Pierce and James were at the harbor in five minutes. The view had been spectacular from the tram and they soon spotted Godfrey's fully loaded yacht awaiting them near the cruise ships in the popular port. It took almost no time to pull up anchor and head off into the warm, still waters of Aegean Sea.

Santorini had once been a round island, but the huge earthquake that formed the harbor had changed its shape in to a crescent shaped island to long ago. The airport was just outside the town, famous for blue roofs and wineries. The grapes grown around the island for the wines were hardy and able to thrive on the morning dew. Pierce had a warm spot in his heart for Santorini and hoped he could stay a few days when he found whatever he was being beckoned to find in Turkey and returned to meet Paul at the small airport.

Pierce had a private two way radio to communicate with Pilot Paul who would wait above at the tiny Santorini air strip on top of the dry island until Pierce returned.

Hungry and tired, Pierce and James ate the huge breakfast the staff of the yacht placed before them.

"How did you get a fully staffed yacht that fast in Greece?" Pierce had marveled earlier in last night's flight to the island. Pilot Paul's skill for making the impossible happen never ceased to amaze him.

"Simple. I called your girlfriend."

"Which one?" Pierce was being a tad sarcastic. He was tired and more than a tad upset with Lioness as the tabloids had even found their way to his private jet. They were more than a bit disturbing last night. Lioness was on the cover of every gossip rag arm in arm with Bart and Tom. Pierce had only been gone two days and the papers were already announcing the breakup of the gorgeous Senator and her Superstar boyfriend, in favor of two gorgeous young studs from the east coast.

"The hot little extra, Barb, you slept with when filming 'Yearnings of the Sun". Who do you think? The rich, beautiful one, the Lioness. Sometimes you are an idiot."

Lioness

"Well, sleeping with Barb was admittedly idiotic. Her only desire was to get pregnant and retire with an MRS degree! No thank you, sir. I'll take an independent woman like Lion any time. Do you know that Barb even poked holes in the condom we used in an attempt to get pregnant? Now I have to run blood tests every six months just to make sure I don't have some deadly disease."

"Darn good thing you met Lioness and quit your running around right after that movie. How did you manage not to get Barb pregnant – you dated her during the entire filming?"

"Vasectomy. Years ago. I'm no dummy. And unlike you, who can not wait to pass on your genes to the masses, children have never been a part of my plan."

"Does Lioness know?"

"Absolutely. But it would not have been necessary. It is not as though Lion and I will ever have any cubs. And believe me, now that I've experienced the treachery of Barb, I am grateful to be one hundred percent faithful to Lion. Which means I am now, sorrowfully, one hundred percent celibate."

Pilot Paul shook his head, lost interest in his boss's love life and went back to work. Paul was a virgin when he and his virgin wife married. Sex with his wife was the only sex Paul would ever know and he had no means or experience to compare it with others. Sex was simply not a very interesting subject to Paul. Birth control, being against Paul's religion, though, he and his wife already had eight children.

Pierce, on the other hand was bored from the sheer volume of sex he had as soon as he became a world famous star. Initially he enjoyed the only real aphrodisiac in the world - variety. But even variety eventually became mundane.

Now Hanson was vaguely aware that there was an entirely new force that was driving him - a force called love. He found himself in angst being half a world away from the powerful woman he loved. The only woman, straight or gay, he could not have at the snap of his long, elegant fingers. He was bored with all the beautiful young "talent". He wanted his older, smarter, more cunning woman – he wanted his Lioness.

Instead, he had found himself waving goodbye to Paul and the white houses with blue roofs in Santorini and was was speeding across foreign seas toward a land called Asia Minor - in a Godfrey yacht that just happened to harbor year round in Santorini. He knew it was so the Godfreys could sail the Greek isles anytime they wanted, but the whole situation felt a little too coincidental to Pierce. Pierce did not believe in coincidence and the fact that the Godfrey's just happened to have a yacht right there to pick him up rubbed him the wrong way. He was on edge all the way to the Turkish bay he loved so much.

It was disturbing, for starters, because Pierce had never known a Godfrey to take a day off work. Ever. For any reason. Especially not for frolicking. They were a family of workaholics. Even when they played in the Bahamas, or training the horses, or adventuring in Puerto Rico, then cruising, they were planning campaigns, doing international banking, and so on. And just how many yachts did they have? He was beginning to yearn to see a Godfrey balance sheet.

Certainly Lioness was not an island person. With her pathological fear of water, her desire to be dead center

Lioness

continents on dry land, and her workaholic attitude there was no way she had ever run around these dry, glorious whitewashed Isles, was there?

Still, it was well known that David adored water and rumored that he loved the Greek Isles, so Pierce figured the yacht must be a David toy. After drilling a few members of the crew, it was revealed he was right. Lion must have called David when Paul called her searching for a yacht. Did Paul work for one of the Godfrey's on the side? Pierce started to feel suspicious of everyone who knew a Godfrey. No, Paul must be totally honest, since he was a Mormon. Still, how was it that Paul had a piece of glass like Lion and Anne? How was it he was able to always solve any problem Pierce threw at him in almost no time at all? How did Paul procure David's yacht, when Paul had never even met David – to the best of Pierce's knowledge?

Pierce looked off the starboard side of the yacht and saw the beautiful white buildings with gracefully rounded light blue rooftops built into the steep island cliffs slowly shrinking from his view. He felt sad seeing the lovely island disappear tried to shake his fears out of his head as he headed out to a Muslim country, not fully appreciating the sinister forces had indeed come to work on the yacht some Godfrey had long since christened the Poseidon.

THE ST. JOHN RUINS

The great yacht with the GP insignia on both the port and starboard sides slipped quietly into the calm Turkish bay just before sunset. The water was smooth as glass and the ship's oil discolored the surface. White birds surrounded the deck as a large charter boats carrying Turkish cargo slipped out to sea. The tall buildings on shore welcomed Pierce, who was surprised at what a modern city this had become since his performance at the Ephesus half round theater so long ago. There was an eerie fog in the air and Pierce sensed trouble. Yet he knew he was seeking something here. What was he seeking?

The red Turkish flag with the crescent moon and the single star were waving outside Pierce's private balcony as the experienced, Greek speaking crew docked the Poseidon . Hanson was mildly surprised to have arrived in the Kusadasi port so soon. It seemed he had taken a short nap, then woke up and they had arrived. Maybe the nap was longer than he thought. He had slept so deep he had drooled. He awakened disoriented and confused rather than refreshed.

Lioness

Even now, as he tried to clear his head by downing coffee and splashing cold water on his face, he felt as if he had been drugged. When he looked toward his only suitcase, he knew instinctively it had been searched. Yes, the crew had put away his clothing in his room, but why? He was not planning on staying long enough to unpack himself.

Pierce nervously looked for the manila envelope his mother had left him. It, too, seemed to be searched, but the papers seemed to all still be there. Wait, he was missing the birth certificates! The cut glass that so resembled Tom and Bart's South American treasure had been left on the plane with Pilot Paul as Paul had seemed so fascinated by it. He had witnessed Paul lock it in the briefcase that never left Paul's side, thankfully. Perhaps Pierce had unwittingly left the birth certificates on the plane. Still, he didn't recall even showing Paul the birth certificates, so where could they be? Pierce felt a loss for him and his infant twin and those birth certificates had made him feel legitimate and somehow connected to the one he could not remember that had shared the same womb as him. Pierce felt a loss at being unable to locate the two certificates, if for no other reason than that it was his only proof Peter had ever lived.

Pierce met James on the upper deck for a sumptuous Greek dinner. Delicious red wine, salad with blobs of amazing goat cheese that melted in his mouth, some sort of lamb dish, cheese pie from the same goat cheese as was in the salad, and three different kinds of baklava for desert. The two men were so full and so exhausted, they decided to retire to their cabins for a full night's sleep before they started on their Turkish exploration.

August Anderson

The cabins were right next to one another, so they bade one another goodnight at their cabin doors. Both men collapsed on their beds and did now awaken for a full twelve hours. When they finally came out of their food induced coma, they were still in the dinner clothes the night before.

"Some body guard you are," Pierce teased the huge Native American who splashed ice water on his dark chisled face repeatedly.

More cold water splashed on their faces and more coffee, still left the men feeling a little groggy, but it was time to get up and at 'em.

Pierce had another huge meal, breakfast of bacon, eggs, and toast on the yacht with James. He carefully tucked away his notes from his mother, threw his limited toiletries and clothing back into his backpack and headed off the gangway with James walking silently behind him. He hit the sturdy wooden dock and walked toward the taxis awaiting on shore. The native taxi was the best they could arrange in a hurry. No limos were available on such short notice in Turkey. A nice taxi was waiting for him dockside so he and James were able to avoid the carpet and souvenir salesmen that were ready to accost every innocent tourist to come ashore from the great cruise ships.

Pierce was relieved that a Turkish gentleman was his driver The driver had never heard of the Godfrey's. He had never seen a Pierce Hanson movie. Somehow knowing the Godfrey's had not touched this country, made Pierce a bit more relaxed.

The red flags everywhere matched exactly a flag that Pierce's mom had so painstakingly glued to his piece of paper. Under the flag, in his mom's hand writing, it simply stated: "Where St. John took Mary for her final days."

Pierce noted that this flag was directly under a flag of Ireland where his mum had penned, "Where Peter was reborn."

Well, it was well accepted among Catholics, even now the Vatican had confirmed, that John had taken Mary after the crucifixion to the Ephesus area of Turkey. Mary's final home was in the hills above Ephesus and the ruins of the chapel in her honor were below Ephesus. And the ruins of St. John's cathedral were about ten miles from there, so that was where Pierce would look first.

What am I looking for and how will I know it when I find it?

As the driver sped up a modern highway, Pierce pondered. Here he was, a Catholic and a movie star, speeding through the arid scenery of a foreign land consisting of 97-98 percent Muslims and looking for something he did not even know its definition. Was he out of his mind?

Seek and ye shall find.

But I know not what I seek!

Like opportunity, you will know it when you see it.

Ooops. Was he talking to himself in his delirious state of exhaustion?

His driver was looking at him in confusion. James was giving him an odd look. All Pierce could think of to say was, "St. John and Virgin Mary."

The driver nodded as if he now knew know exactly where to go and he stepped on the gas even more.

Before he knew it, Pierce was wandering around the ruins of St. John's Cathedral in utter awe. Here where St. John penned his Gospel. Here where Revelations revealed the final vision. Here near where St. Paul had preached and wrote his Letter to the Ephesians. Here where John, obeying the final wishes of Jesus Himself, took the blessed Mother Mary to live out her final days in peace. There, the alleged burial site of John himself.

The thoughts that filled Pierce's head neared the state of a vision, he could so vividly imagine the history that had played out 2000 years ago. At his right shoulder, he felt a spiritual presence and his body froze with chilled goosebumps from head to toe.

As Pierce turned, he heard a familiar voice, "Hello, Peter. I sort of suspected I would find you here."

MEANWHILE, BACK IN THE UNITED STATES

DAVID – THE PRESIDENTIAL DEBATES RAGED ON

It was crystal clear that I was winning the foreign policy debate. All the political pundits said so. I was the star of every television station, every news website, every newspaper and every magazine.

Lioness had presented herself as the pansy-assed woos that she is. She kept saying things like "Freedom through Peace". It was as if she had read her own brochures, bumper stickers, and signs on the way to the debate. Her purple and teal messages were simple and there were only three. Vote for Peace and Freedom. Vote for Lioness. Cut taxes, spending, and regulations.

My sister does not get that life is not that simple. She memorized those three concepts, then had some sort of brain concussion and could argue for nothing but peace that night. Peace was the furthest thing from the mind of the People. The People still believed in the boogie man – terrorists from over a decade ago - and the fear that was cleverly harvested and exaggerated, exasperated and exploited on the back of the 9-11 attack of a decade earlier.

Never before in the history of mankind had just a couple thousand deaths had such political fallout. It caused in a series of wars outside the United States and it caused two hundred million souls within the United States to surrender for free unto there leaders – no battle necessary. How clever was that?

After two thousand victims died honorably in New York and at the Pentagon, two hundred million Americans died without honor by surrendering their souls and all their rights to the government of the United State of America. So, you see, it would not be I taking their souls. Their souls had already been abandoned. Fear and Jealousy? Awesome way to keep the people down with no effort whatsoever!

The two hundred million souls had traded in their lives for a welfare check, television, and a can of beer. Souls came cheap after that fateful morning in 2001. Souls had given up their inner fight, their dreams and desires, their life, liberty, and property in exchange for the phony promise of security of a government busily feasting on its own power.

So the Souls had already surrendered. The Souls of Americans who gratefully gave up their rights, happy to rid themselves of responsibility for anything whatsoever.

The Souls of America were just waiting for a hero to come gather them up and take care of them. The Souls of two hundred million Americans were the real 9-11 victims. When they traded in their rights for security and they found neither. Never before in history did so many people need someone to Save them.

Lioness

I stood before those poor Souls, ready, willing and able to serve. I would save them – I would fulfill their needs. I would love, honor, and protect the people of America.

So there stood I, David Godfrey, ready, willing and able to serve My people. I would protect them from all harm – foreign and domestic. I would guide them and tell them how to live. I would take care of them. My children. All two hundred million who could not sleep peacefully in their beds at night since the twin towers fell to the ground so long ago.

All those Souls, too fearful to even work. No problem, I would redistribute the wealth of those few no good upstarts that were carrying the economy on their shoulders.

I would raise a strong army to protect Souls from enemies beyond the border. I would shore up the border and its patrols so no enemies would infiltrate.

I would see that this government gave My people, My children, My Souls food, clothing, shelter, and health care. They could all have free medical and free legal and free education under my regime. America would be the Utopia wherein most people would not have to work very hard at all to have a truly good life. After all, America is the land of abundance.

I would support the arts, extend pregnancy leave with pay, I would socialize medicine, I would cut the work week in half and raise the minimum wage. After all, corporations and the rich could share their wealth with the less fortunate Americans. There would be a redistribution of wealth the day I was elected.

The masses were cheering for me in the streets. Chanting my name. David, David. Save us David. David, oh David for President. David will lift us from our poverty and from our fears.

Two hundred million people knew this. Well, at least one hundred million people wanted me to take total control over their lives. The other one hundred million were starting to lean my way. It was the remaining one hundred million Souls that ran businesses, were entrepreneurs, that loved to work – that were my nemesis. You know, the one hundred million that believed in self-responsibility, that were workaholics and anti-tax. You know them. They are the greedy bastards that exploit their workers - those ambitious types were trying to start an uprising against me. It was them whom I needed to get under control and fast. You know, the misguided Souls who would follow Lioness or that funny little man, Richard. Those Souls. What are they thinking? Standing in the way of My plans for Utopia – streets paved in gold and a land of milk and honey. All your heart desires just for the asking. Lioness contends, My Souls eventually get sick and lazy and stop asking all together. Richard contends My Souls will only get strong if they do without- some sort of tough love philosophy. I contend My Souls deserve their fair share.

Yuperdoodles, I am going to win this election hands down. The masses needed me. The masses wanted me. I would serve the masses. They would show up by the millions to vote in their new Savior, their new protector. I, David Godfrey, was here to give new hope to the hopeless.

Lioness

I was Robin Hood. I would rob from the rich and give to the poor. And the poor would not even notice the small little tax dollars I would scrape off the top of every transaction and every pay check to run this country for them. As they would be content sipping on their beers after their short work days.

Oh, yeah, I was winning the debates by about a million miles. Between one and two hundred million unemployed, fearful, impoverished poor neglected Souls were cheering me on to victory. Where they were weak, so I would be strong.

"And all you ask is that they give you more than half their earnings in the form of hidden taxes they are not even aware of. And all you ask, is more than half their freedoms, in the form they are not even aware they have," was that the evil Lioness trying to punch a hole in my bubble? I came back into focus on this debate being televised around the world.

Lioness had made the mistake of pointing this out and of also saying the people really had nothing to fear except their own government.

"Your government is robbing you blind and tossing you a crumb. David proposes to take that familiar dance to a new level. Your government does not protect you from your fears – it is your government that is the only thing you should fear. My esteemed brother may claim he will rob from the rich, but don't let class envy fool you. He will rob from you all, to line his own pockets. And the pockets of those who sponsor him. You say you want to work less? What happens when you work less? You live less, you accomplish less, you love less, you become less of a threat to the evil government that is gobbling up your rights and your hopes and your dreams and your stunning free spirit. David would buy your complacency with your own money. I will buy you nothing, but set your free to find your own inner greatness and develop your own magnificent spirit."

I had cited great leaders, great threats, great need for military strength (heck, I sounded more like the Republicans of the turn of the Century than Lioness did!)

Our teen-age travels through Europe with mom had paid off well. Although Lioness speaks seven languages fluently (English, German, French, Italian, Thai, Swahili, and Russian), she was revealing no brilliance in the first internationally televised debate. I was the trained debater. Lioness was merely a successful business woman. Ok. Very, I admit, very successful.

But I had her now. Lioness did not like the bright lights of the public spotlights. The world famous loner was melting where I thrived. It was as if she looked at those bright lights of the studio and lost her genius I.Q. and all her famous panache. She sort of started weaving nervously. I ate her alive. I told you she was not qualified to be President. I trained for it all my life. She is just a businesswoman and should just stay in that role.

Anyway, there I was, totally winning the debate.

That big earned five foot short Libertarian, Mr. Head, kept mumbling irrelevancies about human rights. I had been right in adamantly arguing that no third party candidate should even be let into these debates.

Debates. Ha. It was a run away race I was winning.

Lioness

My idiot sister kept speaking of love and peace and sounding like those damned Hippies we had read about from the Sixties. She certainly would not procure the military vote.

I asserted that America would remain the strongest military force in the world under my leadership.

Lioness blasphemed America right on satellite television asserting that America only thought she was the strongest country in the world because Americans were ignorant. If any of them had traveled abroad as much as she had, they would realize the European Union has surpassed America in terms of quality of life, lower taxes, more modern infrastructure, health care, and so much more. Lioness proclaimed, "While you were sleeping, Asia surpassed you Americans in terms of educations, athleticism, political power, and economic development. While you were watching television, Europe surpassed you in all areas of health and infrastructure. While you were warring, the United Kingdom/Australia/New Zealand/Turkey surpassed you in all aspects of quality of life, agriculture and creative capitalism. While half you were waiting for your 'entitlement'/welfare checks, the Arab nations were becoming ultramodern in architectural achievements and superpowers in terms of war machines. While half you were working three jobs to support the other half of you getting fat, hopeless, and diseased on unemployment and entitlements, the rest of the world passed you by. You lost your freedom, but worse, you lost any desire that might benefit from freedom. You had died while the rest of the world came to life. Arise, Americans. Arise. Travel. Learn. Desire. Seek. Love. Run. Live."

Geez. My own sister was off her rocker. She was proving on live television that she was more qualified for a nuthouse than for a white house.

A moderator interrupted Lion's downward slide and asked the panel what we would do about the high price of gasoline.

I talked of military protection of oil fields. Shit, did I ever sound Republican? I planned on wiping the Republican vote right out from under my sister. I talked of passing more laws and funding more research for ethanol.

Lioness, interrupted, "The truth about ethanol is that it takes 1.2 units of energy to produce the ethanol that will result in 1 unit of energy. If you want to operate in the red for the rest of your lives, you'll go down that road. If you are smart, you'll protect free enterprise while it is allowed to explore ALL alternative sources of energy. At the same time, if Free Enterprise were allowed to drill in Alaska and other "eco-sacred territories", the problem of our energy dependence could be greatly alleviated. Further, there were many, many other forms of energy such as wind power that could be harnessed if only government regulators would stay out of the way. Simultaneously, we need to continue working with world leaders, O.P.E.C. and so forth. There is no subject, from nuclear power, to oil, to human rights that should ever be removed from the jurisdiction of open debate, compromise, and negotiation. When we cease to communicate we experience shortages and war."

Lioness was sounding a little too liberal for her base as well as putting the audience to sleep. I could envision them leaving their televisions for the bathroom and a bag of Doritos while she droned on and on.

Then, the Big Eared Candidate, Mr. Head, opened his big Libertarian mouth, "Over a decade ago, using 9-11 as an excuse, BOTH the Republicans and the Democrats bombed the life out of the Iraqis. I apologize to the Iraqis for this indiscretion. Saddam Hussien was a bad dude running that country, so Republicans and Democrats used this, and the totally unrelated 9-11 attacks, as an excuse to make a power-grab and an oil grab under the pretext of humanitarian concerns. Pansy, fearful people let this crime happen. Spineless political leaders continued to pay for the war until America was bankrupt. As Lioness pointed out, while you were sleeping under the propaganda that America was the best country in the world, not only were masses of Americans falling behind, but the rest of the world was progressing by leaps and bounds. Since the turn of the century, we've been dumbing down America as well as bankrupting her. While we sought to repair and replace and dictate foreign infrastructure we abandoned our own infrastructure. On American money, perhaps based on guilt, perhaps on humanitarian cries, foreigners have better schools and better hospitals than we do in America. And Americans paid for the world's economic boom, while our own system of health care and our system of education collapsed around our ears. Many countries have buildings, airports, and more. All paid for with American dollars and American lives. Bombing followed by reconstruction fell hard onto the hard working, overtaxed, overburdened backs of the overtired Americans. We should have never gone to war in Iraq in the first place. But we broke Iraq, so we bought it. Now, frankly, the Iraqis owe us billions of dollars. We'll take it in free oil, thank you. They have the sweetest oil in the world, and honestly that is why so many people died. Realistically it had nothing to do with terrorism. Surely, all this sacrifice on the part of all people from Americans to Muslims to Jews…it must have been about oil. If that be the case, according to my calculations the taxpaying Americans can only be repaid by giving us all free gas for the next sixteen years."

The debate moderator went dead silent and pale white. The questioning panel went dead silent. The audience went dead silent. I went dead silent. Lioness went dead silent. Even her yellow skin was pale with shock!

What the fuck had Dick Head just said?

Rioting broke out almost immediately world wide. No one would remember my calm, brilliant performance. No one could remember what a dismal boring failure Lioness was. Chaos ensued. That one mouthful from Mr. Head almost resulted in the next world war! Hundreds of Thousands took to the streets agreeing with him and demanding FREE GASOLINE. Hundreds of Thousands of others burned him in effigy. Millions dropped their jaws not knowing what to say or do. Billions gossiped about Mr. Head.

No one remembered that Lioness had made a fool of herself, nor that I had shown clear Presidential thinking. The entire foreign policy debate was ruined before it really even got started. It would be remembered only for the outrage flowing from the lips of that ugly little Libertarian.

I hated him for ruining my moment in the spotlight. Lioness laughed a huge roar at the thought of him and was grateful he had completely overshadowed her pathetic performance.

We all admitted two things.

1. The man was nuts; and

2. *And the man had balls.*

Years Earlier

LIONESS – CURIOSITY

The Lioness paced nervously back and forth in her cage. Withers and haunches moved in rhythm as she paced right then left then right then left. She studied the bars before her, looking for an escape route. Nothing. The small cage seemed impenetrable. She studied her handlers. When she turned her yellow eyes on them and took a swipe through the bars with her mighty paw and roared with disdain, one of the two men peed their pants. He darted away, presumably to change. She focused on the other man. Tall, thin teeth lined in gold and thick spectacles. Wrinkles of a man who had once upon a time lived hard with only a balding head to show for it all now. She hissed at him.

"I'm not afraid of you. I've dealt with a lot worse than you."

"I suggest you let me out right now."

"Only if you tell me why you're here. The only report I got was breaking and entering."

She paced some more. *What the heck, this man probably needed a life. Something exciting to remember and to tell his grandkids.*

A compassionate, almost bored smile crossed her face, "Simple. Curiosity killed the cat."

"Say what?"

"I've always been fascinated by the human brain. Math was my official major, but I did the majority of work toward my PhD in biology. And I adore genetics. Horse breeding. Cat breeding. Human breeding."

The brave jailer opened his eyes a little wide at that one. Lioness ignored him and continued.

"The most fascinating aspect of the human being is his mind. Using only 7% of his brain to think, and a maximum of 12% to carry out the automatic functions of the body, from breathing to walking, what do you suppose mankind does with the remaining 80% plus of his brain."

The man shrugged his shoulders, clearly demonstrating he certainly did not use or intend to use any of the 80%. Not now. Not ever.

"I believe that within that space, not only is there a sixth sense, but there is contained therein the entire knowledge of God. Of the history of the universe. Of the keys to creation. Of mankind's past and of his destiny. I believe we each have pure knowledge inside our brains. The Plan from beginning to end is contained in the mind of every man."

"You almost imply that God Himself is in each man." Her captor's face almost shone with light and excitement.

"In a way, yes. God resides in every man. Every man resides in God. Some call that the Holy Spirit. We are all a part of one another. The universe extends forever outward from the mind of man. And the universe extends forever inward in the mind of man. Cells are made of atoms, atoms are made of subatomic particles and so on and so on. Forever inward. Forever outward. My studies reveal the human brain being dead center of two universes proves the old theory, now totally disdained, that man is, after all, the center of the universe. Not merely the center of the solar system".

"Didn't Galileo or some such prove we were not the center if the Universe?"

"He looked only outside man. He failed to realize man goes eternally inward as well as infinitely outward. Behold, you are not in your body, but your body is in you. All modern science is based on the misconception that we are not the center of the Universe. When, in fact, as children of God, as part of God, I am in the process of proving we are the center of the Universe."

"That doesn't explain why you are in jail."

"Oh, that. Well, needless to say, I am fascinated by the human brain. I am fascinated where thoughts are stored, where memories are stored, what parts control the heart. What parts you can live without. What parts of the brain you must have to function. How to regenerate cells that heretofore they could not regenerated so that if another Christopher Reeve were to sever that small part, I could regenerate his essential nerve cells such that he would not have to live as the inspirational, courageous Mr. Reeve lived his own tragedy unto his death."

"And…"

"And, I first needed to show what drugs, shock therapy, lobotomies do to the brain, hence to the eternal spirit."

"I needed brains. Brains of dead animals. Brains to dissect. Brains. Brains. I needed to know some answers. I broke into the lab where there were fetal pigs, phermeldahyde cats, and oddly, even some human brains were contained in jars. I stimulated, I dissected, I discovered from Friday night until early Monday morning. I found where spinal fluid could be regenerated. I discovered the devastating effect of mind altering drugs. I know where to stimulate to make you laugh or cry. Bottom line, I was cutting, shocking, hooking up to monitors so intently, without sleep for over 72 hours that I simply did not see the guard and the lab assistant enter. I was watching monitors and had my fingers on the vortex of life itself. How could I notice they had entered? I had every cell of my own brain studying the multitudes of brains in the lab. I saw nothing, I heard nothing. I was without sleep for days. I was excited and working outside time and space."

She stopped, tilted her head and turned her eye color to grey, the color of the guard who spotted her and had her arrested. She saw his thoughts were that she was there to rob, but he also wondered why all the mess and stench. She continued talking to the man outside her cage, "Then I sure heard them scream! The first class had entered the lab on Monday morning and called for the campus police. There were dissected parts all over the lab. The microscopes were filled with my slides. The brain parts were on the table, on floors, in the chairs. Electrical wires were strong around the lab for purposes of brain stimulation. Phermeldahyde was spilled all over everything."

"Oh, that is why you stink so bad?"

"Phermeldahyde. Blood. And brains. So you don't think I should invent the perfume?" Her eyes twinkled

Lioness

and turned brown as she looked into her home study and office through the eyes of her young male secretary to make sure everything was running smoothly in her absence.

Lioness had stopped pacing, enjoying the man's company and his listening ear. If only the rest of the world would hear her message. She had just proven every man was an essential part of the heart and soul of God! She had proven the universal link that every man was a part of every other man.

It would be foolish to go to war, that would be like killing yourself.

It would be foolish to hate another human being, that would be like hating yourself.

Since a chain is only as strong as its weakest link, it would only make since for every individual to try to uplift and cheer on to the greatest heights, every other individual. Each positive individual experience would uplift the whole. The universal experience of man, the universal intelligence that man referred to as God. Or Allah. Or….

Mr. Wet his Pants hurried back into the room and with trembling hands began to open the jail cell.

"Say, what are you doing?" his more interesting associate asked, not really wanting the moment with this odd, stinky prisoner to end.

"She is free to go."

"Did someone post bond?"

"No, the School of Mines dropped all charges."

"Why? She openly admitted to breaking and entering."

"Apparently she has friends in high places. Adam Godfrey is her father!"

As soon as the door unlocked the Lioness sprang from her cage into freedom, Glorious freedom. Blessed and Sacred Freedom. It had never tasted so good. She headed for home as fast as a Lioness can run. She had to record her findings.

Her Alma Marta even let her help design the new Biology Building over the next few years. Adam Godfrey's millions of dollars in funding, to make Lion's felony charges disappear, were well spent on the new Godfrey Biology Building.

Lion's thesis was well published in religious texts, but was entirely ignored by all the scientific and medical journals.

Only one part of her findings made their way into the hands of the public. People were slowly realizing that at the urging of the government ("if you don't put your ADHD child on mind altering drugs we will take him from you and do It ourselves") they were turning an entire generation of human beings into drug addicts.

Social services\, my butt, more like social disservices!)

Under the influence of government sponsored programs and government sponsored drugs, girls could only hope to grow up to be Stepford Wives – devoid of all hope. Devoid of all joy. Boys would grow up to be junkies or minimum wage clones – devoid of passion to invent or revolt.

The government was getting what it wanted. An entire generation of welfare dependant slaves that would never question working their lives away and giving it all to the corrupt, power hungry bastards at the top.

Well, the corrupt, power hungry bastards at the top had not anticipated one huge problem – the Godfrey children were on their way up.

LION'S THEME SONG

Lioness decided that no one would read her works. No one would listen to her speak. Yet, they all listened to big brother David. They listened to David and wrote about what he ate for breakfast. Just because he was a newly elected Senator.

Ah, Lioness began to observe. Movie Stars and Politicians. The people listen to them. Even though a good number of them are dildo Idiots with not a thing of importance to say, everyone listens to them anyway.

Well, then, I guess if I am a voice crying out in the wilderness trying to deliver good news for mankind, I'll have to be a movie star or a politician. She was too strange looking for any producer to cast her – just ask the Godfrey's producers. She would follow in David's footsteps. She would run for the U.S. Senate. She did not want to run. She did not want to win. She did not want to leave South Dakota.

What she sought was for her roar to be heard. By the people of the world that she loved.

She wanted the people to hear the good news for all mankind.

Lioness

It took her less than five minutes to determine she must run for office. She never meant to win. She merely wanted to roar.

And roar she did.

LION - ROARING HER WAY TO THE SENATE SPEAKING

OF GOD AND SOULS AND FREE WILL

"I think the very fact of our existence is proof of God's existence. I think you all just hesitate to call our "universal intelligence" by such a name because "Christians" have given the name of Christ such a bad reputation over the centuries. This is, of course, coming from a Christian! But you do not have it call Him God. You can call Him Allah, Nature, Buddah, Universal Intelligence-whatever name makes you comfortable. It is not important what you call Him. It is only important that you call upon Him. It is not as important that I believe in God as it is that God believes in Me."

"Words can not describe the spirit of this universe, so it is not the spirit that fails you, rather it is merely the words to describe It that fails us all.

"When you and your environmentalists describes nature - creative force unlimited....you are absolutely describing "God". Call it "Mother Nature". Call it "Allah" Call It "the Creator". Call it the "God of the Sun or the Son of God." The important part is calling it anything; thereby, acknowledging, not only it's very existence, but it's profound wonderment. It's amazing implications to all mankind."

She continued campaigning, as if running for head preacher, not for Senate! "Now, of course scientists do not believe in God as a man watching over all. What a silly notion for any brilliant mind to buy into. But that does not deny God's existence. It denies only that God is a silly man."

She was embarrassing her brother David, the newly elected Senator, "We all do create God in our own image, so only silly judgmental Christians might see Him as a silly judgmental man!!!!! You are way too smart for that. But even top scientists, in fact, begrudgingly acknowledge seeking souls. A soul so mysterious we can not understand it because words can not describe it, nor can our limited use of our brain capacity analyze it. As Einstein so succinctly stated, "To know the mind of God. Nothing else really matters."

Why did she not speak of welfare, or train lines, or sewer improvent, her brother David pondered. She was running for a political office, yet she talked only of religion. His own sister was nuttier than a fruitcake. He listened to her Senatorial campaign on the radio, appalled and embarrassed.

"Yet, put billions of those souls together and walla - you have a God so mysterious, so great, we can not begin to understand It. Or Him. Or Her.

We all can merely describe the "part of the elephant" we have experienced. That does not mean the elephant does not exist. It merely means, we all only experience our own small bits and pieces of It. Our own existence is proof of our own soul. Proof of soul can not be denied."

"Iam." Lioness concluded that radio interview with the name some call the name of God Himself.

Rene Descartes' renowned explanation for it all raised the famous supposition: "Cogito ergo sum – I think, therefore, I am" has put to rest so many philosophical debates.

Do you not find it fascinating that God's real name is "Iam"?

David was painfully aware of his kid sister's philosophies:

Each of us experiences our own part of the soul of the Universe that we chose and/or dare to experience.

Physicists tell us that matter and energy can neither be created nor destroyed – they simply change form. A soul is a unique combination of matter and energy; therefore, it is safe to extrapolate that *a soul can neither be created, nor destroyed, it simply changes form.*

Do you not see the beauty of this? This means that Science has proven that *YOU ARE ETERNAL.* Since a soul can neither be created, nor destroyed, but simply changes form, it is, of course eternal. You are the soul.

Being eternal, your soul is capable of every possible experience - creative to apathetic - joyous to angry - rich to poor - loving to warring - the choice is up to each soul.

Freedom to choose its own destiny is the glory of the soul. Each soul choses to create its own heaven or hell - its own destiny - its own world view, its own universal view of the infinite eternal universal intelligence that it is an integral part of the whole.

How exciting is that? That means that you can do or be anything in the Universe. You have no limit – except the limit you may put on yourself or allow others, such as your social worker or tax man, to put on you.

All of life. All of eternity is YOUR CHOICE. You can create your own heaven or you can create your own hell. Or you can let others create a world for you that is shallow, boring, and meaningless.

What will you chose?

I've chosen heaven. The amazing power of a galloping horse underneath me; the divine cuteness of babies and Pomeranian puppies; the beauty of the sky ramming clouds against the mountains; thousands of years of history of art and architecture; man's striving to be more than animals, if somewhat less than gods; the silvery moon shining across a quiet ocean. The lightening seeking solace in the earth as sky marries land in a burst of shocking power; oh, infinite rapture. Oh glorious gratitude. Oh, proof of God. Proof of His existence. Proof of His very Greatness. Proof Undeniable and Proof Infinite. Forever deep within me. Forever eternal Outside me.

Forever wrapping around this planet. Forever backwards in time. Forever Forward in time. Exploding in the glory of the Free Will of every Soul to explore its own Infinite Possibility.

God does not exist?!?!? Nay, that is simply impossible. *God exists everywhere and in everything. And you? A sacred and essential part of Him.*

THE ROLE OF GOVERNMENT AND TAXATION

The next interview the Elder Senator heard was a television interview of Lioness that David watched casually on television with a room full of fellow Senators in his Washington D.C. penthouse apartment.

"No way, she'll get elected," said Senator Thomas of Idaho.

"Don't be too sure," responded Senator Jameston of North Carolina, "She has charisma, beauty, and brains. Maybe America is ready for a change."

Lioness came over the airways boldly stating truths that angels feared to state, "The only legitimate role of government is the protection of rights.

"When I say corruption, of course, I do not mean "illegal". I mean "immoral". This rehiring of incumbents as a practice of voters is certainly foolish as well as "immoral". As is giving able-bodied men and women welfare and unemployment likewise "immoral". Lioness was referring to South Dakota's practice of allowing its state employees to retire and get their public retirement benefits, then rehiring said retirees to same or similar jobs. She was also referencing that fact that even a corpse could get unemployment in the state. "Unemployment is considered a career choice for many South Dakotan's," Lioness continued to alienate her voting public, "They should be ashamed. Practices such as this exploitation of the system is the very essence of why we workers pay more in taxes than can ever be "moral". This is why the "leaches in society" now outnumber we "producers in society".

"Do you South Dakota voters ever wonder why you can send an unemployed Bimbo to the House of Representatives and in less than two years she is a multi-millionaire? Where do you think the money comes from? It comes from you – hard working men and women of America. And you continue to re-elect her as she has bought your vote with tax dollars called "entitlements". Then you wonder why two parents working two full time jobs each, can't afford the basics for their family? Because you gave men and women such as your former US representative the job of leader when she was a dismal failure as even a follower. Why did you give her the job over and over again? Because she never met a tax or spending bill she did not love! She temporarily lined your entitlement pockets by bankrupting your children! But you loved her so for all the gifts she gave you. When you should have hated her for all the pockets she robbed to give you those gifts!"

"But she is not the only dismal failure people send to D.C. on empty promises to rob from Peter to pay Paul. She is one of the hundreds of elected officials you should term limit. In fact, you should term limit EVERYONE. Our founding fathers anticipated working farmers serving their country for one term, then returning to work their farms and their factories. They did not anticipate elected pigs making millions of dollars per year taxing and spending Americans to death."

"Ah, now she is alienating everyone in your state," commented Senator Fisch, "I don't think we need to stop her, she is stopping herself from being elected to the Senate."

"But is she brining down my good name in the process?" David worried to his fellow power brokers.

"I don't think so," assured Senator Smythe, "Since she is running for Senate from South Dakota, such a small and insignificant State, no one is paying an ounce of attention to that race. Just hang tight, and this will go away quietly long before you declare yourself a candidate for President."

"I hope you are right." David signed nervously.

Lioness continued roaring over the airwaves, "You say taxes are not all that bad and you get them back at the end of the year? I cry bullshit! You are talking about the income tax, not even facing the medicare and social security that comes out of your paychecks. Then the employer pays matching funds, so that, too, is less money for the families of working men and women. But let's not even talk about payroll taxes, here is where your elected officials are robbing you of 70% of your hard earned dollars to line their own corrupt pockets and to keep the masses re-electing them because of "entitlement money". The masses are being kept down on the blood sweat and tears of working men. Let me read you a list of how your sweet little representatives suddenly have so much money to line their own pockets and toss you crumbs so you will elect them. It is hidden in all those other taxes. Did you know Americans pay:

Accounts Receivable Tax
Building Permit Tax
Capital Gains Tax
CDL license Tax
Cigarette Tax
Corporate Income Tax
Court Fines (indirect taxes)
Dog License Tax
Federal Income Tax
Federal Unemployment Tax (FUTA)
Fishing License Tax
Food License Tax
Fuel permit tax
Gasoline Tax (42 cents per gallon)
Hunting License Tax
Inheritance Tax Interest expense (tax on the money)
Inventory tax IRS Interest Charges (tax on top of tax)
IRS Penalties (tax on top of tax)
Liquor Tax
Local Income Tax
Luxury Taxes
Marriage License Tax
Medicare Tax
Property Tax
Real Estate Tax
Septic Permit Tax
Service Charge Taxes
Social Security Tax
Road Usage Taxes (Truckers)

Sales Taxes
Recreational Vehicle Tax
Road Toll Booth Taxes
School Tax
State Income Tax
State Unemployment Tax (SUTA)
Telephone federal excise tax
Telephone federal universal service fee tax
Telephone federal, state and local surcharge taxes
Telephone minimum usage surcharge tax
Telephone recurring and non-recurring charges tax
Telephone state and local tax
Telephone usage charge tax
Toll Bridge Taxes
Toll Tunnel Taxes
Traffic Fines (indirect taxation)
Trailer Registration Tax
Utility Taxes
Vehicle License Registration Tax
Vehicle Sales Tax
Watercraft Registration Tax
Well Permit Tax
Workers Compensation Tax

"This, my friends is why families are so poor mothers can no longer stay home to raise their children and why both men and women work more than one job just ot survive. YOU ARE THE MOST OVERTAXED PEOPLE IN THE HISTORY OF THE WORLD. Yet none of you has the balls to revolt against our tax system and the wasteful spending of your corrupt governments. Not one of these taxes existed 100 years ago and our nation was the most prosperous in the world, had absolutely no national debt, had the largest middle class in the world and only one parent had to work to support the family."

Lioness looked right into the camera, then continued, "I submit that the middle class is the very backbone of any society; and that because of taxes and regulations our government has broken the very backbone of America. When the middle class disappears from any societs, so does hope. And a hopeless society can not last long upon this earth. Let me put this prediction on the record as history has proven me correct 100% of the time: Within one decade we will experience total economic collapse, if things do not change drastically."

"Let me further ask, when a Representative retires from state or federal government position, why does he or she get a lovely retirement (when the working man gets only enough Social Security to pay property taxes on his home?

"Does a representative who gets a retirement from that office and then gets elected to the Senate later get retirement benefits from the Senate? Isn't that double dipping? What of all the bribes he/she gets while in office? Does he/she sell your vote right out from underneath you? Many elected officials get paid extra for every "board" or committee they sit on and this is not even listed as part of their salary. Why is this double dipping never questioned? Why are not the American people refusing to pay the taxes I just enumerated?"

"I became a Republican because Republicans claimed to be in favor of

LESS government. This means less spending and less regulation. Instead, I witness our current state and county administrations both Republican and Democrat, spending MORE, taxing MORE, and regulating MORE. Therefore, they are not only constantly violating our sacred U.S. Constitution, they are constantly acting in "immoral" ways, and they are, in fact, RINOS (Republicans in name only).

"I can now only pray that you will fire incumbents from both parties in the next election who practice hypocrisy and would tax the working people of America to death."

Of Overcrowded Jails

"If we are talking people whose "drug of choice" merely is different one from your "drug of choice", or a dad who couldn't pay child support, or a Martha Stewart who went to jail ONLY because she was a successful woman, then I can not condone ANY form of confinement."

"The vast majority of prisoners do not belong in jail. Jails must be reserved for violent offenders. Nonviolents? Forgive them. Get them help. Get them out of the jails and free up those beds for the bad guys. But remember the value of true repentance and forgiveness. And judge not lest ye shall be so judged…"

"We must stop being the most jailed society in the history of mankind, while we hypocritically chant that we are the land of the free. Once we free people for disagreeing with those who happen to be out of favor with the corrupt government of our time, the courts and jails will be quite empty. We can put all those resources to bettering mankind through education and health care rather than locking people up like animals."

LION – OF WAR AND PEACE

"When you ask me about wars, you clearly spell out the greatest problem on earth. I have adamantly opposed war since before its inception and will until the very end of time. Most acts of violence could be prevented through compassion and walking a mile in another person's shoes. Americans are not under attack so much as their corrupt institutions. Whatever happened to seventy times seven forgiveness? Whatever happened to peaceful negotiations."

"So, I believe in walking softly and carrying a big stick. Our military men and women deserve better wages, better training, better weaponry, better retirements, and better health care than our elected officials. Our troops are willing to give the ultimate sacrifice, their very lives, and deserve to be some of the best paid, best trained, best retired people on earth. Our elected officials won't even put their own money where their mouths are and need the elected officials are our ones needing a deduction in pay as well as a limit to the number of terms they can feed from the public trough."

"We need the best trained, best prepared military in the world. Then we need to try to never, ever use it. If our elected officials are compelled to declare a war, those so doing should the ones leading the troops at the front line of the battle. If our elected officials are not willing to fight on the front lines because the purpose is so great, then they have no business declaring a war."

"If we used negotiations more and force less, we would have way more money to fund our soldiers than we do now and we could lower taxes and benefit businesses so that we would have still more money for that public trough."

David and his fellow Senators watched appalled, "How can she claim to be a Republican and still be a passifist?" asked one.

As if she heard them from her television interview three thousand miles away she said, "Republicans do not own war. Both parties unanimously, stupidly voted for the last war. Republicans own freedom and smaller government and that is why I run for office as a Republican."

"But let me also talk of peace. In problems facing the entire world, war is followed very closely by our destruction of the planet through pollution and bad military exercises. In my life, I long to see the end of poverty and hunger, the cleaning up of the planet, improvement in health care, and the educating of youth world wide. We could do all this with the human resources and the financial resources we used in the war on Iraq alone!"

"I have no problem with helping the NEEDY. I am a very vocal advocate for education, feeding the hungry, removing the barriers to success, and more. Further, I put my money and the Godfrey money where my mouth is. I DO have a problem with elected morons buying the votes of able bodied Americans with money that should go to the needy. Then, to top it all off, under the PRETEXT of helping the needy, they rob from the hard workers of America who have succeeded and toss the druggies/alcoholics a dime in exchange for their vote (and to keep them from striving for success). Elected officials use the rest of MY HARD EARNED money and YOUR HARD EARNED money on keeping themselves in power and on financing wars, etc. All in the process of REGULATING YOU to death, so that none of the down and out will ever have a chance to climb the ladder of success to challenge them."

David grunted from his viewpoint, "Uneducated, impoverished people raised by incompetent parents are not the problem. Welfare moms are not the problem. Only 16 billion dollars are spent in welfare annually, compared to more than about 800 billion annually for wars. Lioness wants to take food stamps and money for utilities away from families sharing one-room apartments in the inner cities; but she should be more concerned about the 90,000 Iraqis slaughtered in the past decade, the hundreds of thousands who've lost limbs and loved ones, the thousands of US soldiers dead, and all of her tax dollars going to finance the bloodshed. 50% of her tax dollars finance wars, as opposed to the 1% that goes to welfare. The problem is not impoverished Americans - whether or not they are on drugs!"

Lioness was obviously bored with her television interview and was reading the minds of the Senators so far away while she yawned and continued speaking into the cameras, "In war we destroy physical lives. In entitlements, unemployment, and welfare, we destroy spiritual lives. Which has the worst effect on the largest number of people? When we give drug and alcohol money, along with free housing, legal, and medical, people can destroy their own lives. Look at our Pine Ridge Reservation in South Dakota if you want to see the failed experiment called Socialism. Democrats advocate socialism – they always have and they always will. Well, our reservations have some of the worst living conditions in America, not to mention the shortest life expectancy. The Reservations are proof socialism does not work. Yet, they continue to re-elect Democrats year after year on the promise of more free stuff. I do promise them the Black Hills, if they vote for me, because I do not lie to them. I tell them if they turn away white man's modern version of measles contaminated blankets (welfare in modern times), and return to a life of pride and personal responsibility, they can buy the whole state back within a generation! I say this out of love for the great spirits that long to be set free in the Lakota people. I see the failed experiment. The Lakotas, of all people in America, should be voting for a change, not for the same lies of you pretend to be social do-gooder Democrats."

She probably was the first Republican to pick up some of the Lakota votes. But it is hard to teach an old dog new tricks, even when the old dogs way of life is leaving him behind to die young.

Dying before one ever really lives really bothered Lioness.

"If we paid all the people on unemployment a decent salary to work instead of sitting home doing nothing but watch television, reproduce like rabbits, and do food and drugs and alcohol until they achieve diabetes, we could instead pay them to feed the starving, to clean the litter, to teach the children, to perform the arts, and so much more....and we would be saving two sets of lives, the lives of those we paid to work (who can drink and do drugs if they have to get up early to work every day?) as well as saving the lives of the kids they teach or the planet they clean."

Now David yawned, "My hypocritical little sister now sounds more like a Democrat than I did in the election!"

Senator Lilac, the only female in the room nodded in agreement and stated, "We don't have to stop her. She is stopping herself from getting elected. People don't want to hear the truth."

LIONESS – OF RIGHTS AND RESPONSIBILITIES

A Lioness hates to be watched. Pacing. Pacing nervously. Ever pacing to get out of the spotlight. Her mouth was trying to deliver a message of both Freedom and Individual Responsibility.

The hundred wealthy people who might be her supporter in her race for U.S. Senate seemed more interested in the flavor of their $1,000.00 per plate dinner than in what she was trying to explain to them.

Later, though, in the hall behind the dinners, near the stage were 2,000 people who filled the massive civic center and had paid only $5.00 each to hear her message. They appeared to be slowly taking interest in what she was saying. They were at least silent as she continued speaking and pacing.

She plodded on, "You can not legislate morality, you can only educate morality. Then educated human beings must be free to exercise their knowledge, exercise their rights, to rise above their wildest dreams and succeed beyond their wildest imagination. This will not happen because of government. This will happen in spite of government. So the government needs to get out of the way and let the human spirit emerge. The government must shrink if the human spirit is to grow.

"Life, Liberty, Property....they must prevail. They must be honored as sacred by our government.

"Some Rights are so sacred they must be protected from both mob rule and Government Beasts who grow their power by feeding on the rights of man."

"If you wonder what rights could be so important, you need not look any further than the Bill of Rights. There are hundreds of such rights, probably thousands, but here are just a few that must be kept: BEYOND THE REACH OF MAJORITIES, BEYOND THE REACH OF GOVERNMENT. YOU HAVE THE RIGHT TO:

1. Free speech;
2. Freedom of religion;
3. Free press;
4. Freedom to peaceably assemble;
5. Petition the Government for a redress of grievances;
6. Keep and bear arms;
7. Keep soldiers out of your house during times of peace;
8. Be secure in your body, house, papers, and business against unreasonable searches and seizures;
9. Life liberty and property;
10. Confrontation of witnesses against you;
11. Privacy;
12. Jury trial;

13. No cruel and unusual punishment;

14. All other rights not specifically given to the Government by the Constitution.

Cool bunch of rights, huh? Do you know that every one of these glorious rights has been slowly eroded over time by your own Government? Do you know that the powers specifically given by the Constitution are very, very limited?"

Lion stopped to take a sip of water then continued, feeling more like a civics teacher than a Senate Candidate. But she knew she had to make the truth clear in this lesser race for Senate because two years later she would be running for President.

"How the heck did the Government get so powerful then?" the Lion continued.

"You were tricked into trading in your rights for Government's Power!"

Her audience was starting to wake up. Whew. A few might be getting her message.

The United States, being a Republic, NOT A DEMOCRACY, is one of the most important history lessons you will ever forgot.

"You see, in a democracy there is a dangerous risk of mob rule. In a Republic certain rights are considered SO IMPORTANT that they are placed beyond the reach of majorities. Beyond the reach of the government. If you are to have protected rights, you must have certain unalienable rights.'

"A democracy implies that majorities can take your rights away. In our republic, some rights can never be taken.

"But, they are slowly being eroded, so you won't notice they are being taken! They disappear whenever the government raises your taxes. There go property rights when the government demands a building permit for you to add a bathroom to your house. There goes your right to liberty when men who can not pay child support are jailed. Liberty really disappeared when Martha Stewart was jailed over a decade ago. Do you think for one moment it was safer for you to walk the streets because Martha was behind bars? I submit that was a massive abuse of power. Jail is not supposed to be an instrument of revenge. Jail should not be an instrument of self-righteous negative judgment or jealousy. It is not supposed to be instrument of drug treatment. Inprisonment's only legitimate use is to house violent criminals. No other human being belongs in jail. It is a violation of our Bill of Rights to jail anyone else. It is an affront to the God who died that you might live free."

Suddenly everyone was awake. Everyone was thinking. Everyone was shocked. Now she stopped pacing and looked her audience direct in the eyes. Everyone at once felt she was looking right into their individual souls.

"I've talked to you of property tonight and how almost all government regulations take away your sacred property rights. I've talked to you of Liberty and how prosecutors across the country take away that right from your brethren by the thousands daily. The United States jails the highest percentage of its citizens of any country in the history of the world. Yet you call yourselves free? Watch out, it might be the president of a successful company today, but it will be you tomorrow. What right exceeds even that of property and of liberty?

She let the audience whisper and speculate. She had them in the palm of her hand now.

"Only life! Where were you when Ruby Ridge occurred? You should have been protesting in the streets. Where were you when war was declared? Has mankind not evolved beyond mass violence in the past 2000 years. PLEASE do not tell me Jesus Christ died in vain. You CAN NOT go to Christian churches then walk out the door and quietly accept war. Not ANY war, or you take the very life of Jesus in vain. Where were you when the United States declared war on it's own people and burned women and children in Waco. When you sit back and allow collateral damage of any innocent to happen, the blood is on your own hands, my Children."

Ooops. She had lost them. She had gone too far, presenting them with truths they were not prepared to hear. She must change the subject. She must return to a less controversial subject than the subject of life itself. Amazing they could not face something so basic as the fact that life was sacred.

"In the context of abortion or euthanasia, you Republicans stand united that life is sacred, why is it so hard for you to take the final step and say even the life of young, soldiers is sacred?"

People were whispering angrily of a need for defense.

"A need for defense, I recognize. I do not accept a need for aggression. Was it defense that allowed the mobs to nail Jesus to the cross? Was it defense that caused the USSR to eat the souls of 90% of its people? Was it defense that caused us to invade Iraq?"

A hush fell over the room. She needed to lighten and lighten up fast. "You came here tonight to hear me speak on the subject of why our Republic is so important and why we are NOT a democracy, but rather a Republican Democracy. You came here tonight to understand why I run as a Republican. But let us lighten up and all leave this room with a smile on our face and with an understanding of the different forms of government, so each of us can use our minds to understand. I'm sure many of you read this years ago when it circulated the internet, but it applies to this date. I have a simple little brain, and this is a fun and simple way to remember the different forms of government. Please excuse me while I read this to you. It is printed on handouts for you to take home-right by the back door. But before we go on, let's take a little break and listen to a little music from my good friends in the Black Hills Rockin Band."

The Rockins were very popular in the Midwest. Lioness had doubts that they ever wrote a note of music, but they could play music from the 60s, 70s, 80, 90s and 2000s and sound just like the original bands. There was something there for everyone and the music was always up beat and energetic. So, before Lion lost her audience, her friends from the band put on a mini-concert.

After the concert the audience was back with her and all pepped up and happy. The entire party was being televised, so this would also give her favorite local band some publicity while it gave her a much larger and peppier audience that night. At least she now had their undivided attention again. She knew she had to make it light, humorous, and fast.

"Did you enjoy the concert?" Lioness roared out.

Stomping, applauding the audience roared their appreciation. "We have more great music to come after the Rockins take a quick break. Please indulge me a few minutes for this commercial interruption as I self-promote, then we'll get back to the music and get back to having some serious fun."

David and his fellow Senators had turned off their television too soon! They turned it off convincing Lioness would bore her audience to death with the truth. They failed to see her turn the election back to her favor.

The audience couldn't wait to return to the serious fun. But she needed ten minutes to educate them, so Lioness leaped right in, "Please read along with me, then you will understand why you will vote for me in November." Some grumbling, but most were grateful to get a chance to listen to a free band, so they indulged Lioness as she read the internet comedy out loud and added her own comments.

"A CHRISTIAN DEMOCRAT: You have two cows. You keep one and give one to your neighbor.

Ah, if only we were true all true Christian Democrats!

A SOCIALIST: You have two cows. The government takes one and gives it to your neighbor.

This is America today. What do you say we join together and take America back from the Socialists!?!? Just say no to the government taking more than half of everything you make then tossing you back a few crumbs."

The room broke out in thundering applause. She waited until they settled.

"A REPUBLICAN: You have two cows. Your neighbor has none. So what?"

There was some nervous giggling scattered throughout the room. Lioness decided to move on and continued reading

"DEMOCRACY, AMERICAN STYLE: You have two cows. The government taxes you to the point you have to sell both to support a man in a foreign country who has only one cow, which was a gift from your government."

Nervous laughter ensued. A few angry shouts. Lion continued to read the handout to the audience.

"CAPITALISM, AMERICAN STYLE: You have two cows. You sell one, buy a bull and build a herd of cows."

This brought some wild applause and only confirmed exactly who her supporters were. How often she espoused Capitalism. How often fools thought it a dirty word. Freedom. Capitalism. The recipe for the majority of men to reach their full potential greatness.

"BREAUCRACY, AMERICAN STYLE: You have two cows. The government takes them both, shoots one, milks the other, pays you for the milk, then pours the milk down the drain."

"Welcome to our Indian Reservation's" Someone shouted back *"**Welcome to America!**"* "***You got it brother***," she responded. She had them all back now. Everyone here would vote for her.

"AN AMERICAN CORPORATION: You have two cows. You sell one, and force the other to produce the milk of four cows. You are surprised when the cow drops dead."

"And now I move on to the part that almost anyone could take offense at-but please, please take humor rather than offence, here and in your daily lives. Take humor. Live IS fun. Life IS funny!"

Lioness read rapidly:

"A FRENCH CORPORATION: You have two cows. You go on strike because you want three cows.

A JAPANESE CORPORATION: You have two cows. You redesign them so they are an eleventh the size of an ordinary cow and produce twenty times the milk.

A GERMAN CORPORATION: You have two cows. You re-engineer them so they live for 100 years, eat once a month and milk themselves.

AN ITALIAN CORPORATION: You have two cows but you don't know where they are. You break for lunch.

A RUSSIAN CORPORATION: You have two cows. You count them and learn you have five cows. You count them again and learn you have 42 cows. You count them again and learn you have 12 cows. You stop counting cows and open another bottle of vodka.

A MEXICAN CORPORATION: You think you have two cows, but you're not sure where they are. You'll look for them tomorrow.

A SWISS CORPORATION: You have 5000 cows, none of which belongs to you. You charge for storing them for others.

A BRAZILIAN CORPORATION: You have two cows. You enter into a partnership with an American corporation. Soon you have 1000 cows and the American corporation declares bankruptcy.

AN INDIAN CORPORATION: You have two cows. You worship them.

A TALIBAN ORGANIZATION: You have two cows. You load them up with explosives and herd them onto your neighbor's property where you blow them up. Your neighbor dies. You starve to death.

Her audience was laughing. That was good, it was a close call as many people in modern times were humor impaired. Now she dared to ad her own.

"A DEMOCRAT: You have two cows. Your neighbor has none. You feel guilty for being successful. You vote people into office who tax your cows, forcing you to sell one to raise money to pay the tax. The people you voted for then take the tax money for themselves, but give your neighbor just enough that he stays in front of the television and computer, so he never revolts. You feel righteous. Your neighbor feels righteous. You all sue one another. You lose the other cow to the lawyers. Based on the apathy of all, the devil wins the next election."

Suddenly the room went silent, not quite knowing what to think.

Lioness continued, "Are you tired of being taxed out of your hard earned cows? Send me to Washington and I'll cut those taxes in half. Your neighbor will be free so he can earn his own cow, through hard work, honest charity, and loving guidance all of you can, to coin a phrase, BE ALL THAT YOU CAN BE.."

"Lion. Lion. Lion. Lion.," she had her people back. They were stomping and chanting her name. She continued with her "theme speech."

"A COMMUNIST: You have two cows. The government seizes both and provides you with milk.

A FASCIST: You have two cows. Through fear techniques, the government seizes both and sells you the milk. You join the underground and start a campaign of sabotage.

Does this resemble the America you live in today! I will go to Washington and I will take your America back and I will return to you, a land of the Free. The Republic your forefathers died for. The free America we once briefly knew where all Americans thrived. America is a fascist country today. Because we govern by fear. We rob your rights by promises of protection. Promises that we can not and will not keep. I will make it a Free country tomorrow! I will be your campaign of sabotage. I will make sure every American enjoys his life, liberty and property without the interference of a government gone mad with power and greed. I will return your Rights and take from them their Unconstitutional Powers they stole from you over the past six decades."

The stomping of feet and the roaring approval was deafening.

"When I am elected, I will lower taxes, cut regulations, and slice into wasteful spending. Only the violent will be jailed. Opportunity will abound. And you will no longer live in silent fear of your own government. Let freedom ring once again. And let each and everyone of you be truly blessed by the Almighty hand of God, our Father."

She found them. The good people who were starting to realize elements of the truth. They were rioting out into the streets, accepting the truth. From the parking lot, to the newsrooms, they were starting to awaking from the numb fears that back and nearly destroyed the precious middle class in America over the past few decade.

Win the election on the coat-tails of David? I think not. I will win by awakening the passions of the good people of America by giving them the truth, sugar coated with humor.

Lioness quit while she was ahead and introduced the next performer. Ironic, she mused, that it would be someone who rose to fame on the name Madonna!

Lioness won the election for Senate.

YEARS LATER: BACK TO THE FINAL PRESIDENTIAL ELECTION

RICHARD – THE DOMESTIC DEBATE

The big eared Libertarian stood back quietly laughing as he watched the two giants, the Godfrey Siblings, tear each other down.

It was a well established political truth that any loser could win an elected position in America, if said loser was merely quiet and nice and relatively invisible while the two main candidates tore each other to shreds. The people would become so disgusted with the leaders going negative and making up filthy lies about each other that they would vote for a little known underdog in order to not vote for either of the big guys who had made each other appear to be scum from the bottom of the pond-be it true or otherwise. This was happening before Richard's very eyes and before the eyes of the entire nation, glued to their televisions watching the god from Olympus fighting it out with the golden Egyptian like goddess. Ah, the ancients never had myths this good.

The Godfrey battle was being played out on a world stage thanks to the satellite television revolution of the

1980s. The two revolutions that would change the world – satellite television in the 80s and internet in the 90s. After that privacy was a thing of the past and truth died an ugly death – defeated by the sheer volume of untrue mass gossip.

As Richard had been driven to the hall in Chicago, he passed the candidates' signs all over Chicago's street. It appeared the world was indeed divided into three mindsets.

Lioness, the Republican, had her purple and teal signs reading "Cut taxes. Cut regulations. Cut spending. Let Freedom Ring. Lioness for President". That nicely summarized her boring and simplistic political stand. Her shocking, albeit odd, sort of beauty portrayed in her pictures offered stark contrast to the boring, conservative practicality of her message.

David, the Democrat, wanted to associate patriotism with his party for a change. David sought to establish Democrats as respected moderates, while sneaking out his socialist agenda. He wanted to take care of everyone, all the time. He sounded like such a nice guy.

Since the days of Regan patriotism had been strictly associated with the Republicans. David was out to reclaim to the mindless masses to the unearned pride he believed Patriotism gave to those who would never earn their own real reasons to be proud. The majority of Americans, now that the middle class was successfully being destroyed, really had very little to be proud of. Wherever there is a void in honorable acts, patriotism could always be substituted to make people feel justified in their general worthlessness. When patriotism failed, jealousy could always be exploited in its stead. David decided patriotic

Lioness

pride could just as well belong to the Democrats as the Republicans. After all, who said the Republicans had cornered the market on war? And on Patriotism? Both parties always voted for wars and for sending other people's children to their deaths in the name of patriotism, so why not own it and exploit it? War was good for national pride and for the economy. Fear was also good for people in David's opinion.

Naturally, the Male Senator Godfrey's signs were all in Red, White, and Blue. By gum, he was going to be more Republican than Ronald Regan himself had been decades earlier, if that is what it took to win this race. "Americans Standing Strong. Standing Together. Vote Senator David Godfrey III for President." Well, Richard thought, he certainly managed to get all his titles of nobility into it, without saying anything real. Or maybe he was saying "vote for Socialism and Communism in America, but under a much more palatable platform called entitlements".

Still, perhaps David did not need to say a thing. Perhaps like so many successful politicians, David needed no message at all. He simply looked the part. Tall, muscular, good looking to a fault. Perfect, dark penetrating eyes surrounded by just enough wrinkles to reflect his Harvard educated brain was indeed serious. The strong cheekbones, brilliant white teeth.

It was rumored and joked that Senator David could get all the female vote, even if he came out a strong advocate for female circumcism! David had more groupies than the Beetles in their finest hours. Yes, indeed, it was often said David's inner male circles that females voted with their cunts, not their brains, so it was a sure thing David would be president. Hell, he already looked like a king. All they needed to do was put a crown on his head.

Deep in thought, on the drive to the debate, Richard then saw his own signs. In many ways his candidacy had begun as a joke. He was never expected to get this far. In horrid slime green colored letters on a hot pink background, his signs were simple, just as Richard was: "Dick Head for President. For a Change." The hideous, bright, contrasting colors made the sign leap out at drivers. That was good.

Richard's signs were by far the most popular of the political signs although they, too, had no real substance. His political ideology was packed full of thousands of years of substance – borne of suffering, history, love, and profound experience. But his signs were loved - stolen and erected from college campuses to Indian Reservations, to large cities, to foreign towns, to rice fields in China, to the Outback of Australia. Ten of the largest sign companies in the world were printing his signs 24 hours per day and they simply could not fill the demand.

The masses have indeed become disgruntled, yet their humor stays intact. That means there is hope for the masses.

Tonight at the last presidential debate before the election, he could understand why humor was so important. Brother and Sister had gone completely negative in their campaigns and they were going for one another's jugulars. While the two Godfrey Senators scratched and clawed, Richard was smiling at the audience, the cameras, the moderators. Rolling his eyes. Winking. Making funny body gestures like a chicken flapping his wings. And so much more. He was winning over America with his twisted sense of humor while the gorgeous, educated, financially solvent candidates were tearing each other to shreds. Richard was having fun! And the people were being won over to his stark honesty and simple ways. Richard was one of them.

Richard had done nothing to prepare for the debates. His answers on most issues were the same, "That is simply not the role of government". Over and over he would state that the only legitimate role of government was the protection of rights. At least Lioness agreed with that basic philosophy on surface. But being a practical Lion, she then went on to hypocritically concern government with health and education.

The moderator snapped the three candidates right back to the present debate with the age old warn out issue, "How do you feel about abortion?"

Richard: "None of my business, it is not the role of government to interfere with a woman's body. It is between the woman, her doctor, and her God. Judge not lest ye shall be so judged."

David: "I will stand behind Roe vs. Wade as it is the law of the land that none of us can change."

Lioness, who never gave short answers to any question, "There is not a person, man or woman, who is for the taking of a life. In that sense, we are all, each of us, pro-life. On that matter, all Americans agree. Life is Sacred. Here is where we are divided. When does a group of cells become a life? At that very moment, we must always err in favor of life. You may think life begins at conception. You may KNOW it," she pointed to a female audience member. "You may simply KNOW it begins at birth," she pointed to a different woman on the questioning panel.

"I may KNOW God breaths life into a fetus exactly half way through a pregnancy. Whatever we think we know, we somehow know it with a passion. Hence, although all sides agree life is sacred, none can prove with either a religious certainty, nor a scientific certainty when exactly life begins. The Bible is silent on the issue. The Scientists debate the issue. Is it any wonder there is such passionate debate? But we do know two things we can all agree on. One, the life of the woman is sacred. Two, life itself is sacred. Therefore, nothing must ever put the woman's life at issue. Privacy and Liberty are also sacred rights that must never be trampled upon. So as horrible and agonizing as the decision is for a woman, the government simply can not play a role in the debate. Life, Liberty, and Privacy must be protected, therefore the government can not interfere with a woman's right to chose unless and until there is biblical or irrefutable scientific agreement as to when life begins."

Richard: "So that is a fancy long winded way of saying you agree with me."

David: "I think she just said she agreed with me!"

Maybe we will equally divide the female vote after all.

Moderator: "I think she said exactly what she meant and from a woman's perspective. Next question we'll start with Senator Godfrey. What do you propose to do to fix social security?"

David and Lioness both started speaking at the same time. David smirked as the moderator clarified, "I apologize, I meant the senior Senator, David Godfrey".

David took that as proof that on a subconscious level, he was the only real Senator Godfrey. Lioness was merely his kid sister, riding on his coat tails.

David nodded and began, "We have promised generations of Americans that in their elder years, they would not be neglected. Our retiring citizens have served us through wars, depressions, and times of extraordinary change. They have worked harder in their lives to take care of their families and their neighbors than any generations in the history of the world. They have paid into the system and they expect the system to pay them back a small portion of what they have given. I promise all our Senior Citizens on this night that the system will not fail them. Not now. Not ever. Social Security AND Medicare benefits will not only continue, but they will be increased 3 % per year to adjust for inflation."

Half the audience went straight to standing ovation on that vow.

I better stop this right now.

Richard: "Precisely how do you propose to pay for that? The system is bankrupt. The payments you propose to pay out are three times the amount our current generation is paying in. According to my notes, you are proposing to triple taxes on a generation already paying so much in taxes they can now make more money by not working than by working."

That silenced them all.

David, a little nervous explained, "I propose to bring back the death taxes. I propose to raise taxes only on the rich. I propose the rich pay their fair share…"

Lioness interrupted, "It does sound like brother David intends to tax Americans to death. He would tax the rich? Then he better get to taxing himself and all his friends and work associates. When you tax productivity, you crash the economy. He would tax the dead? Then he will eliminate the reason we all work hard – to leave our children better off than we were! He would bankrupt America even further, if he dared to raise a single tax. American's have been taxed to death and we will not take it any longer. The income tax was a hoax perpetuated on society under fraudulent pretenses, and the Sixteenth Amendment should be overruled and the income tax eliminated. You must not tax production another day or another dime. If you are to tax, you should tax consumption, not production. I would eliminate the I.R.S. today and the multitudes of taxes American's pay without choice and make everyone's life easier with a flat 15% nationwide sales taxes on everything but food. You want to live the lifestyle of the rich and famous? Fine, you'll pay one large chunk of taxes! You want to avoid taxes? Fine, don't go shopping for things you can do without. It is time that Americans stopped spending money on things they do not need to impress people they do not like. The consumption tax can be utilized to encourage highly moral behavior and discourage immoral behavior. The power to tax is the power to destroy. Why not put even taxes, put every man's destiny and every man's responsibilities, back into his own hands by letting him chose whether or not to buy something and pay the taxes that go with consumption right back into his own hands? You will kill many problems with a single stone, if you tax consumption, rather than production. You will discourage sloth and waste, it will help alleviate pollution, the energy crises, and so much more. Plus it will give human beings a choice and takes waste out of the hands of the bloated and corrupt bureaucracy."

Hmm. Is that now part of the audience now giving Lioness a standing ovation? Maybe she can take some votes from David on this subject.

Moderator: "Would you eliminate social security?"

Lioness: "Not for a single person that has ever paid into the system. They paid under a promise they would receive and, by gum, that promise will be honored. The money the general fund has been stealing from social security to pay for everything from wars to prisons to pet pork projects will stop flowing out from the moment I am elected. I will veto every piece of legislation containing pork. The general fund OWES the hard working American's who have paid into the system for generations enough money to fund social security and medicare for the next three generations. It is time the US government honored its I.O.U. and its contracts with our seniors and paid all the money back. We told our precious seniors we would take care of them in their elder years and we WILL honor our WORD to them."

There was thundering applause.

This Moderator must have been a David fan. She kept trying to attack Lion on the subject. She was doing the job of David and Richard – so much for fair and unbiased debating.

Moderator: "We hear you saying that rather than letting the general fund take social security money to pay other bills, you will make the money flow the other direction – make the general fund pay back all it has borrowed from Social Security over the decades. Where do you think the general fund will get that kind of money with all the tax cuts you propose?"

Lioness: "Not only should it repay Social Security, it will do so with INTEREST. The people who paid all that money all those years deserve a fair rate of return as they would have received if they had privately invested the same money over all those years. I propose eight percent interest on all the money our government has robbed from Social Security since its inception. This would infuse the system with so much money, I would TRIPLE social security and benefits and medicare benefits and I would have plenty of money to do it. We'll pay back what the fat cat politicians have robbed from hard working Americans for decades. Tripling funds to where Seniors could survive is the least we could do to reward our seniors for a lifetime of hard work. Even still, our beloved elders will not be receiving what a single Congressman or Senator receives in their private pensions their reward for years of sticking it to the people of America."

Now the whole room was standing and applauding the Lioness. David's strong jaw was jutting out in anger as he was gritting his teeth. He simply had to interrupt. First she put him down for proposing a three percent annual increase and now she was proposing a three hundred percent increase in benefits. Could they not see her hypocrisy? That alone would bankrupt America. "First my esteemed colleague, Senator Lioness Godfrey would eschew socialism with every breath she takes. She decries spending programs. Then she says she would increase Social Security! Do you not see her hypocrisy? We don't have enough money in the general funds to pay back what we've borrowed from Social Security."

Lioness: "Of course, we do. All we have to do eliminate all the wasteful spending and pork barrel projects."

David: "So you would eliminate what? Education funds? Highway funds?"

Lioness: "That is what you tax and spend freaks would like the Americans to believe. Education funds are a drop in the bucket compared to our wasteful spending on pork. As are Highway funds. No. I would increase funding in BOTH Education and Transportation, starting with doubling of teacher's salaries. Teachers are the warriors on the front lines battling for the souls of our children. It should be a high-paying sought after profession where the best of the best compete to teach."

David: "Again, 'little miss I'll cut spending', you keep saying you will lower taxes and cut spending, but we've just heard how you are going to double spending on teachers, raise it on transportation and triple spending on the elderly. Might I suggest your inexperience is showing and that your idealism can not possibly work. You are proposing to cut taxes and increase spending. I propose you are the one who will bankrupt America."

Ouch. Yup. I'll just sit back here and let the Godfrey's destroy one another. They haven't even asked, but it is a good thing as this crowd certainly does not want to hear that I would end social security and privatize the entire program as soon as possible.

Lioness: "Don't give me inexperience lectures, Mr. Bottom Feeder. When have you ever worked a 17 hour day in the business world like I have done 7 days per week for 20 years? Idealism can not work? Idealism is our only hope for salvation!"

David: "Blah. Blah. Blah. You've said you would eliminate the income tax and replace it with a national sales tax. How would that work?"

Lioness: "For starters, we could eliminate from the government payroll the jobs of most IRS employees."

Another standing ovation. The moderator motioned for it to settle down as she was quite blatantly a fan of David.

David: "So you are suggesting creating unemployment?"

Lioness "I'm suggesting if all of the accountants and all the IRS agents did not spend their time creating and enforcing the paperwork nightmare called the income tax, those minds would be freed up to make some of the greatest math teachers the country has ever seen. They would not be unemployed, they would switch to more honorable professions and our children and our science programs would all benefit."

David: "You've still dodged the issue of where you are going to cut spending in half in order to pay these teachers and these seniors."

Lioness: "That would, frankly be the easiest task of my life now that I got the line item veto passed through the Senate. As a businesswoman I know where to eliminate spending – cut out all but the necessary in order to be productive and competitive. If the people had ever elected a businesswoman, America would not be facing bankruptcy today-Asian Countries and Arab nations will own America in less than two years if you don't elect me. Where do you think we've been borrowing all our money and sending all our jobs?"

Lioness

Moderator: "I believe those issues were addressed in the foreign policy debate. And I believe Senator David has a legitimate point in asking you what specific programs you would cut today in order to balance the budget AND pay back our loans as you have so often promised."

Lioness: "Specifically: First, I would cut government accounting programs robbing people of their hard earned tax dollars to the bone. It doesn't take much more than a good computer and a hundred data entry people to track 15% national sales tax on every sale except food. Second, I would cut in half the number of prosecutors – state and federal –and half of the jails in the country. We would finally become the 'land of the free' that we lie and tell the good people of America they currently live in. That is so wrong, 'we are the land of the highest jailed in the history of the world and the most fearful in the history of the world'. This must stop, people must be returned to love and joy and acceptance of our differences. Better still we should celebrate with exuberance our differences. Whatever happened to viva la difference? We are a good people and there is no need to jail a higher percentage of our population than any other country in history. We must honor the dignity, freedom and abilities of Americans, not jail them. There is no man who should be in prison for being an acute business person, no woman such as Martha Stewart who should be jailed for lying to the government. The first amendment was supposed to protect both her privacy right and her right not to answer a filthy corrupt government agent – not to mention her 5th amendment right not to testify against herself. The world was not a safer place when Martha Stewart was in jail. What were you thinking? We jailed a woman because we were *jealous* of her for creating jobs and then living the dream we all dream!"

Lioness hesitated, knowing she was losing her audience as they would cling to jealousy, the most powerful and most destructive of all human emotions, so she changed her subject, "Further, no pot smoker shall be worthy of our taxpayer money to prosecute. I would throw no man in jail for failure to pay child support. A child needs time with their father far more than he needs his father's money."

Men everywhere stood and applauded that line.

"In short, jails and prosecution should be reserved only for violent offenders. Only for those who harm the rights of others and are a threat to public safety should suffer criminal prosecution and loss of freedom. If a person harms ONLY himself (I don't care if it is drugs, bad business, assisted suicide, smoking), that is simply his right to be such an idiot. The government can not and must not spend a fortune interfering with the rights of others. Even if we disagree and believe what they are doing to themselves is wrong. Their FREE WILL must be honored. And in staying out of the private lives of private citizens, we will free up enough money to spend on highways, education, and our seniors."

Lioness took no pause before continuing since she now had seniors and men on her side, "Further, we can slash welfare, entitlements, subsidies and unemployment to 1/10 our current spending levels by merely giving benefits to those who truly can not work for themselves. Right now, we pay people who will not work. We need to return to the Original Intent and only pay people who can not work. In fact, double entitlements for the mentally and physically handicapped and we can still slash the budget. Able bodied men and women who are simply too lazy to work or too surly or drunk to hold a job do not deserve welfare and unemployment. Yet these types are taking 9/10s of the welfare and unemployment funds."

"Huge farming operations don't need subsidies, which were passed under false promises to assist small family farmers. Let the huge corporate farms produce in a free market and sell in a free market. This would end world hunger at the same time it saved taxpayers millions of dollars. Let me be perfectly clear 90 % of the people and corporations on entitlements do not need nor deserve entitlements. The only entitlements any healthy adult should have are to the rights given to them by God. You are entitled to life, liberty, privacy, property, opportunity. You are NOT entitled to Rob from Peter to Pay Paul. You are NOT entitled to color television, computers, fancy houses and cars. You are NOT entitled to free legal and medical if you can work to purchase them, but a humane society should provide the basics of life, ONLY if you CAN NOT pay. Note the difference though between can not and will not."

Still, you ARE entitled to the freedom to earn these things through hard work and intelligent business dealings. We most stop rewarding the leaches on society and must allow our hard working men and women the freedom and opportunity to succeed. America needs to throw out all those law books that fill rooms of prosecutors and judge's office and return to its simple foundation of freedoms based on the Bill of Rights.

David had to stop this rampage if the moderators would not, "Might I remind you that your effort to throw out all the laws EXCEPT the Constitution and Amendments through the Fourteenth Amendment, failed to pass in the Senate ninety-nine to one?"

Lioness was not going to let it go and shut up, they had asked how she would cut out waste, so she was going to tell them, "Yes, and look at the pathetic state of America today. If you overthrow our welfare system, you will instantly eliminate 99% of our illegal immigration problems! Further, I could cut trillions out of spending by getting America out of the business of every other country in the world. We are not put on this planet to be the grand manipulators of every man. We need to stay out of the lives of our own people, yes, but also the trillions of dollars we spend trying to control the lives of people in other countries is not only unacceptable, it goes to the root of the causes of terrorist acts against us."

Moderator: "I'm sorry but you are way over any conceivable time limit."

Lioness: "But I have not even begun to enumerate the thousands of painless ways I could cut the budget with resulting economic abundance to our people and our country."

Moderator: "Put it in an ad. We must move on to other subjects."

POLITICAL ADVERTISING

How can one disguise the beauty of a lion?

Her hair was pulled back in a strict bun. She wore a turtleneck sweater under a conservative pin striped navy blue business suit. She wore dark rimmed glasses with a slight tint to help cover her strange eyes. Still, when she looked directly into the camera, there was something about her that mesmerized the nation.

Some love her.

Some hated her.

All were drawn like moths to the flame by her quiet power, an air of warning that something great was about to follow in her wake. Her inner energy could not be subdued of disguised.

Americans did not dart to their refrigerators to grab a snack when this set of candidates appeared for their one minute commercials. Americans dared not budge as the two leading candidates had gone negative and it was a bloodbath. A soap opera about one of America's wealthiest families was playing out in real life before their very eyes.

The television addicted future voters waited until the main feature came back on to go to the bathroom or grab their snacks. They could not wait to hear what was coming next as the rich and the powerful and the beautiful battled for the Presidency of the United States of America. All barriers were down and the gloves were off. Greek god versus his own sister, an Egyptian goddess, and it was good fodder for gossip and for fantasy.

The Kennedy clans stood beside each other through thick and thin. The Godfreys were going for one another's jugular.

The Libertarian candidate sat back and kindly smiled on the people. He was polite, soft-spoken, and slightly amused. He had seen powerhouses destroy one another before. This battle left him in the background, quietly telling the people the cold raw truth without being terribly noticed – for the time being, anyway. He participated, but almost invisibly, while the Godfrey giants attacked one another.

This particular Lioness ad ran a long seven minutes, and was more like an infomercial!

Lioness was again trying to tell the people they lived in a Republic, not a Democracy, and this was very important because some rights were so sacred they must absolutely be beyond the reach of majorities, but in the informercial, she was expanding on the same ideas she had promoted in her Senate run years earlier. Mob rule must never affect the rights granted everyman by God, Himself:

Lioness

BEYOND THE REACH OF MAJORITIES, BEYOND THE REACH OF GOVERNMENT, YOU HAVE THE RIGHT TO:

1. Free speech; This means, not only can you print or say what you want, you can curse like a truck driver, and you have the right to lie and to be rude! You even have the right to say Ugly and Discriminatory things, should you want to;

2. Freedom of religion; Contrary to popular belief, nowhere in the Constitution does it ever say "separation of church and state". It merely states that Congress shall pass no law regarding the establishment of religion. This means you can pray in school, erect a cross wherever you want, print "in God we Trust" on your money and in your court houses, put the ten commandments in a courthouse, and dress however you wish. Let's face it, our founding fathers gave us the right to offend one another. This right is sacred. And Americans need to get a thick skin and live with it. Under my rule, you will not be a bunch of pansies. You will live and let live. Worship or not worship and let other worship or not worship as they see fit. You will be free to express your religion or lack thereof any where, any time any place. And let me tell you something else. There is no such thing as separation of church and state. Religion and politics are married to one another. All political decisions must be based on high moral values. So get used to it.

3. Free press; You will no longer fear a tax audit if you criticize the government. You will no longer fear your right to travel will be limited if you call me an idiot. Your reputation will not be impugned for disagreeing with me or any elected official. I will not use public prosecutors to enforce my own agenda. For the first time since homeland security (which I will instantly eliminate) you can have at it. You will be presumed right and your government will be presumed wrong when I am elected. You are currently presumed guilty until proven innocent. In a government with a Lioness at its head, for the first time in a century Americans will once again be presumed innocent until proven guilty!

4. Freedom to peaceably assemble; This goes not just to that right to gather and express yourself. I promise you will not get on a list of people to be investigated or audited or strip searched at airports just for your gathering to discuss ideas.

5. Petition the Government for a redress of grievances; And while you petition, you will be presumed wrong and the government right. Under my watch, there will be NO WACO. There will be no RUBY RIDGE.

6. Keep and bear arms; This is not just to hunt. Not just to protect yourselves from thieves in the night or rapists. This right is sacred and was given to you to protect yourself from a government gone

Lioness

mad. Might I suggest your government has gone mad?

7. Keep soldiers out of your house during times of peace. In modern terms this means keeping cops out of your home, keeping department of agriculture inspectors, or park services or other weenie assed government employees who've gone mad with powers off your ranches; it means keep social workers and other do-gooders away from your children with their drugs and their badges; it means keep tax collectors and auditors out of your houses and your place of business; Yes, this means ALL government "soldiers" must leave you the heck alone unless you care committing violent crimes.

8. Be secure in your body, house, papers, and business against unreasonable searches and seizures; Might I repeat, time and time again what is so important because you have lost your freedom and dignity in America. You live in fear. You will live in fear no more. Again I say unto you, in my ONE term as President, this will again mean keeping cops out of your home, keeping department of agriculture or park services or other weenie assed government employees who've gone mad with powers off your ranches, social workers and other do-gooders away from your children, tax collectors and auditors out of your house and place of business; Yes, this means ALL government "soldiers" must leave you

the heck alone unless you care committing violent crimes.

9. Life, liberty, and property;   These rights will become sacred again. We will not burn your children WACO style. We will not shoot your wife and child Ruby Ridge style, we will not aggress against nations who have not attacked us, Iraq style. We WILL honor the right to life. We will honor liberty. You will no longer be jailed for failing to pay taxes, lying to the government (after all the government lies to you almost constantly) when not under oath. We will not jail you for keeping secrets, becoming broke or getting rich, making a bad decision, being in an accident, not paying child support or alimony. You will stop fearing a loss of liberty and you will learn to live your life with an abandoned passion. The way you should live a life. And we will quit taking your property for public use just because someone lines our pockets with a lot of cash to do so. The government won't physically take your property nor take it subtly, including your business, by taxing or regulating it to death. Your home, your real estate and your business will once again stand a chance at survival and growth (so the for the first time in a generation your children will be free to live and succeed) because the government will get out of your property under my watch as President.

Lioness

10. Confront witnesses against you; No more kangaroo courts or hidden agendas.

11. Privacy; It will be yours once again when I am President.

12. Jury trial; A jury trial of you PEERS will be absolutely guaranteed. There will be no more licensing boards where your rights are completely ignored – where you are tried and judged by people with vested and financial interests in your losing. Licensing boards nationwide are corrupt violators of your constitutional rights and shall be instantly eliminated the day I am sworn into office.

13. No cruel and unusual punishment; This does not just involve torture. Audits, threats, searchers, violations of your rights, trials without juries, or judges who are prejudiced so you find yourself in a kangaroo court all fall into this category. In other words, fascism and corruption are cruel and unusual punishment, as is the death sentence and so much more.

14. All other rights not specifically given to the Government by the Constitution.

Lioness finished her list, but continued, "Cool bunch of rights, huh? Do you know that every one of these glorious rights has been slowly eroded before your very eyes. One little law at a time has been passed, "to protect you". Yet you are not any safer. You are simply no longer free and you do not even realize it because it happened so slowly. You have lost every single one of your Constitutionally protected rights. Well, I am here to tell you, all those laws passed since the 1800s are unconstitutional and must be thrown out immediately. There are only twenty seven laws I recognize and you can write them all on one page. They are the Ten Commandments and the first 14 Amendments to our Constitution, and the other three are the three laws of Jesus Christ.

"Let me tell you that Jesus Christ walks among you on the face of this planet on this very day. You have only this one chance to make America right in His eyes and your one chance is in this election. Will you chose to follow Freedom and Jesus, or will you sell out your soul to the Devil who promises you everything and always gives everyone the answer they want?"

MEANWHILE, BACK IN TURKEY

THE
BOOK
OF
JOAN

August Anderson

PIERCE IN EPHESUS

She repeated herself in response to his dead silence. "Hello, Peter."

He recognized her in spite of the scarf around her head and bland, loose clothing.

How could that villainess so calmly address him? She certainly had a lot of explaining to do. What was she doing here? How could two people accidentally run into each other on the far side of the globe? This was no coincidence? She must have planned it. Pierce did not see this coming at all. He hated it when that happened.

"My name is Pierce."

"Are you sure of that?"

He ignored the jab. He would not argue with a woman who would not be convinced. "A woman alone in Turkey? You are a lot braver and a lot more clever than I gave you credit for."

"Ah, yes, throughout my lifetimes I would have to say, I have usually been underestimated. We all have, have we not? But the wise among us learn to use that to our advantage."

"To become thieves?" I want my parchment back." Pierce both accused and demanded.

"I am not a thief. I am here to try to locate the parchment."

"You are a liar and a thief."

"No. Honest. It was stolen from the language lab. Just as I told you. You would accuse me, of all people, of being a liar and a thief. I, of all people, hold the Dead Sea Scrolls as totally sacred. I've dedicated my life's work to ancient writings. Wake up and smell the coffee, Peter. I want your parchment back worse than you do."

"The name is Pierce."

"I'm as desperate to find the thief as you are, believe me. I've come half way around the world to find the thief as well as the meaning. It can not be coincidence that you and I have been granted similar ancient writings."

"Great. I've traveled half way around the world in search of goodness knows what, based on that parchment, and you've lost it? And what makes you think you could find any clues to its whereabouts or meaning here of all places?"

"I didn't. I thought I would find it in Rome. The only person at Harvard who knew of the writing was my boss. And he disappeared the same day your document was stolen. It was not difficult to find out from his secretary that he had purchased tickets to Rome. I flew there immediately, but I was two days behind him by the time I decided he was the only one who could have possible stolen your Scroll. Just as I landed at the Leonardo di Vinci airport and was about to take a cab to the Vatican on a hunch, I spotted him with a priest at the airport. Luckily, they were intent on talking and did not see me, so I followed them back to the gate at a safe distance. They pulled out several pieces of paper while they waited for the plane. One looked, from my vantage point, like your parchment. They were hunched over the papers whispering. I stood watching them in confused shock until they got on the plane. They were flying to Izmir, Turkey so I booked the very next flight. Once there, I could not think of where they might have gone. But wondering if they suspected the documents were a link to some ancient holy site, I figured I should go to the only holy sites I knew of in the area. The ruins of St. John are my first stop, then I think I'll go on up to the final earthly home of the Virgin Mary. We simply can not be that far behind them. They've never met you and I don't think they'll recognize me in this veil and glasses, so why not join me? I might need some muscle power to get your papyrus back if we catch up to them. Something tells me they are up to no good."

Pierce shrugged. What the heck. He sure didn't know what was going on, maybe they could figure it out together. And he simply did not have any other plan. "OK, Dr. Johnson, but I don't want to later learn I've joined forces with the Devil."

She laughed, revealing her crooked yellow teeth under the hawk like beak. "Not hardly. In fact, I'm feeling oddly alive and almost holy in the very strangest way. I feel a connection to this place. Almost like I've been here before. Déjà vu? Or a previous life, makes this place feel very familiar. I think I am supposed to be here now, for some strange reason. By the way, my name is Dr. Joan Johnson. You might as well call me Joan and at least pretend like we are friends. And I was able to ascertain something more. Whether or not it was related to the Dead Sea Scrolls, before it was stolen, my technician ascertained its age and its source! It was from a parchment that they used only here on the Ionic Coast about 2000 years ago. Now that I know that, I know exactly what dialect of ancient languages will give us a more accurate interpretation. Further, my researchers verified the material was of the exact same material, age, quality as the original of the book of Revelations! It was right after I learned that, your parchment disappeared."

"Who else would have known that?"

"Besides my research team at Harvard, all of whom remain present and accounted for at the Harvard lab, only the head of my department, Mr. Mathew Champella. Since he was the only person that disappeared when your papyrus disappeared; and since he headed straight to the Vatican, he is the logical choice as our thief. Also, he has worked with the Vatican on ancient documents before, so I had to confide in him about your papyrus when I took it in for testing. Soon thereafter, your document came up missing. When I went to Champella to see if he knew where it had gone I found that he, too, had disappeared! I am convinced there is a connection. I'm also convinced your parchment is not in the United States. I honestly think there is a sinister plot to keep it away from you and I feel so guilt ridden that it was taken when I was in charge. I am determined it will be my life's mission to find and help you solve its puzzle. I have money for I live simply and make a good salary, so I headed here – the only logical place to try to understand it all."

"What makes you think this is a logical place? And why didn't you call me and tell me all this earlier?"

Joan nervously cleared her wrinkled throat before answering, "I tried to call you and your agent said you had gone off to Ireland and could not be reached by phone. Further, I was hoping to get it back and figure it all out before I got the most famous movie star in the world angry at me. Your temper is a little more than legendary, you know. As for logical place, of course, the Vatican was the logical place and Mr. Champella's secretary was good enough to send me in that direction. Turkey would not have been my next stop, but for seeing Champella and that priest get on a plane for Izmir. Once in Izmir, though, logic said there are three sacred places – St. John's Ruins, Virgin Mary's final home and Ephesus. I intend to check out all three places and hope to run into Mathew Champella, who has a lot of explaining to do. I was inexplicably drawn to these ruins first. I almost felt like a magnet being pulled here. And when the workers went to lunch I notice they left St. John's Tomb open and I could not resist darting down there. I fell to my knees down there and noticed a flash of light in the dirt. I scraped away at the dirt and look at this pretty piece of glass I found."

It was Pierce's turn to become ghastly green. For Joan was holding before his shocked blue eyes, an exact replica of the other slices of blue glass encrusted with jewels that all his new acquaintances had somehow run across in their own adventures.

"What's wrong?" Joan worried at the way Pierce was looking at her find.

Pierce began to explain how he was being haunted by similar slices of blue glass with fake gems.

"What makes you think they are fake? I think these are real diamonds, emeralds, rubies, and sapphires."

"What makes you say that?"

"Well, first I know my gems – ancient languages and religions have always fascinated me. Haven't you ever noticed the masses of gold, art, and priceless gems are always owned by churches? And second, I tested one of diamonds for hardness by scratching the glass surface of my watch with it. See?"

Pierce saw the big scratch mark across Joan's watch. "That simply is not possible."

"Why not? Of course if these pieces are ancient, as I suspect they are, they would be made of real gems. They didn't have fakes two thousand years ago when St. John was buried here!"

"The pieces of glass would be priceless if they were real."

"You got it."

"But Bart and Tom are just a couple of kids flashing them around everywhere. They could be stolen. We need to take these in to an expert to test first chance we get. Now I'm glad I'm traveling with my bodyguard. Oh, forgive my manners, this is my bodyguard James, this is the language professor I told you about, Professor Johnson."

"Call me Joan, please. What is that necklace you are wearing tucked in your shirt around your neck?"

Joan was always observing. She always had her antennae up.

James pulled out his necklace which Pierce had never seen as its ornament lay near his enormous belly under his shirt from the time Pierce had known the large man.

There James revealed his own blue glass piece, matching the others and Joan shook her head in awe, "If this is some kind of spoof, I will never forgive you two."

"My ancestors found this while fossil hunting in the Bad Lands of South Dakota," the Native American stated calmly.

Pierce was shaking his head too in absolute wonderment. "It absolutely is not a spoof. I am as surprised as you are. How many does that make? My friend Anne brought one from Thailand. Tom found his snorkeling in Tahiti. Bart in Mexico. I found one in Ireland. Paul, my Pilot found one in Salt Lake City. James found his in South Dakota. You just now found this here. That is seven. Do you think there are others? If so, could that be the reason your boss stole my parchment? Is there a chance he, too, thinks the gems are real and he is looking for these?"

Joan replied softly, "That is a very real possibility!"

Pierce was starting to loosen up and not look upon Joan as a foe now, but possibly she was a friend, an ally. He would wait and see. Something, though, was creeping him out, so he suggested they move rapidly on to the next stop. Mary's final home was what the two decided on with James nodding in agreement.

"My cab is still waiting, we might all just as well go in it." Pierce invited.

They dismissed Joan's cab and gave her driver a huge tip, then took Pierce's taxi up the mountain into the beautifully forested homeland of the Virgin Mary's final home on earth. It was a short drive into the mountains and the views were spectacular. They looked down upon the ancient port where waters had once brought great ships to the base of the ancient city of Ephesus. In modern times the waters had receded and the silt land left behind was now fertile farmland.

The driver Mohammed was explaining, "Our government wants to make it a great bay once again. They are raising money to flood the lands below Ephesus. You can imagine how upset the farmers are down there."

The three strangers looked in the distance toward the port where the Aegean Sea wrapped her beautiful blue green arms around this sacred land. They looked down upon the ancient ruins of Ephesus. The cab driver told them he would take them around this ancient marvel when they were done at the Blessed Virgin's house.

The driver continued as the perfect host and tour guide when Joan noted the burned forest now growing new small trees, "About five or six years ago, back in 2006 I believe, a fire raged through these hills. But it was as if the Sacred Mother herself protected her home, for it stopped just short of there. The Sacred Mother never did die, you know, she was one of the few allowed to ascend unto heaven in her earthly body without having to experience death."

Joan was all ears, "That is what I learned at the Vatican. I was studying there right about the time the Pope finally admitted, and the church sanctioned the idea that this was most likely the final home of Mother Mary!"

As he drove, he chattered, anxious to tell his guests about his native Turkey. And he did seem quite taken by Joan who sat in the front seat beside him. "Call me Mo," he told her as he politely opened the door for her. He was truly happy to find a bright eyed listener in her. She asked all the right questions about the history of his religion.

Pierce and James rode in the back seat and sat quietly listening and becoming more and more fascinated as Joan and Mo began to speak of the commonalities of Islam and Christianity. How both religions held Jesus to be an important prophet and how sacred Mother Mary was to both Christians and Muslims.

Mo continued the comparisons as he drove up the winding road to Mary's final home. "Both religions truly teach men to seek goodness on earth and both are religions of peace. Really, we share so many beliefs. It just happens that our head Prophet is Mohammed; however, honestly 99% of both religions are the same."

Pierce jumped startled when he heard those words. Where had Pierce heard that before? Oh, yes, he remembered that exact same line being spoken years ago when Anne and Lioness were comparing Christianity to Buddhism! 95% of the beliefs were the same. Peace was at the core of the religions. Love was the underlying basis. Eternal life, filled with purpose, was the very hope of religious beliefs. Christians merely believed their great prophet was Jesus while Buddhists believed in Buddha. And again, similar words were spoken when Pilot Paul was in the presence of the blue glass explaining Mormonism. 99% of the beliefs were the same. Life was sacred. Love one another. Peace on earth. Only difference was that Mormon's believed Joseph Smith to be their founding Prophet and in a succession of modern day prophets.

Pierce also vaguely remembered his would be father-in-law, the great Adam Godfrey, visiting Lion's stables one day when they were training horses and making the same statement when he compared Judaism and Christianity. Adam Godfrey had pointed out that they use the same book – the Bible - and the only difference between Judaism and Christianity was that Christians believed Jesus was the Savoir who would come again and Jews believed the Savior was still to come. Mr. Godfrey, too, used those words: 99% of their religious beliefs were exactly the same.

So, Pierce pondered, if all religions are essentially based on the same ideals, but they just learn the truth from different prophets, how can there be religious wars? If the philosophies are for peace, love, eternal life, and understanding, how could there ever be a religious war?

Finally, my son, you understand. There can be no war based on religion. For I, the one great God, call me Allah, Iam, Universal Intelligence, or whatever else, it matters not, rule over all the religions. And you, my children, are all part of one another. When you fight among yourselves, it is like my right hand spiting my left hand. Why would anyone do that? There is, has been, nor ever will be any war ever sanctioned by Me.

Everyone in the car jumped and looked around as Pierce cried out, "Who said that?" They all shook there heads in fear. Mo barely kept the car on the road his hands were trembling against the steering wheel so badly.

When the same voice erupted in their heads again, Mo pulled to the side of the road so he would not drive right off the side of the mountain. Pierce was convinced he was going crazy and thinking out loud as the voice continued.

If 99% of the underlying philosophies of all major religions of the world are the same: Peace, Love, Hope, Joy, Freedom, Brotherhood, Divine Purpose of Everyman, and Eternal Life – how could there ever be a religious war? There simply could not be.

All religions advocate Peace. In fact, all are based on Peace.

Does it matter then, which Prophet you chose as your own? Is this 1% difference worthy of bloodshed? Is 1% difference worthy of ignoring the other 99% of the common truths? Worthy of declaring one another evil? NO. The 1% difference is human error and it does not justify violating the 99% all great religions share.

PEACE ON EARTH IS MANDATORY. THIS IS MY GREATEST COMANDMENT TO ALL MANKIND. LOVE ONE ANOTHER. EFFECTUATE PEACE NOW OR YOU VIOLATE MY GREAT WILL IN EVERY RELIGION.

MARY'S HOME

Oh my gosh, the roar of Pierce's thoughts seemed to shake the entire cab like an earthquake. Looking at the shocked wide eyes of Joan and Mo staring back at him, Pierce knew they heard it, too. Pierce knew Joan, James, and Mohammed were hearing the exact same thoughts. Were they Pierce's thoughts being spoken out loud in an Actor's voice so powerful as to shake the car? Pierce had no recollection of moving his lips -

Mo, the Muslim cab driver, was trembling and sweating profusely. James and Joan just sat there pale.

Looking up, the four travelers eventually realized that where Mohammed had pulled over was the far end of the parking lot at the Virgin Mary's house. Not trusting themselves to drive another inch, they agreed just to get out and walk to the house.

On trembling, weak legs Pierce climbed from the cab and helped Joan out. She was again green colored, ugly, and wobbly. The horrified cab driver shook his head no and said he would wait in the cab for them. Tears were streaming down his face.

It was not quite the height of tourist season and the middle of the week, so there was barely a line to enter Mary's humble home.

It should have been a mansion lined in gold for the pain she endured.

The eternal pain of every mother who has ever lost a child is unbearable beyond words, but this Mother, this Mother raised Him knowing it would be the ultimate sacrifice. How can any mother live with such knowledge? Such eternal agony? Such unbearable sorrow?

As soon as the three guests lit the candles and stood in the entry of he small home, tears flowed down Pierce's cheeks. Jean sobbed quietly beside him. James stood strong, but his expression revealed even he was moved by this small, humble home. Pierce and Joan held hands and were quite a sight - one of the handsomest men and ugliest women in all the world clinging to one another. They entered Mary's main room and they fell upon their knees at the alter of her hearth. Pierce prayed for guidance in fulfilling his Destiny and wondered if Joan, beside him, and James, on one knee behind them, prayed for the same.

They exited through Mary's tiny bedroom and stopped to catch their breath at the rock wall just outside the door. Suddenly their bodies were filled with a restful and knowing peace.

The three came to the wishing wall and Pierce tore his Gucci handkerchief into three shreds of cloth and passed around his pen so they could each handwrite a wish to pin upon the holy wall.

Then, they splashed their bodies with the holy water flowing from the fountain by the wall from head to toe.

Other tourists were looking at the three oddly, but the three knew in their hearts they were going to need all the holy protection they could get as they solved the mystery of the glass pieces and the scrolls.

Somehow, as they wandered off the path and into the forest below, they sensed Mary had been brought to reconciliation with her pain and probably experienced the same calmness of spirit they felt strolling through the uncannily still forest. In some ways this forest felt and smelled to Pierce just like the forest surrounding Lion's home in the Black Hills of South Dakota. Feeling Mary's peaceful and loving spirit, they could go on now.

Their souls were strong and quiet like the silvery moonlight on a totally calm ocean. They were prepared to do what they had to do – following their own instincts. They set out to find their own divine purpose for being here together at this point in history.

All realized that Everyman has a divine purpose. Perhaps it was their destiny to assist Everyman in finding this gift of divinity.

Pierce and Joan agreed that the cab driver should take them to tour the ancient ruins of Ephesus. They had found what they were to find at St. Johns. Then they found their peace at Mary's home. What would they find down below, in Ephesus, besides the ruins of Mary's temple?

Little did they know as they descended the mountain in Mo's slightly shaky car toward The Ancient Wonder Ephesus housed, that grave danger was about to surround their little group.

THE BOOK OF MO

OH ANCIENT WONDER OF EPHESUS

As the cab wound away from the burned forest and down the steep mountain, Pierce laid his head upon the shoulder of James and fell into a coma like exhaustion. His dreams were vivid and wild.

As if seeing a vision, Pierce dreamed of the Ephesus of 2000 years ago. A city of profound beauty overlooking a bay where even the very ships of Troy had harbored.

A city of enlightened, educated men and beautiful, subordinate women. Plays, libraries, whorehouses, public toilets, magnificent operas in the coliseum where even today one could hear a pin drop without the benefit of microphones, bargaining in the streets – all to rival and even put to shame any modern city found today.

Statues to gods, temples to kings, Pierce dreamed of it all in living color.

Globes depicting the world as round were found in Ephesus - a full 1500 years before Christopher Columbus claimed the idea as his own origination.

Galloping up a gold lined street that was covered with roses to pad their horses' hooves, Pierce vividly envisioned Antony and Cleopatra flying into the great city to cheers of wild audiences. Turning toward the hidden tunnels around the coliseum, Pierce viewed a woman even more beautiful than Cleopatra – Cleopatra's own sister. "I am Arsinoe," the dark eyed, dark haired beauty whispered to Pierce in his dream."

Pierce remembered his history that Arsinoe was gorgeous sister of Cleopatra who fled to Ephesus, after being paraded as a captive by the Romans. She had been queen of all of Egypt for a brief period of time. But when Caesar fell in love with Cleopatra and used the entire force of the Roman army to assure Egypt's leader in Alexandria was Cleopatra, how would sister Arsinoe ever stand a chance? Cleo twice married her younger brothers in order to secure legal title to the thrown. Cleopatra would stop of nothing to claim for herself the power and position rightfully belonging to Arsinoe.

"My sister was a harlot who slept with men for power," Arsinoe complained to Pierce in his dream.

"History tells us Cleopatra only had affairs with Ceasar and Antony. And, of course she bore Caesar's child, Caesarian," Pierce was argumentative even in his dreams!

"I saw her with many men over the years. When she wasn't seducing people, she was poisoning them. She and Caesar paraded me in humiliation before the Romans. Caesar exiled me to Ephesus even after I had proven to be a great joint leader in Cypress. To add to the insult, her lover, Antony, later had me poisoned there. You are about to walk upon my ancient bones."

Lioness

History had been no kinder to Arsinoe than had life itself. She had tired of living in the shadow of her sister, Cleopatra, whom she hated with a jealous and purple passion. Ars was by far more beautiful, yet Cleo got all the attention. All the gifts. All the power. All the men. And went down in all the history books. Anthony, Arsinoe's secret lover, should have belonged to her.

She plotted her sister's death even as Antony and Cleopatra's chariots shook the earth as the black stallions galloped straight off the gangplanks of the harbored ship and up the ancient rock roads that belonged rightfully to her. Before Arsinoe could pull off the murder of Cleopatra she planned for after that victory gallop, and claim back all of Egypt, and all else that should have been hers had that bitch not been her sister, Arsinoe felt a burning in her lungs and throat.

In terror, she looked at her own betrayer, realizing, too late, that even her own manservant had chosen the spell of Cleo over her. Imagine, her own servant poisoning her, in favor of Cleopatra! Her last words as she fell to the ground were directed at her manservant, but Pierce in his dream felt like he was there, too. "Why? Asked Arsinoe as she died, "You know such power and corruption must be stopped? Why did you do this to me?"

"I am sorry for your 2000 years of sorrow, but why do you come to me now in this dream?"

"Because you have been chosen to open the door to the era of justice. You are an actor. You were then and you are now. You were my true love way back then. I am here today to warn you that as the night stars guide you in Ephesus, you will be in great danger. Remember to follow the tunnels of the actors to escape this danger.

Between the stage and the temple to honor Mary, you will find what you seek. You will find what belongs to Mohammed."

PIERCE – BENEATH THE STAR OF EPHESUS

James was shaking Pierce off his shoulder, "Quit drooling on me man!"

Pierce awakened with a jolt. The cab had stopped at the top of the 2000 year old ruins of the great ancient city that had just seemed so vividly alive and real in his dream.

Mo parked and locked the cab, and the foursome started their walk past hustling shop keepers at the top of the ruins. Mo purchased four tickets and they entered through the turnstile to the wonders that had moved so many to visit this beautiful land.

Pierce was covered with goose bumps as he walked down the uneven pathway through the ancient ruins. In his mind's eye, he could see Ephesus of old in living color just as he had dreamed, with occupants thousands of years ahead of their time.

Joan was continuing to listen intently, now with a look of total adoration on her ugly old wrinkled face, to

Mohammed the cab driver tell of the history of his proud land, "Call me Mo, please, Saint Joan."

"Oh my" Joan blushed and stammered. The ugly little duckling was being swept off her feet when he bowed and kissed her hand. Surely none had called her saint! Pierce contained his laughter and was lost in his own observations.

The party soon came to the half round marble stairs where the Senate of old once sat. The four climbed up through the tunnel provided for late Senate arrivals to enter at the upper back of the meeting hall so as to not disturb the discussions below. They climbed down marble seats, with Mo offering a hand of assistance to Joan. Were they both glowing?

The four continued down the gentle slope through the remains of great roads, deliberately carved rough shod for horses so that they would not slip. They admired the layout for homes and the market place.

The four laughed at the row of toilets where men apparently sat together for long periods of time with drums pounding so the conversations could not be heard outside the toilets. Great decisions must have been made while leaders were voiding themselves.

Quite symbolic?

Further symbolism was noted by the four in the close proximity of the whorehouse to the group toilets. Across the way were the magnificent remains of the great library, with upper pillars smaller than the lower pillars to give the appearance of distance and size greater than the marvel actually was.

For over an hour they climbed in and round the city, marveling at the art and architecture seen carved into marble by a people of unfathomable talent. Would that modern architects were so clever! Of course, two thousand years from now, people might be starring in wonderment of the architects of the great ruins that were once New York City, Pierce mused to himself.

Pierce knew that he was looking for something, but what?

Arsinoe had whispered in his dream, ". Between the stage and the temple to honor Mary, you will find what you seek."

Pierce was getting nervous and feeling that some of the tourists were starting to stare and whisper as if wondering if were the famous Star he had been before this journey began. Even more visitors, though, were finding James, in his complete Lakota dress fascinating. The two were starting to attract too much attention, so they shot ahead of Mo and Joan for a little while.

Finally Joan and Mo caught up with Pierce and James near the toilets. Pierce and James were already returning across the straight path and level between the library and the Coliseum, realizing they had gotten far ahead of the lovebirds in trying to escape the stares of tourists.

Across from the age old pillars of the library Joan and Mo discussed and admired, "The smaller pillars were placed on the upper floor to give an impression of great size through perspective." Pierce was fairly sure Joan already knew this as she had studied the ancient worlds more than anyone he knew.

But it was funny to watch the fifty some year old Joan blushing like a teenager again as Mo was explaining the line of toilet seats. "Empires were launched, and plots were plotted, from the toilets of Kings and Senators! After, they went right next door to the brothel!"

"Doesn't say much for women of that time does it?" Joan had to comment.

"Actually, to not have to work, to be kept and cherished and served by man, puts women in the very highest position of society.   Both ancient and modern Turks honor women."

Pierce was always a little too blunt and happy to put an end to impossible romantic notions, "What about honor killings they have in Turkey even I modern times? Does that honor women? And I can not say I see Joan as the type of women to be happy wearing a burke."

"Our women modestly cover themselves to protect their beauty as a rare and cherished gift to be looked upon only by worthy eyes of their family. As for honor killings, of course they are wrong. You extrapolate from one or two incidents and make it look like a tradition. Judge not a whole nation based on a terrible act of one. Dare I say policemen beating blacks without cause in America would be a far better extrapolation?"

Pierce was getting agitated, "You claim to cherish women and that you are putting them on a pedestal, while I suspect many a liberated American woman would say you are oppressing them."

"We oppress women? I beg to differ," Mo was not shy about expressing his beliefs to impress Joan, "You Americans have somehow conned your precious and beautiful women into working like dogs to support their families while giving away their precious flower of sex to multitudes of unworthy scoundrels. Who is better to their women, we Muslims who honor and protect their womanhood and feed and care for them and their sacred children, or you Christian men who drug, rape, disdain, and abandon women to do the job of both the man and the woman in the home and outside the home? While you throw away the most valuable and precious and wisest person on earth – the elderly woman – we honor and cherish her. Motherhood is sacred to us. Virginity the rarest diamond on earth. And aging is to be adored, sought after, learned from."

Joan, too, leaped to the defense of her man, "Mo is so right Pierce. When I'm at Harvard, I'm an invisible old hag who couldn't get a date if she purchased it. When I've travel throughout Egypt, Dubai, and Israel, I have felt honored by men. In fact, I actually feel pretty and sought after here. I can't hit a date with a dead cat back home."

Way past the library, whorehouse, and toilets now, the four trekked back to the as the magnificent Coliseum that Pierce had so clearly dreamed of just an hour or two earlier. He paled as he heard someone singing clearly from the stage when the four were half way up the ancient steps. The acoustics were unbelievable here. Looking out over the vast valley of silt where the once ancient harbor had been adorned with ships, Pierce could see just a hint of the modern harbor in the very far off distance. He was wishing he could see the Godfrey yacht waiting for him there. It was dusk, now and with the sun setting, his nerves were getting a little unsettled.

"Did I tell you that Turkey is one of only seven nations in the world to produce more food than they consume?" Mo was groveling to impress Jean. Hmm. Could this Muslim man possibly want an educated American woman.? True, she would look better covered with a veil…..

From the top of the Coliseum the view had magnificent, and the stage impressive, but when Pierce noticed the stars began to come out in the graying sky, he remembered the warning from Arsinoe in his dream that he would be in danger, "Hey, we better move on before it gets too dark to see."

As they descended well worn, ancient marble seats, Mo continued trying to impress his little Saint, "Joan Biaz and Elton John have both performed here in modern times." They crossed the great stage and Pierce could almost here Elton singing to the honor of the deceased Princess Diana, "Candle in the Wind".

The four went through a tunnel on the right hand side that took them to the street below. Very few people remained on the historical site as nightfall approached. Most were using the facilities and wrapping up shopping near the parking lot at the bottom side of this famous dig.

The tourists had already past through the lovely tree lined lane at the bottom of the ruins where the party spotted ancient sarcophagus and the ruins of the temple honoring Mary on the left hand side. Pierce was lagging behind a bit bemoaning that the three sacred sites Joan and he had agreed to visit had been fascinating, yet wielded not a single clue as to why they had come all the way to Kusadi.

At this point Hanson simply wanted to return to Greece so he could fly home to Lioness. He missed her. In spite of those Bart and Tom photos he'd seen in the gossip rags!

Lioness

He saw Joan and Mo heading back toward him.

"What is that?" Joan pointed down to what appeared to be graffiti on the sidewalk.

Mo responded, "In the ancient times when they were killing Christians by the hundreds, the Christians needed a new symbol for Christ. The enemies of the Christians had long since figured out that the fish was the symbol of Jesus, so around here, Christians dared not use the fish anymore as their secret symbol, so they used this."

"What, a fucking pizza is the secret symbol of Christ?" Pierce was doubtful, irritable and exhausted.

"Cool it Pierce," Joan scolded, "Look at the letters above it. It says: Jesus now and forever."

"Are you sure?"

"Something like that."

Pierce looked at the graffiti pizza carved into the sidewalk a little more closely. Oh my gosh! Looking into the circle he saw clearly now what the arms of the pizza actually represented. It was a star with eight arms!

Just as he was explaining to Joan and Mo the profound significance of stars with eight arms sent to guide him at the end of times, Mo spotted a glint of blue light dead center of the eight armed star.

James grabbed Mo's walking stick and began to pound wildly at the center of the pizza. Mo and Joan yelled at him to stop, then wrestled the stick away just as a hole opened up in the very center of the eight armed star. Pierce fell to his knees, stuck his hand beneath the sacred star and pulled out a glowing blue piece of glass – smooth on one side, covered with gems on the other. All four were suddenly on their knees examining it. James looked nervously toward the trees lining the walk toward they exit and shouted for them to get up.

So mesmerized by its beauty and intrigued were they by the finding identical to the one Joan had found earlier, that they did not even realize at first that the loud popping sound was a bullet. They did not even realize Pierce had been hit in the face, until his blood poured down from his gloriously prominent cheekbone onto the deep blue glass.

Mo and Joan simultaneously screamed out in terror and darted for the nearby trees, not only because they suddenly realized that they were surrounded by gunfire, but more because before their very eyes, the most beautiful man they had ever seen had suddenly turned into a hideous bloody monster.

PIERCE – RUNNING

Pierce put his handkerchief to his cheek and darted after Mo and Joan in the direction of the trees.

Running to the shops selling glass with fake gems, lucky eyes, knock-offs of designer originals, and other souvenirs, the gun fire could be felt zinging around their darting bodies. They ran into a shop on their left selling copies of all the famous watch brands and heard the screams and curses of the shopkeeper.

The sound of shattering glass being reined on by bullets filled the shop. "Follow me!" shouted Pierce as he ran out the back door of the shop. They ran down a path that linked the public restrooms with Mary's ruins, then turned left. The bullets again caught up with the four as they ran into the open field displaying ancient Sarcophagus. They crawled on their bellies behind the Sarcophagus – some elaborately carved with lions or grapes, some very plane. No time to admire the artwork on these ancient coffins, their sturdy marble structure was protecting them from the mass of bullets.

Many an archaeologist was going to hate them in the morning. All those bullet wounds on these priceless findings. The bullets finally stopped and the ruckus returned to the area of the shops that were trying to close for the evening. It was pitch dark under the start filled night when four slowly crawled out from their protective tombs and found themselves darting back toward the famous and ancient stage. To the left great series of seats they the darted to shelter in the "dressing rooms" back stage. Remembering his dream, Pierce guided them through a narrow tunnel where James was barely able to squeeze through. In spite of it being pitch black, Pierce was able to lead them exactly through the tunnels as if he had traveled them all his life. He felt like he'd darted through these dark tunnels before.

He found himself passing the room where Cleopatra's stunning sister, Arsinoe, had looked at him with pleading, dying eyes just a few hours earlier in his dream. He seemed to see a ghostly vision of the raging beauty signaling him, "Come this way, my Lover." Shocked, more than fearful, he trusted his instinct and followed her ghost which seemed to be lighting the way through the complex maze of tunnels.

Close behind he could hear Mo dragging a terrified Joan and was aware of James running silently and powerfully beside him. He could feel and hear the breath of the huge Native American.

Most disturbingly as they ran under the ancient city, was the sound of bullets ricocheting off the tunnel walls. How had their pursuers found the secret opening so quickly?

Maybe they yielded lanterns that reflected light off these tunnels such that it made Pierce's insane with fear mind think he was seeing the ghost of Arsinoe from his dream.

Panting wildly, the foursome suddenly emerged from a hidden cave near the Senate chambers at the top of the ruins. They lunged over and out the now closed turnstiles and charged toward Mo's taxi, falling inside just in time to be sheltered from bullets fired out the window of a nearby the car. They sped away, aware of squealing wheels of unknown gunmen in close pursuit behind them.

Mo was a heck of a driver. He was putting ground and invasive action between the cab and the gunman's car. Pierce was dialing his cell phone, trying to reach the yacht to give them the heads up, but without success. He guessed his phone could not find a cell to broadcast from.

As the cab finally squealed up to the dock, two things became readily apparent to the four distraught companions:

First, they were not being pursued by one set of gunmen, but rather two. On one side of them were Turkish police cars. On the other were two black cars with dark windows hiding the identity of their "would be assassins". Both sets were shooting at them and occasionally at one another!

Second, and worse, the Godfrey yacht was absolutely nowhere in the harbor of Kusadasi!

PURSUIT

"Crap!" Jean yelled.

Mo was chanting some sort of prayer to Allah in some ancient language.

"Sheeit," Piece was screaming. Mo whirled the cab around and darted directly between the law enforcement cars and dark cars. Gunning it up onto the sidewalk, one of the black sedans crashed into one of the official cars and the explosion shook the streets. Two down, two to go.

Mohammed drove like a maniac through the back streets of the great city. "We'll go to my cousin's!" he shouted above the noise of squealing tires and sirens. The smell of burning rubber filled the air.

As they whirled around the corner to his cousin's large, walled home, they saw it was surrounded and danger was waiting to entrap them there. Mo slammed the cab into reverse, then started through more back roads, swerving, turning, reversing, plunging forward, grinding gears. He seemed to have lost his pursuers and before they knew it, they were back on the road they started on that morning, heading the opposite direction right back toward where they came just minutes earlier.

Pierce suddenly remembered his Walkie Talkie type transmitter Paul had given him was in the bottom of his duffle bag. Maybe it would work in spite of his cell phone being on the blink.

"May Day. May Day. SOS. SOS. Paul, are you out there? Paul, come in please."

"Pierce" Paul's voice crackled back, "Where are you?"

"We're driving North toward St. John's cathedral. We're being pursued and taking gun fire. The Godfrey yacht is not in the harbor. This is an emergency. I've been shot in the face."

James was on side of Pierce and Joan on the other. Both were using parts of Mo's torn and filthy shirt to try to stop the bleeding as Pierce spoke.

"Roger that. There is a small airport about 45 miles north of Kusadasi. Can you get there?"

Mo yelled to the back seat, "In less than a half hour at this speed."

Pierce repeated the information.

"Ok, I'll be waiting for you,"

"You can't possibly get here from Greece that fast."

"I'm not in Greece. I'm in the air just outside the no fly zone. Pierce, the Godfrey yacht left harbor hours ago without permission and it was blown out of the water. When that came across the wires, I was in the air heading your way, figuring someone on that yacht had abandoned you to trouble."

"Bless you, my man."

"Indeed God has," came the last response from Pilot Paul as radio contact was interfered with, crackled loudly, then faded altogether.

Oh, dear. Did my girlfriend plot to kill me? Pierce had to wonder. Who else could have ordered the yacht away? Who else even knew the Poseidon was docked here? Did she merely want to abandon me in a foreign land? Why? Did it have anything to do with Tom and Bart? Is she having an affair with them? Dizziness, exhaustion and blood must surely be clouding his thought. But really now, is Lioness on the side of light or the side of darkness? Pierce could not help but think these thoughts just before he passed out from lack of blood.

LIONESS ON LIGHT AND DARK

A Lion can see very clearly in the dark. She can see the tiniest speck of light in the darkest of night and can see the dark in the lightest of days.

A Lion can get around better at night than humans can during the day.

Lioness stalked her prey silently through the darkness of the tunnel and out into the pitch dark field. She could do it. She could take him down and save the world from dictatorship. She could see her prey's blood pumping through the jugular she was aiming for. She could do it. She could take her 2000 years of revenge on this spot, this very night.

Revenge is a dish best served cold.

2000 years she had waited. Was not this dish cold enough by now?

Success is the best revenge.

What if I don't succeed? How could a Lioness have self-doubt after all she had accomplished? Because former employees and former tenants said bad, bad lies about her?

August Anderson

It didn't matter. The curse of all females was that they allowed others (parents, jealous women, governments, teachers, employees, tenants, and men) to give them self-doubt. Her doubt now overwhelmed her. She tensed her muscles. She simply must take the jackal before her down by the juggler.

She could do it. She could just kill it. And spare the world of Armageddon. Armageddon had started way back in September 2001, but the American people lived in ignorant, patriotic bliss and did not realize it.

She could do it right now and prevent so much future suffering. Lioness focused on It's jugular vein and started a great leap twoard the enemy of mankind in the darkness.

STOPPED IN MID-AIR

Suddenly, with Lioness in mid flight of her great leap, the lights flooded the baseball stadium and the band struck up the Star Spangled Banner.

"Let the debates begin."

The Lion was five foot in the air just above her prey when it instantly became bright as day. She did what only a cat can do – twisted in mid-air, landed on her feet, with a smile took a bow to the thousands who had witnessed the grandest entry to a political debate in history.

Shit, she thought, I almost gave into my instincts and committed one of the most public murders ever. This would not have been a crime of hate. It would have been a crime of love. But it would have been equally wrong in spite her good intentions. She knew perfectly well the song was right, "the road to hell is paved with good intentions." Yes, it would have been so wrong, not just to deprive the jerk of his life. But it would have been so very wrong to deprive the people of their free will to chose the direction America would take. What if they chose wrong as they had so often in past elections?

Trust the people. People are basically inherently good. Trust the people. Tell the people the truth, then trust them to decide if they want to take the path of least resistance or to follow the path of truth. Trust the people.

Lion shook her mane. One thing she understood – heck she had almost just given into them – was animal instincts. Animal instincts almost always took the path of least resistance.

She had to focus. The preliminary introductions were over and the debate was almost going on without her. She had so very little time to tell the people the truth as she knew it.

"Let's get straight to the question of the decade. How would you fight terrorism? The people of America have been in a state of fear and a state of war for the slightly more than a decade since 9-11 and the acts of terror that have followed since that time."

David was the first to speak, "I will double military spending and I will force the terrorists out from every cave, every corner on the face of this great planet. I will give them a war, like no war before. This WILL be the final war. And we will WIN this war. We will win quickly. We will win once and for all. Swiftly and finally."

The standing ovation lasted for ten solid minutes. The stomping, screaming, applauding was raising havoc with the sensitive ears of the Lioness. "David, David, David for President." The chanting went on and on.

Finally, the crowd became silent as the next candidate stepped up to the microphone and began to speak. For a small man, the little African American Jewish "Heinz 57" (as Governor Head had often described himself) man had a voice that hypnotized and mesmerized, "If only it were that simple. First, let me ask my beloved people not to fear. As one of our former Presidents told us nearly four score ago – 'There is nothing to fear, but fear itself.'"

"I would love to promise you that the war on terror could be won with more bombs. But the truth is, it can not. First, the suicide bombers are not the only terrorists in the world."

"Second, our noble leaders of the past decade neglected to do the most important thing one can do. They failed to ask 'Why?' If you do not understand the 'Why' of any problem, you can not resolve the problem. I'm sure when Lioness gets bucked off a horse, she asks 'Why?'. If she learns the horse fears the color yellow, she can slowly introduce him to yellow objects before riding him by a yellow object and getting bucked off again. I'm sure when Senator David goes to mediate a legal case, he asks himself the 'Why?' of both the Plaintiff and the Defendant in order to find a fair resolution for both sides. Walk a mile in the enemies shoes and you may find he is not the enemy. Communication and understanding and, dare I say Compromise, can resolve so many problems."

"All mankind is a precious part of the great Creator and every one of you are intimately linked to every other life on earth. This chain of potentially infinite greatness can only be as strong as its weakest link. If the human race is to be profoundly great, every one of us has the moral obligation to become our highest self and then to lift his fellow man to his greatest heights. Not to condemn, but to understand. Not to fight, but to compete. Not to hate, but to love."

The Ugly Little Dude is starting to lose them, Lioness realized they don't want a religious lecture. They want blind, mindless patriotic fervor and that is what brother David was always willing to offer the people. Should she interrupt? She wondered. No, I'll let him stammer on a while longer and see what happens.

Richard continued down his politically suicidal Libertarian path, "I, for one, have never been attacked by a single Muslim. I have, however, been attacked repeatedly by my own local, state government and federal government. "When three different cops watch you night and day, when the IRS threatens, when prosecutors sleep with judges? Who is the terrorist?"

Ah, the minorities perked up to this. They knew what he was talking about.

"When you jail a higher percentage of your own citizens than any country in history, who is the terrorist? One out of 32 Americans has been jailed or is on probation. That is what I call terrorism!"

Oooh. The crowd was wide awake now.

"Do you think for a moment, one out of 32 Americans has done something so drastically wrong that they need the guns of power to destroy their lives and reputations? I do not think so. Yet those are the percentages your government has attacked inside your own country."

"When you are robbed of nearly 80% of your income under threat of jail by the tax man - so that your leaders can fund new mansions while they destroy free enterprise jobs while creating more jobs for bureaucrats. I ask you, is that not terrorism? When the attorney general of a state sues the few businesses that bring money into this state, just who is the terrorist?

"When your business is visited weekly by the tax collector or tax auditor, who is the terrorist?"

"When you are prosecuted for telling the truth, who is the terrorist?

"When local fascists search your home without a warrant in violation of the United States Constitution, who is the terrorist?"

"When Martha Steward is thrown in jail for not telling the FBI something that was not the FBI's business, who is the terrorist?"

"When you are thrown in jail because you can't pay your taxes or your child support and bankruptcy won't discharge "government debts", who is the terrorist?"

"When you are arrested because of the color of your skin, who is the terrorist?"

"When you can not put a swimming pool in your yard without a thousand permits, who is the terrorist?"

"When the government takes your family home so its campaign contributors can build condos there instead, who is the terrorist?"

"When you can not speak a word that is not politically correct, therefore you can not seek the truth through the spoken or written word in fear that someone may be offended, who is the terrorist?"

"Let me tell you here and now. The truth is often offensive!"

"Might I suggest that each and every one of my fellow citizens of this great nation has far more to fear from their own layers of government, than from any dark skinned ideologue from a foreign land?"

Holy Shit! He did not just say that, did he, Lioness shook her head in wonderment of the courage of the little elephant man beside her?

As there had been roaring applause for David, there was now dead silence in the stands when Richard spoke. Were the people thinking? Or were they simply appalled? And then he had to audacity to continue!

"It is often hard to tell the difference between good and evil. Idealists do not consider themselves evil. Power mad politicians, who lie about the reasons for going to war - those are the ones I suggest they SHOULD be considered evil. They rob from the rich and give the poor enough money to buy alcohol, but never enough to pursue their dreams. And they pretend that is called compassion? That is evil, my dears, not compassion. It is evil to the rich because they are being robbed. It is evil to the alcoholic or the poor or the unwed mother, because it is enough money to keep these Souls downtrodden. But it is never let them hit bottom so that they might rise to their full and glorious potential."

I better interrupt now, Lioness thought. He has gone on too long. They might stone Richard here and now and David is just standing there with his arms crossed bemused as Mr. Head self-destructs. And the subject of good and evil was, after all a subject Lioness was an expert at.

Lioness interrupted with a roar, "Do you want to know good from evil? Look to the rights given to ALL MANKIND by GOD himself. Sacred rights such as Life, Liberty, and Property. Those who would fight and die for these rights are good. Those who would sneak these from you are evil. Whether they be in a foreign land or in your county courthouse and governor's mansions, it is so easy to tell good from evil. Freedom and rights are good. Life, liberty, property, love, horses. All that is good! Fascists regulators, licensing agents, self-righteous judges, tax auditors, and government regulators. All those are bad. It is really very simple."

Lioness was throwing herself on the hand grenade to save Richard, "Terror? My experience is the sane as Richard's hypothesis. I've only felt terrorized by local and national government agents. I've never felt it when traveling around the world. So where would you have all this money be spent on this so called war on terror? AND JUST WHO WOULD JESUS BOMB?"

"Might I suggest that you would not know Jesus Christ or His Will if he walked among you today?"

"So you who would rush to judgment. You who would rush to war. Just where are you rushing to?"

"And would you surrender to more invasion of rights in favor of more military might? Remember always that when you surrender your rights in exchange for security, you end up with neither."

Stop. Think. Tread carefully here. Fear and Patriotic Fervor are at an all time high in America.

"The ultimate act of patriotism is to stand up for the Bill of Rights and never surrender a single right to a Tyrant. Remember Thomas Jefferson decreed that if a law is unjust it isnot only a man's right to disobey it, it is his obligation to do so! Treat others with respect and love and never surrender a single right. No person should surrender life. No person should surrender freedom. No person should surrender property, privacy, or any God given rights or any of our other rapidly depleting Constitutional Rights without a vicious internal fight against the Tyrants that walk among us."

"Further, might I suggest that sometimes it is easier to die for a cause than to live for a cause? I urge all Americans, all people of the world, to live for the cause of freedom. For that glory that is life itself. Live for the promises of America's dying Constitution. If, in mass, you never let a single authority take your freedom from you there would be no reason to die for it."

Back down. The ones who dub themselves Patriots will be up in arms against you.

Taking a breath, Lioness sought to connect to the audience on a mare human basis, "When a mare gives birth to a foal out in a field in South Dakota, the other mares form a circle around her and the baby. The wolf can not cross through the protective circle to kill the foal until it stands up and is able to run alongside its mother. You are all part of God's sacred herd. Form a protective circle around one another so that none will die for the wolf who would rob you of your life before it has never begun. If they want to throw a war to rob oil, but tell you this has anything to do with your own Freedom, tell your leaders that they and their families should go fight on the front lines first. In all of history, from Napolean to Ceasar, to Alexander the Great to George Washington, the leaders lead the wars. If they want to have a war, they should be the ones to fight it. They should not lie to you that you are fighting for a false ideal, then sit back and let you fight for a lie. If a politician is not willing to lead his troops to battle, then might I suggest the battle is not important enough to give your own life for. Live for freedom. Never ever surrender it. You are born with God given rights. Stand up. Live for these rights. And if all people will question authority, you might find peace will finally come from the pen and not the sword."

"You must have freedom from Tyrants everywhere. From the local prosecutor to the leaders of any unfree land."

Oh my gosh Lioness thought as she stopped in the middle of the thought. I leaped in to save Richard from himself and I ended up sounding like him. I suck at debate. I don't think I will even vote for myself!

There was one feeble hand clapping. Then two. Then four. Soon the stadium was in an uproar and people took to the streets chanting "Freedom. Freedom. Freedom from Tyrants in all levels of government."

David shook his head in disgust. They were following the psycho-bitch and an ugly little black man down the streets and had forgotten his cry to arms just moments ago.

TURKISH ESCAPE

Just a few moments later, Lioness disappeared from the chanting crowd. Thanks to satellite television rioting was breaking out around the world.

On the far side of the world, at a private airport in Turkey, a cat like creature leaped out of a closet in a certain Learjet landing in Turkey. Claws extended and fangs bared, it leaped into the cockpit and killed quickly. When the door to the jet opened to let four panicky people in, the brown blur launched from the plane and flew past stunned audiences toward the hills of Ephesus.

In the brief moment of shock, bullets stopped flying. Four harried people darted from the bullet filled cab into the plane.

In utter fear and awe the gunmen paused as they believed they were seeing a sphinx leap from the jet and gallop toward Ephesus.

In that brief pause, a bloodied, dead body was dragged from the cockpit and tossed onto the runway and the door was slammed shut.

The engines of the jet were already roaring when the gunmen finally came to their senses after hallucinating they saw the Sphinx. Their guns were then aimed toward the plane, but it was too late. The plane became air bound amid a rain of bullets from the ground.

Inside the great Cosmo jet Joan set about doctoring the formerly beautiful face of the movie star. The blood had stopped and it appeared the wound was superficial. It might leave a slight scar, but only enough to be even more sexy she assured the vain man.

"Ouch!" Pierce screamed as Joan dabbed his face with alcohol soaked cotton balls, then with betadine wipes contained in the jet's first aid kit. The red streak of the iodine based substance combined with the old blood to give Pierce the look of a monster. OK, Joan had to admit, it was a handsome monster. She decided to mess with his vanity since he had said so many snide little comments about her lack of good looks.

"Gosh, you better hope you heal or you'll be playing the bad guy in the movies, instead of the handsome hero," Joan harassed Pierce.

"Shut up. It's not funny, wench."

"You can't talk to a woman like that." Mo finally stopped his incessant pacing.

"Sorry." Mo was probably right. And his pacing was probably a result of never having been in an airplane in his life.

Pierce pressed the button to intercom the pilot.

"Take us to South Dakota as fast as possible, please.

The strained voice came back. "Sorry, I can't do that. We've been hit and the plane is going down."

WOMAN PRESIDENT

The Lioness roared.
 The crowd sat silent
"The time to elect a woman president is now. But not because she is a woman. Because she has ideals and thinks outside the box and it is a time for change.

Why now? What is so special about this time in history that we must do things radically different than we have ever done in the past?

Now is a very difficult time. The present is the very strangest of times in all of history:

Courage is now called Gall;
Generosity is now called Stupidity;
Kindness is now called Gullible;
Revenge is now called Justice;
Genius is now called ADHD;
Free Will is now subordinated to Patriotism;
Truth is now condemned as Politically Incorrect;
Discipline is now replaced by Time Out or Drugs.

Pride and divinity of purpose is now sold out for the welfare and unemployment dollar.

Spending is at an all time high.

Freedom is at an all time low.

Government regulations have gone mad.

Taxes are the highest of any nation in the history of the world, but are so cleverly hidden, you do not realize how highly your are taxed. However, you do realize there is never enough money at the end of every month.

A man formerly could support his entire family working a single job. Now both parents work two or three jobs to support their own family and the five strangers' families: two government employees and three welfare recipient families. The workers are literally working themselves to death to support the non-workers. And taxes are robbing the workers blind.

Where should your priorities flourish?

To try to know the mind of God.

To honor any prophet and any religion that would have you become a better person.

To see the glory of God in every man, woman, and child. How could you kill or hate any of his great creations?

To find your own individual divine purpose.

You must be responsible for yourself. Then your family. Then your community. Then all of mankind. You are here to serve. I am here to serve. Not to destroy.

Become your greatest selves, in honor of the great Creator.

You are born for greatness. And I honor you.

You are born for greatness-whether your guidance be Hindu, Buddhist, Latter Day, or Christian of any variety for that matter, Islam, Jewish, and so many more great and honorable religions that would uplift mankind.

God hath spoken to your prophets and each of them is sacred.

God is also speaking to each of you know and you are holy. I honor you. I honor your religion. I honor all who would seek the Great Universal Uniter that created and guides us all. My administration will so honor. And there will be respect, hence peace, among all people in all lands and we will all work together to find the cause of war, hunger, and disease. Then we will work together to end war, hunger, and disease. Let the thousand years of peace and prosperity begin now. We will all work together to find global prosperity based on love and understanding of all people.

And let us celebrate beliefs that are different from our own as they expand our minds and take us into eternity, excited and forever learning. Viva la difference! God loves the differences among the people. How boring and without purpose it would be if any two people were the same? Let us honor and expand our differences. Let us rejoice in the intrigue of different beliefs and different lifestyles.

I come to mankind with an Olive Leaf extended from God to all his prophets and all their people. However any person would seek Him, and in so seeking find in themselves their own greatness, let us rejoice. May we seek and honor Him. There are so many paths to enlightenment – may each man follow the path that is right for him and judge not the path another takes until they have walked upon that path.

May my Administration Serve Him and ALL his Peoples throughout this beautiful planet. May all experience His joy, His Peace and Life, His Liberty and

His Prosperity   Oh what great gifts. Sacred gifts from God must not be taken away by men!

David had to interrupt. She was going too far and the crowd was going to get excited, "Wait. Stop. Senator Lion. With all this individualism you propose and all this slashing of taxes, just exactly how do you propose to feed the hungry, fix the potholes, clean up the planet – all great causes you advocate? How would you fund those if you overthrew our current tax system?"

Lioness was ready. After all, they had rehearsed these arguments around the family dinner table since they were toddlers barely old enough to speak, what more to debate.

Richard commented, "Who among us does not want peace, wisdom and love? And a clean planet and educated children, and good roads?   And to feed the hungry and to cure AIDS and cancer and heart disease? And so much more? But how would you pay for it all?"

Lioness agreed only in part, "All with kind hearts (most of mankind) wants these things. So, you Democrats and Socialists can not pretend to own these things. All mankind owns higher desires. But all man kind is also hindered by lower desire: power, wealth without work, and jealousy. I am not looking to the government to provide these things the same way it has for so long, because they have a mighty poor track record.   So that leaves humane individuals with some responsibility. And the role of government should be limited. And very, very different from the self-serving monster it has become."

Richard focused her, "Answer his question Lioness."

She needed a gentle prod in the right direction and more and more it seemed that she and Richard were helping each other against David. So she did focus, "When you are losing a war, you should change strategies. We are losing the war for health care, quality family time, clean environment, freedom and so much more. It is time to drastically change our approach to every single aspect of governing. If not, there will be no world left for our children. We can be the greatest generation in history or we can be the last generation. We are spiraling down the path toward being the last generation. We need change on all fronts. We need to think outside the box. As a successful business woman, I always think outside the box. Do not condemn it, consider it."

"Says the woman born to wealth," David stated sardonically.

"I have also BUILT wealth - not because of government, but IN SPITE of government. If our government officials are so smart and so wonderful and so protective of the little man, I propose right here and now that all government officials prove they are working for ideals rather than to feed like pigs off the taxpayer money. I propose here and now that all government workers either forego a salary completely and work on the ideal of public service, or, if they can not afford to so work, that they work for minimum wage and see just how hard it is to survive working for low pay and high taxes. I promise here and now that if elected president, I will waive my salary. And I will accomplish all my goals in one term. Then I will do as our forefathers envisioned: having served out of purist altruism and charity, I will return to my ranch and my business having served my country as the founding fathers anticipated. Not as a career, but as a tour of duty, then go back to my career."

Lioness

Richard leaped in supportively, "Political leadership in America was born to serve men such that in Freedom they could serve themselves. It was created to be an act of charity, not a career! And might I say, a career made up of people without the talent to succeed in the world of taxes and regulations they have created for the rest of us!"

Lioness courageously joined back in, "If an individual robbed us of over seventy percent of our hard earned money, he would go to jail. If the government likewise robs us, and we can't or won't pay, it is we, the victims of this deceptive robbery,who go to jail! How backwards has the world become?"

David yawned and rolled his eyes,. His fans giggled, "Easy for a person born into extreme wealth to say….."

Lioness was constantly called upon to address being born into wealth and thought it ironic that her brother, who was likewise so gifted, never seemed to have to justify his birthright. She knew people were jealous of her family wealth and did not give her credit for earning it. They seemed jealous thinking something may have been given to her that had not been given to her people. But they held it against her and let it slide with David.

David had often confided in private, "There is no solidarity among women."

Lioness wanted to prove him wrong on this issue.

She and David both had the image of being Silver Spoons. But they also both knew better. They knew no Godfrey was ever given even a job by their parents. Godfreys were expected to create their own jobs and bring their earnings back to the family pot, not eat out of the family pot.

August Anderson

David didn't care how he was perceived. He slipped from high school to college scholarships, to law school, to a high paying legal job with such ease, money was not an issue for a moment in his life.

Lioness had to struggle and claw her way to the top just like anyone else. But she felt she had to prove herself by working both harder and smarter simply because she occupied a female body. The only reason she made it to the top was that she had worked longer and harder than any other woman alive. In the course of a week, she often accomplished more than many women did in a lifetime. She knew that the family wealth had never been given to her because her parents wanted her to learn a work ethic. She had added and added and added to the family wealth and never been given a dime of it. Lioness had always only given to the golden pot that belonged to the Godfrey Empire.

Public opinion was so wrong and since this debate was being beamed around the world, she wanted this opportunity to clear away the "silver spoon" reputation felt she definitely did not deserve. She had struggled, just like her beloved people had struggled. Oh, how she had struggled. She knew the meaning of work. The meaning of sweat. She fixed fences, cracked ice on stock tanks, cut firewood, cleaned stalls, went hungry, froze her limbs to the point of frostbite pulling people out of ditches in frigid South Dakota blizzards, cleaned toilets in whorehouses, and begged for food in Thailand. Yes, Lioness knew homelessness and hunger. It was part of her training. Part of her strength. Perhaps struggle was the very root of her compassion.

Further, although she dared not say it, for thousands of years she had suffered and borne the unbearable sorrow, and borne the excruciating pain.

Of all people, Lioness personally knew that sweat was meant to pour and blood was meant to circulate.

She pounced on the opportunity this debate had given her, "Since I've earned all of my wealth – every single dime – the hard way…" She had explained it to her audience, now they could accept or reject that she was one of them.

What really mattered more was that each and every one of them realized their own greatness. If Lion could achieve greatness, so could every human being alive.

"All people bear their own burdens," she wrapped up, "But your individual burdens give you your individual strength."

"I have a real hard time with unearned wealth. If one wants the government to rob from those of us who work and give to those of them that do not, then that is socialism. Unemployment, welfare, minimum wage, all of that is socialism. Where the government giveth, they expect money, blood, and votes in return. That is socialism. While the government freely giveth my money away to druggies/lazy slobs/huge farms, and more, they also expect to be able to rob me of my produce and interfere with my productivity. That is socialism. What happens when small business creators have finally had enough? Then who will pay for all that is good in the world - from roads to schools to feeding the poor?"

She was losing them, but continued, "Hard, honest work is what I do and I create jobs for others who would want the same/better opportunities. Opportunities with absolutely no ceiling to what one can earn if they are willing to work and think only half as hard as I did. I've created opportunities for others. Most elected officials only create opportunities for themselves. What I do is called Capitalism. What David performs is Socialism. Viva Capitalism!"

Richard, the Libertarian, piped in, "Viva Freedom. I am here to limit government interference with ANYTHING, for a free man can achieve absolutely anything. Freedom made America great in the past. I will reinstate freedom to make her great again."

Lioness agreed right back, "Here's to opportunity. Self- reliance. Self determined charity. I gladly give my Capitalist earnings voluntarily to hundreds of charities every year. I do not gladly give my dollars to a government to pay Native Americans to become alcoholics or for the bombing of babies in foreign lands. But they take my dollars and do just that anyway."

Richard added in his soft-spoken, yet powerful voice, "Some see government as the solution. I see government as the problem. Hard working, hard thinking people will solve the world's problems. Governments have created the world's problems. They are not here to solve them."

MARY – THE UNKNOWN YEARS

Lioness was attending that very public debate in America as the plane half way around the world began almost imperceptibly losing altitude over the Aegean Sea.

Her alibi was airtight in the death of Paul's co-pilot.

Pierce, Joan, and Mo were in the plane flying rapidly away from Turkey. They were in borderline shock, wanting to sleep, but adrenaline pumping through their bodies so powerfully, their legs were hot, their eyes were tightly wide open.

If they had not been through enough that day, the vision appeared as the plane was crashing.

Pierce assumed it was rational to have a vision such as this before dying, but still his heart was pounding so hard, he was sure the heart attack would kill him before they ever crashed into the ocean.

Mo, simply gave up and fainted. Best to die when you are passed out, anyway, Pierce thought bitterly.

But what was odd was that Joan sat with a peaceful, almost knowing smile upon her face.

Before them stood a vision of a woman of indescribable beauty – arms stretched out lovingly toward them. Her dark wavy hair flowed down past her waist, her smile was soft, holy, and comforting. Her figure small, trim, but proudly erect as if she knew all the world embraced her with honor and love. Her large almond eyes reflected the wisdom of the ages.

"Mary. Beloved of all Mothers. Queen of my heart. What would you have us know?" Joan's voice was way too calm for a woman about to crash into the ocean. And her statement way too familiar, if this really was the Mother of Jesus, Himself, so Pierce thought. Should not they kneel or something? Had they already crashed into the Sea? Was this a vision of a living person that somehow got on the Cosmo Jet in Turkey? Or was she a dream? Or were they already dead and She, the Lovely, standing there to to greet them?"

Pierce had to know, "Pinch me."

Joan complied – hard.

"Ouch!" Pierce screamed. That was going to leave a black and blue mark. At least that eliminated death or a dream. But the two options it left – a vision or insanity – were not necessarily comforting to Pierce.

"Do you see her, too?" Pierce needed to confirm, "Tell me exactly what you see."

Joan whispered in awe as the plane dropping gave her the sensation of leaving her stomach behind and outside the rest of her light weight body. It was the same thing Pierce was seeing, so it confirmed Mary was a Vision. "Hmmm, he whispered bitterly, nobody ever told me there were movies as you approached death." He sat back to watch, knowing in mere moments death would be upon them as the deep dark sea swallowed them whole. He envied James who appeared to be sleeping and Mo for fainting. They did not have to experience the odd slowing of time, nor witness their own deaths.

In the time of a heartbeat, in the knowledge of two thousand years, as if watching a movie in slow motion, yet at warp speed, Joan and Pierce saw "***the rest of the story***".

THE REST OF THE STORY

As the jet plummeted toward the deep dark sea, the vision played out before Joan and Pierce in movie form. Time stood still, so although the jet plummeted, in their dying minds, it all happened in slow motion. Plenty of time for a movie.

In fact, Pierce kept asking Joan, "Where have I seen that woman before? She is so familiar looking."

Joan shrugged, too terrified now to speak. Too fascinated to avert her eyes from the death movie.

Both before and after the personification of God in the form of Jesus, there was Mary. Beautiful, kind, and intelligent Mary.

Mary had been one of the Sisterhood in a little known cult that exists to this very day. Two Thousand years ago, they had existed and been highly respected by the public. They were the healers. They were the light. They were the wise. They were the Essenes Jews living around the Dead Sea.

Essenes were some of the first people to recognize the equality of the sexes. They were an androgynous people whose enlightened ones could be spotted wearing white

Lioness

robes donned by Mary, and later by Jesus. They were the Prophets who were born on the planet to save human beings from the darkness of ignorance and depravity. They would speak the truth with calm demeanor – whether the truth be popular or not.

Essenes wrote what are now called the Dead Sea Scrolls. These scorlls would not be discovered until 1947, but many of the writings would verify much of the Bible.

The Essenes were such marvelous healers, in part because of the salts and minerals that were found in the Dead Sea.

A modern day secret organization of Essenes still exists on the earth and they believe that they are responsible for the final incarnation of the Christ inside all human beings. Two thousand years earlier; however, Mary had schooled both Jesus and St. John in the healing techniques of Essenes as well as in the mysteries of the Universe and being with "The One With No Name", as they referred to God.

Not limited to a single religion, they possessed revelations of past, present, and future. The Essenes were the most advanced spiritualists ever to walk the planet. When Joseph and Mary disappeared to avoid childhood murder of King Herod, they had taken their family to live along the Dead Sea – preparing their Son, Jesus, for the times ahead. Playing with cousin John and learning the ways of the elders, Jesus and his cousin had splendid childhood adventures every morning, then studied religion every afternoon.

In this peaceful and enlightened setting Jesus and Cousin John were spared the terror of King Herod's

Massacre of the Innocents. While Herod the Great sent soldiers on his order to execute all young male children in Bethlehem, to avoid his loss of thrown to a newborn "King of the Jews", his nemesis was safe and growing strong and wise on the shores of the great Dead Sea.

By the age of seven tender years, Jesus was fully prepared to take on his own destiny. But he needed to see the world and learn the ways of other races and religions. The family traveled to Asia Minor and Asia Major. They laughed, they learned. They followed the guidance and the stars of the Great One with No Name.

Jesus had been trained to heal, to work, to speak the truth, to pray. He was ready. At the tender age of twelve, it was time to return to Jerusalem. It was time for Jesus to fulfill his Destiny.

Jesus returned to Jerusalem and the rest of his life, from the age of twelve through shortly after the crucifixion, is the most repeated story on earth.

But what became of Mary? What became of St. Paul? St John? The Apostles? The movie continued. There would be no peace, not then, not now. No peace for the Jews until Jesus was returned to power. No peace for the apostles, no peace for Mary.

Riots erupted. Christians were hunted down by Romans and thrown to the lions. The sacred scrolls were hidden in caves around the Dead Sea. Many writings would disappear completely when the Dead Sea flooded over the centuries. The Essenes were forced to go underground for the next 2,000 years.

John, the apostle, had been asked by Jesus to protect Mary even after Jesus ascended unto heaven, but the job was becoming most difficult.

In the dead of the night, with a sliver of a moon and only the stars to guide them, John and Mary mounted on donkeys at 3:00 in the morning. It was a crisp, cold night and they were wrapped in fur for warmth and to be disguised as they headed North by Northwest.

Hour after hour they rode. The sun came up and night fell again. Stopping for food and water at farms along the way, hiding twice from troops of Roman soldiers, the exhausted and sore twosome, John and Mary, finally arrived at the sea – near where modern day Tel Aviv stands so proudly as an economic powerhouse today.

It was a sleepy, peaceful little fishing village back then. The Mediterranean waves were clean and dancing in the sunlight. They seemed to be beckoning John and Mary onward – to safety, to a new world. It called them to a land where their faces would not be so recognizable.

With a few gold coins, John and Mary were able to persuade a fisherman on a rickety old boat to take them immediately in a northwesterly direction.

Passing Cyprus on their starboard side, they overcame their seasickness. Onward they went with very little to eat, day after day, night after night. Their skin was parched. Their stomachs were shrunken. The nights were bitter cold, but onward the three sailed.

Eventually they arrived in the Aegean Sea – blue green and peaceful one moment, dark and moody the next.

Northwest on a straight line toward Greece, they sometimes fought storms and sometimes fought no winds at all, but Mary insisted she would recognize her final destination when she saw it.

Greek islands were to the left and Ancient Turkey to the right when a violent storm attacked the small vessel at high noon washing it's captain overboard. Helpless, Mary and John tied themselves down to the rickety old boat with ropes as the hurricane force winds picked the small vessel up to the top of a tsunami sized wave. Out of the water they and their old vessel were flung. Wind and waves spun the poor old ship around at unbearable speed. John and Mary prayed for their lives between gasping breaths and vomit that whirled out of their screaming mouths. Suddenly, the remnants of the little ship were flung upon a beach and the storm disappeared as quickly as it had appeared.

Weakly, Mary proclaimed, "Well, I guess this is where He wants us."

They had landed inland, many miles from where the ancient harbor had receded greatly to by the time Pierce landed in Kusadasi on the Godfrey Yacht, some 2000 years later.

Where Mary and John collapsed, they looked directly up to the Roman Empire's second greatest city. Ephesusians would say It was the greatest city, of course. It was on that very site where they landed, that the ruins of the temple to Mary can be found in Ephesus to this very day.

No sooner had they caught their breath than Mary and John were swooped up off the beach by magnificent Amazon warriors and taken to the hills before the Romans could spot them. The Amazons were large, strong bronzed women. They were always painted as one breasted in history, but it was not the case. It appeared that way from a distance as the Amazons were such great Archers, their shooting arms created massive chest muscles on their shooting sides where they would draw their bows with strong arms. This resulted in an atrophied look on the opposite side where they had relatively week backs and arms. The Amazons were kind to Mary and John. After nursing the two captives back to health, the great women released them in the mountains near Ephuses.

Although Mary bore the unbearable sorrow that haunts a woman who has lost her child through all eternity, at least she found her peace in those mountains. She was beloved by the townspeople, who never told the Romans or the Egyptians a word about the lovely lady living in the hills.

Temples were eventually built by the ancient Turks to both John and Mary, but John, of course, had lived a long, public and exciting life. Mary stayed relatively reclusive in those mountains above Ephesus, but John visited often, always bringing food and gifts and tales of his adventures.

After helping establish a small home in the forest for Mary, John soon became bored. He longed to carry on with the excitement of the ministry of Jesus. He wanted to bring the good news of Jesus' eternal life to these people who had taken such good and honorable care of him and of Mary. So off he went, to preach the original gospel of Jesus Christ.

John became pastor of his own church in Ephesus and developed relations with many churches in Asia. He did sneak into Rome once, but his preaching was too dangerous and when he returned to Ephesus John was exiled to the island, Patmos, where he received the book of Revelation. John was a prolific writer as well as speaker and when he returned to Ephesus he lived to be a very old man.

Whereas John's brother James had been the first of the Apostles to die, it is said that John was the last of the original twelve to cross over.

Taking Mary to Turkey had been the greatest accident of John's life. He was glad they crashed there rather in than in Greece.

John and Mary lived long, happy lives in one of the most beautiful lands, even to this day, on the entire planet.

Alexander the Great had embarked upon this great land several centuries earlier and it had become one of the great commercial points in the Mediterranean. But more than a hundred years back, it became part of the Roman Empire

If they avoided the Roman leaders, it was safe for both John and Mary to visit the great city of Ephesus.

John and Mary quietly formed quite an underground of Christians, and it was here that John wrote his gospels.

It was here that John and Paul got together and planted Simon the Zealot's piece of glass that Mo, Pierce, James, and Joan would uncover two thousand years later under the eight armed star at the base of the city.

John wore his part of the sacred mysterious glass with jewels under his robes all the days of his life and into his very tomb.

"What is it – why am I finding these jeweled pieces of glass?" Pierce was able to choke out his first words to the vision of incredible beauty.

"You must learn that for yourself, dear. Besides, right now, you would not believe me."

She continued telling her story, but he Lear Jet was now just feet above the water's surface and was frankly, upside down. James was starting to awaken, his great weight pulling him awake as he was hanging upside down with seat belt attached, but Mo had fainted without seat belt, so brevity had him now firmly planted to the roof of the plane.

Mary seemed to want to entertain them to the very last second, so she continued talking in her silky, kind voice. She had quietly lived in her log home in the forest above Ephesus, virtually undetected by strangers, for the all the remaining days of her life. She mourned the loss of her Son until he came for her at last. She transcended directly unto heaven in her earthly body; hence, her body was never found. Over the centuries very few were ever transcended directly, most often the direct transcenders were mothers who suffered the agony of watching their children die. These silent sufferers walked the remainder of their lives with one foot on earth and one foot on the other side of the grave. On the earthly side, they knew things no woman should know. On the heavenly side, it was easy for them to just to step across death's threshold into the dimension mankind dubbed "heaven."

John? John's temple rose and fell.

Paul? Well Paul's fate was much harsher. Paul got to enjoy the inner walls of Ephesus Prisons!

For Mary, it was simple and peace was hers at last. One day there was a knock on the door. Mary arose from her table and opened the door to a man she did not at first recognize.

With a lurch the plane flipped upright. James was wide awake and in obvious shock. Mo came to.

"Wake up guys, we're going in!"

With the sound of Pilot Paul's voice, the vision disappeared and Pierce and Joan could only look at each other in wonderment. James was starting to come out of his slumbering trance, but the look on his face told Pierce that Mo, even in his passed out state, had somehow shared the same dream!

VENICE, ITALY – ST. MARKS

They had already passed Greece by the time Paul realized they were losing altitude. Later they would learn that small bullet holes had turned into large holes as the wind and turbulence whipped the jet's underbelly.

As they were crashing, the Marco Polo Airport outside Venice had OK'd them for an emergency landing and had a competent staff on standby to put out the jet's small fires and to start making repairs.

Profoundly friendly, the Italians reserved four rooms at the Hotel Danielle for the odd team to stay in while Pilot Paul supervised the repairs. Their every need would be seen to as the Italians simply adored Pierce Johnson and his "Spy and I" series of blockbuster hits. Naturally, they were hoping the next film might be shot in romantic Venice.

Paul looked a little strange. Large bandages were taped across his minor face wound. A white cloth around his neck protected his larynx that had seen the quick swipe of a bullet as he opened the door to throw out the dead body of his co-pilot, release the large cat and picked up the passengers.

After they had landed in Venice, battered but alive, over a divine Italian dinner in a small sidewalk café near St. Mark's Square, Paul had explained his side of the story.

The news had come over the wires that the Godfrey yacht had been blown up at sea. Paul did not wait to hear another word, he got in the jet awaiting Pierce's return in Santorini and headed for Turkey - in spite of lack of clearance and lack of a flight plan.

Just as he approached where he knew the yacht had been harbored, he picked up Pierce's S.O.S. on the walkie talkie type transmitter. Just as he was landing in Turkey, his recently hired, grumpy older co-pilot had drawn a gun on him and ordered him to abandon the mission and return to Greece. Paul was already landing and seeing the shooting from the speeding cars below, there was no way he would abandon his boss to the mess he observed speeding up the runway.

Just as he heard the gun at this head being cocked, this tan blur leaped into the cockpit from out of nowhere and killed the co-pilot. It ran back and sat quietly on Pierce's seat while a trembling Paul opened the door for Pierce and friends to enter the jet, while he stared out of his peripheral vision quite stunned at a sphinx like creature! As soon as Paul opened the door, out went the cat and the dead body. In came four bloodied bodies and off into the wild blue yonder the four stunned people went, followed by gunfire.

Brilliant flight training enabled Paul to right the plane in time to crash land in Venice.

Pilot Paul, it seemed had twice saved their lives in just a few short hours of time.

Fortunately, Pierce had rather superficial wounds and the Cosmo could be repaired. Whoever was shooting must not have been a pro! The five travelers seem to have left the bad guys, whoever they were, far behind them now. Unfortunately, Pierce had an uncanny feeling they would see them again. He kept looking over his shoulder the entire time they were in Venice.

Romantic Venice. Pierce had dreamed of bringing Lioness here one day and trying that marriage proposal again. Surely if he were able to coax her onto a gondola, under the romantic skies and singing gondolier, she could ever not resist.

Instead, here he was with Twidly Dee and Twidly Dumb being the third wheel to Mo and Joan.

James was brooding in the background. As a participant in sweats, visions did not disturb him, but the stares he got in Europe sure did. A man of few words, James dutifully went along with the group, but one could tell he was longing for the peace of the Black Hills. He was silent, brooding, and full of dread. He hated all the stares, whispers, and finger pointing as the huge man in the strange dress with eagle feather adorning his long black braids stood out like a sore thumb in this sophisticated land.

If Pierce analyzed it and had a better attitudes, these would be lovely times in a lovely city with friends. If only his love, Lion, was there, Venice, Italy would be a marvelous place to be stranded. But he found himself in a gondola listening to the rather nice singing of the man with the strong arms cleverly guiding the gondola through the canals, and Pierce tried to look the other direction. For the first time in his life, Hanson was the third wheel in a love triangle and now he knew just how awkward it was.

The fact that James would neither look at Pierce nor say anything did not help ease the awkwardness.

Mo and Joan were oblivious. Starring into one another's eyes, talking about their lives as if the whole world would be fascinated, stealing a kiss, and blushing. It was simply disgusting. They were in love and the rest of the world looked on with envy.

It didn't help that Mo and Joan had been calling Piece "Scarface" all day and were teasingly welcoming him to the world of the plain and ugly. They did not look much better. Joan's thin mousy hair with streaks of grey was standing up all over her head and she looked as if she had been electrocuted. The fine dark brown skin Mo had displayed when he took on the unfortunate role of their cabbie was still pale from shock with a nice greenish tinge to it.

All four had dirty, torn clothes and they determined to go shopping courtesy of Pierce's black diamond American Express credit card as soon as their little canal jaunt was over.

Holy crap! Mo is proposing to Joan. She must have accepted as their poor quality skin is glowing and they are toasting with the gondolier.

"Congratulations," Pierce felt another twinge of jealousy, along with the surprise and shared happiness! He knew he had an obligation to toast the joy of the odd couple who looked like they had just emerged from a war zone. "May your marriage bring you a lifetime of happiness."

He toasted his new friends and finally experienced his own giddy happiness. After all, he had survived the assassination attempt and made new friends, and he was in Italy. He finally let go of his tension and became suddenly become quite silly. "But may you never reproduce, as those would be some gawd awful ugly children."

First the couple glared, then hysterical laughter broke out as the two doused the famous star with every single drop of champagne that was left. Laughing and wrestling the three rocked, but did not tip the gondola, probably because of the huge weight of the bear, James remaining still and silent as the night.

After a shower, followed by shopping for new clothes and totally discarding their old ones, three of the four were feeling even better. James refused to discard his native attires and had not showered. He remained sour in more ways than one.

The others enjoyed there time now exploring Venice – from Boardwalk to Paul would join them for occasional meals. Mostly the four enjoyed playing tourist while Paul supervised the repairs on the Lear Jet.

Pierce enjoyed the new lightness he felt inside. At long last, with his unrecognizably scarred face, he knew the joy of walking the street without being surrounded by Paparazzi and fans. He knew the simple happiness of everyman who was blessed with a private life. He could pick his nose, he could shop for silly souvenirs, and he could laugh without dignity. Physical appearance finally mattered not a wit. He was having a blast being a total unknown in Venice with his two lovebird friends.

It was humorous to have the public not give him a second glance, but to stare instead at his silent, pouting bodyguard.

Pierce's favorite game in Venice became, "let's feed the pigeons". Over and over they would enter St. Mark's square, a mere block from their hotel Danielle, and spend One Euro on a little bag of corn. Holding corn on their hands pigeons would land all up and down their outstretched arms. Surely this was where Hitchcock's early horror flick "The Birds" gave birth! There were thousands of pigeons everywhere. Dropping corn on the ground, the three were so surrounded by birds they could not move for fear of stepping on them.

Mo playfully put some corn on Joan's head and she had three pigeons forming a hat to top off the electrified look. She was simply a horror to view. What did Mo see in her? Mo and Pierce were laughing so hard they were crying. Joan got revenge with corn on their heads and there they were, wandering St. Mark's square without a single ounce of dignity – Pigeons and Pigeon poop on the heads and up and down their arms. They could not stop laughing.

None of the three had ever remembered such a carefree time in all their lives.

Unfortunately, all of that was about to change.

ENTER ST. MARK'S CATHEDRAL

Several days after the emergency landing in Venice Paul finally advised the other four that he was ready to take the Cosmo on a test flight. She was ready to fly and he was interviewing for a new co-pilot. Paul did not speak a drop of Italian, so the interviews were not very successful. Finally, he decided to just let each potential co-pilot take off and land the jet so that he knew they could fly even if he could not understand a word they said..

Back at Hotel Daniele, the four passengers again were freshly showered and shampooed. All but James wore matching Venice t-shirts they had bought on an earlier shopping spree. Joan suggested after the pigeon ritual in St. Mark's square that they should celebrate the end of their stay by going up the clock tower and then visit the famous St. Mark's Cathedral. Paul had advised that he had a few more men to test for position of co-pilot and a few more adjustments to make on the jet, so he would not be joining them.

Besides, he explained, as a former pilot for the now defunct TWA airlines, Paul had been to Venice many times in his life and had no desire to do the tourist thing, again. Paul was missing his family and wanted to get everyone back to the United States as soon as possible. He advised them to wrap up their adventures and join him at the airport as soon as possible. He'd have the jet fueled and ready for takeoff. They could check out of the hotel and he took their new clothes and collection of souvenirs with him to Marco Polo Airport so that they could leave late that afternoon.

"Party pooper," Pierce teased as Paul walked away from breakfast with all their goodies, the only responsible one in the group.

Off the four tourists went to the clock tower. They were disappointed to find that an elevator, not stairs,m would be taking them to the top. On top, their disappointment faded. Their view of the "City of Light"/the "City of Glass" was breathtaking.

The view of amazing buildings floating on the water, sinking slowly over centuries into the ocean that currently housed them, was beyond description. The back doors of homes and little shops lead to endless canals. The sidewalk with bridges undulating along the boardwalk above the canals resembled man made waves. The park leading to the modern sculpture with airport blue light pointed to the stars surely helped Venice the most beautiful city in all the world.

Great debate broke out among the three, for James remained silent as always, with Mo holding fast to his position that Venice was definitely the most beautiful city on earth.

Naturally, Venice was most beautiful to Mo. This was Mo's first time outside Turkey and he was love struck, so most of the real debate was between Pierce and Joan, who had been lucky enough to travel extensively.

Pierce had traveled in his early years just to stay away from Ireland, then he traveled constantly from one set in a glamorous location to the next in his spy movies.

Joan had traveled to great archeological locations as a translator as well as on her own with a fascination with history and religions. Joan had always had a love affair with the past. Pierce was utterly enthralled with the present.

Pierce, naturally opted for Rome. He had fallen madly in love with the city during a movie shooting where he was paid a great deal of money to run up the Spanish Steps, chase a maiden through the waters at the base of the Trevi Fountain, and leap through Rome's ancient coliseum, famous for Christian eating lions. Any catholic boy had to be in awe of the Vatican and St. Peters. And who could argue with the great white building covered in horses and angels? Or dropping behind it into the Circus de Cirque, the ruins rivaled Ephesus for wonderment? Or what view could best the view from atop the Citadel? What was better than Rome's street people posing like statues? Pierce had almost made his home in Rome after shooting a movie there once.

Joan stood steadfast in her contention that Budapest, the Paris of the east, a city her parents sent her to for one glorious week to celebrate her high school graduation as valedictorian of her class, was still the most enchanting city on earth. The Danube River at night with all the bridges and castles lit up as bright as Paris nights were something beyond description. The food would melt in your mouth. And the gypsy music was would haunt her until the end of time. Pierce had never been to Hungary, so he could not make any arguments pro or con.

They were still having this lighthearted debate when they hit the street and crossed St. Mark's Square into St. Mark's Cathedral. It was cool, dark, and silent inside. The exterior light was filtered through the stain glass and the candles cast an eerie glow. Monks quietly prayed and chased away women in shorts while tourists gawked. In silent awe the four explored every nook and cranny of great dark church. Then they spotted the stairway that led them up to where they could go out on the balcony with the huge statues of ancient horses.

The more Pierce looked at horse statues around Europe the more he appreciated how integral the horse was to the history of all mankind. Until everyman began to have access to automobile in the late 1950's horses were the vehicle of choice. They were the war machines. They were the plows for the fields. The interesting thing about the horse statutes throughout Europe, were that these statutes proved from the arched neck and head carriage connecting to powerful rears, that all these great horses from 2000 years ago to modern days were trained in dressage!

Just as something happened during the Dark Ages to make people forget the world was round, a well known fact of ancient time, something happened in the 1950s to make people forget the ancient art of dressage horse training. A horse should develop a powerful rear end for thrusting, jumping, fighting. His power from his rear should flow in a circle of energy up over a raised back for powerful, yet sensitive, support of his rider. His mouth should be soft and face perpendicular to the ground so that the smallest signal could change his pace and direction as if horse and rider were of one mind and body – Sagittarius. His ears must be expressive and alert going back and forth between the rider and the environment. Ears perked in total awareness set above large kind eyes were seen on perfect dressage horses. Strongly muscled body and neck were imperative to survival. Not only did the statutes in Europe display such well-muscled beauties, all ancient carvings Pierce had ever seen of great horses, showed horses precisely in the dressage frame!

Luckily, while Pierce, the horse loving equestrian, was out admiring the carved equines on the balcony of St. Marks, he happened to notice a couple ladders were stretched up from the square below the horses. They were being used by window cleaners to keep the area spotless and pigeon poop-free.

Bored with the subject of horses, Mo and Joan dragged Pierce through the small door back into the upper story of St. Marks where there was a gift shop with very reasonably priced key chains and other souvenirs. While the lovebirds shopped Pierce wandered to the back room to overlook the great dark chapel below.

He strolled casually among the artifacts and paintings while he waited for Mo and Joan to abuse his credit card with still more mementos. What the heck, this may be the only time in Joan's life she could revel in love.

Suddenly Hanson stopped dead in this tracks. There in front of him, hanging on the wall was an eight armed star identical to the ones carved in the sidewalks of the Powerscourt gardens! The bottom quarter of the ancient stone was slightly broken away. The plaque beside the stone indicated that it came from about the 5th century.

He cried out for Joan, James, and Mo to come quickly.

"Look!" he pointed out to his friends who gathered around the display in a tight semi-circle. They recognized the eight arms of a star, just before Pierce grabbed an iron rail that was guarding people from falling to the floor below. He took some solid whacks at the star before Mo and Joan could stop him. Sure enough, just below center he could see the blue glass glowing through surrounding carving. The star was now reduced to and upper 2/3 of a star, but Pierce had what he wanted. He grabbed the cement covered blue object and pulled it out from under the star just as sirens blared around the church and monks began running up the narrow stairs in answer to the cries of the nuns in the souvenir booth who spotted Pierce destroying the eight armed artifact.

"Run" called Pierce.

"We're going to jail for sure," screamed Joan as she took off like a running back.

"Or maybe to hell," anguished Mo as he darted after them.

The four ran out onto the horse adorned balcony and followed Pierce scrambling down the ladders he had spotted earlier. Monks ran out the front door on the bottom floor and chased the thieves down the ladders from the second floor, slowed by their long brown gowns. The spectacle of a dozen monks dashing across the square toward the main canal, chasing the damned Yankees, looked like bats released from hell.

Over the bridges, down the boardwalk toward the canals the four ran. The dark skinned, dark eyed Muslim was torn between oaths and prayers. The skinny, but ugly woman looked green and pale as usual. The big Native American ran with profound grace and silence. Without seeming to take a breath, his strides were easy and rhythmic. And the scarred and bloodied movie star clutched his latest blue glass find ran as if his very life depended on it.

This followed by the human bats was a sight to behold.

All of this was caught on camera from the clock tower above the square and immediately broadcast on all major news stations world wide.

The four ran to the gondola dock and leaped into the first motorized boat they saw.

"To the airport as fast as possible please," Pierce panted as he tossed the boatman a One Hundred Euro bill for extra motivation.

That did the trick. As they raced away from the boardwalk they saw a dozen frustrated monks looking out over the water. Exasperated the monks scrambled into gondolas and other motor taxis and pointed to their fellow Italians to follow the speedboat "Pronto".

Paul was testing a young woman for co-pilot and they were just landing when he again saw his same lunatic friends running down the runway and had a mental flashback to Turkey. He rolled his eyes and started to laugh out loud.

Instead of cars and bullets, as had pursued them a few days earlier in Turkey, they were running from (could it be?) a bunch of monks in brown robes loosely tied at the waist. The site was simply so hilarious Paul was laughing so hard he was crying. The wide-eyed co-pilot almost crashed on landing, bouncing the plane along from side to side with wings dipping right to left. When it stopped before the running comedy team, Paul thanked her, but said no thanks to employment. She ran from the plane just as the wild-eyed foursome ran up the steps. They took off without a co-pilot and saw a single car pull onto the runway and a man step out with a gun and take aim.

"Oh my Gosh," screamed Joan as the plane left the runway, "That is my boss, Professor Champella!"

"Turn around, I want my Scroll back. I'm sure he has it," yelled Pierce above the sound of the engines.

"No way am I going back!" screamed Paul. "He's shooting at us."

An hour later, they were flying on fumes and the radar was out so Paul was desperately planning his flight path and talking on the same air to ground radio he and Pierce had used in Turkey. Paul was desperate to contact comptrollers he could understand in small airports in the heart of Europe. They made it over the Alps and Paul figured he might be somewhere near Austria when the plane sputtered out on its last fumes. They were going down fast and they weren't going to make it to the valley below. The were heading straight into the trees atop a mountain and Paul yelled for the passengers to take crash positions as he was trying to operate the plane as a glider as the fumes of their remaining drops of fuel sputtered them toward a premature end.

Paul spotted a flat green area atop the mountain out of his peripheral vision.

Lioness

"Please fasten your seatbelts and prepare for a crash landing" were Paul's unnecessary words as the jet lurched sputtered and was tossed around like a Frisbee.

"Too late," yelled Pierce. He, Mo, James, and Joan were strapped in their seats with head on knees and hands clasping them downward. Although they all four were rapidly learning all new dimensions of the word pray – begging God for their very lives, this time there was no vision to remove there fear. Pure terror engulfed their hearts.

"Shit!" was the last word screamed by both Joan and Pierce. Mo and James chose to die in silence.

MEANWHILE BACK AT THE RANCH

Lion's feet ached, her hands bled, and her voice was hoarse from a hard day of campaigning. It never felt so good to be back at her ranch for a day of catching up on Godfrey business before returning to the campaign trail.

Lioness looked out her magnificent glass window of the great room of her mansion. She had a perfect view of Mount Rushmore from there. Every year on the Fourth of July she saw the greatest firework display right from her own living room. Thousands drove to Rushmore to see the display that Lion had the privilege of watching from her own front port.

Lion turned on her hot tub, put a slab of steak and a glass of white wine on an adjacent table then lowered her aching body into the warm water. Over the years, she had learned to bathe, shower, and be soothed by bubbles in a hot tub, but frankly, her heart still beat a little rapidly as she forced herself to go in. It was important that she could see clearly there was nothing in the water when she bathed or took a drink. This helped alleviate her natural fear. A Lion would be very stinky if it did not bathe daily, so she had learned to force herself in. And a hot tub felt so great at the end of a rough day.

Lioness sipped on the sweet white wine and slowly chewed pieces of raw red meet as she stared out at the mountain.

Gutzon Borglum had been brilliant to conceive and execute this masterpiece.

George Washington had been guided by divine purpose to form the most sacred of all nations. At least if he had to fight, he fought with his troops, rather than sending other people's children to fight - unlike the modern day lily livered leaders.

Thomas Jefferson's genius was uncontroversial. Jefferson, of all the founding fathers, haunted her thoughts the most as she tried to save her country from the corruption of its leaders combined with the apathy of its citizens. Government by the people had certainly gone to hell on a hand platter over the past century. Government was now a beast gobbling up the rights of Americans faster than she could counter and restore.

Abraham Lincoln's stated purpose was noble and true – to free men from slavery. They never really told of the economic reasons for the civil war. Tragic were the losses. Imperative was the outcome.

Theodore Roosevelt represented America's role in world affairs. It was those affairs that now could assured America had enemies from without as well as from within.

It was not America that had gone wrong. It was America's government. Layer upon layer of bottom feeding bureaucrats feasting on the sweat of the workers were exploiting the American Dream. Regulating and taxing the small business owner until the cross was simply too heavy to him bear, layers of government were destroying America's original greatness.

Incumbents bought votes to remain in power with public funds. Entitlements were numbing the minds of the non-workers with drugs and apathy and causing voting souls to lazily flow down the hill to the depths of hell.

So bubbled the thoughts of the Lioness while the hot tub bubbled around her sinewy body as she stared out at Borglum's magnificent creation that was virtually unchanged since he died in 1941. No other face would be carved upon the granite, but in her mind's eye, she envisioned in the loose rocks below the faces a sphinx like creature guarding the mountain for centuries just as the Great Sphinx of Giza guarded his pyramids along the Nile for thousands of years.

She shook her mane to clear her exhausted mind. Touching the remote, she rolled the television up out of the wall of her hot tub and absent mindedly flipped through some news stations.

She was startled, wide-eyed, and wide-awake. As she flipped from one station to the next, all over the news was action footage of her boyfriend and three others running over bridges in Venice being chased by a gang of monks.

Lioness roared in laughter.

For ten miles, prairie dogs darted to their caves, horses ran into their stalls, mountain goats hugged their kids, and people ran inside.

The roar of a Lion is a terrifying sound.

Lioness

And on this night, Lioness simply could not stop.
Yes, indeed, she thought, the end is definitely near.

THE BOOK OF ANDREW

PIERCE IN HELL

Pierce first gained sight in his left eye, then slowly in his right eye. Blinking wildly he found himself being examined by a large dark Falcon with bad breath wearing some sort of miniature warrior's helmet perched upon his chest and eyeballing his face from three inches away.

The bird from hell twisted his head back and forth to better observe Pierce from each of his eyes. The falcon's sharp beak threatened should Pierce so much as sneeze. The miniature helmet made the vision only more freakish. The rotten breath in his face was unbearable.

The falcon squawked angrily when Pierce even moved his eyes to attempt to get his bearings. He felt the wind from the great bird's wings fluttering for balance, but the angry bird gave no indication he was about to fly anywhere.

Slowly Pierce remembered the plane going in for a crash landing. He recalled Joan's screams, Mo's prayers, a flash of green by the window, and heard his own famous last words rip from his mouth, "Shit. Shit. Shit."

Then it was all over.

This was it.

Pierce had died.

Now the wretched breath of a helmet wearing Falcon, assured him that he had gone to hell rather quickly and rather painfully. He had so hoped for heaven, but his wild days as a movie star climbing the social ladder on the backs of beautiful women must have been more than St. Peter was going to allow into heaven. Pierce had recently dared to hope that the fact that he had listened to his calling, albeit a little late in life, to solve the mystery of the Scroll would have been enough redemption to assure his eternity in a better place than hell, but alas, it appeared a squawking devil bird would be bathing him in fish breath until the end of time.

Well, there was only one thing a man such as Pierce could do when he found himself deader than a doornail and in the bowels of Hades being pinned down by a stinking bird – try to fight his way out!

After all, Pierce was not the type of man to ever surrender to anything. Anything, that is, but the love of a Lion.

Pierce lifted an arm and shoved his loud, fithly tormentor off his chest.

The bird fluttered off him. Hmmm. That arm had worked! How about the other arm? By gum, it was working, too. Right knee up. Good start. Left knee up. So you do have bodies after you die!

"Be still swine, or I'll cut your throat," Pierced blinked up at a devil in a Knight's shining armor holding a sword to his throat while threatening him and calling him a pig in three different languages. Time to test out this new body and quickly – Hanson flipped to the side, threw a leg up to the groin area of the Knight at the same time he grabbed the devil Knight's sword. Leaping to his feet, he took his stance and prepared to battle Satan.

Dozens of birds of hell were diving at him from all directions and he heard the rhythmic approach of thundering hooves shaking the ground of hell and the dim ring of roaring masses circling, applauding and chanting around him. But his mind was focused on the immediate danger of the diving birds and Satan in Knight's armor approaching him with a second sword for a hellish duel.

ROSENBURG CASTLE, AUSTRIA

Pierce drove the Knight backwards and flipped off his face armor with the tip of the sword her had stolen from the devil. He catapulted around behind the Knight and put his sword to his throat, though he knew not if it would pierce the armor or if devils bled and died in hell. The crowd surrounding them was still a blur but was stomping in approval.

The Knight twisted to face Pierce, looked baffled and said in German, "Peace brother. I was just kidding. It is all just for the show." Holding up his hands in an "I surrender" pose caused Pierce to take a shocked step or two backwards.

"Where am I?" Pierce glanced nervously around what appeared to be a castle from about the Fourteenth Century.

"Why, you're at the Rosenburg Castle in Austria, of course," replied his German speaking friend. "Home of the best Falcon trainers in the world. And I'm afraid you've dreadfully interrupted this afternoon's bird show, so if you'll just go along with the performance, we'll get you and your friends some food and wine in a few minutes."

Pierce saw an audience sitting beside a green courtyard that was slightly bigger than a dressage arena. The onlookers were mumbling and applauding – loving the show he had suddenly become an accidental part of. A man dropping out of the sky among the Falcons was way more than they expected for their Three Euros. The courtyard had scatterings of rubble as if from a plane crash and was surrounded by the archways and steeples of a lovely castle on three sides. The fourth side-across from the audience was a steep drop off to a valley far below. And there were birds, huge birds flying back and forth across the courtyard and around the audience as a single black horse bearing a Knight and another horse, a riderless pinto, galloped round and round the courtyard..

The audience was thrilled with the chaos, assuming it was all part of the most exciting bird show on the planet.

An eagle with a wingspan greater than Pierce's "armspan" flew inches above the head of the audience. An owl flew toward the edge of the castle's white picket fence that looked out over the magnificent Austrian valley with mountains on the far side of the great divide. It was near the fence that Pierce noticed Joan, Mo, James, and Paul struggling over the white fence and walking toward him with nothing but torn clothes and Paul clutching for dear to the briefcase containing the mysterious blue glass pieces.

"I saved the Faberge Eggs," Paul stated dryly, obviously in shock. Paul had now dubbed the beautiful bejeweled pieces Faberge Eggs because they looked like detailed gem pieces similar to the eggs only each was placed on identical blue green slices of curved glass. Thinking about it, it flashed through Paul's distraught mind that perhaps the pieces fit together to make an egg or something else- like a beautiful bejeweled puzzle. "Eggs safe, but I'm afraid everything else is gone. I attempted to land in this castle's courtyard., but the plane tore in half it fell over the edge of such a harsh drop. You were thrown from the plane as we went over the edge. The plane caught a wing on that tree and was stuck for a few minutes and we evacuated just in time to see the poor jet plunge to the bottom of valley and go up in flames."

"It was insured, don't worry about that, but how are all of you?" Pierce worried; finally realizing he had not, as yet anyway, died and gone to hell, but perhaps had found hell right here on earth.

"A few scratches, but not a bone broken on one of us. It must be a miracle," Joan breathlessly commented.

"Miracle indeed," said the Knight switching over to English realizing his visitors from the sky were speaking the 'Universal Language'. "When you guys dropped out of the sky right in the midst of 15 flying Falcons we got an overwhelming standing ovation. Best bird show we ever put on. They'll be talking about this one for the next hundred years. Business is gonna explode. Thanks guys. But where are my manners? I am Sir Andrew, the White Knight of Rosenburg at your service."

The motley crew from the airplane stood there in dumfounded silence.

Eventually, Mo found his voice, "What year is it?"

Had they gone back in time?

They were profoundly relieved to hear that they were in the present and the dress was a reenactment of Renaissance times being performed for an audience of tourists in the mountains of Austria in a gorgeously renovated castle.

"Can I show you around me casa and offer you food and wine?"

"As long as the food isn't dead bird," commented Joan dryly.

It turned out it was chicken. Chicken was the standard dish at the Rosenburg Castle's delightful inn. The five plane crash survivors choked it down anyway, realizing their need for strength demanded they eat.

MOONS, STARS, AND FLAGS

Pierce was now convinced of one thing and one thing only. That they did not crash into Rosenburg by accident. He still had the copy of his scroll's translation along with his mother's notes in his pocket. As he chewed on chicken and sipped the dry red wine, he starred at his mum's final notes. Suddenly he saw the pattern. The flags were in the exact order of the discoveries. His mother had indeed, been guided by angels, and he realized now as he looked at the flags she had so carefully copied onto his final directive, that his Mum's flags were of countries where these glass pieces were being discovered.

The dirty and bedraggled actor starred at the first flag of Thailand with its red, white and blue horizontal stripes. Anne had discovered her glass there in the protection of a Buddhist monk.

He recognized the green, white and red vertical stripes of the Mexican flag. Mayan ruins had housed the same blue glass covered in precious gems, possibly for centuries, until Tom and Bart stumbled upon protected by the legends of the ancient Native Americans under the watchful eye of the Sun God.

Paul next eyeballed a flag he did not recognized, followed by two American Flags – red, white, and blues – the familiar stars and stripes. Why, two, he pondered? Wait a minute, Paul and James had discovered their slices of the Egg in America.

Pierce got it! He leaped to his feet, "Do you have a library in the castle?"

Andrew glowed with pride, "Absolutely one of the finest libraries in the country." He led them past the peaceful gardens, up a flight of stairs above the gift shop and into the magnificent huge library. Andrew proudly pointed to the collection of books about trees. The birch book was scribed and covered with birch, the Aspen with actual Aspen. It was the most amazing collection of books the crash victims had ever set eyes upon. Joan, fascinated, stayed in the library with Pierce while Andrew showed the others the great view of the valley and hills beyond from the rooms on the upper floor of this beautifully restored castle. Joan ran her hands in awe over the books with bark, opening them gently. She explored the rest of the library, filled with wonderment.

Pierce agitated. He needed a book with flags of the world. Andrew overheard as he and the gang re-entered the library, "Oh, you won't find something like that here, these books are very old, but come on down to my apartment and we can pull flags up on the internet."

"Duh," Paul shot a teasing glance to Pierce.

Pierce shot back by scratching his forehead with his middle finger. Men always could do in friendship and jest what most women would take as insult. That was one of many advantages to being a man.

Joan stayed behind in the library, saying she was never going to leave that very room in that very castle.

The men all went back down the steps to Andrew's dorm-like room in the castle and gathered around the computer. Pierce set the paper his mother had carefully pasted pictures of flags to next the computer. The men scoured the flags of the world that Andrew had pulled up onto the monitor screen.

After the flag of Thailand that Hanson had recognized from hanging around with Anne, was the flag of Mexico on his mum's paper. He had recognized it from his travels with Lioness when they first met Anne, and her now deceased husband, Bill.

If Pierce's theory was right the next flag, orange, white and green horizontal flag with blue insignia in center, would be from Tahiti, but alas it was not. Ten male eyes scoured the screen for this flag. It was James whose sharp eyes pointed out that it was the flag of India.

That simply was not consistent with his theory. Wait a minute, hadn't Tom discovered his "egg" from Bora Bora in the ancient ruins of a ship from India? Yes, now it made sense!

He starred at the two flag of the United States, with all their stars. Paul had discovered his glass there protected for who knows how long in a sacred Mormon temple in Salt Lake City.

And James likewise had been given his piece from the reservations at Pine Ridge upon becoming a man from his father. It was rumored to have been preserved for centuries in the Bad Lands.

It made perfect sense now as Pierce explained this to the others, "You see, my mother made me a map. Guided by the hands of Angels, so every one of the pieces of the 'Egg' would be discovered in the order of the flags."

"One big egg, then," Andrew remarked as he held the pieces together, "It would have to be a dinosaur egg!"

"Look," exclaimed Paul with excitement, if we glued all six pieces together, it would form almost half of a huge wine glass!"

Andrew joined in, "If there are twenty-four of these, and they are identical in size and shape, they could indeed form a dinosaur egg!"

"I don't think there are twenty four. There are only thirteen different flags on eleven different lines. It this work was guided by angels, it is a map in the exact order we have located and/or will continue to locate pieces of the egg."

At some point, Joan had entered the room and joined in the discussion, "How many Eggs pieces have been discovered by you Pierce?"

"Not by me. By others whom I've met."

"Then you must be the common denominator, Peter," the brainiac of the group irritated him by constantly calling him by his dead twin brother's name. Joan demanded, "Tell us how many are out there, where they were discovered and who has them. This could be a serious clue as to why the Scroll calls you 'chosen'!"

Pierce cleared his parched throat and spoke slowly as he wanted to get it right, "Well, the first one I saw Anne had found in Thailand. Oddly, as she presented it to Lioness, Lion had backed away, eyes large in fear. Next, Bart – one of those two boys we met on Harney Peak just before I took off on this adventure showed us one he had found in the Mexican Ruins at Tulum. Again Lioness backed away in fear mumbling something about Apostle Peter being depicted as crucified upside down in the ruins. It was somewhere near there Bart found his Egg. Third, Thomas showed us one just like it. He had been diving in Bora Bora Tahiti, when he found his on the wreckage of an ancient ship from India. On all those occasions, Lioness seemed to be nervous. Then on the flight over Paul and James revealed their Eggs nearly simultaneously. Next, guided by eight armed stars, I found this in my mother's sacred box housing an Egg there."

The group looked at two identical flags – green white and reddish vertical stripes on either side of what they easily recognized as two side by side red and white Turkish flags.

The seventh line and the eight line contained flags very familiar to Mo, Joan and Pierce.

They housed cut-outs of two Turkish flags-the crescent moon and star on a red background.

"That seems easy said Pierce. The next Egg I saw was the one you stole from the death bed of St. John at the ruins of his cathedral."

"Then I help free number eight at Ephesus," Mo said with pride.

"Then there is another Irish flag," Pierce commented. Does that mean I should have found a second Egg in Ireland?"

"I don't think so," boomed the sharp eyed Native American. The first flag is green, white and orange. Look, it is the Irish flag coloring, he held it up and compared to the computer screen. The one after the two Turkish flags is faded, but actually is green, white and red – the Italian flag."

Lioness

"What could that mean?" Joan pondered aloud.

"What about this theory?" Pierce asked. "After encountering the first five pieces, I found mine in Ireland. Then these two Turkish flags side by side, must indicate the near simultaneous one that Joan found in the St. John's ruins and Mo released from Ephesus. After that we grabbed the one in St. Mark's in Italy. These flags are telling us exactly where we will find Eggs and in the exact order!"

"Far-fetched, but let's use the theory for now! I would then question this, why is it that each Egg seem to come arrive with an individual person, except the Egg in Italy we all discovered? Joan was confused, but excited, "What flag indicates the Egg coming next?"

Andrew's eyes were blurring, so he arose and took out some wine glasses and poured his guests some of the castle's finest wine.

"Look, he pointed out, if we glued the pieces of Egg together, it would form a large, well decorated wine glass – smooth on the inside, decorated with gems in incredible detail on the outside. We have six pieces here and they form one half glass, there are three pieces in America, and we have some flags left. If we put twelve identical pieces together, we would have either half a dinosaur egg, or we would have the most magnificent wine glass ever laid eyes on. Where do you suppose the remaining three pieces are?" Andrew's voice reflected a hint of knowing that made the others nervous. His touch of glee did not seem appropriate unless Andrew was hiding some sort of secret and playing a little game with them.

The next flag had two red horizontal stripes on either side of a white one. "That one is easy, just look out the window," Andrew laughed lightheartedly. They looked at the tall towers on the castle and, sure enough, one flag was the flag of the Rosenburg castle, the other with red horizontal stripes was the Austrian Flag."

All eyes suddenly turned and stared directly at Andrew, "Tell us where it is, dude." Pierce lunged for a sword in the corner of Andrew's room that he had spotted when they entered.

Again, Andrew backed away hands in surrender position, "Chill. I'm friend, not foe!"

Pierce had to grin, for a big old Knight, Andrew was a bit of a lily livered chicken, ready to surrender way too fast in the face of aggression. Pierce had to remember, Andrew was really just a big old kind bird trainer putting on shows for tourists for a living.

Suddenly Pierce got it. HE WAS A BELIEVER. There were no coincidences and the plane crash had not been luck. In fact there was no luck; neither good luck, nor bad luck. Luck had no place in the game. The crash was planned by forces greater than themselves from the beginning. It was destiny.

Destiny trumps lucky every time.

DEER IN HEADLIGHTS MOMENT

Andrew, the Falconer Knight was more than just that, Pierce realized as he starred at the tall, bearded redhead. Andrew was a mountain of a man and probably would have beat Pierce in a dual, if he was not so timid. But Andrew was destined to become a member of this group.

Andrew, in a way, was a fellow actor. And it was not just his ruggedly handsome face and formidable body that struck Pierce so much as the intense green eyes and the booming voice. He was loudly explaining to Mo, Joan, James and Paul all about the art of Falconry and Jousting and all the other fineries of Renascence times with happy voice and waving arms. But his eyes gave him away. Those green eyes were seriously studying the strangers who fell to earth in the middle of his program. He was not stupid. This was the sign from the sky he had been training for since childhood.

Andrew stared and wondered at the group now looking at him accusingly:

August Anderson

Did these guests who dropped from the sky come from the dark side for from the light?

"Why does your castle fly this flag," Pierce pointed to his mum's slight crumpled paper.

"Simply because is the flag of Austria, of course," James said with a slighty celtic accent to his excellent command of English. Pierce got it. He was talking to a fellow Irishman! This big man was in some ways, his own brother! Whereas Pierce was probably from the Black Irish crowd, but got blue eyes somehow, Andrew looked very typically Irish. He had red hair and green eyes.

"See there atop the east tower, she flies. The flag on the west tower, of course bears the ancient coat of arms of the Rosenburg. Please do not look at me like that you guys. I repeat, I am friend, not foe."

"Andrew," I need to know this, Joan's mind was churning. "Are there any sacred buildings around here that might have survived for two thousand years?"

Andrew went stone silent and with narrowed eyes he focused on Joan's ugly squinty brown eyes, then Pierce's large blue beauties. Andrew set his jaw. The room went silent as they saw the movie star and the giant of a man try to stare each other down. You could feel a chill in the room and the wine glasses suddenly had a frost on them as the wine rapidly formed slivers of ice.

"See me outside." Pierce finally hissed after ten minutes of stare down. The freeze lifted from the room. The men went out the front door into a small courtyard where tourists awaited the next bird show.

A fellow actor yelled at Andrew to get into costume, or he would be late.

Andrew ignored him. Pierce and Andrew only saw each other. Timidly the crash victims watched the two powerful actors continue to stare.

"You know why I have come," Pierce stately flatly.

"Yes. And you know I will tell you nothing as I am the protector." Andrew said nervously.

Andrew was remembering his own childhood. Remembering falling. Falling. Falling. Down the ancient well. He was surprised to be alive when he hit bottom and found himself in direct center of what appeared to be a fossil of a large, eight armed star fish. With his own arse hitting hard the dirt covering the star fish still in place after all these centuries, he had cracked open the center and beheld a light so overwhelming he immediately sealed it back up. He had been ten years old. It was twenty one years ago, to this very day. During the two days it took for a tour guide to find him and pull him out of the well, he had suffered horrifying and strange visions. Caused by hunger, he supposed. But he had covered that starfish at the bottom of the ancient well with every piece of rock, dirt, and fallen brick from the ancient monastery he could find. He protected the secret for twenty one years now and he was not about to turn it over to a stranger – even if the stranger did just appear out of the sky like the angel had predicted in the dark damp well so long ago.

"Tell me. Tell me where it is. I know that you know," Pierce demanded of Andrew the Knight.

Andrew silently shook his head 'no'.

Pierce leaped upon Andrew like a lion gone mad from hunger in an Ancient Roman Coliseum.

Pierce's aggression caught Andrew by surprise for the third time in a single afternoon. Pierce was sure a feisty man. Pierce was a clever fighter Andrew had to admit, but Andrew was a way larger man. Pierce punched and kicked and wrested, but Andrew was built like a brick and soon had Pierce pinned in the driveway between the inn and the castle.

The gathering tourists formed an audience that had followed to fight from arena to walkway to driveway. Once Pierce was pinned, they timidly applauded thinking it part of the introduction to the next bird show.

Paul, being of cooler more rational mind, rushed up and opened the briefcase where he had again stuffed the six Eggs as they left Andrew's room to watch the showdown. The light revealed radiated peace as it danced off the diamonds affixed to the smooth form of the blue pieces of glass. The beauty instantly of the Eggs stopped the giant from bashing Pierce's head in with a stone.

"Look, we have brought its friends. We know you have it. Don't you think it wants to be with its friends? They belong together. We, the ones who have found the Eggs belong together. For this it has waited centuries. Take us to it." Paul pleaded.

Andrew and Pierce sat up slowly. What Paul said made sense. They were all in this together. Divine intervention had brought them together for a purpose.

Joan was shaking her head and had goosebumps all over. She continued to dwell on a point she tried to make earlier, but had been ignored. She tried again, "There is something that doesn't make sense here."

"There is a lot that doesn't make sense here," Pierce stated bitterly, "What now?"

"It seems that every single piece of the Egg has come to you with a new person attached to it! Every Egg, but the one from Venice. Who is the owner or protector or the discoverer of that Egg supposed to be?"

The entire group of protectors shuddered as one. They looked about like deer in headlights. They felt the answer was near, but none of them looked up to see a man falling from the sky above Rosenburg for the second time in one day.

This man fell, silently, deliberately with the help of his parachute.

ALTENBURG MONASTERY

The group returned to Andrew's dorm like room in the magnificent Rosenburg Castle. They discussed everything they knew and hypothecated as they formed a plan. Andrew turned off the computer and grabbed his car keys.

It was about a fifteen minute drive to the Altenburg Monastery and Andrew entertained the others with history lessons and stories the entire drive.

"The odd thing about this Benedictine monastery, is that the one you are about to see was built hundreds of years ago. It is a Baroque monastery built in the 17th and 18th century. Totally unbeknownst to anyone at the time, and just discovered a few decades ago, the visible monastery your are about to view was built right on top of an ancient monastery, probably two thousand years old that had been covered by earth for centuries! While fixing the plumbing or electricity or some such, they discovered quite by accident that an ancient monastery lay directly beneath the more recent one you are about to see! The ancient monastery is still being carefully unearthed. This is one of many monasteries on what is called the

Lioness

sea shell path. You will see sea shells all over because the monasteries on this path were marked by sea shells. Each monastery being a days travel by horse, sea shells were placed along the paths and in each Monastery along the trail to guide monks, knights and other travelers from safe haven to safe haven throughout this part of Austria."

"Fascinating." Commented Joan the scholar, "I had read something about that but never had the opportunity to come to this part of the world. "Amazing and beautiful. Whatever caused the thousands of year old monastery ruins to be covered?"

"No one really knows. Simply time, perhaps. Perhaps an ancient volcano or sand storm. But even more surprising, why was a new one built at that exact location two millenniums later? And what a surprise it must have been for the workman who discovered this one sat upon an undiscovered ancient monastery! What if he had not discovered it? Then I would have never fallen into the well as a boy and I would have never recognized these jeweled glass parts you carried in your briefcase, Paul."

"Yup, and the world would be missing one movie star!" they all laughed nervously at Pierce's expense.

They had devised a plan back at the castle. Joan wrapped a rope around her midsection and wound it around her stomach so she looked pregnant. Small garden shovels were tucked in riding boots of Andrew and Pierce. Over the years Andrew had shown many a tourist around the monastery for a small fee, so the monks were used to him bringing in groups and they had never seen him without riding boots, so they would draw no suspicion.

Joan was wadding ropes into her tummy pouch so she once again looked like a skinny pregnant woman.

"I like you pregnant," Mo teased lovingly. He was ready to get this bizarre adventure behind him, marry and make multitudes of babies with Joan. He waited all his life to meet a smart American lady, now he wanted to get on with a family as fast as possible. He hungered for Joan's skinny little body and couldn't wait to make that tummy lump real.

"Shut up," Joan was not quite sure about that baby thing. She believed women spiritually superior to men and that men used family and religion to keep women from ruling the world. She was not sure children were necessary, having never suffered the organized religions philosophy that women are baby making machines.

As much as the sight and sound of the dark eyed Muslim shot heat through her body every time she looked at Mo, she was planning on using birth control for a long time to come. And she had every intention of seeing this adventure, these bejeweled pieces of glass, the mystery of Pierce's scroll through to the very end, wherever it might lead her.

Mo and Paul would be the lookouts – Mo near the stinking bathrooms as you began the quick decent from the Fourteenth Century building to the ancient one buried centuries earlier. Upstairs at the visitor's center were some truly nice restrooms, so Mo wondered why there were stinky ones as you descended from the new Monastery down to the old one.

"Because it is the only passageway to the ancient ruins. It was one of the original bathrooms, far out of the way, until they found the ancient monastery buried beneath," Andrew had no patience for whining. "Don't complain, if trouble arrives, you can easily shout it out to Paul from there while you block people with conversation about the stinky can."

"Great," Paul replied bitterly,

Joan was to wander between the two monasteries like a tourist and also run interference if anyone approached the square surrounding the well of the ancient monastery.

James and Andrew were to provide the muscle power at the well.

After looking around like a bunch of tourists for a good hour, so as to not arouse suspicion, all but Joan left behind sea shells, angels and artwork of would be priests and darted down to the ancient monastery, still being renovated.

Paul stationed himself just past the old toilets, right before the covered square where ancient monks walked round and round on red colored bricks and prayed no matter the weather. The square where the ancients paced in silence surrounded an open, ancient garden housing the well. Paul just prayed no tourist would look down from the modern gardens above into this fascinating "dig" just as James, Andrew and Pierce went about utilizing their rock climbing skills to allow the smaller of the men, Pierce, to belay down ropes to the bottom of the well.

Pierce had ropes attached and was ready to descend when he heard the gun being coked directly behind his head. He looked left and saw Andrew falling to his knees as a result of a blow to the head from a monk, then looked right and saw James falling down like a silent mountain sinking to the sea from a second large monk.

Pierce felt the blow from behind as he, too, was pistol whipped and blacked out sinking to the ground on the ancient garden.

Pierce had no idea how long he had been knocked out when he came to in utter darkness.

He heard a deep booming male voice echoing in his head "Peter. Can you hear me? Peter. Wake up."

He wanted to say, "My name is Pierce, not Peter," as he had so often said to Joan, but he was too parched and dizzy and disoriented to speak. Something was terribly wrong, besides his throbbing headache.

Eventually, in between pleadings from the deep voice of a stranger at his feet pleading for Peter to come to and speak, there was also a strange ray or two of light emitting from above his feet.

It was at that point that Pierce realized, to his complete and total terror that he was hanging upside down from a cross, just as Lion had mentioned the Apostle Peter had done when crucified some two thousand years earlier!

He let out a hideous scream such that the light and the voice above his damp tomb would know he was still alive.

Twisting in Darkness

Out of the darkness he continued to hear, "Peter. Peter. Can you understand me?"

Slowly he got his bearings. He was hanging upside down in the well, his head nearly touching the dirt at the bottom. The well had been dry for centuries.

"Who are you?" Pierce cried up toward the lights and sounds above the rope dangling him by his feet.

"Friends of Andrew. If you do as I say, no one will get hurt. We want the same thing you and Andrew want. We simply want you to bring up his part of the grail as it belongs to him."

Lioness

"If you are a friend of Andrew, why did I see you knock the man out?" Pierce was no fool.

"Because Andrew seemed to decide at the last minute that perhaps you who robbed St. Mark's in Venice were his friends, rather than we, who have searched for more than half our lives."

"How do you know about St. Mark's?"

"We know all you know and much more. If you are the one we believe you to be, we will share the information. If you are not, but are just a person who stumbled across what human kind has launched armies to discover, then I'm afraid you will have to be killed. Come now. Bring up the grail and we will sort it all out on an airplane to your next stop."

"And if I refuse?" he yelled back up.

"Ah, then, I'm afraid you and your friends must die. Time is short. We will not mess around. The wrong people could find us any minute!"

Pierce was angry. He was confused. He had a splitting open, beg to die, roaring headache. "Fuck it, what do I care about some stupid glass."

The descent into the depths of the dark well was relatively easy. They lowered him another foot until his hand touched bottom. He pulled out the garden tools from his boots and the enemy above dropped him a flashlight. Upside down Pierce began to carefully dig. He pulled aside rock after rock, seashell after seashell, and probably a foot or two of dirt. Above, everyone was getting nervous. This was taking too long.

Paul came to, being the first of the group to gain his senses and he was frantic. He sat up and was dizzy. He did not realize that there was a new group in charge of

August Anderson

this excavation now and shouted down for them to wrap it up.

Just as Pierce yelled they must pull him up as the blood in his head was more than he could stand and he literally begged to ascend empty handed, Pierce felt something rough, hard, spiny, and bubbly. It was smooth as a baby's bottom on the opposite.. He cleared away the dirt and reflecting eerily was a familiar turquoise glow from beneath a huge starfish with eight arms. He pulled up Andrew's childhood nemeses and the blue glass identical to all the others that had come into his life in the past few weeks fell out of the central mouth of the huge, bizarre star fish.

Pierce replaced the large starfish, carefully reburying it under the dirt and clasped the blue light that emitted such a lovely hue, it caused the well to emit a turquoise glow. He yelled that he had it, so their attackers pulled him up out of the well. Without offering an arm of support or a care whether the others lived or died, they grabbed the blue glass. For the first time, Pierce wondered if, in fact, the diamonds, rubies, sapphires, and emeralds decorating the glass pieces might actually be real. If so, this would be some valuable old glasswork and it was little wonder others were looking for it. Just how old was it? Whenever and wherever the pieces were located, they all seemed to be in religious relics all about two thousand years old.

Hanson's original group was starting to put two and two together just about the time Joan came running around the corner to the old monastery. She noticed her boss from Harvard had stolen Paul's briefcase full of the Eggs and she leaped on him like an angry hawk. Professor Champella shook her off like a fly. The monks gathered up the ropes and gear while Champella casually walked past the group with all the stolen Eggs. The group eventually got their poop in a group and dashed after him and up stairs leading up to the new monastery.

Pierce needed to see Lioness and he needed answers about the Eggs. "We'll catch a SAS to Copenhagen, then fly KLM to Chicago and Northwest to the Black Hills from there," he yelled as the group took chase after Champella.

"Only one small problem with that theory," Paul interjected, none of us have passports!

THE BOOK OF THEODORE JUDE CHAMPELLA

ONWARD TO EGYPT

"Not to worry," interjected Andrew, "I have friends in low places in Vienna."

They approached his tiny car in the parking lot, totally out of breath. They were still debating whether to chase the Egg thief or return to South Dakota when they spotted the scoundrel. Standing alone, leaning back casually against Andrew's locked car was the thief, Champella. Casually chewing on a tooth pick balanced between his clear white teeth and his right hand, he held the stolen brief case full of "Faberge Eggs" in his left hand. With one leg casually bent as he leaned against the hideous little ugly yellow car, he looked far more like a college professor more than the international jewel thief and gun toting liar that he was.

Tossing the toothpick casually to the ground he spoke to the angry, tired group surrounding him. "We can do this the easy way, or..." Paul snatched the briefcase as Pierce and Andrew lunged angrily at Joan's boss, "Or, as I was saying, we can do it the hard way. The Professor pulled a small simi automatic hand gun out of his pocket with his now empty left hand just in time to stop the angry group dead in their tracks. "I can kill you all without even stopping to cock this little beauty, so tell me, do we work together voluntarily or do I kill most of you and kidnap the rest?"

"Professor Champella," Joan pleaded in earnest on behalf of her friends. "Why are you doing this? None of us have done anything to you. What do you want?"

"What I want, my dear Professor Johnson, is to fulfill our destinies. To complete the mission for which you and I have studied and worked all our lives. I want the rest of the pieces and I want to put it back together for the first time in two thousand years."

"So you shoot at us? And you stalk us? And you steal from us?"

"Ah, I believe you stalked me first. And I believe you stole from me first. After all, you followed me to Rome then to Turkey, was not that stalking? When I found that the piece belonging to St. Peter was missing from the Vatican and figured out where the one belonging to St. John would be located, you had no idea all the research it took, you just followed me and stumbled across it. I let it go, because I knew that one was yours. But when you took another from Ephesus and were joined by the group of unlikely men, I had to take action. And, of course, you stole the one that belonged to me right out of St. Mark's in Venice."

Joan's eyes lit up. "I told you guys an Egg came with a person attached!"

Professor Champella continued talking, "I had already located that "Egg" and had gone to get the help of the monks and the other Illuminati who have sponsored my lifelong search, only to return with permits and proper tools, to find you bunch of thieves taking off with the piece that belonged to me from St. Marks. Who is the thief here, I ask you? Naturally, I would follow you to Austria and learn of all the others when I listened outside Andrew's room. I got the entire story. We know where all but two of the eggs are now. Three are with Lioness in South Dakota, six are in Paul's briefcase right there, the one we just procured is in my pocket. Now it is urgent that we all work together to procure the remaining two. The twelve eggs must be brought together to form a whole, before the rest of the world learns of their existence, or there might not be a rest o the world. Believe me, it is far better that the twelve of us work together than that we fight. I was afraid that you were the enemy until I listened to the story of each of what you all call Faberge Eggs outside Andrew's door. At that point, I realized you were probably each one of the chosen owners, destined to find and return the Eggs. I suspect if any one of us goes missing, or any single piece goes missing quite frankly, the Second Coming might just not happen."

Mo did not understand any of this, "What is Second Coming? What are you talking about?"

"I'm talking about the salvation of mankind and the planet. I'm talking about the identity of the twelve apostles and the Christ figure Himself returning to this planet, but only after the original Apostles come together and drink from the sacred vessel."

"Who are the twelve apostles?" Joan asked numbly.

"Come, come, my protégé, you know that more than anyone as you've studied them all your life."

"Surely you do not refer to Peter, Andrew, James, John, Philip, Barholomew, Thomas, Mathew, James the Less, Thaddeus, Simon, and Judas?"

"Are there is my brilliant assistant. Glad to know you have not lost your memory."

"But what have they to do with the Faberge Egg pieces?"

"Joan, Joan, come on. Think about that one while we drive. It is so simple, you have overlooked the obvious. Although I admit, I did not solve the riddle until I listened to all of you talking about the flags and the Eggs as I stood in the shadows of the Rosenberg Castle listening to you. Andrew, can you take us to Vienna so we can catch a plane out of the country?"

"Why not?" replied a slightly confused Andrew. "And maybe you can explain to us very simply what on earth you and Joan are yapping about on the long drive because the rest of us are very confused."

Pierce was glaring angrily at the Professor, "I'm not going anywhere with this madman who has tried to kill me twice and nearly succeeded, are the rest of you nuts?"

"I know this much," Andrew said to Pierce, "That Egg that you got out of the well has been given to me to protect from the beginning and, by gum, wherever that egg goes, I too will go and I will protect it, even unto death. Now Paul and the Professor are in the car. That means, I'm going wherever they are going. I suspect you are to protect the Egg given you from St. Peter's Bascillica by your mother and the angel, so might I suggest, you don't stand there with your mouth open doing nothing in the middle of the mountains of Austria, but get in the car and do as the rest of us and protect your Egg."

It did make a little sense to the weary and bruised movie star. Standing at a monastery or playing this out to the end? He'd come this far, he might as well see it through. Still he had deep feelings of trepidation mixed with confusion along with many questions and concerns. He addressed his first one to the professor already strapping himself into the back seat, "I'm not going anywhere until the professor returns my Scroll to me."

The professor sounded reasonable and calm, "I'll return your scroll when we find the Egg in Egypt – our next stop. Do we have a deal?"

"Why is that our next stop?"

"Look at your mother's flags. You guys said the red white and black horizontal stripes with yellow ensigna in the center was the next flag after the Austrian reds and white, so I suspect that is where we go next."

"I'm not going anywhere with your dangerous bunch of freaks who will hop in with a gun wielding stranger. I think the answers are back in South Dakota with Lioness."

"I tell you what. I'll make you a better deal. If I don't have to wield this gun to get you to come along, we can go to Egypt where I'll return your scroll when we find the Egg there, and then all of us and all the Eggs will return to your girlfriend together. Do we have a deal?

"And why would I trust a man who tried to kill me twice and has scarred my face so bad with his bullets, my career may be over."

"First, face it. If I wanted you dead, I could kill you right now. Second, All of our former careers are over.

None of us can ever go back to our old jobs. We are forevermore protectors of the Eggs and of the source of the Egg?"

"What is so special about the Eggs? And what is the source?"

"Come on, you're a smart dude. Figure it out. Jeez, I can't believe I'm stuck with such a group of idiots."

Pierce started to take a punch at the obnoxious man right through the back window, but the gun was pointed between his eyes faster than Pierce could take the swing at Champella. The man was quick. "Here is one reason you should trust me," Champella nodded at the gun. "If I wanted you dead, I could have killed you several times by now. The second reason you should trust me is we have all been chosen by history and by forces greater than our individual selves to come together so help save mankind from his ignorant and dark soul. Further, we have all been together on this planet before. The final reason you should trust me, is we are fulfilling destiny together, whether we like each other or not, we are essential to one another until the Eggs acknowledge their mater."

"Not," the nervous Mo finally put in a single syllable word.

"And finally, you should trust me because I am the Illuminati of this rag, tag, group. And you will obviously need me to illuminate your ignorant minds."

"What makes you think we would trust an Illuminati of all people?" Andrew piped in with a question.

"Must I teach you folks everything? I thought Peter there was supposed to be our leader, not me!" Champella nodded toward Pierce.

"What is with you Harvard brats being unable to call me Pierce?"

"Ok, Pierce, then why not let's all be friends, and you can all call me Ted. Short for Theodore Jude Champella."

"OK Professor," replied Pierce not in a friendly mood at all.

"Good, then. Why not get in the car Mr. Superstar?"

"OK, but for the record, I'm getting in under foolishness and lack of any other plan. But if you do not give me back my scroll in Egypt and then take the Eggs and all of us safely back to South Dakota, I swear I will kill you with my own bare hands."

"Ah, like you killed Andrew when he ended up sitting on you back at Rosenberg?" replied Professor Ted Champella with a twinkle in his eyes.

There was some nervous giggling in the car as Pierce got in.

He hated Ted. With a passion. In fact, at that very moment he hated every one in the ugly little uncomfortable car.

ANDREW TO THE RESCUE

"Not to put a damper on all your glee at my misery," hissed the angry movie star, "but we still don't have any passports."

"I told you I have friends in low places. I'll smoke a joint and get the passports in less time than it will take you all to go across the street and get showers and Thai massages. That ought to put you bunch of grumps in a better mood." Andrew seemed a little too calm as he drove them out of the Austrian mountains toward Vienna.

"Perhaps you are the only one not a grump because you are the only one who has had a good night sleep and has not fallen out an airplane today. Further, I don't notice any bullet wounds on your face and neck."

"Ted didn't fall – he parachuted."

How did he know that? Unless Andrew was already sleeping with the enemy, Professor Ted? Either Andrew or Joan, or both, was in cahoots with the professor and when he found out who was the informant, there was going to be hell to pay.

Lioness

Sure enough, before their showers and Thai massages were completed, Andrew was in the waiting lounge sipping on some tea holding passports issued by the U.S. Government. Only Andrew and Joan had Austrian passports. Odd, his two suspects for traitor of the week had passports different from the rest of the group. Andrew claimed his friends were short on covers for the phoney passports and could only make so many U.S. passports.

It also seemed odd to Pierce to be getting "lazy man's yoga" Thai massages in Austria, but they were very nice indeed. Everyone was in a better mood, relaxed and hungry, after the comforting Thai massages.

Soon they were they were headed for the Vienna airport.

Since Paul, through his life of international travel, knew the way to the airport he took the wheel while the others crammed in the limited space of Andrew's hideous yellow car they had grown to hate as they had been packed in like stinky sardines.. Andrew sat in the passenger seat up front, while Ted, Joan, Mo, and James crowded in the back. Mo and Joan didn't mind the tight quarters a bit as she sat on his lap and stole an occasional kiss. But Pierce was crammed up front between Andrew and Paul, who kept ramming him in the knees with the stick shift, while his long legs sought refuge near Andrew's even longer legs. Andrew proudly reached back from the relative comfort of the front passenger seat as he handed out the new passports.

"Meet Joan Johnson of Austria. Yours was easy said Andrew. as he presented Joan with her new Austrian passport. "Congratulations, you are now Austrian. Just remember, Austria, not Australia. No kangaroos."

"I'm not an idiot," shot back Joan, "If you want idiot, look at Pierce, he is the one who turned us all into strangers in a strange land."

"Hey, you helped," bickered Pierce as it dawned on him that he and Joan had developed a comfortable brother-sister type relationship during the course of their illegal activities across multiple international borders.

"Pierce is now Peter St. James." Pierce was handed his new identity and flinched at Andrew's choice of names. Why were his new associates so hell bent on calling him Peter, rather than Pierce? For just a brief moment he had to wonder if, in fact he were the identical twin Peter at birth and that his drunken father did not know which twin was which. Perhaps it was Pierce that had died and the wrong twin, the living one, had worn the wrong name all his life. This was very irritating to Hanson.

"And Mo is now Simon Johnson, Joan's husband".

"I can live with that," Mo glowed at his future wife. Joan melted in his loving look.

It was really quite disgusting, Pierce observed.

"I am Andrew Ferrell Danille, which is my true name. Although my father hailed from Germany, I already had an Austrian passport because my Irish mother, may God rest her soul, had moved to Austria to be with the man she never married and raised me as an Austrian. I grabbed my passport from my room when I grabbed the car keys, so it was one less passport I had to pay my friends to make."

"Great," grumbled Pierce, "When we all get thrown in jail for passport fraud, you will be the only one to go free."

Pierce, looking at Andrew's profile close up with a large nose and beady little green eyes, could not help but think of a ferret. Great, he thought, I'm in a foreign land crammed in a tiny car with a ferret and a snake. He thought of Ted as a sneaky snake in the grass not only because of his actions, but because of the way his tongue darted to the front of his mouth when he spoke.

Andrew ignored Pierce and continued handing out the passports. "And Paul, I couldn't help myself, I got you one naming you Paul Phillip Pilot. Triple P for short!"

"Clever. Thanks," responded Paul dryly.

"James, you are still James Thunderhead because to look at you and your clothing no one would ever believe any other name!"

James nodded and grunted, his usual response to most circumstances and conversations."

"I got Ted a passport indicating he is Theodore Jude. Catchy, huh?"

"Whatever," was the response.

Ted was entirely too casual and cocky for Pierce's taste.

"Now, I had tickets purchased to Cairo in all our new names, in advance while I was at the 'passport office', so we should be able to float right through customs. I'm depending on Peter, here, to pay off my credit cards when we get to South Dakota, cuz getting us all coach tickets maxed out my credit line."

It was Hanson's turn to respond with a grunt.

"You sure speak great American vernacular for an Austrian," Joan, the language expert looked suspiciously at Andrew.

"Chalk it up to four years of undergraduate and three years of graduate school at good old Stanford."

"Stanford, eh? So that is why I don't like you!"

"Joan!" Mo scolded her bad manners. Mo was inherently polite to everyone.

Andrew had an answer to everything. Further, he had handled the passports and tickets just a little too smoothly. Andrew and Ted seemed to know everything the other one knew, and Joan was pretty convinced Ted did not listen outside Andrew's door back at the castle as she had entered later and no man had been lurking. Besides, she thought she'd glimpsed a parachute in her peripheral vision just as they were leaving Rosenburg for the Altenburg Monastery. No, Ted had to be getting his information some other way, and Joan's money was on Andrew being the traitor.

Pierce had narrowed it down to either Andrew or Joan as Ted's little informant, but he, too, knew one of the group had filled Ted in.

Joan did not trust Andrew as far as she could throw him.

IN FLIGHT

Mo slept with his head against the window of the big 747 as they finally headed across the Mediterranean toward Egypt. Joan, next to him, was too nervous to sleep so after she and Pierce, in the seat next to her charted the number of international felonies they had committed in just three short days: passport forgery, assault, grand theft, trespassing, illegal possession of firearms, to name just a few.

How many countries were they wanted in? Probably Ireland, Turkey, Italy, and Austria. Interpol was probably tracking them right now. Hopefully they were not sought after, as of yet anyway, in Egypt or the United States.

After they tired of analyzing how long they might be in jail, they put their minds to work on more useful issues.

Paul, two rows in front of them, was keeping their glass treasures in his briefcase on his lap. James was sleeping with one eye open to guard Pierce as he was always on the job. Andrew was off flirting with the flight attendants. The Professor, directly behind them, kept calling them idiots because the rest of them could not quite figure out what was going on yet.

Pierce pulled his copy of the Scroll's translation and his mother's note and flags out of his pocket.

Joan and Pierce scoured and analyzed endlessly together as the huge jet engines roared. Seeking meaning, or at least guidance, at last they obtained the latter…

They had already acknowledged that the flags were in the exact order that the glass pieces each came into Pierce's life. That meant Pierce was meant to be the bearer, the finder, of the Scroll the Professor had stolen from him. They could only conclude the scroll then referenced him when it said "He Who Finds this is Hereby Called."

The two figured they had pretty much figured out the bottom of the Scroll "Let the Triangle lead you to the moons and stars. Triangles, moons, and stars tended to guide them to all the Eggs. If Pierce were indeed Peter in the translation, that meant he was doing as he was destined in bringing the pieces that would lead to enlightenment together.

"Maybe it means glass pieces that reflect light, rather than enlightenment?" Pierce asked Joan. Joan shook her head in the negative, sure that her Aramaic was accurate when she translated the word enlightenment.

The two also concluded that Pierce somehow picked up a new "friend" or "protector of the Egg", every time he picked up a new Piece of the Egg.

"Well, now you are finally using your brains," The Professor commented dryly when the two in the seat in front of him finally saw some light.

Joan lit up, "There is a relationship between the people, the eggs, and the flags."

"Walla!" exclaimed the professor. "Now how about the relationship between the people, the Eggs, the flags, and the religion of each protector?"

"Yes!" screamed Joan. Let's make a chart. First, the flags, because those are the obvious locations of the eggs." She grabbed the paper

"Oh crap, does this mean we have to go to Australia next?"

Little did Pierce know, the answer to that question would be waiting for him right as he stepped off the plane at the Rapid City Regional Airport.

Beside each flag she wrote the name of the country – which was where each Egg had been discovered. Beside each Egg, she wrote the name of the person who discovered and "protected the Egg". Joan on a whim went to each of her fellow travelers and asked each person what religion they would call themselves. Then beside each person she wrote their religious affiliation. Joan was developing an interesting chart:

Thailand	Anne	Buddhist
Mexico	Bart	New Age Aquarian
Tahiti	Thomas	Agnostic
USA	Paul	Latter Day Saint Mormon
USA	James	Native American
Ireland	Pierce	Catholic
Turkey	Joan	Generic Christian
Turkey	Mo	Islam
Italy	Ted	Illuminati
Austria	Andrew	Christian Scientist

"I don't get it," whined Joan to the professor. "This group has very little in common. Most found their Eggs in different places. And none of us are really the same religion."

The Professor snorted at his understudy. "Look again. Do not look for what separates a man from his brethren. Look for what they have in common. There is where you will discover love and truth."

Joan and Pierce studied the chart and could draw no conclusions. They looked out the window, mentally exhausted.

They had passed the historic wonder of ancient Egypt, where once the great lighthouse guided Pharaohs to their palaces, Alexandria, and were headed rapidly toward the Cairo runways.

As they saw the lights of the great city of Cairo Joan announced that as soon as the Faberge Egg was located she and Mo were going to go back to Turkey to get married and live happily every after.

"What, why?" Pierce was shocked and realized how accustomed he'd become to thinking out loud with her.

"Because in America I have no future and in Turkey I have no past," came her simple reply.

SOLVING PUZZLES

"Let's start with your religion, then," Pierce demanded of Ted who kept insisting religion was relevant to the entire fiasco, "What are the basic principals the Illuminati adhere to? All we know is anyone who reads Dan Brown novels - and who doesn't read Brown these days – his novels are great - thinks Illuminati are pretty bad dudes."

Joan agreed wholeheartedly, "Yes, aren't you a bunch of fascists wanting to take over the planet and destroy large portions of the human race? And further, why didn't you give a hint of this when we worked on so many projects over so many years?"

"I didn't know you were one of the twelve until just a couple days ago."

"One of what twelve?"

"Figure it out."

"That is what I'm trying to do here."

Pierce interrupted. He wanted to know what this man whom he simply did not trust was up to. But the fact that Joan seemed ignorant of the true nature of her boss made him start to trust Joan a little more.

"Come on, tell us why any Harvard Professor would be a secret Illuminati."

Ted leaped in enthusiastically as if he had been waiting to explain himself to them. "As you know, from reading Brown, the all seeing eye on the back of the U.S. One Dollar Bill is an Illuminati symbol. The eye is above a pyramid. These are ancient clues that our forefathers put before us to guide us to the Eggs and warn us when then end of America was facing her people.

"Through meditation and deep thoguth, we Illuminati have become the enlightened ones. We have had a close relations with the Masons over the centuries. Now I know we have a reputation of wanting one world government. But what is wrong with that? That would eliminate wars. You like the sound of the United Nations, right? So why do you judge negatively the fact that some among us want one world government. With technology and air travel, the world has become small indeed and it is time."

"Aren't you the enemy of the church?"

"Come. Come. I have solicited the help of the Vatican itself in locating these Eggs. Of course, I never let on that I was Illuminati. I even had Joan infiltrate the Vatican for an entire year under the disguise of a nun who unfortunately died, but looked a good deal like Joan."

"Did you kill Sister Julie?" Joan teared up.

"Now, now. Sister Julie died of a heart attack. You know that. And you never hesitated to pretend to be her and infiltrate the Vatican."

"But that was when I thought my research was going to good purposes, to serve Christianity. To learn of the ancient times and beliefs. I didn't know I was serving the devil when you sent met there."

Lioness

"Now, really, must you be so judgmental. Illuminati are not evil. We are enlightened and we want to bring our enlightenment to the world. Really now. Monarchies? Aren't those way outdated in modern times. And let's face it. What about the modern church? No women priests? Surely you bristle at that Joan, being the modern woman you are?"

Joan argued, "You seek to destroy the both the church and the monarchs of Europe."

"No. We seek to bring all the world into modern, realistic times. We seek to unite the world."

"But don't you control all the money in the world already?"

"One language. One currency. Or better, a cashless monetary system. One government. What is wrong with that?"

"Who would be the one and all powerful leader of this one world, is what is wrong with that. Where are the options? Free will? What if an evil man became the leader? Where would be the checks and balances? Where is privacy in a cashless system?" Pierce nervously protested.

As he spoke, Ted's tongue darted excitedly in and out of his mouth as if thirsty. With his beady little dark eyes and dry, almost scaly skin, he reminded the Movie Star even more oof a snake than he had earlier.

"What you call checks and balances, I call wars and dissension."

"What you call dissension, I call expression of free will." Pierce shot back.

"What you call free will, I call a fantasy. The people don't want to work as hard as free will demands of them.

They want their basic needs fulfilled for them by a great and benevolent government. Free health care, food, clothing, shelter. What government shouldn't give that to its people."

"In exchange for what? And exactly who will build these free farms, hospitals, and homes? If not free men who learn and grow through struggle, then it would be slaves. Are you suggesting that in exchange for one great caregiver, they would sell their souls and become slaves?"

"That system built the pyramids we are about to see, didn't it?"

"Oh look," screamed Joan excitedly as if on cue pointing out the window and they descended, "the great pyramid of Giza!"

What excited Joan at that moment, filled Pierce with painful trepidation.

LIVING KINGS

"Figure out your Scroll and I'll return it to you," Ted urged Joan and Pierce as the plane circled round and round awaiting landing instructions in Cairo.

Pierce placed Joan's translation of this scroll on the tray tables before them.

"Ok, let's hypothecate," Joan began. "The Second Coming will begin at the end. That seems obvious. Jesus will reveal himself at the end of the world as we know it."

"Excellent," proclaimed her boss.

"OK. So are we at the end. This is when there are five living kings before and one after. That does not make sense."

"Maybe it does!" It was Hanson's time to get excited. "There could only be one time in history where there are living kings coming before and after. Think of it, kings come to power only after their predecessor dies. The only land with King after King would be America. She has President after President. And for the first time in History, there were five living Presidents during Bush and

Clinton reigns. And there has been one president since that time!"

"Ok. So it is the time for the Savior to be identified!" Joan interjected. "And Pierce, what if you are actually Peter and it was Pierce that died as an infant!?!?"

"How could I recognize and identify The Savior?"

"Maybe your Godfrey connections?" Joan thought out loud?

"Bringing pieces together could lead to your enlightenment," Ted hinted.

"We know how moons and stars have been guiding us…" Pierce had his doubts. Yet the pieces of the puzzle were sort of starting to gel in his brain.

"When right is left and left is right;

Then night will be day and day will be night; And truth will be revealed to all who are bright," teased Ted.

Pierce wanted to turn around and bitch slap the man.

CAIRO

The rag tag group checked in to the Meridian hotel on cash Pierce's procured back in Vienna from Black Diamond American Express, which somehow had stayed on his body throughout the grand adventures alongside his mother's final notes to him.

They each had their own room and took advantage of the expensive swimsuit shop near the lobby and went for a swim. As they swam round and round the circular pool, they could not help but gaze at the dark form of the three magnificent pyramids raising up before them as if it only natural that a city be outlined by such mystery. It caused them awe to be in a swimming pool and gazing up at the three pyramids just outside the city as they swam such a nice pool.

They exhaustedly themselves, then eventually fell into their beds, knowing that tomorrow would be another one of those unpredictable and out of control days they had all learned to deal with that week.

The next day did not disappoint that expectation. After a divine brunch on the second floor restaurant of the hotel, they set out for the only logical place.

They knew they were to be in Egypt because of mum's flags. Logic and the Illuminati Professor both convinced the group that what they were looking for would be at the Pyramids. Surely the Sphinx was guarding their secrets? Their eleventh slice of Egg?

It was just awful to see all the garbage along the Nile as they took a cab toward the pyramids. Poverty. Filth. Traffic. When compared with Istanbul, the third largest city in the world, or Venice floating with its cute shops, or the organization of Vienna around its circular center, Cairo was a tad chaotic, albeit exciting and dangerous could also describe the aura of Cairo.

One could see the glory of the great Nile that fertilized and fed magnificent Egypt all the way from Alexandria, south to Lake Nassar and beyond. What gifts, what secrets, what richness the Nile blessed the beautiful Egyptian desert with. Why would she be treated as a dumping ground in this great city?

Joan commented, "Poverty and pollution. The result of individual responsibility combined with pride being eliminated from men."

Did she see Ted cringe at her comment?

This was soon overlooked as they rounded the corner and standing proud above this great and ancient city was the Giza necropolis. It filled their vision, as if springing up directly from the mystery of the ancients themselves. It took away the breath of everyone in the crowded cab. Beautiful shadows of theses mysterious structures made of perfect isosceles triangles, fit together with precision for the purpose of – well that debate ran on for centuries.

And the Sphinx – what secrets did he guard?

Lioness

The group of five men and one woman marveled at the size of the cat body with the human face. Pierce shuddered as the Sphinx reminded him of his Lioness that he now missed beyond words. The huge creature stood guard over the largest pyramid at Cairo, the Pyramid of Khufu and they wondered what still undiscovered secrets it guarded. What history had the Sphinx watched unfold over the centuries? Did he guard the piece of the Egg the group now sought in this marvelous and magical country called Egypt? They could almost taste the history and the legends as they stood before one of the seven ancient wonders of the world.

The mathematical precision of the pyramids left Joan and Ted in profound awe. The sheer size of the huge rocks left even James shaking his head wondering how they were crated and stacked. So many treasures had been robbed from these ancient ruins. How many remained buried in the city still beneath the sands?

The group bemoaned that someone had tried to ruin the face of the great Sphinx.

Pierce, Andrew, James, and Ted eventually were allowed into the narrow passage of the Great Pyramid and it was a really cramped fit for the three larger men. Ted, at 5 foot 7 with the skinny build and look of a snake darted and squirmed in happily while the rest suffered and tried to breathe in the very limited and hot, smelly air. Body odor surrounded them in the narrow, thick stone passage with no windows. At last they made it to the King's Chamber and the now barren sarcophagus. The four searched the huge granite blocks for moons, stars, any clue as to why Pierce's mum had pasted onto their map of flags, a flag of Egypt, but found nothing.

Pierce was becoming claustrophobic, "If it was ever in here, it would have been robbed a thousand years ago by any one of a million visitors or a thousand archeologists who've come before us. Let's get out of here."

The others agreed. They all had a spooky feeling they were not welcome in this chamber in the very heart of the pyramid.

The group spent the rest of the early afternoon in and around the all the pyramids, searching anywhere for a star with eight arms that might guide them to the next part of the sacred egg.

They found absolutely nothing.

They were also being totally mobbed by Egyptians trying to sell them everything from belly dancing outfits to singing toy camels. They loaded their arms with trinkets.

On the mountains behind the pyramids, several of the group even braved riding a camel. Joan had never laughed so hard in her life as she nearly rolled over her camel's head when it stood up and when it got back down for the mounting and dismounting because in both cases her brown old beast rolled on and off its knees to accommodate the rider, as it was trained to do.

Pierce thought as a horseback rider, there would be nothing to riding camels. He, too, almost rolled when his yellow camel stood up. It snorted, spit, growled, and glared. Unlike horses who travel on opposite diagonal legs, his camel tried to rush toward the desert pacing with a strange movement where both right front and hind moved forward, then both lefts. It left the normally erect rider rolling from side to side and laughing so hard he almost fell off.

The rest of the gang took a pass on the five dollar camel rides in favor of guarding Paul and the briefcase housing all the treasured pieces of their Faberge Eggs. They might be worth a dime, they might be priceless, but all the members of the party agreed to treat them as priceless until they learned the truth about them..

The non camel riders did participate in a jolly photo sessions standing above the hill pointing a finger on top of the distant pyramids which made the great, huge pyramids look small. There were the extra fees charged by everyone for everything from photos of Pierce and Joan on the camels (the owners refused to let them off their camels until the camel masters were paid more money) to the photos of them holding down the great distant structures in the distance.

They took it all in good humor. They all had plenty of cash thanks to large cash advances on Pierce's limitless American Express Card.

Pierce was beginning to get nervous about charging on his card simply because Interpol could locate him so easily if need be for his many crimes in the European Union. Hence, he had procured an obscene amount of cash at the Vienna airport and was paying for everything in Cairo in cash from hotels, to meals, to photos. If Interpol were looking for any of them, it would be in Vienna, in the heart of Europe, not Northern Africa.

After exploring all the pyramids, even examining the little ones for the wives, looking all around the Sphinx and every studying aspect of the Giza people, sands, and more they looked one last place. There was a sort of ship like structure beside the great pyramid. People speculated everything from it was used to carry great boulders up the Nile to the building site of the pyramids to it was a spaceship such that the Egyptians could return to their ancestors in the stars. There were many who still believe original man was placed on the planet by UFOs and the space men bred either ape women or snakes to populate earth. In any case, the group bribed their way on to the amazing ship, yet found not a single clue as to why they were in Egypt.

Eventually, they wandered back down to the gift shop by the Sphinx, they were a hot, tired, dirty group. And there was no sign whatsoever of moons, eight-sided stars, or slices of bejeweled eggs.

They were about to head back to the bus and cab parking area to return to their hotel, when they looked back at the view of the Sphinx guarding the largest of the pyramids.

They all seemed to notice him at the very same time. A guard wearing a gun and white head wrap like the one Andrew had purchased back at the camel festivities sat proudly on a pure white camel. He was a man of elegance that simply took one's breath away riding high and proud in full military uniform. He stood out like a sore thumb from all the other camel jockeys. He was proudly posed on a magnificent pure white camel, and the camel shone an aura of white that almost had the effect of snow-blinding the group. The camel master sat high between the Sphinx and the Great Pyramid and looked directly at the rag tagged group from the back of one of the proudest animals they had ever seen.

And with the flair of an aristocrat he was waving them to come hither.

THE EMPTY SEARCH

The six were drawn to the glowing white camel and his rider like moths to a flame.

The rider's deep clear voice did not disappoint, "I hear you have been asking everyone about eight armed stars," he boomed in a voice of pure leadership and authority.

The parched group only nodded yes, mesmerized by the dark skinned beauty of the man and the effect of the setting sun on the magnificent glowing white camel before them.

Pierce could not help but worry they were going to jail. The others just dropped their jaws and stared in awe at the magical beauty of the sight of the handsome man on the greatest camel ever seen.

"Well you won't find anything here. Where you want to be is Memphis."

"Tennessee?" Andrew asked, his ignorance showing.

"No Memphis, former capital of Egypt. There are new explorations in some of the step pyramids in that area, and the eight armed stars you speak of have been baffling many archeologists," the man spoke in near perfect English.

"Will you take us there?" Joan blurted out, knowing this elegant man was meant to be part of their party.

"Ah, as the sunsets now that would be too dangerous. I would be happy to take you in the morning. I assume there will be a nice gratuity in it for me?"

Pierce could not help but think the Egyptians sure were not subtle about asking for money. He did not care, he wanted to find the Egg and get back to South Dakota as fast as humanly possible, "I'll give you a thousand dollars in the morning when you pick us up at the Meridian, and another thousand if we find what we seek, and a part interest in what we seek."

The proud soldier was too busy gulping. This would keep him in his apartment for years and his camel in the best of stables. He did not care what they sought, he would provide two cars, armed guards and a tour anywhere these people wanted to go.

"The Meridian at ten in the morning then," he finally managed to say, barely containing himself from jumping off his camel to do a happy dance.

The group was happy to have a divine diner buffet and swim again in the shadows of the pyramids that night, in spite of the fact they had an eerie feeling they were being watched. They knew they should talk of why they had seen scrolls, what their eggs could mean, how Pierce's mum came to put the flags in the order she did, the meaning of it all. But frankly, they did not know who watched or listened and they were so drained from the days activities they simply wanted to fall into the cozy beds and sleep like they were in a coma. It was agreed Paul and the Eggs would move into the same suite as Pierce and James because instinct said the eggs should be watched all night long. They were each going to take a four hour shift of keeping their eye on the briefcase, then they would meet in the morning with each man having had a full eight hours of sleep.

Imagine their horror, when at four in the morning, Paul went to relieve James only to find James sound asleep in front of the television with no briefcase on the coffee table where it was to stay the night.

Further the room reeked of an odor of dead flesh And scattered about the room was what looked to be mummy wraps like they had viewed throughout their Cairo adventures.

Paul let out a piercing scream which awakened James and brought Pierce running.

"Shit, shit, shit," grumbled Pierce.

"I never fall asleep on the job," James shook his head in confusion. He felt drugged.

Looking at the stinky old rags Paul asked, "What on earth is this smell?"

"Look!" Pierce pointed to something gold in among the rags.

"Oh my gosh, - it is a gold star with eight arms." proclaimed Paul. "Whoever left it has stolen the Eggs. Better call the others. Whatever it was, it must have come in through the window. The three turned toward the open window letting in the hot dry air of the dark Egyptian night. In spite of the night's heat they shuddered at the thought they had a visitor that night who may have traveled through history to leave them this clue.

INVASION IN THE NIGHT

James, the bodyguard who had failed to guard for the fist time in his career with his hero, was finally awake enough to take it all in, "Wait, don't call the others."

"But our Eggs are gone. We must call them." Paul protested.

Pierce was not quite as convinced. In all the years James had been his huge silent shadow, Pierce had never known him to make a mistake such as this. "What if one of the others was the intruder?"

"A traitor among us?" Paul sounded doubtful.

"Of course there is a traitor among us," Pierce was convinced. "Our only questions are, who is it? And how many traitors are there among us?"

"After all, who else knows we are even here?" James backed Pierce up.

"At the very least, our camel jockey does," Paul asserted, "And probably all his friends by now."

"He knows we are here, but how would he know that we might have something valuable in the briefcase?"

"Maybe by the way you cling to it all the time?"

Lioness

"Maybe, but, my guess still would be a traitor in our midst."

Paul sank to the couch across from where James had fallen asleep on duty. James had slept in the easy chair across from the television. His face in his hands, he moaned over the loss of his briefcase full of sacred treasures they had come so far to collect.

James moaned over the terrible stomach ache he was enduring.

James was also very oddly groggy.

Pierce was pacing nervously. Then it caught Pierce's eye. James had spilled the milk he was drinking last night right beside his left arm. The milk had eaten a hole in the carpet!

"James, what is the last thing you remember last night?"

"Sitting here watching the news and wondering if I could ever learn Egyptian. I had gone to the bathroom and returned to this seat where I had a couple of cookies and some milk….wait a minute, as I took a sip of milk, I smelled something foul, felt a pain in my gut and the next thing I knew Paul was yelling."

"I think someone tried to poison you. Look." Pierce pointed at the carpet. "Something was in that milk that ate a hole in the carpet."

"No wonder I feel so groggy. I simply would not fall asleep on the job," James was relieved to know he had not slipped up, but rather foul play had made him let his guard down.

Pierce was thinking out loud, "We need to tell the others, and watch their reaction to see who the guilty party is. Then we'll search his or her room and I'll be we will find the briefcase."

"Not necessary," the big Native American smiled smugly, "Now I remember. Before I went to the bathroom, as soon as I went on duty, I slipped them under the cushion of my chair. Unless our culprit was strong as an Ox and could lift me, I suspect our eggs are right where I left them when I went to the restroom."

The big brown proud man, stood up wobbly from the effects of his poison encounter and lifted the cushion. There was the briefcase, he had roosted on it like an immovable hen all through the night. Good man, thought Pierce. When Paul opened it and saw that all seven eggs were safe and sound he danced a happy dance. It was hilarious to see the little round Mormon man who looked like a Koala shaking it madly. James the Bear and Pierce the elegant Cheetah joined right in.

James doing a Native American pow-wow looking rain dance, Paul doing a Koala jig, and Pierce, waltzing with himself, they looked like three lunatics. Lack of sleep will do that to a person.

They danced round and round laughing until they fell on the couch exhausted.

"Now we must form a plan." Pierce said.

"Maybe not. Let's flush the stinky mummy rags down the toilet and keep the star in the pocket of my briefcase and not say a thing," Paul said. "Let's act like absolutely nothing happened last night and just see who acts suspicious or accidentally says anything – about poison, about milk, about mummies, about open windows, about golden stars, about the missing briefcase – anything that might be said that will point out who the perpetrator of this murder attempt might be."

"Ah, you may be right. Pretend like nothing happened last night and see if any of our fellow travelers spills the beans," James nodded in agreement

At least these were two good men that Pierce could trust with his life – or so he thought.

THE BOOK OF MATHEW

MEMPHIS

Before they knew it, there was a knock at the door and Mo, Joan, Andrew, and Ted were inviting the other three to the same great brunch they had enjoyed the morning before. Scrambled eggs, meat, cheese and even layered Greek baklava desert prepared the group for the adventure ahead.

Over breakfast the group talked of how much information they should share with their new camel friend. They agreed to tell the story basically as it happened, but to totally leave out the part about the Eggs. Just in case the Eggs had value, there was no need to tempt anyone to steal the Eggs. They were going to simply say they were looking for eight armed stars as an ancient symbol of Jesus, in hopes of finding ancient scroll. So they had their agreement just in time.

The proud man on the camel, and two associates, now dressed in suits, yet obviously packing heat on their shoulder straps under their suits, joined the men and Joan just in time for desert.

The man who sat so regally on the camel the previous night introduced himself as Mathew, originally from

India, out of American missionaries who had converted to Hindu on their mission. Mathew's parents had stayed in India for two decades. Rather than convincing any Hindus to convert to Christianity, his parents had become Hindu and eventually exiled themselves to and thrived living in Egypt. Matt had been there since he was ten years old and had few memories of Indea. He was a Hindu, as were both his friends, although he had been in India for all the parts of his life and his friends had never left their native Egypt!

They took two cars south and were impressed that they were riding in Mercedes. Mathew's obvious rank in his guard position was obvious both from this camel and his car. The two cars were obviously official cars and traffic parted way for them all the way south to Memphis.

Paul, James, and Pierce carried the briefcase in the car with Mathew and told them their story, while Mathew drove and talked of his own history. The four suspected traitors: Joan, Mo, Ted, and Andrew were in the Mercedes directly behind with Guy and Samuel, Mathew's two friends. They were native to Egypt, but converted to Hindu and that is where Mathew met them as teenagers.

They all went to the academy together and were guards, fully entrusted by the Egyptian government to carry guns and to protect pyramids. The group was as familiar with pyramids from Memphis to Cairo as any but archeologists and other scientists who made a life out of studying and excavating. If anyone could help them solve the riddle it would be these proud, handsome men.

After telling Mathew as much as they were comfortable telling him, about flags, notes, papyrus, scrolls, moons and eight armed stars and how they came to be a group, so that he could be as useful to them as possible, they sat back and enjoyed the lovely sites along the drive that essentially paralleled the Nile. They were surprised at the varying sizes of pyramids they would sometimes spot in the distance.

Mathew told of his growing up and of his Hindu beliefs….

THE STEP PYRAMIDS

As they drove toward Memphis, Pierce questioned Mathew about some pyramids he viewed outside his right hand window. Mathew said those were step pyramids that had only recently been the victims of digs and might be worth visiting on the way back from Memphis.

The group had a great time playing tourist in Memphis as they learned more of the ancient former capital, admired the Alabaster Sphinx, stood in awe of the sheer size of the Colossus of Ramses, heard more of Egypt's fascinating history – especially regarding ancient scrolls that had been dug up along the Nile. Still nothing, though that would tell any one of them why they might be in this marvelous land.

After a lunch break in the lovely and relaxing gardens at Memphis, they decided to head back empty handed to their familiar hotel in Cairo. Disappointed, they agreed they could finally all fly home to the United States in the morning. A dejected Ted, gave Pierce his scroll over lunch! Ted assured Pierce it was in perfect shape and that he had made he had many copies of the papyrus-like scroll, but that this was Pierce's original.

The group examined the papyrus and marveled. They broke out in goosebumps in spite of the hundred degree desert heat. They wondered if it was the same material as the recently discovered scrolls that purported to be additional books of the New Testament that were recently discovered by a farmer along the Nile.

Eventually, the tired group got back in the patrol cars to head to the hotel by way of the Cairo museum that housed so many King Tut artifacts.

As they traveled north toward the great city, Pierce followed his whim and told Mathew to radio their friends in the other car and tell them they would meet them at the busy Cairo museum in a couple hours. Joan radioed back that would be fine as she was dying to examine the Rosetta Stone in the museum. Mathew told them and to go on ahead. Then Pierce had Mathew turn over to those new digs that had been mentioned on the way down to Memphis.

There was one great step pyramid – step being in layers rather than directly up to the point of the adjoining triangles. James, Matt, Paul and Pierce wandered around and stared in wonderment at the parts of an ancient city coming to life before their eyes. They were able to wander from room to room in these relatively new digs surrounding the Step pyramid, as well as explore several different tunnels into the pyramid and around the ancient town that had been buried under silt and sand for centuries.

They view several mummies in several different small dark chambers. In one room they came across mummies of two dogs that looked like small greyhounds on either side of their master, now a human mummy.

"Look," cried Paul as he pointed to a mummy with part of its cloth missing atop a sarcophagus right beside another unraveling mummy on top of a sarcophagi's decorated all over with eight armed stars.

The stench was the very same smell in their hotel suite the night before.

"Mathew, we must examine this mummy."

"I can not let you touch an Egyptian heirloom! I would be fired and perhaps jailed."

"Please. You must. That mummy is protecting something that belongs to us. Something that perhaps belongs to you. I'll bet it does. My instinct tells me you were the one who owns the treasure we came to Egypt to find."

"What treasure do you speak of?" Mathew shook his head wearily, nervously.

"Show him Paul," demanded Pierce.

When Paul opened the briefcase and showed him the seven eggs irradiating a light of their own and looking like a treasure greater than any pirate might ever dream of, Mathew jumped back covering his eyes. Slowly, separating his forth and fifth fingers, he peaked through the narrow opening at the light filling the previously dark room to a brightness that shown of a night on the Vegas Strip. Then he slowly approached. After what felt like hours, he spoke, "You think there is a treasure such as these for me? Hidden by this mummy?"

Pierce and Paul nodded. James had taken a powerful stance by the small doorway of the small room they had crawled through earlier. James would not allw a tourist or scientist to enter until the matter was resolved.

In one sudden, swift movement, Mathew was atop the mummy that was atop the star decorated sarcophagus slicing wildly with a knife he had worn strapped to his legs under his pants. He hacked away the filthy, ancient bandages in a clean stoke from neck to groin. Matt was now a wild-eyed maniac looking for gems he had been assured were his heirloom. He had forgotten his official rank as he yanked apart to mummy's rags from neck to groin. On the left side of the mummy, directly above the heart, he saw the light. In only a moment he had freed another Faberge Egg, identical to the ones in the briefcase.

James heard voices approaching, "Run!" he yelled to his fellow grave robbers and the four men departed the step pyramid like bats out of hell.

On the way back to the museum they decided not to tell the others of the find. But to say Mathew wanted to return with them to the United States to try to look up his relatives he had never met. He had four cousins in Kansas and he thought he should tell them that his parents had died, but that he remained alive.

The others bought the story without question. They remained saddened that there were no clues in the museum, but all had agreed the group would stay together until all parts of the Egg were together.

The next morning they headed, in accordance with their agreement, back to South Dakota. Four men secretly elated. Three men and a woman who had been kept in the dark and felt they had failed in their mission, feeling totally depressed and defeated.

A stressed out Ted said they had to research the papyrus found by the farmer along the Nile, then return to interview him and search all the secrets of the Nile until they found what they were looking for. Then as soon as the Nile gave up her treasure, the group must go on to Australia, in accordance with Pierce's mum's map.

The four with a secret said nothing and slept most of the way home.

THE BOOK OF MARGARET

AUSTRALIA

Sister Margaret Mary Meade, or 3 M as she had been affectionately named by her loving Kindergarten students is St. Martin's academy north of Brisbane Australia, had four separate claims to fame

Sister Meade was pure Aborigine. Generation after generation of these Australian Outbackers formed union after union amongst the heated desert lands known for poisonous spiders, snakes, and an occasional Roo. They were not privileged to cuddle Koalas or ride Camels. Sister Meade's family tree was lined with skilled boomerang hunters and survivors of all type. Until one day, in the early 1900s the missionaries discovered them. The Meade family went from scantily clad desert survivors to bible thumping servants of the Lord and his Catholic Church with all the standard passions of the newly converted.

Sister Margaret's second claim to fame was that she topped the scale at over 400 pounds. She loved to eat. She had no desire to exercise. Chocolate bars were not safe within ten miles of her. Her darling little Catholic girls loved Sister Mary's soft layers of fat surrounding them with lovely hugs and they could get lost in her long flowing black robe.   No modern nun attire for Sister Mary. No, siree, she adored her own shaved head and the fact that her large body felt so comfortable in her loosely flowing gown.

The third thing people noticed about Sister 3M was the cross around her neck.   True, it was a large and plain wooden cross that would have caught not a second glimpse from anyone, but for one thing.   Against the wishes of all who trained her, 3M insisted on wearing a crucifix of another style on the same chain with her cross. Handed down carefully and worn around the necks of generation after generation of Aborigine men, this instrument had been used to start fires, skin snakes, protect from demons. And it was easy to find the Meade Aborigines from miles away – for the necklace reflected an amazing array of lights from the jewels and always seemed to give off a laser like turquoise shine.   Many people caught staring at Sister Meade's chest were found wondering what that necklace would be worth if those were real gems. Surely they were not, were they? 3M never had it appraised. She did not care its earthly value. She knew its heavenly value. She knew the great white spirit had handed it to her great, great, many great grandfather thousands of years back and the family had protected it with their very lives through this very day.   It had saved their lives and they had saved this magical glass for generations.

In fact, her brother died when a thief tried to steal it right off his neck. Which was how 3M came to be the first woman in the family to ever wear it. She was the only one left in the Meade clan when her brother was laid to rest, so the ten year old orphan, pulled it off the corpse's neck and promised to wear it to her own grave – or until

Lioness

God removed it from her neck. She was the first woman to ever have the sacred boomerang of glass and gems around her neck. In the orphanage she grew closer and closer to God and could be heard talking aloud to him if you listened at her bedroom door. Oddly, some swore they could hear God talking back to her.

Now the first three notables about Sister 3M were blatantly obvious. But only the children of the orphanage knew Sister Meade's dirty little fourth secret.

SISTER MEADE'S FINAL SECRET

Sister Margaret Mary Meade's dirty little secret was that she loved a man! She loved him to a distraction. She loved the way he looked. The way he sounded. The way he danced. The way he thought.

She loved him with all her heart and was about to leave the orphanage itself for this man. She had tickets to America. She would join him and follow him to the ends of the earth.

For years upon years, her girls loved 3M and found her secret simply delicious, for after all, it is the forbidden fruit that tastes the sweetest. And for 3M to love a man was indeed forbidden. But to love this particular man was beyond all reason.

Yet, the girls at the orphanage encouraged it. Developed it. Learned from it. Love, oh pure forbidden love, from a distance. Passion. Humor. Determination to touch her love. The girls lusted vicariously right by their favorite Sister's ever loving, huge side.

They brought her magazine articles about him.

They tucked tabloids with him on the cover in with candy bars and carried them to 3M.

They rented all his movies on video and long after the evening prayers sat in a circle around Sister Margaret, enjoying popcorn and spy movies that were far too spicy for young Catholic hearts.

They formed their own fan club and wrote to him weekly.

Yes, the group of virgins, led by Sister Margaret, loved every breath that Pierce Hanson ever took and every word he said, whether accurately reported or not.

And tomorrow, Sister 3M was flying to Rapid City, South Dakota and she was going to meet the love of her life, if it was the last thing she did on this planet. It had come over the wires he was flying there to meet his girlfriend from some sort of adventure in Europe and according to her calculations, since he would have a layover of 5 hours in Amsterdam, she could arrive in the small airport a good two hours before he did and she would confront him with her full confession of love.

Yes, Sister Meade was crazy as a loon. But then, are not all the greatest people on earth crazy as loons?

DISSAPPOINTMENT AT THE RAPID CITY AIRPORT

The twenty nine hour flight, including layovers, from Cairo ended up taking thirty eight hours. First they missed the flight on SAS airlines from Cairo to Amsterdam because the extra suitcase full of souvenirs put them overweight. They had to get out of the check-in line, go to a special room where they were explained weights, pay an overweight luggage blackmail fee and by the time they presented it to their check in friend again, they had missed the plane.

They felt as if they were treated like criminals just for having too much luggage.

"This is why I fly first class or in my own jets," Pierce snarled.

The delay caused them another seven hours in Amsterdam, waiting for a plane to Chicago. In Chicago they all breezed through customs except Joan. Now, the entire group of unshaven men with obviously phony passports traveling on one way tickets who looked like a group of terrorists passed right through.

Joan, a scrawny harmless looking professor from Harvard was pulled aside, interrogated for hours, luggage searched, and more humiliations that she would ever tell Mo for fear he would have a heart attack. The only saving grace in the Chicago fiasco was no one had asked anything about Paul's briefcase. How it flew right through customs they would never know and were too afraid to ask. Were they diamond and artifact smugglers along with all their other crimes? The press knew they were on their way home from criminal participation in Europe and it was all over every gossip rag from here to Australia, so why didn't the customs agents stop them?

Yet, even more amazing was that Ted with the knife strapped under his pants, and Matt with the gun under his suit, cleared security at every stop.

Only Joan drew suspicion, and only Joan was without sin among them! Made Pierce vow to never fly commercial again!

By the time they finally landed in the small Rapid city Airport, they were catching colds and downright exhausted.

Pierce walked up the narrow exit hoping the balloons were something from Lioness. They were teenage girls awaiting the arrival of a girlfriend. In fact, his red, tired, blurry eyes sought any sign at all that she had missed him and was there to greet him. Heck, he was lowering his standards so fast, he just wanted a sign she knew he even existed. He was so disappointed, he felt kicked in the chest. He thought of nothing but her from the moment he came off Harney Peak and headed for Dublin. Had she even given him a single thought while he fled from death time and again? He had missed her every moment so bad it hurt. Had she even noticed he was gone? Was it time to rethink their entire relationship? Was it time to stop loving her?

He signed autographs for his fans who obviously tracked his every move and cared more than his woman and took the escalator down a floor to dejectedly to pick up his luggage. In Chicago he had called ahead for his long stretch limo to pick them up. After their luggage was loaded and the dirty group of tired travelers hoisted into the back, he directed his driver to take them all to the Godfrey compound near Keystone.

"Don't you think we should clean up in a hotel, first?" Joan protested.

"No. We have issues with Lioness. She knows more than she has told us about these Eggs," he patted the briefcase still on Paul's lap. "She has some serious explaining to do – about a lot of things."

"You are just so anxious to see your girlfriend, you want us to be tortured and cramped up for still another hour?" Andrew snarled, just as miserable as the rest of them.

"The Godfrey's have a pool and plenty of private rooms for everyone. You'll bet resting and showering in far better conditions than any hotel in town."

"But the last time anyone was a guest of a Godfrey, the entire yacht was blown out of the water, or have you already forgotten that? It was only about a week ago!" Paul reminded. Was it less than a week, he wondered? It felt like a lifetime ago.

The group was so busy arguing among themselves, they did not even notice the creature in black that had followed them out of the airport and drove an inconspicuous rental car a short distance behind them all the way to the Godfrey estate.

THE TERROR OF SEXUAL BETRAYAL

Pierce felt his head explode as he burst into Lioness' living room from his travels totally unannounced and uninvited. Before his weary eyes, his greatest terror was unfolding. The terror of sexual betrayal of one you love. It has driven many a lesser person to madness, to murder, to building walls around there heart that could never again let another in. Pierce felt all those things as he beheld the sight in Lion's Great Room of her mansion.

His Lion had her head back in Barth's hands and he was giving her a wet, sensual massage. Thomas was knelt down at her feet, running his hand up her long golden thighs to the golden triangle even he had never been allowed to explore.

No wonder she had not missed him, she had taken on two young lovers while he was away, risking his very life.

Pierce grabbed a poker from the fireplace and charged before any of the three sluts had even noticed he was there, "On guard you bastards!" he yelled as he leaped toward his enemies."

GATHERING OF STRANGERS

In one swift, shockingly strong motion Lioness whirled to face him and grabbed the poker out of Pierce's strong hand, tossed it to the ground. She threw her arms around his neck and started passionately kissing him.

Bart and Thomas were on the ground laughing hysterically with tears coming out of their eyes as they roared outrageously at what they had just seen.

A filthy movie star covered with scars and bandages challenging them with a fireplace poker for, of all people, the love of his lady.

Apparently he did not know how much she loved him or how she spoke of no man except him or how she glowed at the very mention of his name. They found it so amusing that lovers could live in such blindness.

Pierce pulled away from the kiss he had so longed for and prepared to fight Bart and Tom, the two rolling balls of hysterical laughter, to the death.

"So the tabloids were right, you scumbags, you are having an affair with my woman. And you, Miss Lion, what kind of whore are you to be having affairs with two men at a time, both half your age?"

Now Lioness was laughing, too, and could not help teasing the love of her life. "That is why I have two. If you add their ages together, they are the right age for a good juicy affair."

She had a lifelong reputation of being a merciless in her constant teasing.

Seeing hate in Hanson's eyes, she sobered herself enough to explain, "Oh my silly and precious Love, they are not MY lovers. They are GAY lovers of one another."

"Then why were they all over you when I walked in unannounced?"

"Well, let's see, Bart was washing my hair for tonight's debate and Thomas was taking in my skirt for the debate because I've lost so much weight while your were away. I have not eaten for days for the missing of you."

Tom piped in, "Had you not returned today, Lioness might have starved herself to death."

Bart finally quit laughing and stood up. After all, he had to finish her hair. "She has been working herself to death at the same time she has been in constant worry over your travels. Do you know the last news shot we saw of you was a bunch of monks chasing you down the streets of Venice? Bad boy! Lion kept leaping into your brain to see what you were viewing, so she saw you all over Austria and Egypt, yet she had to keep coming back to her own brain to bark out orders and prepare. You know the election is upon us and your absence is really causing her to blow it. She said you were on an important mission, but I said you should wait until after the election."

"After the election would be too late," Lion purred at her dirty and bloody boyfriend.

"How about you explain to me and all my friends what you know and we'll tell you what we've been doing and learning. And then let's never part again."

"Bring your friends in. Make the introductions and make them comfortable."

After everyone came in and introductions were made, Tom showed them all to rooms and asked the maid, Marion, to feed and care for them. Tom and Bart had to finish getting Lioness ready for the debate at the Rapid City Civic Center, so they all promised to spend the next day together discussing the mystery of the Eggs. Lioness had promised that it would all make sense in then morning.

After she left for the debate, though, the figure in black that had followed the group from the airport let itself into the house through the unlocked back door without a single exhausted person noticing.

EXCERPTS FROM THE FINAL DEBATE

LIONESS: Let's see, some creepy assed greaseball mental moron fascist pig bureaucrats who work for the government because they are too incompetent to hold a real job or run their own business, interferes with my businesses daily in attempts to ruin me through taxes and regulations. Hmm. Do I want them, the same body police interfering with my reproductive system?!?! I DON'T THINK SO, BATMAN."

RICHARD: "TAKING AWAY RIGHTS IS NEVER THE ANSWER. How dare one take away from Man what God Hath given Man?"

LIONESS: "The solution to poverty and overpopulation is easy. We currently use welfare to pay poor women to reproduce without discrimination. The more kids she pops out, the more money and other freebies we throw at her (free medical, free legal, free housing, free drugs). I know a gal with 5 different children from 5 different men getting over $100,000 of MY TAX DOLLARS per year (and she certainly is not spending the money on her children or on birth control!). Quit giving people financial incentive to reproduce like rabbits and they will think twice about it. PLUS, for every ONE person that really NEEDS (I would never deny the TRUE NEEDY) welfare and unemployment, TEN are ripping off the system because they are simply lazy and insipid. Anyone who wants welfare or unemployment should be put to public works as volunteers: at our schools, fixing our highways, picking up litter, etc. Let's give people pride in work. Let's give them a hand up not a hand out."

RICHARD: "Might I remind you there is nothing in our Constitution that says we can interfere with a person's body. In fact our reproductive choice is sacred and protected under all three: LIFE, LIBERTY, AND PROPERTY. However, there is likewise NOTHING in our Constitution that says people are entitled to welfare and unemployment."

DAVID: "Again, you propose to take food from the mouth of welfare moms, as if that will help anyone. I will end starvation, not create more of it. I will add to entitlement programs. I will increase taxes on the rich to pay for it. The rich have plenty of money. They can afford to pay way more Social Security taxes and take way less out."

RICHARD: "The trickle down effect of that will be to tax the middle class until there is no more middle class. The rich have lawyers that will find the loopholes. Or they will simply shut down their businesses and retire to a warm beach somewhere. David's plan will cause massive unemployment and elimination of small businesses. There will be no one left to pay for all his social do-gooder programs."

LIONESS: "The problem I defined was OUR GENERATION spending our country into bankruptcy. Further, while I'm giving Constitutional Law lectures, please study Article 9, Section 4 of the US Constitution under "POWERS FORBIDDEN TO CONGRESS".

Apparently Congress has never read how many powers are forbidden it. I repeat. Our Constitution is a limitation on power. In fact, this country was founded on the very ideal of limiting a government's power to tax. The Income Tax was always Unconstitutional. It was only On Feb. 3, 1913 that the government defrauded the masses into accepting the 16th Amendment for a 'TEMPORARY TAX THAT WOULD NEVER EXCEED 10% OF A PERSON'S INCOME FOR THE LIMITED PURPOSE OF FINANCING THE WORLD WAR. The Constitution was designed to extremely limit a grant of power to form a very limited government. It was a FAR GREATER LIMITATION OF POWER on said government than it was a grant of power. On one tiny page called the Bill of Rights, you will find the greatest limitation of power that pen ever put to paper. You should not surrender those rights so easily. You have surrendered virtually all of those rights to your many layers of government. Why? What have you received in return?"

DAVID: "They have received streets, highways, education, medical care, protection from terrorists, police protection, jails and retirement benefits for starters."

RICHARD, "The terrorists shot their wad a long time ago. Our population is way over-jailed,. Most people can not live on public retirement benefits and they never saved for retirement expecting that Big Brother would take care of them. You could take care of streets, education, and public safety on less than one hundredth of the money currently being wasted by our many layers of government."

LIONESS: "If the bureaucrats can crawl inside your reproductive track what is to stop them from crawling inside your brain for a lobotomy (oh, ooops, they already give chemical lobotomies to our children under the pretext of a fake disease -ADA/ADHA); or crawling inside your business (oops they already do that under the guise of tax audits, OSHA, and more). YOU, the American Public, should be irate when the government takes a single right. Instead, you sit back in fear pissing your pants, giving away our rights, saying "oh, protect me, protect me" to greedy corrupt elected officials who only possess half our I.Q. and none of our morals! The only thing they protect, is their ownre-election. If you were smart, you would never vote in an incumbent."

DAVID: "Since I've earned my meager amount of wealth the right way, the honest way, through hard physical labor - just ask my calloused hands, frostbitten toes, my scarred ankles, I have a real hard time respecting unearned wealth. But I have no problem with helping the needy and curing the sick."

LIONESS: "If one wants the government to rob from those of us who work and give to those of them that do not, then that is socialism. That is what David proposes to you tonight. Unemployment, welfare, minimum wage, all of that is socialism. Where the government giveth, they expect money, blood, and votes in return. That is socialism. While the government freely giveth my money away to druggies, lazy slobs, huge

Farms, and women who don't practice birth control, they also expect to rob me of my produce and interfere with my productivity. That is socialism. Soon we Worker Bees will crumble and quit under the pressure of taxation and regulation. Then who will pay for all that is good in the world - from roads to schools to feeding, educating, caring for, uplifting and clothing the truly needy?"

DAVID: "Lioness is right there. Hard, honest work is good for the soul. It is true what the Prophet Gibran said, "Work is love made visible." Hard work grows the soul. I'm not saying painful work. I'm saying joyous work. Where you follow your own passion with such happy enthusiasm, free from government interference, is where you find your destiny. Your happiness, purpose and personal growth directly result from whatever work you perform and can say at days end that you wonder where the time went!"

LIONESS: "It is odd, that I must continue to defend my earnings. What I do, along with all other entrepreneurs, is provide jobs for others who would want the same/better opportunities. I create opportunities with absolutely no ceiling as to what one can earn if they are willing to work and think only half as hard as I did. I've created opportunities for others. Our elected officials only create opportunities for themselves. What I do is called Capitalism. What David proposes is Socialism. Viva Capitalism!

RICHARD: "Viva Freedom. To heck with government interference with ANYTHING! Stop interfering with life by sending people to war. Stop requiring building permits, property taxes, controlling the price of oil. Stop.

Stop big government right now or there will be no more tomorrow."

LIONESS: "The world is on the brink of environmental disaster. Half the world is looking at Armageddon as we speak. And America is on the edge of total economic collapse right now. We have taxed and regulated all our great businesses and great ideas right out of the country. While all other countries tax and regulate our products so they can not leave our shores, they grab all our ideas and jobs with open arms."

DAVID: "My sister is a Capitalist Pig."

LIONESS "Here's to opportunity. Self reliance. Self determined charity. I gladly give my Capitalist earnings voluntarily to Doctors without Borders and to hundreds of other charities every year. I do not gladly give my Capitalist Pig dollars to a government to pay Native Americans to become alcoholics or bombing of babies in foreign lands. But the government takes my dollars and under the pretext of doing good, the government does great evil. Some good around the world. But also Great evil around the world."

RICHARD: "Might I suggest that could be prevented if every time we filled out a tax form, we the people of a true democracy, got to check which box we wanted our tax dollars to go to. I might check the boxes: feeding the poor, curing cancer. You might check the box to pay the IRS and your local sewer inspector. David might check the boxes for funding more jails and police. Lioness might check the boxes for education and health care. Would not that be a much better system than having the politicians overspend on free travel and getting re-elected time and again (via pork) and tax us to death for wars and bridges we don't really need or want?"

LIONESS: "I see government as the problem. David and Richard have not had enough government interference in their lives yet to realize how wrong and stupid and wasteful and corrupt most of those bureaucrats are. Hard working, hard thinking people (capitalists) will solve the world's problems. Governments have created the world's problems."

DAVID: "Do not degrade Socialism. Socialism is borne of idealism. Absolute kindness. Absolutley wanting to uplift the needy. We all want that. We all love our brethren and want the best for them."

LIONESS: "But socialism in practice creates a government that feeds on the rights and dignities and hopes of mankind. It robs the man of his money, his ambition, his self-reliance, his pride, his opportunity for greatness; hence it robs the man of his greatness of spirit – his very soul – his desire to become close to godliness. So I ask you; who loves people the most? Those who would give handouts? Or those who would give jobs?"

RICHARD: "Christ was born, lived, and died and was all about freedom and forgiveness. The most basic freedom of all is the freedom to do with your own body whatever you want. Years ago, back in 2006 your own State of South Dakota sent men to your own capital, Pierre, to launch an affront against women that must never be accepted. They voted against the right of women to date whomever they love with their prehistoric alienation of affection laws. They decided they owned women's bodies when they ruled against a woman's right to chose. Women should have arisen finally found their solidarity and taken those elected officials down. Instead, the women of South Dakota re-elect and promote the same hypocrites time and again."

LIONESS: "Richard is correct. Politics was created in America by our Founding Fathers, not to be a career! It was to be a service you performed once out of moral highness, then you were to get back to your work on your farm like our Founders did. Your government has utterly destroyed your Founding Father's Original Intent. I will take us back to our very foundation, if I am elected. To the Foundation that Created the Greatest Country in the world at the Hands of Men, I nspired by God Himself. I will rule over a Real Constitutional Party. A real party by the people and for the people. A real country based on freedom and sacred, God Given Rights!"

RICHARD: "I believe the Constitutional Party already exists (it is called Libertarian); however, maybe Libertarian is so associated with legalization that it should change it's name to Constitutional Party. Should you decide to establish a true Constitutional Party, COUNT ME IN AS A FOUNDING MEMBER!"

LIONESS: "It is way past time to revolt against the politicos who have stolen our country and our rights out from under us.

DAVID: "This spoken by a politico. Are you not a Senator running for President, oh yeah hypocrite?"

RICHARD: "She probably has not been "In" long enough to get corrupted. What others tout as experience, is code word for bought and paid for over years such that they are now absolutely corrupt. Let us all elect relatively inexperienced politicians. Experienced politicians have no experience with how hard Americans work, how impossible it is to fill out a tax form, how terrible it is to try to get a building permit to house a family, and how difficult it is to earn a meager living. The very CAUSE of homelessness or lack of affordable housing is the LOCAL government. Government causes all problems, it does not solve them. The idiot morons in government who are experienced have long since infiltrated our businesses, our bank accounts, and our homes. Now they've gone mad to infiltrate our bodies and infiltrate other countries; all under the pretext of security, they send young people to die to steal oil."

LIONESS, "I admit the South Dakota government has long since gone mad with power. Once our glorious governor signed a bill saying cops can stick you with a needle and TAKE YOUR BLOOD on the MERE SUSPICION of drunken driving.

Accidentally ease through a stop sign? Roll up your sleeves and let some filthy power hungry corrupt cop give you AIDS! Swerve slightly to grab your cell phone and you can have hepatitis for free. What fun! Don't want AIDS or hepatitis from a corrupt cop? Welcome to jail. Of course, they had to raise taxes again to pay for more jail cells. When will the madness ever end?"

RICHARD: "And let there be no mistake about it, what our Congress is currently offering not only will bankrupt America, it is not a defense budget - it is a war budget - and there is a huge moral difference between defense and war. Imagine what we could do to feed the starving, clean up the planet, educate the masses if only all that money were put to good and honorable purposes. Then, I would not have such an issue with taxes! You can not have a war on terrorism, as terrorism is not a place."

DAVID: "I would fund Ethanol research to help alleviate all the problems related to our appetite for and dependency on foreign oil."

RICHARD: "Ah how you mix the truth with lies. The truth is, we must support alternative energy. The lie is that ethanol is the solution. It takes 1.29 units of fossil fuel energy to produce 1 unit of ethonal energy. This does not account for environmental damage done by the tractors, ethanol refineries, and more. The oil companies are laughing their way all the way to the bank when our politicians, who are owned by oil companies, support ethanol. It is a negative energy proposition that makes us feel good about ourselves!"

LIONESS: "Both Capitalists and Socialists have loving hearts that want the best for the people and the planet. But Capitalism will solve these problems with individual brain, hearts, responsibility, and loving works. Socialism says "If we give the government everything - our rights, our money, our souls, they will solve these problems. The government will not solve your problems. It is in the business of keeping the masses down. Socialism is a tried and failed experiment. Socialism gives a man a fish, then lets him hunger. Capitalism teaches him to fish and encourages him to become his greatest self such that he might both feed and teach others. America's current system is Socialism with dangerous doses of Fascism thrown in! David would take us over the brink and into Fascism. He will use Socialistic ideals - feed and educate the world (what we all want) - to rob us blind, then they spend it on war, ethanol subsidies, and jails instead. Our elected officials already use Fascist techniques - keep us scared to death - to get away with robbing the sweat of our brow and jailing our unique thinkers."

RICHARD: "Of course I am opposed to the death penalty. It is not possible to be a Christian and not be opposed to the death penalty. Jesus' stand on the death penalty was made crystal clear when he said 'May he who has not sinned throw the first stone.'"

LIONESS: "I am a Republican. I am a Republican because I believe in less government. I do not live in a Democracy, I live in a Republic. It is a Republic that recognizes there are some rights that are so sacred, they must be placed beyond the reach of majorities. A true democracy is dangerous as it can result in mob rule and mass hysteria."

DAVID: "I would raise taxes on the rich to pay for health care for the poor, do a better job of collecting taxes, such as capital gains taxes, and put an end to poverty.

"LIONESS: "The only way to end poverty is to end welfare and entitlements. You must not give a man a fish, but rather teach him to fish. Creating self-reliance and strong, hopeful rugged individualism never came from robbing the rich to give to the poor.

DAVID: "We can have the best of both. We can give to those who can not work and to those who can work, we can give a fair wage for doing work-from cleaning up litter to providing day care, whatever their talents and interests, they can earn a living while learning to care for themselves, then their families, then society."

LIONESS: "So you would have the government be the great and all knowing employer of us all? Katrina should serve as your reality dose on how good your governmnt is at fixing problems. NOT. They create problems for the most part, they do not fix them. So I

August Anderson

say starve the Beast. Take back our money and our rights, and we'll fix the problems ourselves. May I remind you time and time again how the Beast that is our government keeps you down with their multitudes of regulations and taxes? Remember these taxes are the cross that crushes your every dream:

Accounts Receivable Tax
Building Permit Tax
Capital Gains Tax
CDL license Tax
Cigarette Tax
Corporate Income Tax
Court Fines (indirect taxes)
Dog License Tax
Federal Income Tax
Federal Unemployment Tax (FUTA)
Fishing License Tax
Food License Tax
Fuel permit tax
Gasoline Tax (42 cents per gallon)
Hunting License Tax
Inheritance Tax Interest expense (tax on the money)
Inventory tax IRS Interest Charges (tax on top of tax)
IRS Penalties (tax on top of tax)
Liquor Tax
Local Income Tax
Luxury Taxes
Marriage License Tax
Medicare Tax
Property Tax
Real Estate Tax

Septic Permit Tax
Service Charge Taxes
Social Security Tax
Road Usage Taxes (Truckers)
Sales Taxes
Recreational Vehicle Tax
Road Toll Booth Taxes
School Tax
State Income Tax
State Unemployment Tax (SUTA)
Telephone federal excise tax
Telephone federal universal service fee tax
Telephone federal, state and
local surcharge taxes
Telephone minimum usage surcharge tax
Telephone recurring and non-recurring charges tax
Telephone state and local tax
Telephone usage charge tax
Toll Bridge Taxes
Toll Tunnel Taxes
Traffic Fines (indirect taxation)
Trailer Registration Tax
Utility Taxes
Vehicle License Registration Tax
Vehicle Sales Tax
Watercraft Registration Tax
Well Permit Tax
Workers Compensation Tax

I am aware that I am repeated myself over and over verbatim from earlier talks, but when Jesus spoke in the bible, stories repeated contained the most important lessons. When America's Founding Fathers repeated themselves thrice, it was because they really meant it. What they repeated was how important, Life, Liberty, and Property were. The Founding Fathers are Angry beyond all words as they gaze down from Heaven and see what the bureaucrats have done to the freedoms they fought so hard for. Especially the Freedom from Taxation without Representation. There is no way all these taxes are representative of the will of the people. The Corrupt Government of the United States has completely usurped our Bill of Rights. They have hijacked the political parties and turned them into monsters devouring the blood, sweat, tears, money, pride, life, property, and freedom of the American people. This insatiable beast is ever expanding at the cost of bankrupting and illegitimizing America. I've come to take America back, with the full backing of God, Himself."

RICHARD: "I have never, in all my life feared a terrorist. Yet, everyday of my life I have feared my own government."

RICHARD: "You can not have a war on terrorism. Terrorism is not a place, so how can you bomb it?"

RICHARD: ""It is not a defense budget, it is a war budget that is bankrupting – financially and morally – our great nation."

LIONESS: "The Old Testament illustrated the failure of ruling by law. Jesus reformed this ancient system of strict obedience to laws and replaced it with a system of love, hope, forgiveness and grace. Jesus only espoused three laws: First, Love one another; Second,. Do Unto Others as you would have others do unto you; and Third, Judge Not Lest Ye Shall be so Judged. If mankind has so much difficulty just honoring those three simple laws, what makes you think mankind can honor the tens of thousands of laws on the books already passed by everyone from Congress to your local City Counsel?"

DAVID: "You claim to be anti-war, yet you and I worked together to help save Ellsworth Air Force Base years ago.

LIONESS: "We all helped save Ellsworth Air Force Base behind the scenes years ago because it would have crashed the economy of South Dakota to lose it. But that is because South Dakota lives in a negative economy. It expects more from the federal government than it gives to the Federal government. An economic Black Hole can not survive forever. This is why I work so hard to give South Dakota fresh money, rather than recycled money. Fresh money is exactly sixteen times as valuable to any state as recycled money. Fresh money coming into a state from other states and countries gets distributed over and over again – to the truckers, farmers, bankers, waitresses. Those, in turn, distribute to insurance salesmen, farmers, grocery stores, and gas stations. Whose workers, in turn, distribute to gas stations, laundromats, local governments, homeowners, butcher shop, and so on. In turn, they have money then to give to maids, house builders, candidates, and so on. At each step down, that fresh money I bring to the state, gets taxed by each of those dozens and dozens of taxing agencies, over and over and over, until it all eventually becomes government money. In the meantime, I have given you hundreds and hundreds of jobs for every little bit of money that I bring in from out of state. Until, after about sixteen generations of the money being turned around from proud worker to proud worker, one way or another until the government has siphoned it all off in the form of any of our multitudes of taxes. Without business people bringing fresh money into the state there could be no government. There could be no entitlements. There could be no jobs. Governments should kneel at the feet of its small businesses, farmers, hardworking families and beg them to stay. Instead, governments are regulating them to death and I see in the near future total economic collapse unless entrepreneurs are invited into this state and into this country and enticed to stay here through limiting taxes and limiting regulations. All other countries of the world are enticing business away from South Dakota and away from America. Why is America prosecuting and persecuting and taxing our businesses away? Because the masses are jealous of those who would succeed? Americans are the great creators of great ideals and are hard working, money making machines. Why does our government drive away business rather than welcome it with open arms? Hard thinking, hard working, peace loving, families supporting ideals can create heaven on earth. On their own initiative, rugged free thinking individuals can save the world, if the government will get out of the way and welcome those of us bringing in fresh money. Recycled/government money has already lived fifteen of its lifetimes and will disappear shortly. Only fresh money makers – those of us who bring in new ideas and sell them around the world to bring in new money can save the South Dakota's economy and the U.S. economy this late in the game. Recycled government money has only one or two spending cycles left to it and will totally dissipate without fresh money. Fresh money has sixteen spending cycles before the government has every drop of it to send out to its chosen ones. Governments at all levels should bow to its knees in honor of those who bring fresh money unto it. If all the farmers, engineers, businesswomen, landlords, home builders suddenly quit because they are sick and tired of regulators, tax auditors, building permitters, and other worthless agencies harassing them, the world would collapse in an instant. Right now 95% of all new businesses fail. We 5% who hold up the entire economy are thinking of retiring. What then? When I am president, America will become a land of the free once again, so that 95% of all new start-up businesses have a chance to succeed! That is why I will eliminate layers of government, give tax breaks to one and all, and eliminate regulations and regulators from our alleged land of the free.

THE GATHERING OF ANGELS AND DEVILS

Initially there were fourteen of them gathered at the Godfrey table the next morning. It was the fateful day before Anne would be discovered murdered, covered in blood at the Watergate Hotel.

David and Lion's mother, Eve Godfrey, knew how to be the perfect hostess. She had thrown magnificent political parties for both her children for years. She invited all three candidates to a lovely breakfast along with Lion's new friends. She looked at the way Lion and Pierce glowed and moved close to each other with the pride only a mother knows. She wished that Lioness would marry the handsome movie star that made her so happy, but she was also aware of the reasons Lioness could not marry.

Pity, she thought.

Now that Hanson had such scars across his face and his neck that he would probably never get another movie part, it would be a great time to raise her some grandchildren. Pierce might get parts now as the bad guy.

But obviously Lioness was deep enough to not let the man's beauty, or lack current lack thereof, effect the loving way she looked at him. Hanson still had that magnificent tall, trim well muscled body, even Eve had to notice.

But Eve shook her head sadly knowing there would never be another Spy movie. There would never be a wedding. For Pierce would, of course, be dead. She knew it would rip to shreds even the heart of a Lion. But Destiny always fulfilled Herself.

The large oval shaped rosewood table in the Godfrey mansion had become a familiar feasting place for each member of the Godfrey family. They dined individually or in groups of two, three or four at a time at this table for decades and it was here that great debates took place nightly.

But this morning, it was at Pierce's request, command and invitation that they gathered. They all knew deep in their guts that their gathering here today was going to be something very different from any breakfast any of them had ever had. It was two weeks before the presidential election and somehow all three candidates had taken the time out of their busy campaigns to meet here today. That indicated to the others that this was a meeting with the magnitude and importance of international peace talks.

The invitation had issued the night prior immediately following the local debate, during which time, a creature in black had descended upon Pierce in the privacy of the Lion's den. All involved scrambled to clear their mornings for this feast. Each guest knew in their heart their attendance was essential and that this would be the most important breakfast of their entire lives. All

August Anderson

Fourteen arrived sharply at 9:00 and introductions were made around the house.

They gathered in the large Godfrey dining hall. Central to the room was the famous rosewood table, ornately carved with roses and angels and seven matching, thickly cushioned chairs on each side, with another at the foot of the table and one at the head. Soft, plush white carpet covered the natural hardwood floor and Joan could not help but wonder how they kept it clean.

Paul marveled out loud at the incredible artwork that adorned the high wide walls of the magnificent dining haul.

All the paintings had a French Impressionistic flair and were of unicorns. It was unlike any artwork Paul had ever seen in all his years of traveling around the world. Paul and his wife loved art and were minor collectors with what little money was left over after caring for their eight children.

Eve graciously explained, "All the pieces in the entire mansion were done by the famous South Dakota artist, Avonelle Kelsey." Eve gave Paul a quick private tour of some of the other rooms. Huge paintings explored vibrant colors. A hint of Vincent Van Gogh was seen in every work of art. Paul vowed to save his money to buy one of Avonelle's original works.

Meanwhile Ted and David greeted each other as warm, long time friends. This shocked both Pierce and Joan who were sipping Champaign with sugar cubes bubbling up as they melted at the bottom of the fine crystal glasses.

"How do the two of you know each other?" Pierce asked accusingly

"I was David's freshman counselor, then his friend, throughout his many years at Harvard. David was brilliant at everything he did and has always been like a son to me," he replied casually but you could see the obvious deep affection that results only from years of friendship.

David spoke to the entire gathering, "Everybody let's sit, I'm hungry!" He took his place at the head of the table and asked Ted to sit beside him at his right hand side. Just before Ted sat, Anne offered him a warm hug, remembering Ted vaguely from their wedding, which Pierce had not attended because he was shooting a jungle scene in South Africa at the time. Anne then sat beside her magnificent looking husband at his left hand side. Ted realized again, what a stunning couple they were. David with his dark curly hair with graying touches and Anne with her sleek dark mane with highlights in red cut to perfectly emphasize her high cheekbones and large brown eyes that slanted upwards ever so slightly. Then the neck, the elegant swan neck was likewise accented by the layers of her perfect haircut. Elegance and class were defined by Anne.

Ted had met Lioness off and on over the years as well as at the David and Anne wedding. As and as he starred across the massive table to her at the exact opposite end of the table, he could not help but think how much he disliked her. She had always made him nervous. How could she and the magnificent Anne be best friends? Anne's sleek coif showed never a single hair out of place. Lion's scruffy blond mane never had a hair in place. Anne's was precisely cut and sprayed to accent the lovely face and neck. Lion's long hair flew out every which direction.

Anne had the neck of a swan while Lion's neck was brown and insignificant. Anne had a cool calm blue Aura about her. It blended so nicely with her husband, David's, silver aura. Lioness had a purple and teal aura. Odd, he saw that Richard had a teal and purple aura. Those two oddballs were the only two he had ever seen with these colors in their auras. Two purple auras side by side, now that was against all odds. One in a billion, maybe?

Shit, what if they had united and this just doubled their power?

Ted could feel his own yellow aura growing pale at that possibility.

Lioness had placed that awful little Libertarian Richard at the foot of the table, completely opposite David.

Hmm or was that the head of the table?

Richard sat directly across from the magnificent hero David. That, too, Ted saw represented a stark contrast. David was tall, well muscled, handsome powerful and arrogant. Richard was small, big eared, big nosed, and humble.

As Ted stared at the Lion who sat opposite the huge table from him, having placed herself between Richard and Pierce Ted saw Lion's eyes turning purple, then blue, then green, then brown. He was covered with goose bumps as he knew precisely what she was doing. She was quickly looking out from the brain of each of the guests. Seeing what they were seeing. Thinking what they were thinking. She was reading their minds uninvited.

He was covered with chills and shut down his brain so that the Lion could not see inside it. Valcon like mind-control was an art of all the Illuminati and he was not going to let her see what he knew. He knew what was about to be revealed to every one in this room and once it was revealed, the destiny of the world would likewise be revealed. Once revealed Destiny would be sealed.

When he asked Andrew to sit beside him, Ted was covered feeling chilled from head to toe. He was dizzy and he was feeling Lioness pawing at the block of his brain. Trying to get in, her eyes had turned black, like his, and she was looking at him so hard he was about to faint. He had to remain strong. He had to protect David with his very life.

Matt felt awkward not knowing this group very well and still wondering why he was there, so he took a seat beside Andrew. Tom sat to his right with an empty seat between them. Naturally beside Tom was Bart. At that moment Eve and Paul returned to the great dining room so Eve sat Paul beside Bart promising she would sit between Richard and Paul so they could talk art as soon as the maids had breakfast ready to serve.

Naturally, James sat to the right of Pierce, always the good body guard. Joan had taken up a conversation about the Thai language with Anne a little earlier, so she seated herself to Anne's left. Mohammed sat with his beloved Joan to his right. There was an empty seat between James and Mo, who both sat quietly until Eve entered the room with Paul.

It was as if they all recognized Eve at the very same time. Pierce, James, Mo, and Joan turned to each other in complete shock that very instant. Mo, felt himself slipping toward a faint.

"It is her!" James gasped.

"Yes," cried Joan.

"Now I remember why she looked so familiar!" whispered Pierce. But for the modern hairdo, Lion's mother looked exactly like the beautiful vision of Mary those four shared as their plane was crashing in Europe.

THE FINAL SEATING ARRANGEMENT

Lioness had stopped knocking on Ted's mind's wall as soon as Eve took her seat and the food was served. The Lion finally relaxed and seemed to radiate happiness with her purple aura around her golden head while David's dark hair with silver streaks reflected his usual intelligent, somber silver aura. Although it was breakfast, David refused to remove his dark sunglasses.

Lioness started to speak, "Thank you to each and every one of you for coming here at the invitation of Pierce. Everyone here is an essential part of a very important puzzle. Some of you have already figured out your part. Others have figured out bits and pieces of this two thousand year old puzzle. And still others are in complete darkness, but were brave enough to follow pure instincts such that they could show up here and learn the secret for which mankind has search for thousands of years."

Ted squirmed. David showed no reaction as he already knew what his sister was going to say. He just was unsure what his glorious wife was going to do when she found out. David's end of the table had its work cut out for them and they were sweating bullets of sulpher. The end of the table with Richard surrounded by Eve and Lioness looked profoundly calm.

Naturally, Adam Godfrey who was seated far away, three stories above the family dining area, in the security offices of the mansion was watching the entire undertaking on the monitors that were beaming the happenings far below him in the house. Arthur calmly noted the suffering of David and knew both his children were about to suffer more, much more.

Adam realized from the camera directly above the center of the Rosewood breakfast party that the group below looked as if they were seated in the shape of a cross. From the cameras in the four corners of the room it was hard to tell if Richard were at the head or David. With seven people on each side, it sort of mattered how the guests scooted their chairs.

David, Ted, Andrew, and Matt were obviously nervous. Anne, Joan, and Mo remained confused and tense. Seven guests were ill at ease.

Adam saw that Richard, with Lioness and Pierce to his right and Adam's lovely wife, Eve, sitting by Paul, Bart, and Tom revealed seven serene people.

James was stoic.

If it was going to be seven against seven, then Adam was quite sure his wife and daughter's side of the table would win because James Thunderhead, the big Indian, would surely follow Pierce. On the other hand, Doubting Thomas had always been hard to call for he had a history of swinging both ways. He could easily scoot over to

David's side of the table and bring his love, Bart, with him. If that were the case, David would win.

But there was one more factor. As if right on cue, at the very moment where Adam was setting high up above questioning his own family, in floated the creature in black that had followed them from the airport and let itself into the house of the Lion, uninvited and unnoticed from the night before.

THE FIRST BREAKFAST

Adam and the guards at the monitors jumped in their seats three floors above as a huge blackness filled the dining hall. The diners and servants, three floors below, literally leaped to their feet and released a collective gasp followed by dead silence as the blackness wobbled toward the table now piled high with steaming eggs, omelets, blueberry muffins, sausage, steaks, bacon, coffee cakes and so much more.

Eve darted around behind the table past Richard, Lioness, and Pierce, appearing to place herself between the danger and her daughter, as any good mother would do. But she had a smile on her face, only her husband spotted through the cameras from his vantage point above.

James whirled and placed his own mountain of a body between the darkness and his master employer, Pierce.

Eve was the first to speak, "Margaret, my love. I was wondering when you would get here. We saved a chair for you and I've been stalling until you arrived". The large black being pulled back her nun's habit to reveal her kind, jolly, loving fat round face. She sported at least three chins The brown eyes peering from the layers of skin giving Sister Margaret's face the distinct look of a kangaroo filled with merriment. Pierce could not help but notice the nun's arms looked small and devoid of the flab that covered the rest of her body as she held them in front of her to hug first Eve, then Lioness who had darted to the large women's side. Yup, Hanson concluded those black robes barely covered humungous and powerful legs to carry all that weight. He could not look at her in this morning's light as anything but a big friendly Kangaroo. Richard greeted her with a fond hug, too. From up above, Adam Godfrey relaxed as soon as he realized it was only Sister 3M even larger than ever. And he was sure who 3M would side with. He shook his head laughing. The whole world would soon know 3M's greatest love, second to only God Himself. Adam had known who his Aunt Margaret loved for years now. The girls at the orphanage confided this to him soon after Pierce's first movie hit the shores of Australia.

As Eve asked James and Mo to make room between them, 3 M laughingly pushed James over beside Mo and stole James' chair so she could hoist her large frame right down beside Pierce.

Lioness chuckled knowing now Pierce was surrounded by the two women who adored him most in this world and Pierce had no idea his biggest fan had just arrived.

Adam shifted in his chair nervously as did David, three floors below the audacious true head of the Godfrey family, the one and only Sir Adam. There were now seven people on David's side of the table. James, Mo, Jean, Anne, Ted, Andrew and Matt. There were seven on Richard's side of the table: Tom, Bart, Paul, Eve,

Lioness, Pierce and Margaret. "Let the games begin," Adam sighed as he watched from above.

As if she heard Adam announce the time was upon them, and perhaps she did, Lioness, spoke while the others ate, listening quietly. "I believe there are twelve of you here, gathered all together for the first time in two thousand years that hold the keys to the mystery of the secret grail".

THE MYSTERY UNVEILED

"Two thousand years ago, after the twelve Apostles drank from the Holy Grail, Jesus in his infinite wisdom knew that men would hunt and kill for the secrets the grail contained until the Second Coming. He had the grail made to his special order long before that night and as soon as the Last Supper was coming to its unforgettable close, he divided the grail into twelve parts. He gave each of his twelve Apostles a piece of the grail and instructed them to see to it that each piece was taken to the far corners of the world so that no one finding a single piece could access its powers and unveil its secrets. He said the Angels would bring together the pieces of the Grail and all its powers when the twelve apostles gathered together to dine again upon planet Earth. This would only happen when the Christ was ready to reveal himself at the end of history as we know it."

Eve nodded to Paul to go ahead and do as they discussed earlier when they were viewing artwork in the other rooms of the Godfrey mansion before breakfast. He stood and passed by Bart and Tom. At Matt Paul, the guardian of the briefcase, reached in and grabbed Matt's

Faberge Egg found at the step pyramid and handed it to him. Then he handed the Faberge slice from the well in Austria to Andrew. Then the slice leaped in his hand and dropped to the floor when Paul took out the Egg belonging to Ted. It was the slice the group had stolen from St. Mark's in Venice, Italy.

When Paul walked behind David and bypassed him, David's eyes burned behind the dark glasses. David kept dumping saline in them and it was the only time in David's life that his sister had ever noticed him even tremble.

Proceeding clockwise around the table, Paul passed by Anne, too and then handed Joan her slice of egg from St. John's near Ephesus and Mo his from the sidewalk of Ephesus itself. He passed by James and Sister Margaret, handing Pierce the slice from Ireland that had lain with St. Peter for so long until the Angels freed it and gave it to his mum.

Lioness continued to talk in a mesmerizing, perhaps even hypnotizing voice, "Exactly two thousand years ago to this day twelve people sat with Jesus Christ himself. The meal came to be known throughout history as The Last Supper. Yes, at that time they shared wine, the blood of Christ, and Bread, the body of Christ. But there are reports not contained in the Four gospels that tell of man other things the twelve shared with Christ. Most important, of course, were the final words of wisdom he would import on them. To go tell Mankind of the Glory of God. That Christ was indeed the Son of God and through him all men could be saved. This we all know from the gospels. But there were other gospels. There were other religions. Other prophets. Other lessons the

Lioness

twelve were to learn about. The love of God was to be spread across the planet. The message of peace and love was to be taken to gentiles, heathens, jews and all mankind. Hope was to be a gift for all to enjoy. Eternal Life was an absolute. For live has always been and always will be. That was not the question. The question was, how would each individual man live his own life? Would he realize what a gift his life was? Would each man life it to its greatest glory? Would men and women explore every piece of the world with excitement? Watch all their sunsets with a grateful heart? Love with abandoned passion in spite of heartbreak? Risk public humiliation to always speak the truth? Live with the energy and spark, often called the holy ghost, of God that is a piece of every man? Would they realize they are not in their mortal body, but that their mortal body is inside their eternal souls? Would they know that the path least taken, might be their individual path to greatness? Would they have the courage to follow rightness even if it meant leaving the group behind? These and so many other lessons were imparted on the twelve apostles that faithful night?"

When Lioness paused for a deep breath, Tom interrupted, "But what has that to do with us?".

"Only everything. You see on that fateful night the famous goodbye bread was not the only thing that was broken and shared among the twelve Apostles."

"We know. So was his blood, the wine they drank from the Holy Grail," piped in Anne excitedly as she had just finished figuring out the puzzle for herself and nodded to her boss, Ted. He knew that she knew.

"Yes. And once the grail was emptied of His sacred blood, He broke the grail itself into twelve pieces and instructed the Apostles to take the twelve pieces of the holy cup to the far corners of the earth. He then gave Mary the golden base that held the pieces together which she has worn as a bracelet ever since. They were told that the golden base decorated with eight armed stars would forever be their secret symbol of Him and His Second coming. When he came again, the eight arm star would unite them and their pieces of the Holy Grail and they would know it was Him by his very blood."

"Let me guess," said Pierce with the light of his piercing blue eyes brightening up the entire room. The bright light of knowing what was about to be presented left him feeling so excited and energetic he could almost float outside his own body, "Each of the twelve pieces of the grail is blue green in color and looks like it curves like the bottom half of an egg! It is covered with priceless gems – diamonds, rubies, sapphires, emeralds and more. These gems are on slices of glass that shines of the color of the ocean when the sunlight reflects the blue green aura of the universe right back up unto eternity,"

"Absolutely," proudly purred the Lion.

"But why break it into twelve pieces? What if pieces came up missing?"

"Jesus knew the grail was priceless that men and armies would look for it, fight for it, kill for it, and do anything to fin it. Hence, no one man was to be trusted with the secret of the Grail until His return. No one man was to find it and enlist it's power. For in the Blood that fills the Grail lies all knowledge, hence, all power in the Universe. Jesus wanted the men he trusted and loved the most to carry each piece as far from each other piece as humanly possible. And to order their descendants to carry it far away and protect their pieces with their lives. Jesus also wanted the golden strand to be taken away to be protected by his mother because he knew that each individual piece would be drawn to the golden bracelet like moths to a flame."

Quit unexpectedly the elephant at the end of the table spoke, "Apostles, I call upon you now to present your pieces."

David almost fell out of his chair as Pierce was the first to set his "Egg" in front of his plate. Margaret pulled her necklace off from around her neck and was the first member of her proud aborigine family to surrender her heirloom in two thousand years. James did likewise of his Native American "hand me down". Clockwise around the table they laid out their priceless gems. Mo, then Joan. Then Anne, who now understood what Bart and Tom understood – why Lioness forced them to take back the gems they had tried to give her. They were each one of twelve that were to surrender these Faberge Egg pieces to the whole of their own free will and only when the twelve gathered back together again.

David had no Egg to surrender, but felt like he was on fire as he watched them place the pieces counterclockwise on the table. He tried to will his friend Ted to keep it. He placed the thoughts in the head of Ted, Andrew, and Matt that they should run from here immediately with pieces in hand. They should run from this overly hot room and sell their eggs and live happily ever after. But again, Ted's egg acted as if it had a will of its own and flew onto the table in spite of Ted trying to cling to it. This scared Andrew so much, he tossed his glass from the well onto the table. Matt's slice from the pyramid quickly followed. Tom trembled as he put his glass in the center of the table too, followed by Bart and finally Paul. Twelve pieces of aquamarine glass adored the great rosewood table glowing upward toward the camera above from which Adam looked down on the group.

Adam had his answer.

Good would win over evil in the end.

Eve raised her Champaign glass and said, "Let me propose a toast. To all women who have endured the eternal pain of losing a child. May they know in their heart of hearts that one day, they will all be reunited with their children. And their reward for bearing the unbearable sorrow of losing a child will be eternity with their maker and their child."

Lion raised her glass, "And may I toast every woman who has morphed into a man. For every woman who becomes man is automatically given the keys to heaven."

"How does a woman become a man?" cried out Joan, only desiring the keys to heaven.

"She not only bears the children," explained the Lion, "she brings home the bacon, and fries it up in the pan. Glory be unto the single mother who raises her children with the help of no man for she will be returned a hundred fold the unconditional love she has given. But woe unto the man who hath abandoned his family whether it be to lust, television, drugs, alcohol, or welfare. For that man shall suffer all eternity without knowing the joy of unconditional love. And the lightness of being in infinite freedom."

Pierce's turn to offer a toast, "Here is to every life lived to the edge of its limit. To all who escape the chains of a government or a family gone wrong and who would live every day of their life on the very edge. To all who would take their passion to the point of no return. Those with the courage to live the live others only dare to dream – to them is given eternal freedom to live spectacularly within His great light."

Margaret lifted her glass, "To all those women who would love faithfully and forever whether or not they stood a chance of the man they love even glancing sideways at them. Let the fact that they have the courage to openly love be the reward in and of itself. Love need not be reciprocated to have eternal value. Love is enough unto itself."

James proposed a toast, "To the great spirit that is a part of Everyman. No matter what we name Him, may he uplift Everyman and fill Everyman with the desire to be as great as he can be. May we, in our moments of aloneness and silence, speak to Him knowing we are never really alone and that we will all one day return to the Spirit in the Sky."

Mo the raised his glass, "To Allah and Mohammed, and all the Prophets that would promote the brotherhood of man. May we understand your greatest message was that of Peace."

Joan then raised her glass, "To the Inclusionary God that originated all churches, not the Exclusionary self-righteous hypocrites that often fill those churches!"

Anne rose her glass, "To my husband David, and my best friend Lioness, may the best man win."

David picked up his glass of Champaign and dumped it on his lap in disdain of this bunch of crazies and to put out the fire that was burning in his crotch as his gorgeous wife, Anne, rubbed his muscled inner thigh under the table.

Pierce looked at Lioness who had worked like a dog to create jobs for multitudes, who had built and painted houses with her own paws to create affordable homes for the homeless to rent at below market value, who had traveled to the far corners of the earth to live her life to the fullest and to somehow bring this group together at this point in history. Suddenly it dawned on Pierce, his Lion, although the most beautiful woman he had ever seen, had in her lifetime morphed into a man. For she lived her life, right down to being a Senator, an entrepreneur, and running for President, not as a woman but as a man. No wonder they could not marry, he thought bitterly, for neither one of them was gay. Hanson then turned to the woman who sat on his right and saw big soft kangaroo eyes gazing at him through two thousand year old lives of love. At that moment the sexiest man alive fell in love with a 450 pound aborigine woman.

He barely heard Ted's Toast, "Here's to the future President of the United States of America, Senator David Godfrey!"

Andrew toasted, "Here's to He who brought the twelve together on this day. Thank you for honoring your promise to us the night of The Last Supper, that we could live to see your Second Coming. Thank you for bringing us together on this day so that we might witness your glorious return."

Matt picked up his glass and said, "To all of those who have lived time and time again, striving for perfect Karma such that they could move off the circle and into the great light of the Universe, your time has come."

Tom raised his glass, "Well, I'm not sure I understand, or even want to, what everyone is saying, but here's to a great breakfast and to the final Revolution."

Bart rolled his eyes, then looking at Tom, "Here's to Love."

Paul raised his glass, "Here's to eternal life. That we have existed from the beginning of time and will exist to all eternal, all a part of one another, all a part of God, may we realize that whatever we do unto one another, we do unto ourselves and unto Him. To the God in everyone."

The toasts had gone the full circle.

What about Richard and David skipping their toasts, Tom questioned silently to himself?

THE CUP RUNNETH OVER

Eve reached out and placed the eight sided star a mummy had left in the Cairo hotel room on the table. She then removed her golden bracelet and placed it upon said star.

Paul had handed the mummy's star to Eve earlier when he was privately viewing the Avonelle Kelsey originals in the other rooms of the house. She had slipped it into her pocket explaining that it had been left in Mary's final home above Ephesus two thousand years ago. Although Matt's Egg had originally been taken to India the Pharaoh who owned the step pyramid with the eight stars had found pieces of the New Testament never published along the Nile. These documents guided him to the located both of those treasures and had promptly searched the world and stolen them. They were buried with him in the step pyramid just north of Memphis, Egypt. However, when his mummy had been recently unearthed, but not unwrapped Pierce's guardian angel recovered the stolen treasures and unwrapped the eight armed star to deliver to the Cairo search party that night. Intervention had been required as they were search for Matt's Egg in all the wrong pyramids when they searched Giza. Giza was the wrong era and much too public for the treasures to have been laid to rest there.

Eve had confided everything to Paul during the tour and was telling the group this story now as she placed the star and her bracelet midway between Pierce and Bart on the table.

Paul was a little more ready for all that would take place the breakfast. "So, you see, although all the Apostles kept written records of their travels and their secrets, not all of these writings were included in the New Testament. Their records, and other ancient scrolls are still being discovered from the Dead Sea to the Nile. Many are hidden in the Vatican. So, when the angels want to point people toward Jesus, they have used eight armed stars to guide people.

Adam from above, and the group below noticed that Eve's gold bracelet on the star had been placed on the table such that its light shown out in the form of a gold glowing cross across the table. As soon as Eve placed the star on the table, some sort of magnetic force began slowly pulling all twelve Egg pieces to its center. Eventually the pieces formed a tight seal that looked like a rather large glowing aqua colored, gem studded half egg. The grail had formed itself back into a cup for the first time since broken two thousand years earlier.

Then the Faberge Egg, now Holy Grail, filled itself with a red bubbling liquid that looked and smelled of blood.

It creeped out most of the people at the table so bad that Mo passed out and Joan vomited. Bart turned white and Thomas became a believer.

"Now what?" Pierce managed to croak out to Lion and Eve.

"Heck if I know," said Lioness flatly and somehow they believed her.

Much discussion was had by everyone after Mo and Joan recovered.

The movie star got it at last. "Ladies and gentlemen, I present you with the Holy Grail. The reason it had never been discovered by crusades of men, generations of seekers, is that it had been broken down into twelve different pieces and removed to seven different continents before Christ even arose from the grave!" Some gasped with shock, others passed knowing glances at one another.

David unmoved said, "Bah, humbug," but for the first time in his life, looked a little pale.

Lioness gave a bored and sleepy yawn as Lionesses tend to do.

"Should we drink from the cup?" shyly trembled Margaret.

"Count me out on that one, I'm no vampire," cried Joan, looking like she was going to vomit again.

"Who's blood is it?" whispered Tom.

"Duh," responded Paul. "Surely it is the blood of Christ."

As Pierce spoke his eyes circled the table clockwise speaking of each one there, beginning with Paul, "Why would the blood of Christ bring together a Mormon (Paul), a New Age Aquarian type (Bart), an Agnostic (Tom), a Hindu (Matt), a Christian Scientist (Andrew), an Illuminati (Ted), a whatever David believes in, a Buddhist (Anne), a Generic Christian (Joan), a Muslim (Mo), a Native American (James), a Catholic Aborigine

(Margarite), an Irish Catholic (me), a woman who looks like a vision of Mother Mary and three potential leaders of the world –Richard, Lion and David?"

"Wait," said Margaret. "There are the twelve of us coming together from all around the world. Jesus scattered his twelve Apostles around the world to spread His word. Why would he not bring them back together before his return?"

"I see sixteen people at this table," Tom looked completely doubtful, more like his normal self again.

"But remember," Margaret who had actually studied Catholicism rather than being a "Jack Catholic" like Pierce often referred to himself. "When Judas betrayed Jesus, Judas was excommunicated and there are many who thought they added a thirteenth Apostle to bring the numbers back up to twelve. Some scholars and historians believe Mary was added at that time as the thirteenth Apostle."

Tom was not to be convinced, "That explains thirteen of us being necessary to bring back the Grail and the Blood, but what about the extra three people here?"

"Maybe some of us are just here to take notes or serve food or something," Bart was as confused as his friend.

Pierce reiterated, "Why would the Grail and Blood bring together all these different religions from all over the world?"

Paul whispered his answer, "To deliver the message that at the end of times all religions would unite! That maybe no one religion was completely right, but if you combined all religions of the world, therein you might find spiritual truth. Remember when God told Joseph Smith that none of the religions were completely right?

Maybe He was simultaneously saying all of the religions of the world had some, perhaps many. things right! Maybe when the commonality of good – peace, love, respect, honor, kindness, compassion, self-responsibility, non-judgmentalism, individualism, acceptance, joy, hope - of all religions join together to bring about a united and enlightened world, then is the time for our Leaders to return."

"Maybe at this time, it is time to unite for the cause of peace and all things good that Paul just enumerated?"

"Is the thousand years of peace upon us? Or is Armagadeon upon us?" Joan asked.

"Maybe that depends on who we elect for president?" Tom gasped.

Now the twelve looked suspiciously at all three candidates who had offered nothing to the discussion and nothing to the glowing light of the grail on the table.

"Might it be that the blood of the grail flows through one of the three candidates?"

"No surely that is not possible," muttered Mo.

"There is only one way to tell." stated Joan flatly. "They must all three submit to a genetics tests. We can take a sample from the grail and sample from our three silent candidates here to Harvard's genetic labs and they can run a full comparison panel in less than a day."

"What if one of these three is a match?"

"Well, then, we have an answer to our most pertinent then question, don't we?"

"No. We have an answer as to the identity of one candidate. Who then are the other two?"

At that question, the blood of the thirteen non-candidates at the Godfrey table ran cold with speculation and fear.

WHOM CAN YOU TRUST?

Eventually, as each looked nervously around the table, Ted finally spoke up, "I have to get back to my classes and get caught up on mail at Harvard. I'll take the Grail and the blood samples and call you all with the findings."

"Over my dead body," hissed Pierce. "Do you think we are going to trust you with the greatest finding in the history of the world."

"Don't worry," David soothed with his great, deep voice, "I need to return to my law office in Boston, I'll keep an eye on Ted."

"Like we can trust the two of you!" roared out the Lion.

"I'll go, too," said Andrew.

"I don't think so," said Pierce, "You've been the puppet of Ted since the moment we met you. Who is to say you, David, and Ted are not some sort of co-conspirators?"

"Who would you trust?" Richard finally spoke, his voice soothing and trusting as his calm brown eyes searched Pierce's flaming blue ones.

"Me, but I've been called back to London to reshoot a fight seen from my lastest flick and I need to leave today. Let me see, I think we can all trust Anne as she is friends with everyone here. I know we can trust Margaret."

"Ha!" replied Ted. "Sister 3M is in love with you. She'll find for your side."

"Just who says there are sides?" snapped Hanson, "I thought we were all in this together."

"Not if you don't trust me," replied the Professor.

"I trust you as far as I can throw you," replied Pierce.

"Then that is your problem, not ours," said Ted.

The movie star's quick Irish temper was getting the best of him again, "I'll make myself your problem, if you wrong us again in this lifetime."

"In this lifetime? Ah, so you acknowledge I am right about reincarnation," the table finally heard from Matt, the Hindu.

"No. I don't know how that slipped from my mouth. My jury is still out on the reincarnation issue, I told you that."

"Is not everything we hypothecate today proof of reincarnation?" Matt rested his case.

THE ANSWERS AT LAST

After much debate, the group finally came to a compromise. They would send seven people to monitor the tests. Ted, Andrew and David needed to go to Boston anyway, so they would represent that end of the table. Lion had to go to Washington and Richard to Sacramento to host parties for their largest financial supporters.

Bart, and Thomas were filling in for Lion at the Godfrey mansion daily until the election, while Lion made her final campaign swing. Pierce was returning to London with James. Paul had to get back to his wife and kids. They all agreed that Margaret, Joan, and Mo could go represent the group on Lion's side of the table fairly and offset the Ted, Andrew, and David union.

They all voted and agreed that both sides trusted Anne to be the ultimate arbitrator, so she would receive the lab findings and Anne would be the one to present the findings to each member of the two groups as soon as the lab made a match.

The Grail and its contents would be locked in the Godfrey safe that only Eve could access.

Lioness

The blue-green bejeweled challis had a magnificent aura of light touching all at the table that was enhanced by the golden light around the eight armed star and golden base.

In fact, everything but the food at the table and every person sitting around the table had their own aura such to Adam and the guards looking on from security cameras above, it looked like the goblet was the sun and the auras surrounding it were rainbows. The goblet appeared to be the pot of gold at the end of the rainbow. The guests all seemed to have some circular lights above their heads that looked almost like halos.

The three candidates donated blood to syringes yielded by Eve. She was glad she had studied to be a nurse, before her husband Adam swept her off her feet so many years ago. Had it really been more forty years ago? It seemed like only yesterday.

The group split up, promising to meet the day after election day, as everyone was going to be unbearably busy until then.

Anne promised to identify the results of the blood tests in person first to each of the candidates, then to the others of the groups, and finally to everyone else in the room, but she was not to tell another soul until after the election.

Lion made a suggestion, "Let Anne only reveal the results to David, Richard, and me, please before the election. Sixteen people is just too many. If the secret got out before the elections, the magnitude of the knowledge might sway the election. The people of America must chose the next president based on what is in their hearts and in their minds and in their souls. They must be free to choose. We must not scare the people, ever again, into giving away the gift that is free choice."

The group begrudgingly agreed that they would all wrap up their businesses and their lives and would meet the day after the election, knowing whatever blood evidence was presented on the date would change not only the course of the own lives, but the course of the planet.

They did not know how they would survive the curiosity. How could they wait for two whole weeks to know the outcome of the future of mankind?

The same way everyone waits. Mankind has waited two thousand years. You can wait two weeks. Keep so busy and so productive that time flies by and you forget you are waiting.

DEATH REVISITED

Lioness had made it back to her D.C. apartment, called Pierce on the Code Red, which meant a huge emergency and they must meet immediately. She was packing and searching her brain for her memory when the FBI showed up at her D.C. condo to discuss the murder of her sister-in-law!

The press would not be far behind.

She could run. No. If you run you have to run the rest of your life.

She could lie. No. If you lie you have to lie the rest of your life.

She could kill. No. If you kill you have to kill the rest of your life.

She had to follow the principals she had followed all her life. Work hard. Tell the truth. Accept responsibility.

"Come in," she said to him. When the press showed up fifteen minutes later, she graciously let them in, too.

"I honestly don't remember," she said over and over.

"Convenient loss of memory," quipped Barnett from the Times who had always been jealous of her.

"Maybe," she sighed, "But true."

"Are you going to take her in to be charged with murder?" asked Thomanson from the Tribune."

"Not yet. We have no evidence and she is not a flight risk. There is no where in the world she could run and not be recognized."

Lioness trembled. He was so right about that.

While the other two candidates finished the final time before the election, the Lion that had read so many minds stayed inside and tried to read her own mind. It was blank. When she tried feebly to search her boyfriend's mind, she saw absolutely nothing. She had heard his plane went down somewhere in the Atlantic soon after he had responded to her Code Red.

The Lion was in shock. All her life she had known all the answers. She was from the light. She was here to bring to the light to mankind. She had purpose and drive. She was on a mission of greatness. She had the all the answers.

Now, for the first time in this mortal body, she ha no answers, only questions. All her powers seemed to have evaporated. Suddenly she felt like a weak, unpopular middle aged woman with Alzheimer's. Is this what all lives boil down to, she wondered?

Now that the two people she loved the most in all this world, Anne and Pierce, had probably died, possibly because of her, she came to doubt all that she knew to be true.

Eventually she was flown back to her bed in the Black Hills, shaking violently, peeing herself, and rejecting food. She lost her power and her looks. She had lost everything when she lost her love. There really was no more reason to live. Hope was gone. Man can not live without hope. Without his divine purpose there is little left.

Her internal pain was beyond anything she had seen from the eyes of any person. And she had looked out through the eyes of thousands of souls in her lifetime, but never had she seen such anguish.

Never had a person hated herself, like the Lion now hated herself.

Never had a person wronged so many in the course of a single evening.

Was she the Judas of the group?

She tried to see through Anne's eyes. She saw nothing. Anne was dead.

But dead does not exist. Life is eternal.

Lion argued with herself day and night, night and day. She had passed over the edge into a madness that can only known by parents who lose a child.

A priest came to the house to offer his services. She heard Eve say, "She does not need a priest."

"Does she need an exorcist?" she heard someone else ask in the dark fog that was all that was left of her brain.

"That might kill her," Eve whispered having never left Lion's side.

The papers were having a field day speculating about her. Richard and David quit campaigning because no one was interested in anything other than the murder of David's wife and the sudden disappearance of the most popular movie star in the world.

Lion would never walk again. She crawled like the snake that she was on her belly to use the bathroom initially. Eventually she quit even crawling. She did not care if she soiled her bed or her self. She just lay in her own waste in agony while she waited to die and spend eternity in the hell that was too good for her.

She thought of the employees she tried to help. They all cursed her when they were fired or quit and now rejoiced at her agony. She would get what was coming to her now. She thought of all the people she had provided with affordable housing that cursed her when she evicted them after months of non-payment. They cursed her while in that life she was the one who had cleaned up their filth, their garbage, their remains. She wondered how they could live like that. Now she knew. Absence of pride and purpose. They always blamed her somehow. Blamed her through jealousy because she was rich and proud? She only had the best intentions.

The road to hell is paved with good intentions.

Lion was on the road to hell. She had to eventually be transferred to Rapid City Regional Hospital where they were keeping her alive with feeding tubes. Initially she had pulled out the tubes, to hurry her trip to hell, but eventually she was too weak to even fight that.

One day, she heard the voice she had talked to right after the infamous murder in D.C. The FBI agent who had come to arrest her for murder before she collapsed was in her hospital room. Eve was screaming at him to leave her daughter alone, but his assistants and the nurses subdued Eve with sedatives and removed her from the room instead.

Tom sat on the side of the once beautiful woman's bed and spoke directly to her, "Lioness. You must wake up. You must listen to every word I am about to tell you.

You did not kill Anne. You tried to save her. I have her suicide note right here."

As he began to speak, Lion's memories came flooding back.

FROM MURDERESS TO HEROINE IN LESS THAN A DAY

Once the FBI informed the press of the facts, Lioness went from Murderess to Heroine in less than a day.

Damn, thought David, I almost had one of them eliminated. Somehow in his heart, though, he would always blame Lioness for Anne's death.

Lioness was slowly learning to eat again. Making herself stand erect, then walk, then run.

Before she knew it, election day was upon them, and she actually had a shot at becoming President. She was pale and emaciated, but everywhere she went she was greeted with hugs and applause. People were certainly forgiving. Mankind was worth saving.

She forced herself to fly to D.C. on election day and try to look her best. She still looked anorexic, but she would be there for her people whether she won or lost.

The Libertarians were holding their big election day party in the same city for it was the first time in history, they might actually win a presidential election.

In honor of David, still in grief from the loss of his wife, the Democratic celebrations were all shifted to Boston at the last minute. David did not look much better than Lioness.

Mr. and Mrs. Godfrey stayed home in South Dakota as they refused to show favoritism to either of their children.

Lioness kept sending her mind out to look for Pierce, but it kept coming back with the same blackness that greeted her when she sent her mind out to Anne. How could the black shield that protected those who no longer had bodies from those who remained behind in their wretched containers of flesh that impenetrable Lioness wondered.

Not impenetrable, my child, simply one way. Two way communication would interfere with the human race's free choice to believe or not believe. You would not have Me deny My children the glory that is faith would you?

Lion's head ached constantly. But she kept analyzing her memory of that final fateful night when she lost her mind two weeks earlier. A mind in pain was better than no mind at all she mused to herself as she remembered.

She had entered the Watergate a superstar to rival her own boyfriend. She was blinded by the cameras as she was hailed future president of the United States from all her fans and supporters. She floated into the room with the grace, beauty and class of Grace Kelly becoming queen of Monaco so many years before.

Where before she only remembered waking up in the blood covered bed, now she remembered it all. She enjoyed the tributes, the excitement, the handshaking until her hands bled. Her speech, followed by individual conversations with her most faithful followers left her hoarse.

At last she decided to turn in, and was relieved that she had the penthouse waiting right upstairs in the hotel for her.

Just as she was about to turn in, she heard a knock on the door.

A panic stricken Anne was in front of the peephole. Lioness opened the door to let her in surprised to see Anne looking unkept for the fist time in her life. Anne sported black eyes and a swollen lip. Her hair was a total mess and it was obvious she had been beaten by someone.

Lioness had been so busy that night leaping in and out of the minds of her constituents and saying all the right things, that she had not given a second thought to Anne or the blood panels. Lion already knew what the bloodwork was going to reveal. So did David and Richard, of course. But the three also knew that short of scientific proof no one would believe it, so scientific proof Anne was about to come across.

Perhaps Anne was a bad selection, Lioness thought as she saw her dear friend standing there before her in a frenzied panic.

Lioness sat Anne down on the bed and stroked her hair, trying to smooth it, while calming her best friend.

Eventually Anne's hysteria calmed slightly. She was able to gasp out her findings.

"Yes, so, my beloved sister. I already know that," Lioness replied quietly. "But here is what you did not learn from the blood test. The exact identity of all the others."

When Lion told Anne who each of the sixteen were at the Godfrey breakfast that morning, Anne started screaming, "No. No. No. Please. Please. Please. No. No. No."

Anne started going into an epileptic type fit, throwing herself backwards on the bed.

Lioness was grabbing Anne's tongue and holding her down and trying to soothe her, "Now, now Anne. It is not your fault. You have done nothing wrong. No one can help who they love."

Anne set up suddenly, "You must go downstairs right this minute. You must go downstairs and tell the world what you just told me."

"You know I can't do that. We've all made a promise. Not until after the election. Not until after a free people have chosen their own destiny."

"You MUST tell the WORLD right now, or I will," Anne attempted to blackmail Lioness as she strode determinedly toward the still open hotel room door. Lioness leaped on top of Anne and held her to the floor."

"I love you Anne, but you know I can not let that happen." Those were Lion's last words before the blow to her head from behind knocked her out cold.

Never leave a hotel door open.

Anne's suicide note was brief but to the point. I know whose blood the Grail contains, therefore I know who speaks the truth to mankind. I will tell all the candidates and I will insist they warn the world. Then I will kill myself for having twice betrayed them all.

Lion never got the chance to tell Anne that she was not the great betrayer.

THE FINAL CHAPTER

At precisely 7:00 p.m. Pacific Time the polls in California closed. It was 10:00 p.m. Eastern time. Political pundits were at their microphones around the world. The internet, the television stations, the radio stations –all were poised to announce state by state, electorate vote by electorate vote, the outcome of the most closely watched election in history.

For the first time in any living man's memory there was at least three way dead heat between at least THREE main candidates. This also meant, any of the "third party candidates" actually stood a chance.

Mankind did have a choice. The days of choiceless elections were over now, mostly thanks to Richard Head's candidacy. The people were free. They were no longer limited to Democrat or Republican. Sister or Brother. There were three distinct philosophies on trial before the American people. Even candidates from the Independent Party, Green Party, Peace and Freedom Party and others had a chance thanks to the chaos the Godfrey's had created immediately before the election.

And the American people were to be the judges of who would be America's final leader, the last leader of the free world, simply by casting a vote.

99% voter turnout was predicted.

Apathy and laziness of the voting public had disappeared at long last in this election.

Prior elections had only 42% of the eligible voters showing up or even caring about the election results. This year, because of the turn of recent events and the shocking differences between the candidates, early polls indicated most of America's eligible voters were turning out to take control of their own Destiny

The votes from Maine had been tallied. The winner of Maine's four electoral votes was David.

Crap. The reception on the television just went out worldwide. Those stupid vertical color lines were on the television. The people ran to the radio. Absolutely nothing but white noise. Computers world wide shut down. Staff leaped to the cell phones and land lines. Nothing. No dial tone. Nothing.

Was America under attack?

The next world war was over and done, and so was the human race. The stag at bay was at bay no more..." Samuel Hoffenstein.

There was dead silence in his room full of advisors. Then someone pointed to the television. Computers flashed. Radios blared. Across all forms of media the very same message magically appeared. Choreographed by someone who must surely have gained access to all satellites in space.

The message was clear throughout the world, on every screen in teal print on a purple background. The same message was simultaneously aired around the world in the famous, deep sexy voice of the world's most popular movie star, the now deceased Pierce Hanson.

Side by side Lioness and Richard stood looking out at the Washington monument. Lightning lit up their faces. Washington D.C. had never seen such a storm. Slowly, they became aware of their staffs urging them to listen and to see. There was no mistake. From beyond the grave, the voice of Pierce was announcing:

On this night, your Savoir is returned to you.

As quickly as the communication world had been shut down. It was restored. Political analysts were frantically analyzing how a world wide communication failure could have occurred.

Eventually, the baffled world turned back to the election results.

Lioness prowled to the private room back room where she and Richard would watch the election until it was over. Richard was sitting casually on the couch, barefooted and watching the line-up of seven televisions all basically reporting the same thing. He was a little too casual, Lioness thought to herself.

Earlier they had prayed together, "Lord, thine will be done."

Oh, how she wanted to interfere with the votes, but she remembered the great vote in heaven millenniums before and how the majority of spirits of all future men and women had voted for Free Will. She dared not interfere.

Senator Lioness Godfrey quit pacing, found some microwave popcorn and heated it up. She only burned a few kernels in the bottom and gave her face a bit of a steam when she opened the bag and then handed it to Richard. She pulled some sacred Sesame oil out of her purse, dipped her mane in it, knelt before Candidate Head and cleansed his feet with the oil and her hair. She crawled up beside him on the couch to watch the future unfold.

Maine count was done just before the blackout. They already knew David had won those four electoral votes.

Initial broadcasts speculated the split second electronic blackout might effect the voting machines, but it seemed almost like it was the world's imagination. All electronic equipment world wide was up and running smooth as a purring kitten.

Vermont's three electoral votes were hands down for Richard.

Massachusetts' twelve were looking like a clear win for David's.

The surprise was that both New Hampshire's four and the huge Pennsylvania's twenty one delegates were going to Richard, as was Ohio's twenty. History was a being made. For the first time ever, a Libertarian had a chance at the Presidency of the United States! The people were clearly stating they wanted more of a choice than just Democrat or Republican in future elections. The people clearly were telling the world that the lines between Democrat and Republican were as imaginary as their convictions. The people were telling the press they wanted Third Parties in the nationally televised debates. They wanted variety, independence and equality.

Virginia's thirteen electoral votes and North Carolina's fifteen delegates easily were going to go to Lioness by a landslide.

At the last minute, David lost New York and the Peace and Freedom candidate from New York, whom nobody had ever paid an ounce of attention to outside the state, swept the thirty one New York electoral votes right out from under David – a major blow.

Rumor abounded that there were going to be an unheard of number of faithless electoral votes - electors who cast their vote for someone other than the one whom they have pledged to elect.

There were no longer blue and red states. There were states in the color of rainbows.

The importance of California's fifty five electoral votes had never been so painfully clear.

Voter turn out had reached its highest percentage in one hundred years. The voters were awake, angry, involved and they were not going to take the "same old same old" anymore.

It was anybody's horse race. The heart and soul of American was at stake. The future of the planet was at stake

Good versus evil was on display before the very world. All eyes were on the American voter to see which would be chosen.

And all the eyes of the world were on the voters of America to see if they could even tell the difference between good and evil anymore.

THE END

ABOUT THE AUTHOR

August K. Anderson, a former lawyer and one of the country's top equestrians, is the long time CEO of Golden Quest Enterprises and the founder of Cheval International (www.chevalinternational.com), a globally renowned equine products company. August's favorite quote regarding her writings? *"a deity inspired list of mandates that when embraced can transform the ordinary into the extraordinary"*

August was the principal political force behind *Keeping the Masses Down*. Her ideals formed the foundation for this motivational, life-conquering manual. She has also penned several other fiction and nonfiction books, Including:

- *Love Letter from God*
- *A Bridge Over Troubled Waters*
- *The Equestrian Green Book: An Objective Guide to Valuing Horses.*

Printed in the United States
88878LV00001B/1-48/A